"A Plague of Cholera" and Other Stories

Judaic Traditions in Music, Literature, and Art
Ken Frieden, *Series Editor*

Select Titles in Judaic Traditions in Literature, Music, and Art

Café Shira: A Novel
    David Ehrlich; Michael Swirsky, trans.

Diary of a Lonely Girl, or The Battle against Free Love
    Miriam Karpilove; Jessica Kirzane, trans.

From a Distant Relation
    Mikhah Yosef Berdichevsky; James Adam Redfield, ed. and trans.

Jewish Identity in American Art: A Golden Age since the 1970s
    Matthew Baigell

*The People of the Book and the Camera: Photography
in the Hebrew Novel*
    Ofra Amihay

A Provincial Newspaper and Other Stories
    Miriam Karpilove; Jessica Kirzane, trans.

The Rivals and Other Stories
    Jonah Rosenfeld; Rachel Mines, trans.

The Tears and Prayers of Fools: A Novel
    Grigory Kanovich; Mary Ann Szporluk, trans.

For a full list of titles in this series, visit:
https://press.syr.edu/supressbook-series
/judaic-traditions-in-literature-music-and-art/.

A Plague
of Cholera
& Other Stories

Jonah Rosenfeld

Translated from the Yiddish
and with an Introduction by
Rachel Mines

Syracuse University Press

∞ The paper used in this publication meets the minimum requirements of the American National Standard for Information Sciences—Permanence of Paper for Printed Library Materials, ANSI Z39.48-1992.

For a listing of books published and distributed by Syracuse University Press, visit https://press.syr.edu.

ISBN: 9780815611646 (paperback)
       9780815657026 (e-book)

Library of Congress Cataloging-in-Publication Data

Names: Rozenfeld, Yonah, 1880–1944 author. | Mines, Rachel, translator.
Title: A plague of cholera and other stories / Jonah Rosenfeld ;
       translated by Rachel Mines.
Description: First edition. | Syracuse : Syracuse University Press, 2024. |
       Series: Judaic traditions in literature, music, and art |
       Includes bibliographical references.
Identifiers: LCCN 2023043546 (print) | LCCN 2023043547 (ebook) |
       ISBN 9780815611646 (paperback) | ISBN 9780815657026 (ebook)
Subjects: LCSH: Rozenfeld, Yonah, 1880-1944—Translations into English. |
       LCGFT: Short stories.
Classification: LCC PJ5129.R598 P57 2024 (print) | LCC PJ5129.R598 (ebook) |
       DDC 839/.133—dc23/eng/20240214
LC record available at https://lccn.loc.gov/2023043546
LC ebook record available at https://lccn.loc.gov/2023043547

Manufactured in the United States of America

Contents

Acknowledgments

I extend heartfelt thanks to Solon Beinfeld, Helen Mintz, Seymour Levitan, Gene Homel, and the expert members of the Facebook group Yidforsh for their kind and invaluable assistance. I would also like to thank Deborah Manion and her colleagues at Syracuse University Press who assisted with this publication.

This book is dedicated to Lillian Green, the grand-niece of Jonah Rosenfeld, who is justifiably proud of her "Uncle Yoyne" and thrilled that his stories are again being read and appreciated.

Introduction

Jonah Rosenfeld's understated psychological horror stories, with their themes of loneliness, mental fragmentation, fear, and death, are rewarding and also unsettling. Rokhl Kafrissen, in an article in *Tablet Magazine*, states that "Rosenfeld's stories are not for the faint-hearted . . . but for all their darkness, I can imagine readers powerfully connecting with them, relieved to see their own hidden pains reflected and honored."[1] Jonah Rosenfeld was an astute observer and analyst of human psychology, and his stories demonstrate a sensitive and nuanced reading of the human psyche. He was far ahead of his time in his intuitive understanding of the workings of the unconscious mind.

During his life, Rosenfeld's critics—even those few who admit to disliking his work—were unanimous in their observations that the author's psychological approach to his characters was unique in the Yiddish literature of his time.[2] Rosenfeld's stories, with their focus on his characters' internal worlds, were written around the same time that Freud was developing his psychological theories, and his writing seems steeped in Freud: plot is subordinate to character, and "events . . . occur in the character's thoughts, associations, memories, fantasies, reveries, contemplations, and dreams."[3] While other

---

1. Rokhl Kafrissen, "Return of the Thief."

2. See, for example, articles in the Jonah Rosenfeld Archive, RG 647 (boxes 1–3), YIVO Institute for Jewish Research, New York, by I. Varshavski, Sh. Niger, Sholem Stern, Moyshe Katz, M. Osherovich, Sh. D. Zinger, and others.

3. *Encyclopaedia Britannica*, s.v. "psychological novel," https://www.britannica.com/art/psychological-novel. Early writers in the genre of psychological fiction

Yiddish writers used elements of the psychological approach in their fiction—Sholem Aleichem's stream-of-consciousness monologues are one well-known example—Jonah Rosenfeld is unique among Yiddish writers in his consistent depictions of his characters' subconscious associations, emotions, and motivations.

Some of Rosenfeld's critics have suggested that Rosenfeld was a psychoanalytical author, even a Freudian.[4] For example, G. Sapoznikow's 1958 Freudian analysis of Yiddish writers noted that Rosenfeld, "who had no school but his boss's workshop and no experience of life except Jewish poverty, found the same path [as Freud] to the deepest mysteries of human nature and illuminated them with the light of his remarkable psychological intuition."[5] There is, however, no indication that Rosenfeld was familiar with Freud's writing—and quite a bit of evidence, including his own admission, that he was not: "Everything I wrote, I tore out of myself. I've never read Freud. Everything must come from the self."[6]

While we cannot know how much Rosenfeld was aware of Freud's ideas—which he may, after all, have encountered secondhand through reading or conversations with friends and colleagues—there is no doubt that the author, whether intentionally or coincidentally, through his own powers of intuition and observation, developed a number of Freud's ideas in his fiction, predominantly the hallmark element of his style: the impact of subconscious thoughts and motivations on human behavior.

Typical Rosenfeldian characters exhibit powerful emotions, but with little or no understanding of themselves, they sense their feelings

---

included Fyodor Dostoyevsky, Leo Tolstoy, Henry James, James Joyce, and Virginia Woolf.

4. See, for example, I. Varshavski, "Jonah Rosenfeld's Yahrzeit," *Forverts*, Oct. 21, 1945, and many other articles in the Rosenfeld Archive.

5. G. Sapoznikow, *Fun Di Tifenishn: Eseyen*, 51. Unless otherwise indicated, translations from Yiddish are my own.

6. Quoted in S. Dingal, "Jonah Rosenfeld: A Month after His Death," *Der Tog*, Aug. 9, 1944, Rosenfeld Archive.

only dimly, as though peering through a nebulous haze of fragmentary thoughts and images. Lacking insight and unable to access their emotions, they may try to reason their way to understanding themselves and their predicaments, but logic alone is insufficient, and their attempts to make sense of the world and their place in it usually end in disaster. For example, Mr. Zafran, the protagonist of "A Singular Man," is a likable character with one major tragic flaw: a stunning lack of insight into himself and others. Mr. Zafran is in love with the tailor girl Manya. But his lack of empathy and mind-boggling insensitivity destroy any chance of love as, for reasons unclear even to himself, he embarrasses Manya in public, gaslights her, and attempts to manipulate her into lying to save his own skin. Middle-aged Mrs. Belemer, in "A Respectable Woman," strikes up a flirtation with her son's friend. She is not only unaware that her overly familiar relationship with the young man is unwise, but even less aware of why she is flirting with the young man, though the reader knows she is lonely in her marriage and thinks herself no longer attractive.

Like Freud, Rosenfeld was an explorer of human psychology. Unconscious thoughts and motivations play a key role in character and plot development. Typical Rosenfeldian characters are alienated, detached from their own inner lives and the families and communities in which they live. Rosenfeld wrote about those who are left out: the poor, the uneducated, the lonely; those with little or no self-awareness and few resources in a hostile world that is changing rapidly around them. Like many of today's individuals who struggle to stay afloat during times of chaos, Rosenfeld's characters are challenged by evolving gender roles, sexual mores, culture clash, the loss of stabilizing traditions, war, and pandemics. Rosenfeld's stories have no cheerful endings. He provides no solutions to his characters' dilemmas, no redemption to comfort the reader. His are bleak stories for uncertain times, for a world beset by loneliness, uncertainty, and constantly evolving threats. In short, they are stories for today.

A brief examination of Rosenfeld's tragic life may shed light on his unique approach to his writing. Unfortunately, little biographical information is available, and even less is accessible in English. His

youth and childhood were marked by poverty, deprivation, and bru-
tality; his writing career was cut short by interpersonal conflict; and
his life ended after a long battle with stomach cancer. With no background in literature, and few—if any—role models, Rosenfeld nevertheless taught himself his craft and became a successful and popular
author. His difficult life and his relative lack of literary influences
forced him to observe and analyze others. Through observation, he
learned to understand not only the people around him but also himself. Rosenfeld's own mind and experiences, with few early outside
influences, were the source of his literary achievements. Therefore,
no deep understanding of Rosenfeld's literary works is possible without understanding the author himself.

Jonah Rosenfeld was born around 1880[7] and spent his first
years in Chartorysk, Volhynia, Russian Empire (present-day Staryi
Chortoryisk, Ukraine). According to Shmuel Niger's introduction to
Rosenfeld's posthumous anthology, *Geklibene Verk*, the shtetl, which
comprised about 150 households, was poor, its inhabitants trapped
in hard, monotonous lives. Rosenfeld's father was a *melamed* who
also taught German, but his salary was insufficient to support a family of seven children, and young Jonah's mother also had to work
outside the home to help make ends meet.[8] As a child, Rosenfeld
barely got enough to eat, let alone decent clothes or shoes; he didn't
even have tefillin on his bar mitzvah.[9]

Rosenfeld had a traditional religious Jewish education: cheder
(religious elementary school) until he was twelve, followed by yeshiva.

---

7. Rosenfeld's birth date is uncertain. The date of 1880 is according to I.
Varshavski, "Rozenfeld, Yonah," col. 347. According to Rosenfeld's tombstone
in Mount Carmel Cemetery in Glendale, New York, his date of birth was 1881.
Finally, according to Rosenfeld's widow, his date of birth was 1882 (letter from
Chaya Rosenfeld to G. Sapoznikow, Aug. 23, 1953, Rosenfeld Archive).

8. Shmuel Niger, "Yonah Rozenfeld: Byografish-Kritiker Araynfir," 1.

9. T. Ts. Goldberg, "Jonah Rosenfeld," *Der Tog*, July 15, 1944, Rosenfeld
Archive.

He was bright, and his parents hoped he would become a rabbi.[10] Tragically, however, before his thirteenth birthday, his parents died of cholera—possibly the same epidemic as the one fictionalized in "Di Kholyere" ("A Plague of Cholera," in this volume). His brothers sent him to Odesa to apprentice to a lathe operator, and Rosenfeld worked in that trade for the next ten years.[11]

The apprenticeship system in Russia at that time was cruel and inhumane. Apprentices were more or less bought and sold like slaves; they virtually belonged to their boss and were unable to look elsewhere for work until their term of apprenticeship ended.[12] Rosenfeld's boss, Avrom Kohen, seems to have been particularly sadistic, and the years that the orphaned adolescent spent under his yoke, as the author later described in his autobiographical novel, *Eyner Aleyn* (All Alone), caused him great suffering. Young Jonah was overworked, inadequately fed, and made the butt of practical jokes. The greatest torment for a sensitive young man was that Kohen and his family treated their apprentice as though he were subhuman: they refused to call him by name and taunted him at every opportunity. According to Rosenfeld's later recollections, his boss "beat me for four whole years with sticks and poles, but despite that I came out alive, unharmed."[13]

Writing eventually saved Rosenfeld from his hardscrabble, slavelike existence.[14] During his years in Odesa, he read and wrote nothing. He had no one to write to, and he had no idea that such a thing

---

10. "Jonah Rosenfeld Dead at the Age of 63," *Forverts*, July 10, 1944, Rosenfeld Archive.

11. Varshavski, "Rozenfeld, Yonah," col. 347.

12. A. Mukdoyni, "Books and Writers," Rosenfeld Archive. The clipping omits the newspaper title and date.

13. Jan Schwarz, "The Trials of a Yiddish Writer in America: Jonah Rosenfeld's Autobiographical Novel," 193.

14. M. Osherovich, "Jonah Rosenfeld: The Life and Writings of the Yiddish Writer," *Forverts*, July 12, 1944, Rosenfeld Archive.

as literature existed—that one could write for no one and everyone, just for the sake of writing. But one day, when Rosenfeld was around twenty-two, he was feeling especially lonely and, sitting down to write a letter to someone he barely knew—a married cousin of his— he found his literary inspiration: "This hand, which had never written anything to anybody, this hand, which from the age of twelve years on . . . had never held a pen, just kept going and going."[15] This was the beginning of Rosenfeld's literary career.

In 1902, Isaac Leib Peretz, the renowned Yiddish author who encouraged and helped many writers to publish their first works, was visiting Odesa. When Rosenfeld heard that Peretz was in town, he got up early and rushed to the great man's hotel to meet him. When he arrived, Peretz was still sleeping. Rosenfeld woke him and proceeded to read him a story he'd just written—a story about a banker. Peretz asked the young lathe operator if he knew anything about banking. On receiving a negative reply, Peretz encouraged Rosenfeld to write about his own life, adding, "If I haven't heard about you five years from now, I'll curse you for waking me up so early."[16] Rosenfeld's first published story, "Dos Lernyingl" (The apprentice), appeared in St. Petersburg's daily Yiddish newspaper *Der Fraynd* two years later.[17]

After this literary debut, Rosenfeld devoted himself to writing, apparently with great success, publishing stories in various newspapers and literary journals. His first collection, *Shriftn* (Writings), appeared in 1909, followed by two more collections: *In di Shmole Geselekh* (In the narrow alleys) in 1910 and *Nakht un Toyt* (Night

15. Niger, "Yonah Rozenfeld," 2.

16. L. Kussman, "Jonah Rosenfeld: From Odesa to New York," *Morgn Zshurnal*, July 13, 1944, Rosenfeld Archive. Kussman adds, "But the person who first discovered Rosenfeld as a writer wasn't Peretz, but a friend most people have never heard of. His name was Pines (I don't remember his first name). He was a character. He'd walk around in a heavy, old, ripped coat of an indeterminate color, even in summer, his pockets loaded down with books. . . . This Pines met me once and told me he'd met a Yiddish Dostoyevsky and took me to meet him." The "Yiddish Dostoyevsky" turned out to be Rosenfeld.

17. Jan Schwarz, "Rozenfeld, Yona."

and death) in 1912. In 1914, Rosenfeld moved to Kovel, Poland, and shortly after that to Kyiv, Ukraine, where he lived during World War I.[18]

Although Rosenfeld was now married and supporting himself as a writer, his troubles continued. In January of either 1919 or 1920,[19] Rosenfeld was forced to leave Kyiv amid the violence and chaos of the Bolshevik Revolution and the ensuing Russian Civil War, and after a dangerous and harrowing journey of more than a month he made his way to Kovel, then part of the independent Second Polish Republic. He describes his journey in two autobiographical stories, "Grenetsn" and "Nazad."[20] While details of the stories, such as thoughts and conversations, are clearly fictionalized, the basic plot elements are probably true. Rosenfeld's widow, Chaya, who was with Rosenfeld during the escape from Kyiv, later assured the writer Gershon Sapoznikow that the events in Rosenfeld's autobiographical writings took place as he described them.[21]

"Grenetsn" opens as Rosenfeld and his traveling companions (his wife, Chaya, and a mixed group of Jews and Gentiles), who have paid a Ukrainian guide a huge sum of money to help them escape Ukraine for relative safety in Poland, endure an anxious week in Kyiv, in those years a region caught in the grip of murderous violence,[22] waiting for

18. Jan Schwarz, *Imagining Lives: Autobiographical Fiction of Yiddish Writers*, 176.

19. Jan Schwarz (*Imagining Lives*, 176), possibly following Shmuel Niger ("Yonah Rozenfeld," 8), gives the date as 1919, but Rosenfeld's dated diary entries of his journey correspond with the year 1920.

20. "Grenetsn" and "Nazad" appear in Rosenfeld's *Geklibene Verk*, vol. 1, *Grenetsn* (Vilnius: B. Kletskin, 1929), 63–118 and 119–204, respectively.

21. "I can assure you that in his autobiographical stories, sketches, and notes, Jonah Rosenfeld was always honest and true to reality as he remembered it" (letter from Chaya Rosenfeld to G. Sapoznikow, Rosenfeld Archive).

22. Ukraine was the battleground of three major armies: the Red, or Bolshevik, Army; the White, or antirevolutionary, Army; and the Polish Army. About a million people, including one hundred thousand Jews, lost their lives in Ukraine during the years 1918–21. Jews "were singled out for persecution by virtually

the train that will take them on the first leg of their journey. Following their escape from the city in an overcrowded, unheated boxcar, there is a tense, week-long sleigh journey from town to town, including an overnight stay in one village where Rosenfeld and Chaya are horrified to discover that their Gentile hosts (who are unaware that several of their guests are Jewish) have recently participated in a pogrom in a neighboring shtetl. As the refugees leave this village, glad to escape with their lives, their sleigh drivers become lost in the woods, and the travelers are forced to shelter overnight in a barn where Chaya is terrified by the discovery of a corpse. Eventually, the refugees reach the Polish border. The Gentile travelers are allowed to cross, but Rosenfeld, his wife, and another Jewish traveler are turned back.

"Nazad" picks up the story as Jonah and Chaya Rosenfeld leave the border with no idea what to do next or where to go, as it is too dangerous for them to remain in Ukraine and impossible to cross into Poland. They find temporary shelter with a series of householders who are willing to put them up, but can find no way out of their dilemma. During this time, they negotiate with various officials, some of whom offer to help (for a price), but the couple does not know whom they can trust. They suffer a series of setbacks as various plans fall through. They are also terrified by witnessing an incident in which two peasants accused of burglary are arrested and one is forced to execute the other. The day after this traumatic event, Rosenfeld and Chaya are themselves arrested, ostensibly for having "suspicious" documents in their possession. They are locked in a prison cell and fear for their lives, but are released later that night and taken under guard to the train station—where, miraculously, they are met by a friend from Kovel who has brought papers that will allow them into Poland.

In 1921, after spending about a year in Kovel, Jonah and Chaya Rosenfeld emigrated to New York. Rosenfeld became a major literary contributor to the leading American Yiddish-language newspaper, the *Forverts*, where he worked, writing prolifically, until 1935.

---

everyone." Jeffrey Veidlinger, *In the Midst of Civilized Europe: The Pogroms of 1918–1921 and the Onset of the Holocaust*, 15–16.

After the traumas and difficulties of his time in Europe, this time was probably the most stable and satisfying period of his life.

Peace and stability, however, were not to last. In 1935 the editor of the *Forverts*, Abraham Cahan, refused to continue publishing Rosenfeld's stories, and Rosenfeld was left without an audience for his work. Various reasons for the rift have been suggested. According to I. Varshavski (a pen name of Isaac Bashevis Singer), Cahan felt that Rosenfeld's stories set in America were inferior to those set in Europe. Rosenfeld had a different opinion of the quality of his more recent stories and refused to revise them to meet Cahan's demands.[23] Hillel (Harry) Rogoff, one of Rosenfeld's contemporaries on the *Forverts*, claims that the issue was Rosenfeld's style: "It became difficult for the reader to follow him, to understand what he wanted to say. His style became complicated; his sentences, long and confusing. Even his admirers had to admit it took an effort to read him."[24] Others suggest that hostilities arose owing to personal differences between the two men.[25] In any event, Cahan's "nastiness toward Jonah Rosenfeld . . . became a subject for gossip in Yiddish intellectual circles."[26] Between 1935 and his death in 1944, Rosenfeld published relatively little: a handful of stories in the journal *Tsukunft*[27] and his autobiographical novel *Eyner Aleyn*. Rosenfeld was at work on a companion volume to *Eyner Aleyn* at the time of his death. A letter from his widow, Chaya Rosenfeld, dated August 23, 1953, mentions "a manuscript of a few hundred printed pages about his youth which has not yet been published."[28]

23. Varshavski, "Rozenfeld, Yonah," col. 347.

24. Harry Rogoff, *Der Gayst Fun Forverts*, 73.

25. See, for example, M. Osherovich, "Jonah Rosenfeld: A Few Words for His Tenth Yahrzeit," July 14, 1954, Rosenfeld Archive. The clipping omits the name of the newspaper.

26. Irving Howe, *World of Our Fathers*, 533.

27. See Schwarz, "The Trials of a Yiddish Writer," 204.

28. Letter from Chaya Rosenfeld to G. Sapoznikow, Rosenfeld Archive. According to Jan Schwarz ("The Trials of a Yiddish Writer," 205), Rosenfeld's unpublished manuscript resides in the same archive.

In 1937 Rosenfeld had surgery for stomach cancer. He was given only a short time to live, but Rosenfeld—as always, fiercely independent, arguing that he knew his stomach better than his doctors did[29]—devised his own plan of treatment: a special diet; long walks on the boardwalk from his home in Brighton Beach, Brooklyn, to Seagate; and daily year-round swims in the ocean.[30] He outlived the time his doctors had given him and seemed well for the following seven years, but in the spring of 1944, following the death of his good friend and colleague Israel Joshua Singer (the brother of Isaac Bashevis Singer), his health took a turn for the worse.[31] Jonah Rosenfeld died in New York on July 9, 1944.

One might think that a man with a traumatic childhood and youth, a man with no secular education and no access to the world of ideas until adulthood—a man who, when he did eventually find his voice, wrote about child abuse, family dysfunction, exploitation, and loneliness—would be an unhappy, humorless individual. That, however, seems not to have been the case. Rosenfeld's fellow writers described him as an eccentric[32] who preferred his own company to that of others, but he did have close friends, supportive colleagues, and a lifelong, devoted partner in his wife, Chaya. Temperamentally,

29. Yitskhok Horowitz, "An Evening with Jonah Rosenfeld: On His Tenth Yahrzeit," Rosenfeld Archive. The clipping omits the newspaper name and date, but presumably appeared in July 1954.

30. Niger, "Yonah Rozenfeld," 9.

31. Yitskhok Horowitz, "Jonah Rosenfeld," *Yidishe Kempfer*, July 21, 1944, Rosenfeld Archive.

32. Melech Ravitch describes Rosenfeld as "an oddball, in his writings and also in life. . . . For an hour at a time he'd play the madman, waving his hands around wildly, winking and blinking and talking as if he'd gone out of his mind. If you answered him the same way, as if you'd gone crazy yourself, he wouldn't be surprised—he'd just play along. . . . The oddball world of his stories, which are literary psychological experiments, isn't entirely his invention; somewhere deep in his soul he experiences that world." Melech Ravitch, "Yonah Rozenfeld," 269–70.

Rosenfeld was a seeker, constantly striving to understand the world and the people around him.[33] However, despite his best attempts to understand people, he trusted few of them; he had learned as a child that he could depend on no one but himself, and even in later life he remained stubbornly independent and somewhat of a recluse. According to A. Mukdoyni, Rosenfeld was "the most solitary of men, but he was never lonely—he had his own chaotic, tangled-up world, all to himself. . . . He avoided the world around him—no good could come from it. He was suspicious of people, and for good reasons. . . . He was used to being alone and to the protective walls he'd put around himself."[34]

Jonah Rosenfeld seems to have been as independent in his art as he was in his personal and professional lives. There is a general consensus among his critics that he had few, if any, literary influences. Isaac Bashevis Singer claimed that Rosenfeld had none at all,[35] while Moyshe Katz explains, "He kept to himself and read very little in the way of literature. He didn't want to be influenced by other writers, and maintained that the best writing comes from within." That a writer of Rosenfeld's insights and abilities had no literary influences seems incredible, and the YIVO archives do in fact produce a scattering of writers whom Rosenfeld admired: among Yiddish authors Abraham Reisen[36] and Dovid Bergelson (who seems to have been

33. According to M. Osherovich, "Jonah Rosenfeld thought every person was a riddle, almost impossible to understand. He sought to portray their most deeply buried secrets. In his thinking as well as in his writings, he was original: in both was an odd mixture of deepness and naiveté." Osherovich, "Jonah Rosenfeld: Life and Writings."

34. A. Mukdoyni, "Jonah Rosenfeld's Place in Yiddish Literature: A Word at His Fresh Grave," *Morgn Zshurnal*, July 12, 1944, Rosenfeld Archive.

35. Yitskhok Bashevis, "Jonah Rosenfeld and His Place in Yiddish Literature," *Forverts*, July 5, 1964, Rosenfeld Archive.

36. Moyshe Katz, "Jonah Rosenfeld: On His Tenth Yahrzeit," *Yidishe Kultur* 17, no. 7 (1954), Rosenfeld Archive.

a special favorite),[37] and among Russian writers Leonid Andreyev[38] and a few other post-1905 authors. An article by Yohanan Twersky mentions that Rosenfeld enjoyed Chekhov for his sense of humor, his interplay between comedy and tragedy, and his insight (all markers of Rosenfeld's own literary style), while he found Dostoyevsky "too monotonous" and Maupassant, whom he read in Russian translation, "too focused on male-female relationships, not deep enough."[39]

Setting aside the question of who (if anyone) influenced Rosenfeld's writing, it is clear that the author's approach to his art derived mainly from himself. His childhood loss of his parents, his adolescence of poverty and abuse, his solitary nature, his lively imagination, his powers of observation, and his innate abilities as a storyteller inspired him to produce stories of a rare, dark power: stories that convey anguish, loneliness, the search for belonging, and the struggle to find meaning in a world that is often cruelly rejecting. Rosenfeld's popularity as a writer indicates that his stories found a response in the minds of his Yiddish-speaking readers, many of whom were also grappling with displacement, loss of culture and tradition, and rapid social change. One hundred years later, in a world challenged with pandemics, climate change, political and economic chaos, mass migrations, and changing social and gender roles, contemporary audiences can still look to Rosenfeld's writings for insight into their own anxieties and uncertainties.

BIBLIOGRAPHY

Howe, Irving. *World of Our Fathers*. New York: Harcourt, 1976.
Kafrissen, Rokhl. "Return of the Thief." *Tablet Magazine*, Sept. 30, 2021. https://www.tabletmag.com/sections/community/articles/return-of-the -thief-sholem-aleichem-moshkele.

37. Yohanan Twersky, "Jonah Rosenfeld," *Tsukunft* 49, no. 9 (1944), Rosenfeld Archive.
38. Katz, "Jonah Rosenfeld."
39. Twersky, "Jonah Rosenfeld."

Niger, Shmuel. "Yonah Rozenfeld: Byografish-Kritiker Araynfir." In *Ge-klibene Verk*, edited by Chaim Grade, 1–9. New York: CYCO-Bikher Farlag, 1955.

Ravitch, Melech. "Yonah Rozenfeld." In *Mayn Lexicon*, 5:269–71. Tel Aviv: Veltrat far Yidish un Yidisher Kultur, 1982.

Rogoff, Harry. *Der Gayst Fun Forverts*. New York: *Forverts*, 1954.

Sapoznikow, G. *Fun Di Tifenishn: Eseyen*. Buenos Aires: A Komitet, 1958.

Schwarz, Jan. *Imagining Lives: Autobiographical Fiction of Yiddish Writers*. Madison: University of Wisconsin Press, 2005.

———. "Rozenfeld, Yona." In *YIVO Encyclopedia of Jews in Eastern Europe*. http://www.yivoencyclopedia.org/article.aspx/Rozenfeld_Yona.

———. "The Trials of a Yiddish Writer in America: Jonah Rosenfeld's Autobiographical Novel." *Prooftexts* 18, no. 2 (1998): 187–206.

Varshavski, I. "Rozenfeld, Yonah." In *Leksikon fun der Nayer Yidisher Literatur*, edited by Shmuel Niger and Jacob Shatzky, vol. 8, cols. 347–50. New York: Congress for Jewish Culture, 1956–81.

Veidlinger, Jeffrey. *In the Midst of Civilized Europe: The Pogroms of 1918–1921 and the Onset of the Holocaust*. New York: Metropolitan Books, 2021.

Translator's Notes

Like any translator, I have had to consider a great many stylistic choices in my translations of Jonah Rosenfeld's stories. The strategies I selected reflect my goal, which is to make the stories accessible to readers who may not have any prior knowledge of Jewish or Yiddish culture. My central concern was how to most effectively reproduce Rosenfeld's words and sentences in English, a language very different from Yiddish in its vocabulary and cultural connotations.

I began by assuming that Rosenfeld's intended audience, those individuals who read his stories in the first half of the twentieth century, would have found his Yiddish familiar and natural, the language they spoke every day. Therefore, I decided to translate Rosenfeld's colloquial, idiomatic Yiddish into a colloquial North American English that reflects present-day vocabulary and idioms. While remaining as faithful as possible to the words and sense of the original, I wanted to avoid the overly stilted, awkward wordings that result from a too close adherence to Yiddish vocabulary and syntax. Above all, the stories must be believable, relatable, and enjoyable. To this end, I have had to make a number of decisions.

First of all, vocabulary. There are words in Yiddish, as in all languages, that assume cultural knowledge on the parts of users and listeners. Words and phrases that have specifically religious connotations, such as *shul* and *mitzvah* (a synagogue and a religious obligation, respectively) are obvious examples, but they are not the only ones. Even more or less secular words such as *goy*, *mensch*, and *golem*—to suggest a few examples familiar to many English speakers—carry deep cultural associations and connotations. What to do with such words and expressions, with their associated freight of history and tradition? There is no generally accepted rule. Most translators of Yiddish have a number of choices, each with its limitations.

One option chosen by many translators is the use of explanatory footnotes or a glossary. I have chosen to avoid footnotes because they interrupt the smooth flow of the text. A story, I believe, should be a pleasure to read and not (or not only) an academic exercise. Similarly, although a glossary may be helpful to many readers, it shares with footnotes the weakness of interrupting the narrative flow as the reader flips back and forth in the text.

An alternative option is to insert a "stealth gloss," that is, a brief explanation that appears in the text of the translation. Stealth glosses may be acceptable under certain conditions. First, they must be absolutely necessary for the reader's understanding. Second, they must be as brief as possible and should never disrupt the flow of the narrative. Here is an example from the title story in this collection, "A Plague of Cholera": "Carrying the etrog and lulav, plants symbolizing the holiday, Gabriel trotted down the festive streets." The words "plants symbolizing the holiday" do not appear in the original Yiddish, since Rosenfeld's audience would have been perfectly aware of the words' meanings and rich cultural connotations. Most modern readers, however, would be mystified without an explanation.

Some Yiddish words have found their way into English, and when they appear in the story I generally retain them, using the spellings in *Merriam-Webster's Online Dictionary*.[1] Such words include *chuppah, havdalah, mezuzah, mikvah, minyan, rebbe, sheitel, shiva, shofar, sukkah, Sukkoth,* and *tefillin*. Although these words "count" as English words, at least by virtue of appearing in an English dictionary, many are not in common use, so I have used stealth glosses to briefly define them when necessary.

Yiddish is written in the Hebrew alphabet, and therefore personal names which have no English equivalents must be transliterated into the Latin alphabet used in English. For transliteration, I

---

1. https://www.merriam-webster.com/.

have used the YIVO guidelines.[2] *Ey* is pronounced as in *day, sleigh*. *Ay* is pronounced as in *high, dry*. *E* is pronounced short as in *bed, elm*. Word-final *e* is never silent. It is pronounced similarly to the final vowel in *banana, sofa, Rosa*. Finally, *kh* represents a guttural sound similar to the final consonant in *Bach, loch*. Stress in Yiddish words, including personal names, generally falls on the first syllable (YOSHke, SHEYNdele, ELye).

In a few cases, when an English equivalent for a Yiddish word is unavailable or unsatisfactory, and when context makes the meaning clear, I have chosen to retain the untranslated word. One such example is the Yiddish honorific "Reb." I could have translated the word as "Mr." However, "Reb" is used differently—it precedes the first name, not the surname—and it has a warmer, less formal connotation than "Mr." Therefore, I have left "Reb," when it occurs, in the original Yiddish.

A few Yiddish words that are now used in English merit a brief mention. In North American English, the word *goy* is generally pejorative. In the Yiddish of Rosenfeld's time and place, however, the word did not have negative connotations, but was simply a neutral descriptive term for a non-Jew, who could be a neighbor or even a friend. In keeping with Rosenfeld's original Yiddish, I have used *goy*,[3] *Christian*, and *Gentile* more or less interchangeably.

Another common Yiddish-English word, *mitzvah*, has also changed in its connotations. To most English speakers, a mitzvah is a good deed, and the word can refer to almost any helpful act. In Rosenfeld's time, however—and to observant Jews today—the word is much narrower in scope and refers to a religious obligation. Thus, in "A Plague of Cholera," when the Jews of Chartoryisk decide to marry the two orphaned outcasts to each other, they are not doing so out of the goodness of their hearts, but in order to fulfill a religious obligation, the sacred covenant of marriage.

2. https://yivo.org/yiddish-alphabet.

3. Plural *goyim*.

One final Yiddish word I would like to mention here is *hoyf.* Following common usage, I have translated *hoyf* as *courtyard.* Unfortunately, the word *courtyard* is a rather grand term to North American ears. The courtyards of Eastern European towns and cities are simply open spaces, often (but not necessarily) paved, surrounded by houses or apartment buildings, the residents of which share the space in common. Typically, the courtyard will have at least one entrance to the street for vehicles and/or pedestrians, usually with a gate that can be locked for security.

Finally, while this issue is not something translation can address, the observant reader might notice a discrepancy in chronology that appears in the title story, "A Plague of Cholera." On Erev Rosh Hashanah, the day before Rosh Hashanah (which begins, like all days according to the Hebrew calendar, at sunset), three men go to the mikvah, the ritual bath. A few hours later, clearly that same evening, people gather in the synagogue. Yet the narrator tell us the synagogue scene occurs on the day *following* the events in the mikvah. Perhaps the error crept in as a result of newspaper serialization, with the author losing track of chronology. Whatever the reason, it does not distract from the power of the story.

I have organized this collection into six sections, each roughly corresponding to one of Rosenfeld's various themes: transitions, mortality, the roles of women, the roles of men, rivalry, and the role of the writer. Some overlap, of course, is inevitable, but I hope that this arrangement will be useful. Section titles are inspired by some of the volume titles of Rosenfeld's two major collections: *Gezamlte Shriftn* (New York, 1924, six volumes) and *Geklibene Verk* (Vilnius, 1929, eight volumes).

"A Plague of Cholera" and Other Stories

Section 1

Between Day and Night

These four stories are studies in transitions: from childhood to adulthood, from health to illness, from life to death.

The protagonist of the haunting story "On the River-bank" is fourteen-year-old Miriam, the daughter of a blind father. Raised in poverty and ignorance, Miriam's only acquaintance is the young ferryman who lives nearby. One summer, an inarticulate kind of romance blossoms between the two, inciting Miriam's father—who is not only physically but also spiritually and emotionally blind—to jealousy. Rosenfeld shows us that human potential cannot develop until basic needs are met, including the need for companionship and the language in which to express oneself.

Looking back on pogroms in Europe and foreshadowing the Holocaust, "The Old and the Young" explores the after-effects of severe trauma on family life. The father, Mayer Wolf, is clearly suffering from what we would now identify as post-traumatic stress disorder following the murders of his wife, his father, and his son. As Mayer Wolf gives in to his despair, his adult daughter, Gitl—less affected by trauma, perhaps owing to her youthful resilience—dreams of falling in love and starting a new life.

"A Pair of Glasses" follows an interview between a psychiatrist and a young woman who is obsessed with a pair of sunglasses given to her by a stranger in a chance encounter before his apparent death by drowning. The glasses come to symbolize the mysterious spiritual connection between the two young people. In this story, Rosenfeld invites readers to contemplate the responsibilities that strangers have for each other and the debts that the living owe to the dead.

"In a Dream" is a noir mystery ahead of its time, with a decidedly *Yiddishe tam* (appeal to Jewish tastes and sentiment). In a few short pages, we encounter a hot-blooded young woman, a middle-aged adulterer, a marriage plot, a dying woman, a ghost (or is it?), and a baffled, frightened community. As in many of Rosenfeld's stories, the veil between this world and the next is porous, and the living and the dead exist in close proximity.

On the Riverbank

The day gradually faded into stillness, and a cool, melancholy evening settled in. Thin clouds veiled the sky. A few scattered drops of rain quietly pattered down as the shadows deepened almost imperceptibly, as if the day were a patient so wasted by tuberculosis that the end, when it comes, comes unseen. A river—the most desolate feature in all the landscape—wound gloomily through the darkening scene, a dull, sad mirror into which a corpse had just looked or from which a drowned man had just crawled. Even the frogs that chorused at dusk were silent: a solitary croak sounded now and again, but the others didn't join in and it died into stillness. This meant the night would be cold. The frogs know—they can sense such things.

Miriam, fourteen years old, was sitting in a little boat moored to a stake near the shore, washing the little yellow mushrooms she'd just picked in the forest. Holding her sieve full of mushrooms over the water with one hand, she rinsed them with the other, dropping them into a pot next to her in the boat. Beyond her outstretched hand holding the sieve, she could see a round black blob wobbling in the water, contracting and then flowing out like a puddle of ink as if trying to untether itself and swim away. Miriam knew the shadow was her own head reflected in the water, but she was still afraid to look at it.

The night deepened. The forest that stretched more than a mile inland on the far side of the river had long since congealed into a thick black mass from which an eerie, mysterious darkness seemed to flow upward into the sky. When Miriam glanced in that direction she couldn't believe that just a short time ago she'd left that menacing

3

forest and would soon go back. Now she was relieved to be out of its reach. Closer to hand, scattered here and there along the riverbank where they'd been tethered on long ropes all day, horses stood with heads lowered as they grazed, as black as shadows or photographic negatives in the gloom. The tearing sounds as they cropped at the grass carried clearly to Miriam's ears. Once in a while one of the livelier beasts gave a short hop across the grass, pivoting on its haunches as its mane fluttered like a black flag in the wind. One horse right next to the river was mirrored upside down in the water, its reflection clearer and more sharp-edged in the gloom than the original. It seemed to Miriam that the real horse was the one in the water, while the one standing above, as if stuck by its hooves to the one below, was the water horse's shadow.

On the far shore of the river, right across from Miriam, the ferryboat floated like a turtle on the water, its rope stretching from one shore to the other. At Miriam's distance, the rope looked like an incredibly long, curved stick half-submerged in the water with each end poking into a bank. A few yards from the ferry stood a little shack without a door or windows, just two black holes in its walls: the taller door hole looking toward the ferry and the window hole, a third the height of the other, in the wall facing Miriam. Right now the shack was empty; the red-haired young man who spent his days and nights there had gone to synagogue for evening prayers and to say kaddish, the mourners' prayer, for his father. Later, when he got back, he'd lay a big fire on the shack's dirt floor, and everything would light up like a miracle. Miriam had never been in the shack after sundown—she sometimes peeked inside during the day, but she'd never had the chance to do so at night. Still, she knew the shack would be much nicer at night than it was in the daytime. The fire drew her with its mysterious power. Every evening she watched its fluttery, trembling brightness through the window hole, and it beckoned like a magic spell: *Come, Miriam, come to me—there's no point sitting there in the dark with your blind old father.* Miriam often thought about the red-haired ferryman. He was a good man. Every day he took her across the river and back again, and he wouldn't let her pay.

But even so she was a little afraid of him and refused to go into his shack for any reason. She felt a bit uneasy whenever he was around, though vague longings stirred within her when he wasn't. Normally, a girl like her would confide in her mother, and maybe that's why Miriam was starting to miss the mother that by now she'd almost forgotten.

Miriam felt loneliest in the evenings when the sun started to set on the other side of the river where the cemetery was. The "other side" terrified her. The vague, nebulous thought kept going through her mind that everything and everyone that left this world was still there, on the other side—everything that lived went there to die, and the road through it was possessed by an infinite mystery, its very air haunted by fluttering ghosts. Even the birdsong that filled the cemetery and its environs was freighted with ghastly secrets. Though Miriam seldom took the path to the other side, she'd seen dead animals on it, and she found it quite natural that their bodies would be on that sunset road and nowhere else, because everything that died must find its way to the other side—its final resting place.

When Miriam was finished with her mushrooms, she clambered out of the boat, and, dragging her feet, she reluctantly walked toward her little house, which stood a few yards back from the riverbank. Its dark, hunchbacked windows, set into the wall just a foot from the ground, gazed inward with sorrow, as if the little shack had turned its back to the world and was looking into its own soul, where shadows and poverty came together with a completely different sort of element, the human one. Yet, for all his differences, the man inside that house was as blind as the darkness and poverty that surrounded him.

"What could he be doing in there?" Miriam asked herself.

"Nothing." Miriam heard the voice in her mind as clearly as if someone had answered her unspoken question, and the thought of that nothingness made her shudder. As she neared the shack, her steps grew even shorter. Her bare white feet were pale on the dark mossy earth, and the night was so dark she seemed to be walking on a pair of feet unattached to a body.

As she hesitated on the threshold, Miriam noticed someone walking down the hill that loomed high behind her house, topped by its tall white church that looked less imposing at night because its brass cupola and crosses were swallowed up in the darkness. The girl was overcome by a vague sense of unease, though she scarcely knew why—it wasn't as though she'd never seen anyone walking down that hill before. But she instinctively felt it was someone she knew well—and even before she recognized the man she felt a sudden shock, and the thought leaped in her brain: "It's the redhead, the ferryman." The sight of him made her sad and happy at the same time.

"Good evening," called the ferryman. He walked over to her, stopped, and glanced at her hands. "What have you got there?" Miriam made an awkward gesture, raised her hands a little, and wordlessly showed him her basket of mushrooms.

The ferryman stuck his hands into his pockets, making his jacket gape a little in front, and smiled directly at her. The smile and his friendly greeting made Miriam feel flustered—this was the first time anyone had looked at her that way, and the first time anyone had ever said "good evening" to her.

"Are you about to cook dinner?" he asked, still smiling.

"Yes," she answered, and was instantly sorry, because it seemed to her that wasn't quite the answer she should have given him.

"If you like," he said, "you can come to my place"—he jerked his head toward his dark little shack—"and cook there. I'll light a big fire. It'll only take a second."

Miriam felt something clutch at her heart. Just a few minutes ago she'd been thinking about going into the ferryman's house, but now a new feeling rose up within her: a visceral determination that she, as a woman, shouldn't give this man what he wanted from her. "No. I don't want to cook in your house."

Footsteps sounded in the dark enclosed porch nearby. Both young people turned to its open door. A few seconds later, a hand appeared in the doorway, waved around in the air, and clutched at the door frame. The hand was followed by a large, blurry white something that paused on the threshold and asked, "Who's there?"

"It's me," Miriam said quickly, throwing a confused, apologetic look at the ferryman for having refused him.

"I thought you were talking to someone. Is somebody there?" the old man said, his voice soft, yet demanding an answer.

The ferryman put a hand to his mouth and bent over a little, trying to smother his laughter. "Good evening to you, Reb Shmuel!"

The old man's vague sense of discomfort at hearing his daughter speaking to some stranger on his own doorstep dissipated, and a delighted little smile appeared on his face. "You must be the redhead, the ferryman, eh? You rascal," he chuckled, though at the same time a sad thought crossed his mind—he'd quite naturally thought the voice wasn't the ferryman's but Leyzer's, the young man's father. At the same time, the blind old man was pleased that he hadn't been too far off the mark.

"The ferryman!" the red-haired young man repeated cheerfully. "You recognized me! Do you remember how you'd twist my ears because I used to be so rowdy in synagogue?"

The old man chuckled. "Of course I remember! Such a temper! What a naughty little brat you were!"

"I still am, Reb Shmuel!"

"Still?" the old man asked, a smile in his voice. "So come here then, I'll show you what happens to a brat like you!" He reached out with one hand. The ferryman chuckled heartily and offered his ear, and the old man, with a loud mock growl, gave it a twist. The younger man, who wasn't hurt in the least, bellowed like an ox, pulled his ear free, and rubbed it as if it were frostbitten. "Oh, Reb Shmuel, I thought you'd forgotten how. Help! It hurts, it hurts!"

Miriam's father, with something more important on his mind, changed the subject. "Did you earn any money today?"

"I did—thank God!"

"Good. But a thoughtful young man with money to spend would have brought me a packet of snuff," the old man wheedled. "I haven't had a taste of snuff for two days."

"Thanks for reminding me," the ferryman replied. "Tomorrow I'll bring you a packet of snuff—first class. In the meantime, how's about a smoke?" Not bothering to wait for an answer, he took a square tin out of his breast pocket, opened it with a resounding snap, and began to roll a cigarette. Even though the old man didn't smoke, he'd been taking snuff for a long time and couldn't resist the lure of tobacco. The ferryman rolled a couple of cigarettes and passed one to Reb Shmuel, who took it between two fingers and put it to his lips. Then the younger man lit a match and held it out to the old man. The glow of the match lit up the old man's face. It was a small, pale face, consisting mostly of a nose and a pair of blind, staring eyes—the rest was wildly overgrown with long gray hair. The skin beneath the eyes cringed and quivered in the light of the match; the old man was afraid of the flame, which he could dimly see and feel right before his face. The greasy bill of his cap, pulled down over his eyebrows so that his face resembled a ruin with shuttered windows, reflected the light of the flame, just as his eyes did—a double reflection.

The ferryman managed to light the old man's cigarette just before the match burned out. Then he struck a fresh match and lit his own, the light illuminating a face very different from Reb Shmuel's: a young face with plump cheeks and a thick blond mustache trimmed short. Puffing at his smoke, the ferryman looked across at Miriam, who was standing nearby like a helpless lamb, her hands fidgeting with her basket. Her face was visible in the glow of the men's cigarettes, and her big blue childlike eyes bore a confused expression, as if she didn't know where to look. Long black shadows extended from the feet of the two young people and stretched along the ground, their heads lost in the surrounding darkness.

"Hey! Ferryman!" A voice cut through the fresh air, followed by a distant echo.

The ferryman stood there calmly, as though the voice were calling someone else, his eyes resting on Miriam while he thoughtfully puffed on his cigarette. With each inhalation the orb of his face appeared as if materializing out of the night. Eventually, the old man asked why he wasn't heading for the ferry, adding, "Now I know you really are a lazybones. You did the same thing last night. I was sure you were sound asleep. I heard someone yelling his head off for you—my Miri heard it too. She said, 'Papa, do you hear someone calling the ferryman?' I thought you were sleeping, but now I know you were just too plain lazy to get up."

Miriam felt a stirring of dread. She remembered the shouting—she heard the same thing most nights, and every time she was reminded of a scary story her mother had told her many years ago, about a demon who haunted this man, Moyshe Leyb, in an effort to spirit him away. Moyshe Leyb had had dealings with the evil ones, but after he tried to cut himself loose from the gang of demons, one of them appeared every night to seduce him back. Everyone around could hear it calling, "Come here! Come here! Come to me!"

"Hey! Ferryman!" The voice returned, shouting even louder than before. The owner of the voice was barely visible in the dark, but his black shadow, much more vivid than its original, lay reflected upside-down in the river.

The ferryman hastily said good night and disappeared into the darkness.

It was a beautiful summer morning a few weeks later. The sun lavished its dazzling light over the shabby, half-ruined shack where Miriam stood before a little tin mirror, which she'd bought at the fair for two copper coins earlier that morning, braiding her thick blonde hair into two plaits. A surge of unfamiliar feelings was shouting in her heart—everything within her brimmed with incomprehensible joy, as if she were a fledgling spreading her wings for the first time to launch herself, twittering, into the boundless blue ocean of air. Hands quivering with excitement, she combed out her hair, braiding and rebraiding it while the sense of passionate sweetness, intensified by the sight of her own reflection, poured through her body. She moved gracefully, not at all like a girl who'd grown up in abject poverty in a lonely tumbledown house by the riverbank. A woman had woken within her, a woman fully capable of the flirtatious gestures and refined feelings that God grants to women, no matter where or in what society they grow up. Girls like Miriam are like dazzling, multicolored wildflowers that spring up and thrive in filthy places rank with weeds, and one can't help but wonder: How do such beautiful flowers grow in such ugly surroundings?

Because of the fair, Miriam hadn't gone into the woods that morning, and in any case she'd decided to stay home for the rest of the day to do laundry, which had collected in a considerable amount. Today, even more than usual, she was repelled at the idea of touching her father's dirty underclothes, and she used a stick of kindling to toss them into the tub.

The day was hot, and it was stifling inside Miriam's tiny one-room shack, a quarter of which was taken up by the heating stove. The two beds, one with a screen between it and the oven and the other set at a right angle to the first, were unmade; the dirt floor, pockmarked with holes pecked by the chickens Miriam's mother had kept, was unswept and wet from the laundry. Miriam stood at the washtub with her sleeves rolled up over her pink elbows, energetically toiling away at the heavy work. A fire roared in the stove behind her, and all around were big black earthenware basins full of washing. The air was saturated with smoke and steam, which drifted leisurely out the open door into the shadowy porch, eventually finding its way from there into the open air outside.

The old man was sitting outside on the bench next to the door, basking in the sun and listening intently to the livestock pastured on the broad green meadows on the other side of the river: cattle lowing, horses whinnying, pigs squealing. Even though his vision was long gone, the beasts were there, life-size, in his mind's eye, as if he'd photographed them and filed their images in his head before he'd gone blind.

The black veil before Reb Shmuel's eyes became thinner, more porous. Pictures began to emerge through its fabric, each one clearer than the one before, until the entire world in all its glory stood before him. But just as he was starting to think his vision had actually been restored, a black blot expanded through his awareness, plunging his brain into darkness. Everything, as if by magic, vanished. The old man's face crumpled, and feeble tears appeared in his unseeing eyes.

His entire being filled with an unspoken prayer for death to come quickly and take him. But a wave of horror instantly followed; since he'd lost his vision, he was even more afraid of death than he'd been when he could see. His tears flowed more freely, streaming down his cheeks to lose themselves in his white beard. Now it seemed to him— he was almost convinced—his prayer would be granted and he'd die at any moment. He began to tremble, hands shaking feverishly and one leg jittering back and forth as if it had a life of its own. Finally, his voice thick with tears, he called out to Miriam. He had to call almost a dozen times before she came outside. She'd never made him wait so long before.

Today, more than any other day, Miriam felt her old father as a heavy burden. But when she finally appeared in the doorway, her cheeks flaming from the heat indoors and eyes lit up as though she'd just downed a few glasses of wine, to see her father shaking with fear, she ran straight to him with an anxious cry: "Papa, what's the matter?"

Reb Shmuel silently pointed at the empty space on the bench beside him. Miriam sat cautiously, never taking her eyes off him. The old man didn't move for a few minutes, but then, as if he'd just remembered that Miriam was there, he slowly turned, silently put his arms around her, and squeezed her tight to his chest, his blind eyes staring off into the distance. A chill ran through Miriam's flushed body. She felt her father's cold hands through the back of her thin blouse, which she'd unbuttoned at the front for work. Beneath the blouse she wore only an undershirt, below which nestled her little breasts, round as apples. And deeper yet seethed her revulsion for the withered old man. Everything in her screamed at the touch of his icy hands, and she shuddered with a new, unfamiliar kind of fear.

"Papa, maybe you should go inside," Miriam suggested, hoping he'd let go of her, but the old man didn't reply and she didn't ask again. She tried to wriggle away, but his grasp was too tight. Giving up, she sat quietly with her father for some time. Both were absorbed in their own thoughts—the old man's of dying, and his young daughter's of living. Death and life clutched at each other: the young girl resisting, wishing to escape death's cold arms, and her old father holding tight, absorbing the girl's youthful freshness, inhaling her warm young breath. Eventually, the old man started to feel a bit better, as though death were in retreat, overpowered by the strength of his daughter's vitality.

"The wash water's getting cold," Miriam said, her voice faltering. She renewed her efforts to squirm free, but Reb Shmuel still wouldn't release her. When he did finally let go, the old man's sallow face bore an expression of terrible sadness. He could sense Miriam's distaste, as if he were some stranger, and it seemed to him that his last ray of sunlight had vanished. The bright, luminous world was gone forever—he'd fallen into a frightening, dark abyss where no living soul was to be found. The old man burst into tears, wailing like a small child. Miriam had been his for so long that she didn't even know anyone else—but not anymore.

As for Miriam, she felt better the minute she'd freed herself from her father's arms. She ran straight back into the house and over to her little mirror where it sat on the table, losing herself once more in her reflection, her big blue eyes shining with the happy excitement of a girl on her way to a wedding. The mirror was more than a mirror—it was a mediator between Miriam and her long-suppressed emotions, and the longer she gazed into it, the stronger and steadier her emotions grew, until eventually, after she'd left the mirror and turned back to her work, she heard an unexpected sound: her own thin, soft, resounding voice. Miriam was singing . . . while her father sat on his bench outside the house and wept.

The sun climbed over the woods, red as molten iron, its first beams lighting up the church spire and the tall poplars surrounding it. A thick mist began to rise along the length of the river, and a damp fragrance wafted from the forest. Pools of water somewhere off in the distance saturated the air with their sweet, subtle smells, as if somewhere nearby, hidden from view, was a young woman who'd just woken from luxurious sleep, her body emanating a fresh-smelling, pleasant warmth.

From the town at the top of the nearby hill came the sound of gates creaking open and shut as herders led their animals to pasture. A short time later cattle appeared on the hillside, straggling down the well-trodden paths. They forded the stream, the water splashing and rippling around their legs. Behind them, little groups of geese lingered on the slope, cackling companionably to each other, until at length they launched themselves, shouting into the deafened air, and flew off. Some settled on the water, while others landed on the meadows, craned their necks in various directions, and finally began grazing the grass.

Miriam walked down to the water, wearing a short skirt to her knees and a thin, brightly colored calico blouse. Her head and feet were bare, and a basket dangled from one hand. She was on her way to the meadow to collect feathers shed by the geese—it was the first chore she did every morning. Today she was a little late, and as she stood on the riverbank, dabbling one bare foot in the water while she tried to decide whether to go on or turn back, she noticed the red-headed ferryman getting into a little boat moored next to the ferry. He carried a fishing rod and was clearly on his way to go fishing, but catching sight of the girl, he broke into a wide grin, jumped out of his boat, and called, "Miriam! Good morning!"

Miriam didn't answer—even she didn't know why—and now she felt twice as shy. Ignoring her silence, the ferryman went into his little shack and emerged a minute later. Dangling from his hand by one wing was a dead goose. The young man walked straight over to Miriam with his goose, grinning broadly. When he got to her, he said, his voice strangely eager, "Look, Miriam, here's a present for you! I found it today in the meadow."

Miriam stared at the ferryman in astonishment, glancing uneasily at the goose, which he was brandishing in the air right in front of her face. But her surprised expression faded as she suddenly realized what he meant and why he'd brought her this bizarre gift. How many times had the poor girl walked in the meadow, stooping low to the ground time and again, gathering feathers one by one, until she'd finally managed to collect "a goose's worth"? Oddly, though, she made no move to reach for the dead bird—a heavy, oppressive feeling held her back. Perhaps, if it had been offered by someone other than the ferryman, she would have cheerfully taken her gift and remembered that lucky morning for a long time after. But now all she felt was outraged humiliation. In her wide eyes, no longer child-like but not yet a woman's, a flame of anger sparked to life, though she couldn't have said why—she just knew the goose's carcass made something in her turn inside out. She felt as though she'd suddenly entered an alien world full of gray and revolting things. Miriam, just starting to bloom into womanhood, found herself waking from sweet dreams to crushing disappointment. Too young, she'd come up against the harsh reality of her banal, ugly life. The bad luck that had always plagued her, unmasking itself at her happiest moments, was playing yet another practical joke on her, and her entire being protested—she couldn't and wouldn't reach out to take the gift. Doing so would be a betrayal of her finest, purest emotions. Poor, unfortunate child! Other girls, had they not been so poor, were given flowers—and she was offered a dead goose.

The ferryman saw she was lost in thought. "Don't you want it?" he coaxed.

Miriam didn't answer—she didn't know what to say. Her eyes overflowed with tears like drops of dew that glittered in their millions on the tips of blades of grass under the rising sun.

She couldn't hold back any longer. "It makes me sick!" she shouted, shuddering all over with disgust.

The red-haired ferryman was stung. "If you don't want it, you don't have to take it," he said sulkily and flung the goose into the river so hard that it sank in a shower of water droplets that glittered like rainbows under the sun. A moment later the carcass reappeared, all but the head that dangled in the depths. Expanding rings of water raced with eerie speed across the river's surface from one bank to the other. Miriam turned and burst into tears. What was the matter with her? Even she didn't know.

The ferryman stood there, looking at Miriam's back. She was crying so hard that her braids trembled from side to side. Eventually,

he circled around—though he couldn't see her face, which was buried in her hands—and asked, his voice soft with sympathy, "Are you
all right? I can get it back—it's not too far to reach."

Miriam said nothing. The dead goose floated on the water, surrounded by hungry shoals of minnows and a few larger fish. From
time to time you could hear a quiet splash.

Miriam stood there unmoving. Eventually, she wiped away her
tears, hesitated briefly, suddenly took a step, and fled home.

One evening Miriam returned home from the forest loaded down
with pitchers full of berries she'd picked in the woods. When she put
down her haul and turned to look into her mirror, she was shocked
to see it was no longer on the wall where she'd hung it before she'd
gone out. She gazed around blankly, with dwindling hope, at all four
walls and finally concluded that someone had gotten in and stolen
the mirror. What else could it be?

"Papa, who's been here? Has someone been inside while I've been
gone?" She turned to the old man, who was lying, fully clothed, in
bed, with his legs propped stiffly against the wall like a couple of
wooden beams.

"Not a soul," the old man answered curtly.

Miriam was devastated. She couldn't imagine where the mirror
had gone. Could her blind father have taken it down from the wall?
If she'd left it on the table, he might have taken it from there, but
surely not from the wall—and why would a blind man want a mirror
anyway? The very thought depressed her: a blind man, a mirror. She
glanced uneasily at the old man, and despite her confidence that he
couldn't possibly know anything about her loss, she was tempted to
ask if he'd noticed the mirror anywhere. But she didn't ask—something held her back.

Miriam poured her berries into a big clay basin, sat down at
one end of the table with her back to the window, and began to
measure out the fruit with a glass, pouring the berries back into
the empty pitchers one glassful at a time. She measured out thirty

glasses—almost two gallons. Then, sticking a finger into her mouth to help her concentrate, she calculated that if she left half a gallon of berries at home and sold the rest—she could sell them for sure— she'd end up with about . . . if she got four copper coins per quart, and there were six quarts . . . how much per gallon? . . . per quart? If she got six tenners, that'd be thirty coppers, minus six, which left twenty-four . . .

The thought cheered her up. "Papa, would you like some berries?" she asked.

Her father turned his furrowed face to her but then remembered it was time for afternoon prayers. He slowly lowered his feet from the bed, stood up, and walked unsteadily across the room, his raised hands fumbling for the way and his bulging eyes straining to see. He touched the bench on which stood a tin basin and a jug of water, poured some water over his fingertips, and in a soft, sorrowful voice began his prayer: "And the Lord spoke unto Moses, saying . . ."

Miriam threw her moth-eaten shawl around her shoulders and picked up the berries, about to go out and sell them, when suddenly a tall shadow passed across the walls. She looked through the window and saw the red-haired ferryman. A moment later, he walked straight in, carrying a woven basket under his arm. Miriam's heart began to beat hard. She was thinking about the mirror, wishing she'd been able to look at her reflection before he arrived, and for some strange reason it suddenly occurred to her that the ferryman must have sneaked into the house and taken it from the wall.

The young man stood in the doorway with a curious, amused expression on his face, looking at the berries. Then he walked straight over to the basin and upended his basket into it. "Here you go," he said. "I don't need them."

Miriam knew the ferryman had gotten the berries as payment from the young wives and girls he'd ferried across the river, though he'd never taken anything from her. Now, right out of the blue, he was giving her something that belonged to him. Miriam understood that he hadn't done so purely out of pity, and she smiled at him bashfully.

Miriam and the young man stood there in silence, the ferryman gazing at her intently, his lips twitching in a barely discernible smile. Reb Shmuel stood off to the side praying the Eighteen Benedictions, his blind face turned in the couple's direction. His lips moved silently, as if he weren't praying at all, but rather sending them some kind of secret message. It was all very odd. When the old man finished his prayer he lapsed into silence, and then, turning to face the young people, he put a hand into the pocket of his torn coat, his face tightening into a sad, serious expression, as if he'd found some mystical object there. Then he took his hand from his pocket and showed them the mirror. Miriam stood there in shock, as if her own soul lay in her father's pale, lifeless hand.

The blind man was rubbing the mirror between his fingers. "What's this?" He had no idea what it could be, this thing that had blazed on the wall in the rays of the sun like a lantern. He'd thought it really was a lantern, burning in the daytime. He had just enough sight to tell the difference between night and day, especially if the day was bright. But why on earth had a lantern been lit when the sun was shining? He went over to put it out, but what he touched wasn't a lantern—it was a flat, cold thing that went dark the moment he put his hand on it and flared up again when he pulled his hand back. Puzzled, he touched it once more and the light was extinguished, only to return when he moved his hand away. The mysterious object did the same thing repeatedly until he took it down from the wall and tucked it into his pocket.

"What's this?" the old man asked again.

"A mirror," the ferryman answered, glancing uneasily at Miriam. He took it from the old man's trembling hand, looked it over, and with a bemused little smile offered it to the girl. But Miriam shook her head. She didn't want it, she was afraid of it. She had her reasons.

Summer was imperceptibly drawing to a close. The days continued hot and the nights warm, though the birches were beginning to yellow and the willows' long, delicate leaves were pierced with holes.

Blackberries had vanished from the woods to be replaced with red lingonberries. The goslings and ducklings that had recently thronged the river and its lush meadows were no more. They'd grown up, and now you could barely tell them apart from their parents. Other creatures had matured as well. Mothers no longer cared for their young, and the young ignored their mothers—they forgot each other, and each congregated with its own kind. Miriam was growing up also. Her small breasts were now fuller and rounder. Her face looked more like a young woman's than a little girl's, and her eyes were different, too; they'd lost their childish softness and glow and now looked grave and thoughtful. Behind those eyes, an adult brain was at work. Though Miriam wasn't fully aware of it, she knew ill fortune dogged her every footstep, never leaving her for a minute, and likewise she knew her existence lay in the hands of two people—a young clear-sighted man and an old blind one. Both shadowed her, and she was equally afraid of them both. Two incidents involving both men had left deep, lasting impressions within her: one man, like a blind magician, had found her lost mirror, and the other, on a bright summer morning, had offered her a dead goose. Yet she found herself at the door of the red-haired ferryman's little shack several evenings a week. She never went inside. Sometimes, when the ferryman tried to insist, she scared him by saying she'd go away altogether if he wouldn't let her be. Then he'd leave her on the threshold and go back to sit on a log by the roaring fire, arms crossed over his chest, while she stood with one shoulder leaning against the doorway, gazing into the flames.

"You've grown into a young woman," he said to her once, but she pretended she hadn't heard.

A few times he put some potatoes into the fire to roast for her, but only once did she oblige him by accepting his offering. The old man never let her stay long. She'd hear him calling her name, and though she never answered, she'd run off immediately. Even so, her father would keep shouting, "Miriam! Miriam!" his voice disturbing the nighttime silence and the deep, dark forest echoing his call: "iam, iam." In the town atop the hill, people who weren't used to hearing shouting at night were taken aback. "What's the old guy yelling about?" His voice sounded hopeless, as if he were calling to someone who'd died, or as if he'd lost his mind and was calling the name of some imaginary person. The townspeople had completely forgotten young Miriam. It never occurred to any of them that next to the old skinny tree a young sapling was budding who might be in danger in the dark night. But where could she go?

The old man would be standing on the porch, in the doorway, afraid to venture outside, his white beard like a faint beacon, motionless in the darkness.

"What do you want—what are you yelling about?" Miriam would demand, and sometimes she'd add, "Just like a baby! I can't leave you alone for even a minute."

The old man fell silent, keenly alert to her words. She sounded just like a grown-up! He was amazed—his mind's eye told him she was still a little girl, maybe eight years old. But, he thought uneasily, she wasn't the child she'd been before summer. She'd never before left him all by himself at night, putting out the lantern before she went. He hated that. She thought he wouldn't know when night fell. He *did* know, but he'd never tell her that—he enjoyed keeping his secret. Recently, he thought she'd been trying to hide something from him, and a vague jealousy gnawed at him. He was jealous of her and the light: the bright, visible world.

"Where are you always disappearing to?" he demanded.

Miriam didn't answer—she just stood there a few minutes and then sat down on the bench outside the door and gazed intently at the bright window of the ferryman's shack, listening to the whispering of the river and the stillness of the night. Twenty minutes later she heard footsteps, and a figure swam out of the darkness. It was the ferryman—but no matter how stealthily he walked, the old man heard his footsteps and sensed his approach. He listened for some time and finally asked, "Who's there?"

"No one. Who do you think?" Miriam said, her voice sullen.

The old man lapsed into a listening silence. He knew someone was standing there next to his daughter, but he feigned ignorance.

Let her think he had no idea, he thought with a certain satisfaction. He'd pay her back, an eye for an eye. Just let her try to trick him—he could trick her right back.

One night, after Miriam had gone to bed following yet another such exchange, the old man shuffled over to her side and began touching her, running his hands down the length of her body. She lay there motionless, paralyzed with mute shock as his fingers crawled like cold worms over her warm young skin, each one leaving a horrible, chill trail of cold that made her hair stand on end. The blood that warmed her limbs retreated somewhere inside, and her shivering skin prickled with pins and needles. She couldn't help but imagine that a corpse had crawled out of its grave and was touching her with its dead hands, making her shudder—especially when the cold fingers stroked her female parts. The house was silent and dark, and the world outside the window over Miriam's bed was silent and dark too. The only sounds in the darkness were the muffled chirp of a cricket and from time to time the squeak of a mouse.

Finally, with a heavy groan, the old man drew back and lay down in his own bed. A few minutes later, he spoke: "Light the lamp, Miriam."

Miriam hesitated. "Why, Papa?"

"I'm going to die . . . tonight."

Miriam's father didn't die, not then and not for a couple of weeks thereafter. But from that night on, he stopped calling her home—she could have been lost out there in the dark for hours on end, for all he knew—and he spent more and more time in bed. And then one morning, when Miriam got up, she was shocked to see him lying there with his mouth frozen open and his eyes closed. She let out a little scream. From under the ripped old overcoat the old man was using as a blanket, a rat emerged, jumped to the floor, and vanished.

That same night, Miriam let the red-haired ferryman kiss her— her very first kiss.

The Old and the Young

The snow reached almost halfway to the top of the cellar apartment's window when old Mayer Wolf got up at dawn for work. The minute he saw the whiteness piled up on the other side of the glass, he was struck by the odd notion that it wasn't actually snow, but rather a pair of nameless ghosts—spirits from some unknown, faded world—that had come to visit him and were waiting outside with their pale backs pressed against the windowpane. It was no colder inside than it had been yesterday, before the snowfall, but he could still feel the snow breathing its icy breath through the glass.

It was dark in the house, and Mayer Wolf couldn't decide if the snow was making the inside darker or the outside brighter: it had to be one or the other, he thought; it couldn't be both. It seemed, however, that the darkness inside and the daylight outside had come to a tacit agreement to find the middle ground, and in the shadows of the courtyard the snow blanketed the earth like the pale dregs of a dark night—or a lifeless dawn.

The old man walked into the kitchen and looked glumly at the sewing machine that stood in front of the window. He struck a match on the black stove—it was still faintly warm—and lit the tin lamp with its sooty glass, after which he washed his hands and said the blessing. Then, in a soft, mournful voice, he began the morning prayers.

When Mayer Wolf sat down at the sewing machine, the first thing he saw was the image in the two snow-covered bottom panes of the window: an indistinct figure that, since it was his own reflection, should have looked exactly like him but didn't. His white beard was invisible in the white mirror, and though his black jacket and hat stood out distinctly his face was wraithlike, a foggy blur with a pair of glasses glittering on the misty, barely visible nose.

The old man suffered from a strange malady: he was afraid of mirrors. He'd had this fear ever since the pogrom in which his wife, son, and elderly father had been murdered. Mayer Wolf's hair and beard had gone gray overnight from grief. The first time he'd seen himself in a mirror, with his silvery beard making him look just like his dead father, something in his brain gave way, and he started screaming that the reflection wasn't his own. And for some reason that confusion still lingered. His father, it seemed, hadn't been murdered but had taken possession of him, hiding inside him or somehow becoming him. Mayer Wolf no longer knew whether he was his father or his father's son: most likely his father, he thought, or maybe he was both at the same time—but if that was so, then who had been killed?

The old man sat working at his machine with a disquieting awareness of the eerie figure, only its upper half visible, sitting across from him, imitating each of his movements. This impersonator, which must have arrived with the snow from some faraway world—a dead white world—was now peering at its white-haired counterpart through the window and calling him away . . .

Mayer Wolf knew the ghostly image was really his own reflection and was surprised that it had no beard. Why not? Where had it gone? And then a new thought struck him: the image must be his younger self, enveloped in an outer appearance of hoary old age and returned in a dream, having fallen along with the snow from the heavens above. The old man sat working, still glancing up from time to time, but now the fear he'd felt when he'd first seen the reflection was slowly fading: he was seeing himself as a youth. His fear dwindled from one glance to the next until he was staring at the blurred figure, astonished to realize it wasn't himself but his son—of course, it was his murdered son, who for some reason was wearing his father's jacket. It was his son, looking just like his father, Mayer Wolf, when he'd been a young man, and Mayer Wolf looked just like his own father, and all three were somehow, simultaneously, one being. All three were amazingly identical, and all three lived inside him . . . or perhaps it was he who lived inside the other two? And although Mayer Wolf knew that the image across the room wasn't really his son, he couldn't escape the disorienting sensation that he was sitting here in the kitchen, watching his son reflected in the window.

A wave of depression overwhelmed the old man. He couldn't work anymore. The kitchen was still freezing cold. A white strip of snow, packed into the gap at the bottom of the door that opened to the outside, breathed its melancholy breath into the dark, dirty kitchen, filling the room with an icy chill.

Mayer Wolf stood up from his chair and noticed that the reflection's head, which was either his son's or his father's—he still couldn't decide—had vanished. The black jacket, visible from the shoulders down, was all that remained. The head was gone, effortlessly detached from the body, and for some reason it suddenly dawned on the old man that this was an omen: he was about to die. The thought didn't particularly bother him. In fact, it felt perfectly natural, and the idea he'd just had—to go back to bed—seemed somehow connected with the omen he'd just been given, because never before in his life had he gotten up in the morning and then gone straight back to bed.

The old man stood motionless for a few minutes and then slowly walked into the dark room he'd left a half hour ago, tiptoed over to his bed, took off his boots and heavy jacket, and crawled under the covers.

Gitl, Mayer Wolf's daughter, woke up early. She sat up in bed, looked through the window, and saw the snow outside. A joy she'd never felt before rushed through her, making her forget her abject poverty and even the fact that she didn't have warm winter clothing. Naked, she jumped out of bed and crossed to the window, a delighted smile on her pale lips. The courtyard was so beautiful! And the rooftops—completely white! It was just like a holiday! And look—there were a couple of boys making a snowman. Gitl envied them—if she'd been a bit younger, or if she hadn't been the poor tailor's daughter, she would have run outside to help.

Gitl remembered that the lodger, who'd moved in just yesterday, had asked her to wake him—after his first night in a new bed, he was afraid he'd sleep in and be late for work. Full of happy energy, she knocked at his door and a few minutes later heard his sleepy mumble: "Oh. Uh." The girl quickly pulled on her blouse and under-skirt, at the same time glancing into her father's room, surprised to see he was still sleeping. Then she ran into the kitchen to tidy up a little before the young man, whom she didn't yet know properly, came in to wash.

Gitl began by mopping up the black dye stains that the clothes drying on lines overhead had dripped onto the floor, and just as she was finishing, the lodger—a lively looking man in his twenties—walked into the room. The two young people smiled at each other for no reason in particular, and the lodger asked, "Have you been out-side yet?" Gitl caught the meaning behind his words and answered with spirit, "Amazing—just look at the snow!"

They stood there a few minutes, he with his arms crossed over his chest, she still holding her grimy rag, both looking out the window with cheerful smiles. At length he remarked, "It's a perfect day for sledding."

"It certainly is," she agreed.

"Too bad it's a workday," the young man said regretfully, and Gitl, again hearing his unspoken words, remarked, "It would be nice to go for a walk later, in snow like that."

The lodger seized his opening. "If only there was someone to go with."

Gitl understood from his words and his smiling look that she was that "someone," and, hiding her pleasure, she averted her eyes.

Right after the lodger left for work, Gitl went into his room and made his bed. She did so with pleasure, and especially enjoyed fussing over the mattress, which gave off a fresh, masculine scent. Afterward she stood there a few minutes, looking over the room as if she'd never seen it before, overcome with the desire to make it attractive—not for his sake, but . . . She didn't think it through, but she had the vague idea that she wanted to make his room more feminine, breathe herself into it, mingle her breath with the masculine scent that filled the room. She wanted to surrender a part of herself—she wanted to imbue these walls and this air with her female being.

After Gitl finished cleaning the room, she went to her father and, feeling a little worried, woke him up. The old man opened his eyes, and she said softly, "Papa, get up. It's so late already."

But Mayer Wolf, glancing out the window at the untrodden snow, couldn't even contemplate getting out of bed: a sense of blinding, frightening despair smothered him, falling over him like the blanket of snow in the courtyard, and it seemed as though it wasn't snow he was looking at, but piles of corpses, tangled together, their white shrouds covering the earth.

He hesitated a few minutes. "I'm too tired," he answered at last.

Gitl tried to cheer him up. "Papa, just take a look outside."

"What's going on outside?" he asked with a confused look.

"Look—see how white everything is!"

The old man fixed his dull eyes on her, but Gitl didn't notice. She was looking out the window where, it seemed, the whole world was covered by a white veil, just like a bride under the wedding canopy, and Gitl was filled with a joy that she'd never felt before. Inarticulate hope filled her soul. Something drew her, tugged her into a white, new, faraway place: vague, happy thoughts, like chicks warming themselves under their mother, jostled each other and comfortably nestled together. Her heart was beating harder than usual, and her blood flowed with a sweet, easy warmth, showing from time to time in her face and touching her pale cheeks with color.

"Papa!" she coaxed. "Just look at the snowman they made."

The old man turned to the wall and waved her away. Gitl put on a shawl, went outside, and rubbed her face all over with the freshly fallen snow. She was thinking about the lodger who'd just moved in.

A Pair of Glasses

A good friend of mine, a doctor of psychiatry, told me this story recently. Not too long ago, he'd seen a young woman who wanted his advice on what she should do about her husband, who was insanely jealous.

The doctor told this woman she was wasting his time—he couldn't help her. He thought that would be the end of it and motioned to his assistant to let in the next client, who was waiting in the reception room. But the young woman stopped him: "It's not what you think, Herr Professor."

"What do you mean, it's not what I think?" asked the doctor. "You said your husband is a very jealous man. Jealousy is a psychological problem, true enough. But if you're about to tell me you've given him no reason to be jealous, what can I do to help? You should have told him to come see me—otherwise, he'll have to get over it on his own. Why are *you* here?"

The young woman said her situation wasn't what the doctor thought and asked him to hear her out. He offered her a seat, returned to his own chair, and said, "Go ahead, please."

The young woman gave a little smile and said all in a rush, "My husband is jealous of a pair of glasses."

The doctor wasn't particularly surprised. A woman can get jealous if she smells another woman's perfume on her husband or if she finds a stranger's hairpin in one of his dresser drawers, so why shouldn't a husband's suspicions be aroused by a pair of glasses? And obviously, if his wife is hanging onto a pair of glasses that belongs to some other man, he has a reason to be jealous. But at the same time, the doctor was curious to know more.

"Why is he jealous of a pair of glasses?"

"Because, um . . ."

The doctor could tell his client had more to say on the matter, but she clearly didn't feel comfortable telling him. He decided to make things easier for her: "Whatever happened isn't important. Maybe your husband can't stand it that you have a pair of glasses that belongs to an old friend of yours, or maybe . . ." He trailed off.

The young woman jumped up from her chair, raked her fingers through her hair in a graceful, impatient gesture, and practically yelled, "What friend? What are you talking about?"

The doctor said he hadn't meant to imply anything at all. He understood perfectly well that wives could have friends and still be faithful to their husbands. He was about to go on, but his client interrupted. "I didn't even know him!"

"Who didn't you know?" the doctor asked in confusion.

"The man whose glasses they were."

Now the doctor was completely stumped. Why would a woman hang on to a pair of glasses that belonged to some strange man? If this young woman expected anyone to believe *that*, there had to be something wrong with her. So, looking straight into her lively, bright eyes, he said, "Excuse me, young lady—you came here asking my advice, and if you *want* my advice, you need to be frank with me. You need to tell me about the man with the glasses: Who is he, what's your relationship with him, and why, of all things, would you want to keep a pair of his glasses to remember him by? Can you answer those questions?"

The client hesitated for quite a long time. Eventually, she said, "It's very difficult, Herr Professor. If I could just explain it all to my husband, he wouldn't be jealous. I've tried again and again, but I can't."

And insofar as she succeeded in describing what happened, here's the story:

It was a hot summer's day. She was lying on the beach reading a book, surrounded by hundreds of legs walking and running all around her. Suddenly, she noticed a particular pair of legs—they were bare, with bare feet—standing right beside her. Next to the legs was an outstretched hand, and in the hand was a glasses case. She glanced up from her book, and there was a man wearing a bathing suit. When she tilted her face higher to get a better look at the tall figure, the stranger said to her—he spoke in English—"Can I leave my glasses with you?"

She couldn't see his face properly because the sun was in her eyes and looking up made them water. But there was no need to get a good look at him; he wanted to give something to her, after all, not the other way around.

"All right," she said. "Leave them here."

The minute the stranger left, the young woman returned to her book and immediately forgot about him and his glasses. A fair length of time passed before suddenly, with a little shock of unease, she remembered that some stranger had left a pair of glasses for her to take care of.

Without quite knowing why, she picked up the glasses case, sat up, and began looking around for the stranger, scanning the crowds around her, hoping to spot him. But here's the remarkable thing: she was looking on the sandy beach because that's the one place she was absolutely certain he wasn't. If she'd been sure that he *was* there, after all, she wouldn't have been so worried and wouldn't have had to look. She knew perfectly well she was searching the beach as a way to calm her anxiety . . . but it wasn't working. So she thought things over: Even if her fears were true, so what? Even if something *had* happened to him, what did it have to do with her? Why should the fate of this stranger be more important than the fate of any of the other strangers for miles around who were swimming in the sea?

With that thought, she stretched out on the warm sand again and turned back to her book. But she couldn't concentrate. She read a paragraph and had no idea what she'd just read. Something kept nagging at her.

The worst thing was that she didn't know what time it was, nor did she know what time it had been when the stranger had left his glasses with her. The young woman went on to tell the doctor, taking some pains over her explanation, that when you're on the beach in a bathing suit, you lose track of time. She believed that was true of everybody, not just herself. Normally, most people can estimate what time it is, but hardly ever when they're lying on the beach sunning themselves—then time seems either to fly by like a flash or, on the other hand, to drag out incredibly slowly.

As the young woman thought it all over, she succeeded in calming herself down for a while (she wasn't sure how long). But then her worry returned, along with a sense of annoyance with the whole situation. All right—so what if the man had drowned? Why should she care more about him than any other stranger? She read almost every day in the newspaper that someone had drowned somewhere or other on one of the New York beaches—did that bother her? So why was she bothered now? Had this stranger suddenly become more important to her than any of the others, just because he'd entrusted her with his glasses?

As these thoughts ran through the young woman's mind, she opened the case to find a pair of large dark-green sunglasses that looked almost black against the dark plush lining. Their color depressed her. She had the vague sensation that a pair of eyes was peering up at her from the vast depths of the sea . . . such dark, cloudy eyes . . . a pair of eyes that looked like glass, and a pair of glasses that looked like eyes, had accidentally fallen from the hands of a stranger into her own, and . . . and now, for the first time, the question entered her mind: What should she do with this pair of glass eyes?

The sun was already far in the West. The noise of the crowd was dying down, their voices fading. From time to time a cool breeze stole over the beach, a reminder that night was waiting in the wings. It must be around six o'clock—time to go home, she thought, because her husband was expecting her at seven, and he'd worry if she was late. She should go down to the sea to wash off the sand that was clinging to her, but the thought of wading into the ocean filled her with fear—a fear of the mysterious, a fear of the supernatural—a man had just drowned in that sea, and she . . .

The young woman shivered. "Herr Professor!" When she'd gone swimming in the past, she'd never felt any connection to the men who happened to be in the water around her. But now, standing on the shore, her mounting dread stopped her from wading in, because . . . well, because she had the feeling she'd somehow be united with him, the man with the glasses—if she went into that sea, she'd become one with the man who had drowned. "Herr Professor, tell me: Am I crazy? Or not?"

The doctor reassured her. All of us, he said, are liable to erotic fantasies under certain conditions, but . . . "Rest assured, young lady, there's nothing wrong with your mind."

"So why do I still have the glasses? Why don't I throw them out? Why don't I smash them to pieces, when my husband—whom I love very much—wants me to?"

The doctor reassured her again. Any sensitive person, he said, would feel the same way in the same situation, and they wouldn't be able to throw out the glasses, either. He couldn't tell her exactly why. And if he were to suspect that either one of the married couple had something wrong with them, he'd suspect her husband. "Why doesn't he want the glasses in the house? What did he tell you?"

"He didn't say anything. He just says he doesn't want them around. He doesn't want them in the house."

"And he's jealous, you say?"

"I think so. If he wasn't jealous, why would it bother him?"

"If he's jealous, send him to talk to me."

As the client was about to leave, the doctor remembered something. "There's just one last thing, if you don't mind my asking. In everything you've just told me, there's something I still don't understand. Did the man with the glasses really drown? He could have just forgotten about his glasses, or maybe he didn't come back for some other reason."

The young woman replied that the next day she'd read in the newspaper that someone had drowned on that beach.

"But how can you be sure it was him?"

She thought it over a few minutes. "I'm sure," she said firmly.

I'm sure—what more could the doctor do? If she hadn't been so sure, he could have given her some advice, though he still found the whole thing puzzling.

What really happened? And even if the drowned man really *was* the man with the glasses, so what? Does the wife really need to keep them, given that her husband's making such a fuss about it? Well, who knows. Will we ever understand the human soul?

In a Dream

Zelik the cattle dealer had been scurrying frantically from house to house since early morning. He'd been trying to gather a minyan, a prayer group of ten men, to go with him to the cemetery and beg forgiveness from his dead wife, Freyda, who'd appeared to him the night before and ordered him to marry Zelda, Nekha the baker's daughter. Some of the men told Zelik there was no need for a minyan—it was enough to have three pious Jews interpret his dream—but the cattle dealer swore that, as sure as he was a father to his children, he *hadn't* been dreaming: he'd seen the ghost with his own two eyes. True, he'd thought he was dreaming at the time, when he'd heard her voice: "I am Freyda, your dead wife, and I order you to marry Zelda, Nekha's daughter." But Zelik wasn't the kind of man to be frightened by a dream, so, after thinking things over a few minutes, he got dressed and went outside—where he was shocked to see the very thing he'd least expected. The minute he laid eyes on his wife, she started to drift away. He unthinkingly followed, and they went on like that, Freyda in the lead, Zelik trailing behind. Of course, he wasn't happy about the whole business, but to go home meant turning his back on the ghost—a terrifying prospect. So he walked on, telling himself, "What difference does it make? If I die, I die. That's the worst that can happen."

In short, Zelik followed the dead woman to the cemetery. When she stopped at the cemetery wall, he stopped too, waiting to see what would happen next. What happened next was this: she clambered over the wall and disappeared.

At the same time that Zelik was rushing from house to house trying to collect a minyan to take to the cemetery, Nekha the baker, shawl flung over her shoulders, was also rushing from house to house. Nekha was looking for her daughter Zelda, the very Zelda whom, just that night, Zelik's dead wife had commanded him to marry. Nekha had no idea where her daughter had gone. She wasn't in bed, and Nekha hadn't heard her leave the house.

The townspeople didn't have to be particularly superstitious to be shocked by that night's events. Everyone was caught up in the fear of the unknown. Even the teacher, the freethinker, couldn't explain what was going on, and people mocked him. "*Now* he doesn't have a thing to say, does he, the wise guy?" they jeered.

It was winter and pouring hard. Wooden houses, stone walls, and fences were black with water. The snow underfoot looked like a grater: packed hard, dirty, full of holes. The weather was truly ugly, and Zelik had a hard time collecting his minyan. No one wanted to go all the way to the cemetery on the edge of town through such awful weather.

Finally, a little group gathered on the street, Zelik in the lead. The men trudged along, bundled up, hunched into the wind, a black umbrella tossing over each head. Pale faces with frightened eyes peered from the windows. Nekha the baker was still running around wrapped in her shawl, terribly upset, trying to find her daughter. From house to house she went, but nobody had seen Zelda or knew where she was.

Three women lived in their little house on the Gentile side of town: the grandmother, her daughter, and her granddaughter. The grandmother was an old woman in her seventies. For years now her burial shroud had been waiting in the trunk, the same trunk in which her granddaughter kept her trousseau of hand-stitched handkerchiefs and embroidered tablecloths. The time was right, and they were both prepared: one to die, the other to marry.

Nekha, the younger mother, and her daughter Zelda made their living from the loaves and rolls they baked. Early every Sunday morning Zelda, with her kneading trough full of bread, appeared on the path that the peasants took from church, where she sat on the porch of Zelik's house. Zelda was a healthy-looking young woman with a shiny round face like one of the rolls she'd just taken out of the oven. Her eyes were sharp, like those of a clever wild bird. Her lips were juicy-red, and the nostrils of her broad nose fluttered with every breath like a young mare's.

Zelda never went out on weekdays. She was hard at work, kneading basins of bread and troughs of challah. At night, all alone in her room, the young woman would toss and turn in her lonely bed. After such nights she'd wake up angry and irritable, hair a mess, face flushed, eyes burning as if she'd come straight from Gehenna. She'd squabble with her mother and grandmother and sleep away whole Saturdays without even changing the sheets or her clothes.

On Sundays, though, long after Shabbas and its festivities were over, Zelda would get up early with a smile on her face. Sunday was her favorite day of the week. She worked Sundays, as she did every other day except Shabbas, but on Sundays she got to keep the money she earned. Even more precious than her earnings, though, was Zelik's porch. Oh, how she loved those summery Sunday mornings; how impatiently she looked forward to them! The sun and the porch . . . she was all alone in the natural world, all by herself with the sky above and the wooden boards below. Here, her sorrows forgotten, she surrendered with joy to her passionate feelings. In her cramped, overheated house she went through life in a fog. But here, outdoors, on Zelik's porch, she knew what she wanted and to whom her heart was drawn. It was drawn to Zelik, that forty-year-old man who had children older than her. She was crazy about Zelik. His big, hairy hands like paws, his tigerish eyes, and his thick, red lower lip drove her out of her mind. His slightest gesture attracted and excited her—a forty-year-old man forged from steel and iron, his neck burned copper by the sun, his thick black hair threaded with gray. Whenever Zelik was around, Zelda practically glowed. His black beard alone, with its stiff, wiry silver-white hairs that blended into his thick mustache, conjured up the image of firm, deep-rooted, masculine strength.

Zelik had a sick wife, Freyda, who spent more time in bed than out of it. She was a wreck: skinny, shriveled, skin and bones, as dusky and dry as a wooden grave marker. Zelda was overjoyed that Zelik's wife was like that. That's why Zelda was sitting there on his porch; it was her strategy for finding her way into Zelik's heart.

He was always the first person out of the house in the morning. There he'd be, this powerful, lusty forty-year-old man, without a thought for his sick, dying wife, nudging Zelda's back with his booted foot, to which she'd respond politely, "Good morning, Reb Zelik."

"Well, look who's full of the devil today!"

"Would you like a roll, Reb Zelik?" With those words, Zelda's face flushed deeply. As Zelik kept prodding her with the toe of his boot, she went on, "Go ahead, Reb Zelik!" Then, without turning around or looking at him, she said, "See how fresh and pink they are—practically bursting!" And Zelik, wearing his thin silk yarmulke over his tousled hair and an unbuttoned shirt over his hairy chest, would bend over Zelda from behind, leaning his knee into her back. He'd reach around her, grab a double handful of young flesh, and, tugging and squeezing, say over and over, "Now these are rolls! What a pair of rolls!" while she bit at his big, hairy hand.

After Zelda had sold all her goods, she'd visit Zelik's house and help his daughters with their housework. On Sundays there was always a gathering of traders from out of town, so there was plenty of work to do. In a couple of hours, Zelda would give the whole place a thorough cleaning, but she'd get offended if Zelik tried to pay her. Her particular aim was to please Freyda, his wife. Zelda wanted the sick woman, who knew she was dying, to keep her in mind before the end.

The cemetery wall, streaked wet with rain, looked even gloomier than usual. The black, naked trees, visible a long way off, loomed tall with silent mystery, and among them were grave markers: stone slabs with rounded tops and black and gold lettering. Here and there were larger tombs with their low, sharp-peaked roofs poking out of the snow. Long, white drifts covered the ground. From a distance they looked like shroud-clad corpses that had clambered out of their graves and were lying next to them on the frozen earth.

Gabriel, the synagogue caretaker, opened the door of the little hut where the dead were prepared for burial. One by one, the ten men were swallowed up in the gloom, and then, singly and in couples, they emerged from the other door into the cemetery. Gabriel, in the lead, walked hunched over, his back rounded, clutching his walking stick. His feet sank knee-high into the deep, crusty snow, so that he looked much shorter than he actually was. Nevertheless, he strode ahead bravely, as if he were the one in charge—the only man there who knew anything at all.

Suddenly, Gabriel stopped, both arms reaching out before him.

"Gabriel!" shouted one of the men. Gabriel didn't answer, and everyone realized he was too terrified to say a word. At this, his nine followers became one—one man with nine heads and paralyzed limbs and tongues.

"Sh'ma Yisroel!" Gabriel shouted the prayer, in a voice that didn't sound like his—it was a voice screaming from an open grave. He turned back to the others and pointed with his walking stick: "That's her, lying there! Look!"

"Freyda!"

"We're here . . ."

"We're a minyan . . ."

"We beg you . . ."

"Freyda, go to your rest!"

"We're here to apologize . . ."

"Your husband, Zelik, son of Yekhiel . . ."

"He begs you, before the whole community, to forgive him . . ."

"He says . . ."

"He says to you . . ."

"Go to your eternal rest!"

"He says he will marry Zelda, Nekha's daughter!"

Huddled together, step by faltering step, the men walked over to Gabriel where they could see the dead body sprawled over the low, sharp-peaked stone roof of the monument it had fallen across, legs on one side and head on the other. In a moment Gabriel was next to the body. He looked once and again, then quickly stepped back and moved forward once more. For the last time he looked into the dead body's face and then cried out in a voice that didn't sound like his, "Zelda!"

An hour later a fresh grave lay next to Freyda's. They laid Zelda inside in the same position they'd found her. She was so stiff that they couldn't even straighten her out.

Section 2

In the Shadow of Death

The threat of death is a constant presence in Rosenfeld's fiction, ranging from the metaphorical—the death of love, culture, security—to the death of individuals and entire communities. Two stories in this section portray the lurking threats to life and safety in uncertain times and describe the reactions of ordinary people to impending catastrophe.

"In Transit" is probably set around 1919 or 1920, during the Bolshevik Revolution, during the Russian Civil War following the Bolshevik Revolution, at which time it was often dangerous to be either Jewish or communist—and doubly dangerous to be both. Two young Jewish women, caught up in the chaos, are observed by passersby in a train station. In a few short pages, the story encapsulates the complex interplay between political, religious, and social groups and examines the conflicted loyalties of ordinary people.

The title story of this collection, "A Plague of Cholera," though set in 1893, foretells elements of the coronavirus pandemic that began in 2019. Many elements of the story will resonate with readers: the rumors and fears of impending catastrophe, the rationalizations—"either there was no plague, or, if there was, it was nothing to worry about"— the townspeople's suspicion of government and medical authorities, and the threats to life, established traditions, and daily routines. As the plague advances, it becomes clear that certain segments of society—women, the elderly, the poor—suffer disproportionately, while members of the wealthier classes buy themselves out of danger. Social divisions are exposed: Christians against Jews, pious Jews against the less pious, older women against younger, rich against poor.

This sprawling story, whose plot does not follow a continuous arc, is presented as a series of vignettes. The experience of reading is similar to following the daily news as a pandemic spreads from family to family, community to community, while government authorities and self-appointed experts argue about what, if anything, must be done to vanquish an invisible and inexorable enemy.

In Transit

The winters had been terribly cold for two years in a row. All Europe was frozen solid, and in the lands where winter was typically hard, things were even worse.

I'd just left Zamość, a city in Poland where I'd given a literary reading, and since I had to change trains, I was about to get off at the next town.

The wind-blasted trains pulling into the station were grizzled with snow. White, frozen streaks peered gloomily out of every crack and corner, and the cars' dark panels were plastered with big snowy patches. Their windows were so glazed with frost that no glass was visible—they didn't look like windows at all, but rectangular sheets of ice fixed into the walls. One got the impression the trains in their white mourning veils were grieving the miserable cold that oppressed the earth and its people, expressing the anguish of a frozen, snow-covered world. They looked like refugees from some terrible foreign land that was even whiter and icier than this place they'd escaped to.

Because of the dreadful cold, the trains were running behind, often by as much as the journey from one place to another would normally take, and sometimes even more. Nevertheless, the trains pulling into the station seemed to be bustling along as if trying to make up for lost time.

My train pulled in slowly. There was a great deal of jolting and screeching accompanied by the ear-splitting shrieks of the cast-iron brakes, and I couldn't help but think that the train's agonized arrival was a result of its being fifteen minutes late—a long delay for a short journey that normally took only thirty-five minutes. It was the train's lateness, I thought, that made it screech and jerk back and forth so violently it could barely haul itself into the station.

With every backward jolt of the train, the passengers lurched back too. They bore their discomfort with silent resignation, and I mused about how inconsequential people were, how helpless in the face of nature, despite their intelligence and technical achievements.

It was a few minutes after ten when we finally arrived. The cold bit so hard I couldn't even tell where it hurt. The snow squeaked loudly, impudently, under the feet of the couple of dozen passengers who disembarked with me, as though the icy winter were trumpeting its absolute power over us with a jeering melody. A full moon encircled by a huge pink halo hung overhead, illuminating the empty, pale landscape around us. It was as though a bright white dream of dead worlds had poured into the sky and flowed into a thick crystalline layer on the ground below, which only in summer could you call "earth."

The station was jammed with people from trains that had arrived before mine. They were sitting at two long tables set up end to end, drinking tea and eating. The newly arrived passengers took off their outer wrappings and heavy furs and found places where they could make themselves comfortable. Those who didn't manage to find seats perched on their luggage. Some went to the serving station and drank their hot tea while standing at the counter; others, evidently having lost patience while waiting for their train, milled through the crowds. Almost everyone was smoking, and the smoke drifted slowly, floating in the warm, bright air above our heads, clustering in dense clouds around the gas lamps in fixtures attached to the walls, hovering like a pall of misery over the heads of the passengers, a visible reminder of the impatient boredom of people who've been plucked out of their homes but can't get to wherever it is they want to go.

For a few minutes after I entered the waiting room, the door kept opening and closing. Whenever the door opened, the freezing outdoors air spat an icy blast of fog inside, each blast driving one or two people ahead of it. Each new cloud of vapor settled at everyone's feet, chilling their legs, and everyone in the waiting room would glare at the newcomers and their accompanying streams of cold air as if they were unwelcome invaders, members of a hated and hateful occupying army.

Among the last of the new arrivals was a group of four: an armed soldier followed by two young women, with another soldier bringing up the rear. They stood by the entrance, all bunched together in a corner between the door and the wall, and it was obvious they hadn't arrived together by accident. Anyone could see that the girls were prisoners and that the two soldiers had escorted them here under guard.

Still standing by the door, the girls put down their bundles and began to take off their outer clothing, helping each other unbutton the shawls that crisscrossed snugly around their chests and fastened at their backs. They worked quickly, their expressions carefree and confident, and as they chattered and smiled at each other, I began to doubt my earlier conclusions. Could they really be prisoners? If the men with them had been Jewish, you'd have thought they were two Jewish girls who'd come with their uniformed boyfriends. And the girls *were* Jewish—you could see it in their faces and hear it in their speech: they were speaking Yiddish. It's hardly worth mentioning that the language they were speaking was a surprise in this place, where the majority of the population was Christian, but even more surprising was *how* they spoke. Their voices were fearless and unconcerned, and they paid no attention at all to their guards.

"Communists." One young man, obviously Jewish, half-whispered the word to his companion. He glared at the girls and a few minutes later added, "Why the hell are they speaking Yiddish? Would it kill them if the Poles don't know they're Jewish?"

Glancing around at the Christian passengers, I noticed—and this surprised me—that not one of them was sneering or laughing at the prisoners, the Jewish communists. I didn't hear a single word mocking the girls—only interest and curiosity. Maybe that was why the young man was so angry; the fact that the girls were speaking Yiddish was provoking nothing but curiosity among these Christians.

In an area where there were so few Jews, the Polish majority had probably never heard anyone speaking Yiddish. That in itself must have lessened the hostility you'd expect them to feel toward Jews in general—let alone Jewish communists.

The girl prisoners carried on, minding their own business, chattering away with one another so casually you'd think they were in their own familiar, comfortable house in their own hometown with nobody paying them the least bit of attention. It was just as though no one else was around, just the two of them. You can imagine two young women being so completely focused on each other only when they're sitting cozily side by side on a bed in one of their bedrooms. So when the young man's next remark came, it was right on target: "Look at them—they seem so happy. You'd think they were on their way to a wedding."

After a short pause, his companion asked, "Where are they being taken—do you know?"

"What do you mean, do I know? Of course I know," the first man said, offended that his companion thought he might not. "They're on their way to Siedlce—Siedlce Prison. Have you heard of it?"

"No, I haven't—so what?"

"If you don't know about Siedlce Prison, you're as dumb as an ox."

"And I suppose you're the smartest guy in town?" Now the second man was offended.

His observation had merit—his talkative, know-it-all companion certainly *looked* like the smartest guy in town, at least according to the beard he was sporting. He was clean-shaven over his cheekbones and under his chin down to his neck, but the shaved part was divided by a narrow strip of beard, a hairy ribbon winding between the two shaved halves of his face. Just this beard alone proclaimed its owner's intelligence: instead of shaving once like everyone else, he shaved both halves of his face separately and kept some of his beard into the bargain.

"Don't you think they're giving Jews a bad name?" continued the young fellow, who was clearly the son-in-law of some wealthy man. He added in an undertone, "You know, I'm really surprised that none of the goyim here are harassing them. If I were a goy, I'd tell those girls a thing or two about their filthy communes. Girls like them . . ." Then he spat out a word that people say and write down, but which can't be published.

While he was talking, one of the girls and one of the soldiers left their corner and made their way through the thick crowd to the food counter, and as they were passing the garrulous young man he loudly repeated the filthy word he'd said before. The girl glared at him, but she and the soldier didn't stop. When they reached the food counter, she had a glass of tea and a bite to eat. On their way back, the girl looked straight into the eyes of every person she passed, her own eyes burning. Then her gaze fell on the man who'd just blurted out that unprintable word, and she smacked him across the face.

There was an outcry, and a wave of people surged toward them, as if a crowd of newcomers had suddenly poured into the station to set off a riot, and in the noise you could hear the young man's voice, out-and-out provoking the Poles to attack the Jewish prisoners: "*Psiakrew*! The hell with them! Damned snot-nose little bitches, and already communists! *Cholery takie*, damn them to hell!"

Who knows how things might have turned out if, at that precise moment, we hadn't heard the heavy, ponderous approach of the train pulling into the station? Everyone rushed to put on their heavy fur coats and, grabbing their bags, crowded toward the doors.

A Plague of Cholera

The year was 1893, and the cholera pandemic was advancing across Russia. The plague gathered force as the summer set in, increasing in strength with the longer, milder days and extending its reach across cities, towns, and villages. As the weather grew hot, the death toll increased. In places where the epidemic hadn't yet arrived, the population waited in terror. Rumors that people were dying in their hundreds and thousands spread from distant cities and towns, the numbers of victims increasing with each telling—and the dead, people said, weren't laid to rest with the usual rites. In some areas, Jews couldn't be buried in Jewish cemeteries according to Jewish laws, or even properly prepared for burial. Instead, their corpses were covered with quicklime and flung into their graves.[1]

The plague arrived in the town of Chartoryisk shortly before the end of summer, but its citizens had started to worry much earlier. No one could talk about anything but the cholera and the tallies of victims it had claimed in one city or another. Some Jews believed the numbers were accurate and some didn't, but everyone knew there was a kernel of truth in the rumors. Even the people who said it was all nonsense scoffed only to make themselves feel better.

The peasants took things more calmly. They didn't trust the travelers who brought the horrific news, so they really meant it when they said, "Nothing but fairy tales—pack them up and take them

---

1. Four excerpts from this story appeared *In geveb: A Journal of Yiddish Studies* (May–June 2023), https://ingeveb.org/texts-and-translations.

away when you go." Nevertheless, they enjoyed the stories, smoking their pipes and sneering at the fairy tales they didn't believe in.

Chartoryisk was so small that deaths were rare, usually fewer than two or three a year, and each person who died was mourned for weeks and months afterward. The Jewish burial society would sit around with nothing to do, their shoulders missing the heft of a coffin. But the town was so small that hardly anyone died.

There were a few old men who'd sit and watch the younger people and still have plenty of time left over. So it was a terrible shock when it happened.

It began very slowly, without fanfare. A goy—a Christian, that is—who lived in the Christian neighborhood came down with all the signs of cholera. The Jews did their best to convince themselves and the goyim, too, that he'd simply stuffed himself with too many unripe vegetables. And when this particular peasant managed to get better, that proved they were right—because everyone knew that if you ate something contaminated with cholera, you'd die for sure.

Another week of summer passed after the peasant's illness and recovery, and during that week the fruits on the trees and the vegetables in the gardens got riper and riper, and, as they did every year, the town's Jews and Gentiles ate what the trees and gardens produced. This year, they ate even a bit more than usual because a notice had been posted forbidding people from eating raw produce. The poster had come from the government, and no one liked or trusted the government.

As usual, people from the surrounding villages brought their "forbidden fruit" to the town's market, and the town's police force, which was made up of a village constable and the chief of a Cossack squadron, began to turn back wagons carrying the illicit goods. A couple of these wagons belonged to particularly independent peasants who refused to obey government orders. The constable or the Cossack chief would personally drag their wagons to the river, leading the horses by their bridles, and order the owners to tip their goods into the water.

The state of unrest increased. The scofflaws had started it, but the confrontations provoked by that pair of authorities, the constable and the Cossack chief, made things worse. Every day there was some sort of uproar: one day it was a peasant breaking some regulation; the next day it was a Jew dumping garbage outside his house. Every day the constable wrote up official reports, and every day someone was dragged away and locked up in prison until he could pay the fine for whatever crime he'd committed. Of course, there was always somebody who could bribe the constable with a few coins so he wouldn't have to pay the fine, and that convinced the lawbreaker's family and neighbors that the new rules had nothing to do with cholera, but that the constable had made up the whole thing so he could line his own pockets.

So it went with the police and the ordinary citizens, and so it went with the plague, which struck again in the Gentile neighborhood. It grabbed a peasant, and before you could blink, he was gone.

There was a typical Christian funeral. The peasant, surrounded by burning candles, lay at rest on the table for three days in a house crowded with people. Bad smells came from the living and an even worse smell from the corpse. Candles burned day and night, and icons glowed on the walls, their holy faces looking down askance at the goyim, who prayed their Christian prayers to these saints with non-goyish faces while the dead man lay on his back, his craggy, uncovered face yellowish with black hollows under his closed eyes.

After the usual three days, the body was put into an oak coffin, and there was a funeral with a priest and a deacon, wax candles, and the ringing of church bells. As always, there was a procession to the cemetery, even though people knew that the peasant's death was far from ordinary and they shouldn't perform the usual rituals for him. Even Jews, seeing the coffin, were relieved that the dead man was getting a typical funeral because, although everyone knew what he'd actually died of, the display of normalcy was proof that the cholera hadn't come to their town after all. Furthermore, both victims—the sick peasant and the dead one—were goyim from the goyish neighborhood, so it was clearly a matter that didn't concern Jews. And if it didn't concern Jews, it couldn't be cholera, because everyone knew that wherever the cholera went, it killed Jews and goyim alike.

One of the town's Jews was Yitskhok Aron, and one of the Jewish houses was a special house: Yitskhok Aron's house. Yitskhok Aron was different from other Jews, and his house was different from other Jewish houses. Yitskhok Aron was one of those rare souls who'd grown into his middle years while remaining as young and carefree as a bachelor. He'd been a mischievous boy and a clownish young man, and he stayed mischievous and clownish even after he'd become a husband and father. He was a jokester. He poked fun and laughed at everything and everybody, and everyone (including Yitskhok Aron) thought he was the cleverest man around. Even his house gave the impression of being cleverer than other Jewish houses, because it didn't have a back—all of it was the front. The house had windows and doors on all four sides. Yitskhok Aron himself lived in one half of the house with his wife and children, and in the other half lived a feldsher, an unlicensed doctor who treated the locals, who had as many rooms to himself as his landlord did for his whole family. That's why Yitskhok Aron was considered wise: he'd built a unique house, and he had a tenant who was a feldsher, a Christian who spent his days running around the meadows hunting wild ducks. Because he had a Christian feldsher for a tenant, people thought of Yitskhok Aron differently than they thought of the other Jews in town. Because of the tenant's Christianity and his status as a feldsher—an intelligent, educated man—a glow reflected on Yitskhok Aron, the Jew. People considered him more refined than other Jews, and he was also an expert on diet: he knew which foods were healthy and which were unhealthy. He wouldn't touch cholent, the traditional heavy bean stew eaten on Shabbas, but instead dined on cold fish and cold, thoroughly baked potato pudding made with goose fat.

Yitskhok Aron earned a steady income in rent from the feldsher's half of the house: seventy-five rubles a year, enough for Yitskhok Aron and his family to live on for half of each year. And it didn't cost him anything to heat the house, either—heating galore! The feldsher's half of the house, and the landlord's too, was as warm as the inside of your ear. As the saying goes, "Christians love the heat," and so did Yitskhok Aron. The heating stoves burned scorching hot until long after Passover in spring, and sometimes all the way up to Shavuot in early summer.

Yitskhok Aron was the first Jew in town to wear a short jacket instead of the long coat worn by most pious Jewish men. His neighbors had never seen a Jew wearing a jacket before, though they knew it wasn't his own—he'd borrowed it from the feldsher. Well, that was forgivable, they thought—it certainly wasn't Yitskhok Aron's fault that the Christian had a short jacket. They also forgave Yitskhok Aron for wearing sunglasses with blue lenses on bright summer days. They were the feldsher's, too—he had two pairs, and he'd lent one pair to Yitskhok Aron. If the lenses had been some color other than blue, that would have been fine with the neighbors too.

Yitskhok Aron's house was different from other Jewish houses not only because half was occupied by a Christian, but also because the doors on that half had no mezuzahs on them. The feldsher's part of the house was thoroughly Christianized, feldsherized, hospital-ized, and goyishized because of the goyim who came from town and the surrounding areas for treatment and bottles of medicine. When summer came, peasant women would drag their little kids to the feld-sher to have them vaccinated, and often you'd see wagons in summer or sleds in winter on their way to the feldsher's: some Christian man or woman bringing a husband or wife for medical care. There'd be a face peering out of the straw bedding, the face of a long-suffering invalid who already looked more dead than alive.

"So, Yitskhok Aron, what d'you hear—what's the news?" Everyone wanted to know about the peasant who'd just died: Had he died of cholera, or for no particular reason? Yitskhok Aron must know, because, after all, he had a feldsher for a tenant. But Yitskhok Aron didn't know. He just replied, looking mysterious, "You have to be careful. Keep yourself safe!"

Time flew by. It was Elul, the last month of summer, the month leading up to the High Holidays: Rosh Hashanah, the first day of the new year, and Yom Kippur, the Day of Repentance. The bright, beautiful morning air carried the sacred sound of the shofar a long way from the synagogue, and little by little the Jewish townspeople began to believe the blasts of the ram's horn would protect the town from the plague. They became more pious. One or two women would occasionally wander into the women's gallery of the synagogue, which was almost always abandoned on weekdays. They'd stand there in the empty, spacious women's section, praying the midweek prayer along with the men.

The sun lovingly, faithfully warmed the earth, putting everyone in a good mood, though many knew they shouldn't enjoy the mild temperatures—on the contrary, they should be praying for the cold to set in before the cholera arrived, hopefully early enough to keep it away altogether. But it stayed warm, even quite hot in the daytime, so they had no choice but to accept the fine weather and hope it would come to nothing, just as nothing had happened so far. People had forgotten the events in the Gentile neighborhood, given that there was nothing to remember—because, after all, those things had happened to goyim, not Jews.

One of the Jews sitting on a wooden bench outside his house, warming himself in the late-summer sun, was seventy-five-year-old Hersh, a heavyset man with a big wide beard who'd served in the army of Czar Nicholas I. On another street, Notte Hershl Leybs likewise sat in the sunshine, whiling away his days. Notte was a very young man, so skinny and bony that his clothes hung on him—he was practically a skeleton wearing a pair of pants and a long coat. All you could see through his overgrown beard were his nose, his eyes, and the hollows beneath them. Everyone knew that these two men would soon die, the first of old age and poverty and the second, despite his youth, of tuberculosis—doom was written all over his face.

As though the two men had gotten together and made a pact to die of the plague that struck fear into everyone, even those who weren't old or sick, Hersh and Notte came down with cholera within a couple of days of each other, and both died that same week, leaving two corpses to bury. A few people were annoyed they'd chosen to die of the same disease that, in other places, killed the young and healthy, but they also took comfort in the fact that the pair had already been good candidates for the Angel of Death. Certainly, things would have been simpler if they'd died of what should have claimed them—the older of old age and the younger of tuberculosis—but, people thought, they were doomed to die anyways, and that's why they'd died of the plague—which, after all, hadn't killed anyone else.

"And what about the goy?"

"The goy? Didn't he just eat too much?"

But the invader had its own methods. As if assuming larger-than-life powers, it got to work everywhere at once with the apparent intent of confusing people so they couldn't figure out what was happening or even be sure the disease was among them. And the game didn't end there. The plague attacked a healthy middle-aged man who came down with all the symptoms but recovered. After that, most people shrugged off the whole thing, saying there were only two possibilities: either there was no plague, or, if there was, it was nothing to worry about. If the cholera had been in town as long as people thought, and if during that whole time it had killed only one peasant and a couple of Jews, one an old man and the other an invalid (not to mention someone who'd become ill and recovered), there was no cause for concern. It would all blow over.

One fine day a disturbance broke out—a real uproar. From inside someone's house came screams and shouts for help, and people rushed over to see what was going on. "What is it? What happened?"

"Sheyna Khaya is sick!"

The onlookers weren't so much worried about Sheyna Khaya herself. But they *were* frightened because she was a healthy young person. Now everyone knew trouble had finally arrived.

Seconds later, the little house where Sheyna Khaya lived was full of people, with another throng milling around outside. Among them was Yitskhok Aron, who'd slipped into the crowd like a stranger, his grim face shadowed by the blue lenses of his sunglasses. Without saying a word, he pushed his way over to a window, waved off the people crowding around, picked up a stone, and started bashing at the plaster around the window frame. The dry substance flaked away, showers of chips bouncing off the glass. Having freed the window, Yitskhok Aron opened it, stuck his head into the room, and yelled, "Idiots! Barbarians! What are you crowding around for—this isn't a klezmer concert! Get out of there, or I'll bash in your heads!" He was horrified by the hullabaloo going on inside and outside the house. What was needed was quiet, especially for the sick woman's sake.

But Sheyna Khaya was going downhill with frightening rapidity. Within a few minutes this beautiful woman in the full bloom of life was unrecognizable, under sentence of death: her eyes fallen shut, black hollows beneath them.

The next day, twenty-four hours after Sheyna Khaya had fallen ill, her bed was empty and she was gone. The world went on without her. A memorial candle, together with a glass of water and a little rag, stood on the window sill, the sad little flame pale in the daylight. That evening, a group of men gathered for a prayer minyan, the men slipping into the house in succession as though counting themselves off one by one.

A few days after Sheyna Khaya's sudden death—her household was still in mourning, a minyan tiptoeing in and out every morning and evening—in a house quite far from hers, history, like the punch line of a bad joke, repeated itself: one minute a strong, healthy woman was walking around as usual, and the next minute everyone heard she was sick in bed. Her family was doing everything they could to help, but she was already well on her way out of this world.

That evening, one of the sick woman's relatives, on his own initiative—he hadn't asked her husband or children—ran over to Yankl the Postman's house and told him to harness his horses. A few minutes later this relative was in the wagon, and he and the driver were on their way to a nearby town where a doctor lived. They returned with the doctor first thing in the morning, before dawn, but it was already too late. The men, without even getting out of the wagon, were preparing to turn back when someone ran up to them and asked the driver to bring the doctor over to his house. This man and the doctor were longtime friends—they'd known each other a good ten years, ever since the doctor had started caring for the man's wife, treating her with medicinal powders and various remedies. Though she was still alive and not in immediate danger, the whole town knew she'd never fully recover. Her family never called the doctor specifically for her, but they always asked him to look in on her when he came to town for some other patient, so none of the townspeople thought it was unusual for the doctor to be seeing her now.

The doctor examined his long-term patient. At first glance he knew this was the end. Suppressing deep sorrow, he said there was nothing to worry about, that she was in the same condition as always—however, they should rub her with alcohol and apply hot water bottles and warm sand compresses. Now the family understood there was something deeply the matter with the sick woman— not the usual trouble at all—and one man caught the doctor by the arm as he was leaving. "Doctor?" The man's tone was frightened, but he said nothing else.

After leaving the sick woman's home, the doctor waited outside for the feldsher. When the two men met, they were already thinking along the same lines, both with the same idea in their minds. They walked together for a while, preoccupied with their urgent medical matter, while the horses, the wagon, and the young Gentile driver waited. The beasts tossed their heads with the stolid impatience of horses compelled to stand in one place, and their harness bells rang out as if to warn everyone that something strange and ominous was happening in their midst. The sound made the listeners anxious— something uncanny had slipped into town under cover of the jangling harness bells, a lurking, ever-present danger waiting to track down its prey—and it looked like the doctor, who'd been in such a hurry to get here, had arrived too late. On the one hand, no one would mind if he stayed—they could always use a doctor's services—but on the other, since he was about to leave anyway, it would be better if he went immediately, taking the ringing bells away with him, because the bells were making everyone nervous. People were already saying that the doctor and the feldsher had decided to treat the fresh corpse with quicklime.

Back in the dead woman's house, there was so much screaming and wailing that the roof almost came off. The family rushed around in terror. A couple of people, surrounded by the horrified screams of the living, carried the mute corpse outside and, neglecting the usual ceremonies, laid it on some planks with poles attached, covered it up, fastened it down, and hoisted the poles to their shoulders. Gabriel, the synagogue's caretaker, ran up and, frantically pushing his way through the crowd, loudly rattled his tin box for collecting donations, shouting, "Give to the poor! Charity will save you from death. Charity will save you!"

Just then, the doctor and the feldsher drove by in the postal wagon, accompanied by the wild ringing of harness bells that told everyone the wagon was carrying away the doctor, a very important person in a very great hurry, who'd just rushed into town and was now rushing away again—but it would have been even better if he hadn't had to come at all. It was good that he was leaving, but on the other hand—if, heaven forbid, you might need him—it would be better if he didn't live so far away.

The harness bells rang out, growing fainter with distance and intermingling with Gabriel's cries: "Give to the poor! Charity will save you from death. Charity will save you!"

The postal wagon with its clamoring bells was back in town, and with it a little group of strangers: Christians with intelligent faces who looked less like the local goyim and more like Jews who preferred to dress like Christians. Their clothes didn't mark them as special, but they clearly weren't ordinary folks who'd just happened to drop into town. The strangers had obviously been sent by the government for official reasons that had to be hidden under everyday Christian clothing. The only thing out of the ordinary was their hats, which had dark-brown velvet hatbands and little badges in front: five badges on five hats firmly pulled down over five foreheads.

The wagon drove up to Yitskhok Aron's, stopping in front of the feldsher's half of the house, and all five strangers with their five pairs of legs jumped down from their high seats and one by one disappeared inside. A few minutes later the village constable and the chief of the Cossack squadron came running. The Cossack chief, who had discreetly removed his hat as a sign of respect, helped the driver pull down the baggage the five men had brought, carrying each piece into the house with the reverence usually reserved for sacred relics that belonged in a church.

Though they were more interested in the feldsher's half of the house and the Christians inside it, the locals congregated around Yitskhok Aron's half, gathering one after another until a few minutes later quite a crowd had sprung up. Before they could find out who the five strangers were, the crowd already knew why they had come— and for this reason they felt both better and worse about these men than about any other government official they'd dealt with before. It was clear these men's activities would affect both the living and the dead. No one could tell what the strangers' plans for the living were, or what the results would be—but for a long time, everyone had known what they planned for the dead. They'd come to do both good and bad things, and while their terrible intentions for the dead might have good results for the living, no one in the crowd could deny it was evil to pour quicklime over a corpse. The very thing the officials were planning for the dead—in order to benefit the living!— could, in fact, make the situation even worse: it's no small matter to desecrate a dead body.

The constable, looking frazzled, popped outside once or twice. He seemed scared to death, as if he'd completely forgotten that he, like the visitors, was also a government official. He had the air of a rooster who'd stumbled into an unfamiliar yard full of bigger, stronger roosters. The crowd stared, rejoicing in his downfall. "Zdrastvuyte, gospodin uryadnik," they jeered. "Well, hello, Mr. Constable!"

Every once in a while, Yitskhok Aron stuck his head out the window and yelled at the crowd: Why were they loitering around? Even though he was at home in his own house, he was wearing his yarmulke as if he, not the feldsher, were entertaining important guests. He appeared to be a man among strangers and his own people alike, as though he'd just stepped out of a military recruitment office full of officials and Jews. He waved the crowd away, telling them it wasn't a good idea to stand around gawking: under the circumstances it was best not to gather in large groups.

"They're salters. They're here to use quicklime," people said darkly, suspecting that Yitskhok Aron was in the know but didn't want to say.

Battle commenced the next day. The five officials, accompanied by the village constable and the Cossack chief, went into every house where the plague had struck to disinfect it. First they sprayed a pungent liquid onto beds and tables, walls and ceilings. Then they flung open doors and windows, carried out anything that had been in close contact with a plague victim, doused it with kerosene, and burned it. Sheets and straw mattresses, pillows and bedcoverings smoldered and smoked, and the stink of charred feathers filled the air. Guards were posted on the roads to stop people from entering or leaving town. For those who did manage to slip in or out, piles of straw were placed all around to be used as kindling. Any items brought out of town would be burned, while the travelers themselves would be "baptized" with disinfectant from head to foot. New ordinances were posted with lists of rules about cleanliness and threats of large fines and long prison sentences for disobedience. Another set of ordinances spelled out a complete list of forbidden and permitted food and drink. All the mandates emphasized that as soon as a case of cholera was discovered, it must be reported at once to the sanitary station.

That same day, two goyim dug a deep hole in the middle of the marketplace. Then they went to the bathhouse and chopped the boiler free of its walled-in enclosure. The boiler, sterile inside from decades of scalding water, was hauled with great fanfare to the marketplace where it was ceremoniously lowered into the hole, its empty, concave interior facing upward to the sunny sky. The constable and the Cossack chief rousted about a dozen goyim—men and women—out of the surrounding houses and ordered them to fill the boiler using shoulder yokes with buckets attached. The goyim hauled bucketful after bucketful of water and dumped them into the boiler. While they worked, a fire was lit underneath. As the wood burned and the water heated to a boil, smoke and steam filled the air. When there was enough boiling water, the constable and the Cossack chief ran from one house to another, knocking on windows and yelling as though trying to wake the people inside. A crowd of peasants gathered to scoop out the hot water: men and women, married and single, came running from all sides with jugs, cups, clay and cast-iron pots, and rusty tin pitchers. Shouting with excitement, they stood around the boiler in a cheerful, noisy circle while the steam silently swirled out of the enormous cauldron and sailed over the heads of the crowd, so that it looked like everyone, breathing in unison, had puffed out a thick cloud of fog.

It was a strange thing, though: despite the weapons the five officials had brought to fight the plague, people grew increasingly anxious as time went by. As they watched the sanitation process, even the few heretics who'd refused to believe the cholera had come to town were now convinced.

While the Christian medical officers carried out their scientific mission against the plague, the two groups of common folk, Jews and Gentiles, began their own campaigns. Jews began to spend extra hours praying loudly and fervently in the prayer houses, and Christians prayed in their own way according to their own religion. There were many street processions, the priest at the fore in his mantle and tall hat, a cross held at his breast, and peasants following with their crosses, holy pictures, banners, and wax candles, in exactly the same formation as if they were going to a funeral—in fact, the watching Jews thought it very strange there was no coffin in their midst. The priest babbled in some foreign language, and the deacon, walking behind him, recited from a book (from a distance it looked like a Jewish prayer book), repeating whatever the priest had said. Their voices—one coarse, the other squeaky—were accompanied by the shrill voices of children, who, in honor of the ceremonial occasion, wore clean sandals, their legs wrapped to the knee in spotless white rags wound about with new ribbons. The peasants, bareheaded, had smeared their hair with some sort of nasty-looking oil that glistened in the sunlight as a sign of Christian piety. Their Jewish neighbors, who usually found these spectacles strange and distasteful, now accepted them, knowing full well the reasons. The Christians were brothers in misfortune, so the Jews refrained from scoffing at their delusions and patiently tolerated the ringing of church bells.

The sanitation officials carried on with their mission, and so did the plague, which swept across town from day to day like a conflagration. Just as a wildfire leaps across a wide gulf to devour a house no one thinks it can reach, people living right next to a case of cholera escaped while those down the street, or even on the next street over, succumbed.

Every day there were more mourners and more orphans. A new row of fresh mounds of earth appeared in the cemetery. People began to lose faith in the countermeasures, and some grew to suspect the officials themselves. A rumor started to make the rounds: if the officials got hold of a person with cholera, they'd kill him themselves to prevent the plague from spreading further. So the Jews kept their mouths shut when someone in the family fell ill. If the sick person died without the help of the Gentile murderers, at least everyone could be sure he'd been kept alive as long as possible. Also, the body could be sneaked out of the house and its dignity defended from the desecration of quicklime. So, as soon as victims closed their eyes for the last time, their bodies were slipped outside and carried through back alleys to the small building in the cemetery where they were cared for according to Jewish customs and rites. Those who were discovered with a "stolen" body suffered a cruel fate. The body would be torn out of their hands, and the Christian officials would promptly deal with it in their own unnatural way.

While Jews were doing everything in their power to keep their dead safe from the quicklime, goyim did the reverse. When one of them came down with the plague, their near and dear ran straight to the authorities. The goyim couldn't understand why Jews got so upset about a little bit of quicklime sprinkled over a corpse. For them, it was just the opposite: when a peasant lay dying, a friend or relative ran off to get quicklime, and the minute the victim died, they'd treat the body with some and hold back the rest to make whitewash. In just a few days you'd see the dead person's house all brightened up. Every peasant family did the same: a freshly whitewashed house was a sign that one of its occupants had just died. Each corpse left behind a house that looked more festive and cheerful than before.

So there were many Christian bodies and many whitewashed houses. But after every Jewish victim there was only a memorial candle and a window looking out to the street with the sorrow and fear of death.

The Jewish woman who'd been sick for ten years died too. She'd withstood the plague for a few days, and so, because the disease—which had vanquished so many younger and stronger people—didn't kill her immediately, people figured she'd stay alive, possibly for years, with this new ailment on top of her many others. Her husband and children weren't much surprised when it happened, but people outside the family were annoyed that she'd chosen to die when everyone else was dying too, when she could have done so any number of years ago instead of dragging things out until there were more than enough corpses to go around.

She died without fuss, and her body was surreptitiously carried out of the house, taken to the cemetery, and laid in the little building to be readied for burial. Outside, not far away, a fire was lit and big clay pots full of water placed in the flames to heat. The dead

woman's husband and children were there, together with a few synagogue assistants. Inside the building—a windowless room with two
openings, facing each other, as doors—Shmendrik the tailor and his
daughter sat next to the body, sewing her shroud. People walked in
and out, doing whatever needed to be done for the dead woman.
Somewhere in the distance, among the tombstones in their fenced
plots, among trees, saplings, and tangles of shrubs, two bearded Jews
were digging a grave, while the widower watched the fire to make
sure it kept burning and that the water in the pots was heating. The
dead woman's children, young men and women, wandered around
the cemetery, their feet tangling in the long grass that was growing
thinner and drier with the end of summer. They walked aimlessly,
not speaking or looking at each other as if they were angry, from
time to time glancing up at the dark little building whose blank, open
doorways gaped like the frozen mouth of a corpse. They could see
their mother with Shmendrik the tailor and his daughter sitting next
to her, working on her shroud, their shiny needles running through
the white fabric one stitch at a time.

There was a sudden commotion. Shmendrik and his daughter
burst into the open air, terrified out of their wits. The tailor muttered
the prayer "Shema Yisroel," his lips pale with shock.

They'd heard the dead woman make a sound. If, in other circumstances, they'd heard the same sound from a normal, healthy
person, it would have been funny—but from a corpse? Everyone was
horrified. The two grave diggers came running with their spades in
their hands, and everyone crowded together at the doorway to beg
the dead woman's forgiveness for whatever they'd done to cause her
evident displeasure: "Freyda, please forgive us! We beg you three
times! Freyda, your husband begs forgiveness! Freyda, your children
beg forgiveness!"

The only good thing was that Freyda had done what she'd done
before they'd washed her body to prepare it for burial. So, grateful for her timing, and also to do their duty by her—as though she
were blameless, and the fault lay with them and all of humanity—the
women treated Freyda's body with far more care than they treated

more typical, well-behaved corpses. When they were finished, they laid the clean, white-clothed body into the caretakers' arms. But the moment the grave diggers began to lower her into the grave, exactly the same thing happened. One of the members of the burial society forgot to be frightened. "Stop it, Freyda, that's enough!" he snapped. "We forgive you, but we're asking you nicely, cut it out!"

So Freyda's body had to be ritually purified for the second time and her white shroud washed. After they finally got her into her grave, they hurried to cover her up with spadefuls of earth.

This business with Freyda cast a pall over the entire town. People saw it as a bad omen: surely the plague was about to run riot. The dayan—a judge in the Jewish religious court—had been rummaging through prayer books and biblical commentaries since the start of the epidemic, looking for remedies and cures. He was a wise and devout man whose studies and piety made him forgetful, a man who'd never achieved much except, once or twice a year, to pronounce an excommunication on one or another shopkeeper for selling candles and kerosene when only he, the dayan, had the license to do so. This dayan knew he was a weak and ineffectual judge who got no respect despite being the oldest man in town, and he longed to be seen as a bold, decisive leader. So now he took charge, directing everyone to obey the religious laws to the tiniest detail. Every day he found new scriptural verses for people to recite before and after prayers and at various times of day. He ordered people to hang garlands of coal around their houses as a remedy against the plague and found other remedies as well. Finally, this dayan, worried about what had happened with Freyda, decided on a commonplace solution, one that any Jew, not just a scholar, could have figured out for himself. He ordered a minyan to go to Freyda's grave and ask for forgiveness.

Yitskhok Aron was alone in standing up to the dayan and his followers, but he stuck to his own position: none of these remedies would work, he said, and the only thing that *would* work was to be careful, to protect oneself. That, of course, was what the Christian sanitation officers were saying, so hardly anyone agreed with him. To them, Yitskhok Aron was like a stone lying off the main path, separate from other Jews and allied with the Christians: he was on the officials' side and gave the same advice, repeating everything they said. Worse, his neighbors complained, he didn't become even a hair more devout. In fact, it was just the opposite—he'd completely stopped going to synagogue during the week and was away when the shofar was blown. That's how *he* protected himself—by staying away from people. Instead of trusting in God, said the gossips, Yitskhok Aron put his faith into avoiding the plague's powers of infection.

The next day a minyan consisting of the dayan and nine other men went to the cemetery to beg Freyda's pardon. They circled her grave seven times while reciting various prayers and passages from the scriptures. Finally, one man stuck a key into the freshly dug dirt over the grave and commanded the earth to seal itself up. The words were hardly out of his mouth when they heard a woman screaming off in the distance, a howling wail that rent the air. The sound came from a quiet, empty field, a wide, dusty expanse of earth that belonged to a stranger, and though no one could identify the voice that was nearing the cemetery with such horrifying lamentations, it had to belong to someone they knew—a familiar voice transformed by some appalling misfortune, some dreadful calamity that had befallen its owner. Each of the men, hearing that unrecognizable voice, was terrified it belonged to his wife or someone else in his family. They all sprinted toward the screaming woman to see whose wife, mother, or daughter she was and came face to face with her just outside the cemetery's entrance gate. She was the wife of one of the men, come to wail and beg God for help at her family graves on behalf of their daughter, who'd just been struck down by the plague.

People couldn't help but notice that a good 80 percent of cholera victims were female, so some of the older pious women began to work in secret, scrutinizing their sisters for sins—particularly those tied to women's matters. The cabal began by tracking down women who weren't sufficiently scrupulous in the mikvah, the ritual bath. Hudya Leah, the mikvah attendant, reported on every woman, from the youngest, who'd just begun going to the mikvah, to those old enough to stop. When it turned out that all the women were performing the rituals correctly, the conspirators started looking for other, more severe, sins. Because, who knew? Maybe an adulteress . . . ? No—the pious, God-fearing women were too timid to imagine that one of their own could do such a thing. But there had to be *some* reason the plague was attacking mainly girls and women. So the conspirators began to seek out less serious sins. The Living God can send down punishment for small as well as more egregious misdeeds, and surely someone had to be guilty of some trifle.

One of the cabal, Leah "Letochka" Pantofels, leaped into action. She knew if she looked hard enough, she'd find somebody somewhere who was sinning against God, His holy commandments, and His holy scriptures. So she set out to inspect her neighbors' sheitels, the wigs that religious tradition ordained for married women. She looked so long and so hard that she eventually found a young woman whose sheitel was the merest pretense: her neighbors assumed she was wearing a proper sheitel, but actually her own hair was showing. She combed her hair and blended it into the wig so skillfully that out-of-towners, unfamiliar with her habits, would think all the hair was her own. So Leah dropped in on her clever young neighbor and took pains to convince her that wives, maidens, and little girls were dying because of her. At last the young woman broke down and let Leah shave her head right down to the skin, and then she—Leta, Letochka, Leah Pantofels—strode victoriously through the marketplace, waving the bundle of hair and shouting for joy, as though she'd vanquished a great witch, robbing the sorceress not only of her hair but of her demonic power as well. At the market she told everyone that she'd halted the plague in its tracks.

During this time of crisis, most people did their part: Some vowed to recite psalms after their usual prayers for the rest of their lives; some decided to fast on Mondays and Thursdays. Some went to the cemetery to wail and plead for God's help at their family graves;

others opened the Holy Ark in the synagogue to beg for salvation. All these efforts—vowing, fasting, graveside laments, pleas before the Holy Ark—were made by poor people. Those who were better off tried to buy themselves out of danger through charity. When her only daughter fell ill, one rich woman had the entire length of the cemetery fence measured. She then bought the equivalent amount of linen and divided it among the poor. That's how she managed to tear her only daughter out of the clutches of the Angel of Death. This rich woman began with small vows: she promised to donate a pound of candles to the synagogue, a cover for a Torah scroll, and a curtain for the Holy Ark, but she soon took things further until she drove the Angel of Death away from her daughter. Not everyone, however, could do as she'd done. Some poor people couldn't afford to donate even one candle. They couldn't do a thing for their dying loved ones except cry and scream, and that's why they carried a grudge against their wealthier neighbors, who could buy themselves out of death's grasp. Anyone could see there were more illnesses and fatalities among the lower classes, and the poor knew it was the promises and charity of the rich that allowed them to evade destruction.

Those who were well-off, however, had their own problems. Not only did they have to feed their poor neighbors, but they were consistently nagged to provide burial shrouds for the dead. According to the rationale of the wealthy, poor people shouldn't bother burying their dead in shrouds—which, according to the cholera laws, they weren't supposed to do anyway—especially since they had nothing to make them with. After all, the wealthy reasoned, it was more humiliating for a dead person to be buried in a stranger's shroud than to have no shroud at all. So some of the town's upper crust made plans to leave—to escape the poor, who were growing in numbers each day, and the plague, which was also growing in power and tightening its grip on the town.

The number of people saying kaddish, the mourners' prayer, was on the rise too: there were old men, middle-aged men, young men, boys, children of three or four, and even children too young to speak. These tiny mourners stood on chairs like a row of baby goats to repeat after their fathers, word by word, the prayer for their dead mothers. When the older boys and adult mourners had finished saying kaddish, the little kids kept bleating into the silence, over and over, "Amen. May His great name be blessed forever . . ."

You could have heard a pin drop. The congregation listened in silence, reverently absorbing each word as though it bore the whole weight of a child's desolation and loneliness. People watched the little lips moving, remembering the young mothers who'd been alive just a short time ago. They ached with pity for the mothers who'd died so young and for the little children, who were far too young to be motherless, and each listener, wishing only to help the souls of the dead women and their surviving children, repeated fervently, "Amen. May His great name be blessed."

The High Holidays drew nearer during those dark days, and no matter how people felt, they needed to prepare. Many had to interrupt shiva, the weeklong mourning period after a death, to buy food and supplies for the holidays. Widowers went to the same stores where their wives had so recently shopped. Some of these men had unhappy encounters that bothered them for a long time after.

Several widowers had been living on credit for years on end. They'd calculate their debts every few months, pay off their bills, and then go back on account. Without warning, one shopkeeper, closely followed by a second—as though they'd reached a joint decision— stopped giving credit to these trusted longtime customers. Why? They wouldn't say. The customers had to figure it out for themselves. One widower looked a shopkeeper right in the eye and retorted, "So you've signed a contract with God? It's not just me who could die any minute—you could be next." Humiliated, the man went home, found something he could pawn, took it to a different shopkeeper, and in return got some food for the holiday, as much as his family needed. But even then he couldn't stop worrying: maybe he'd taken too much food; maybe some of the people the food was meant for wouldn't live long enough to eat it.

By the afternoon of Erev Rosh Hashanah—the day before Rosh Hashanah, the Jewish New Year—the whole town, even those few untouched by the plague, knew that this Erev Rosh Hashanah would be different. Half a day still remained before evening, half a day of the old year until the new one began, and there was nowhere to spend it. Only a few hours remained of this last day before the holiday, and with the bathhouse shut down, the men couldn't enjoy their weekly soak. Some went to the river, but a dip in the river couldn't offer the pleasure of hot water, a massage with a willow switch, and plenty of steam. They all missed the bathhouse: you could see longing on each pale, thirsty face. How could they take off their weekday clothes, their grubby underwear, and dress their parched, unwashed bodies in clean garments? Their homes were prepared for the holiday, but men in their everyday clothing loitered restlessly in the streets, feeling underdressed and out of place as the festival arrived, like ragged paupers invited out of charity.

Bored and at loose ends, some of the men wandered downhill to the bathhouse, just to see what it looked like; hanging around would at least pass the time they would have spent bathing. They walked around the building, peering in through the windows and glancing up at the chimney, but no steam fogged the windows; no smoke puffed from the chimney. The bathhouse was as deserted and silent as on an ordinary weekday. The big tub hung over the well; it was dry inside and cracked, every gap expressing desolation and abandonment. In short: a cold, arid, silent bathhouse wrapped in cold, arid, silent gloom.

Three men walked up with changes of clean clothes under their arms. They'd come for their ritual bath in honor of the new year, though the mikvah's water was unheated. The three looked bleakly at the bathhouse's vast, empty interior, which seemed oddly foreign, as though they'd never seen it before. An unidentifiable atmosphere pervaded the place, a strange smell that lay heavy on the scrubbed benches and thick-planked floor. The men stared at the ruined corner where the boiler had once stood, the gaping hole in the wall with its smashed, crumbling stones and chunks of mortar, bone-dry from years of intense heat. The once-familiar room looked frighteningly alien.

A few minutes later the bath attendant appeared. He was carrying a couple of buckets with cracks in them in an aimless sort of way, as though he had no idea where the buckets had come from or where they should go. Like a man possessed by an evil spirit, he was frowning angrily. The visitors greeted him with a volley of complaints: Why was the mikvah cold? "You could have at least warmed up the water!"

The bath attendant defended himself—he had no coal for the furnace, he said. Where was he supposed to get coal, since the mikvah couldn't heat up by itself?

"That's no excuse. Why didn't you come to my place? I could have given you some."

"It's a terrible thing," said one of the visitors, a pious Jew and esteemed scholar, "that these bath attendants know so little Torah. If you weren't such an ignorant young lout, you'd know very well what people do on Erev Rosh Hashanah."

"Well, yes . . . but no scholar would want to be a bath attendant," his companion interrupted.

Every word rang out loudly, as if the vast, echoing space were helping them speak and hear more clearly. The men stood in the center of an unhallowed emptiness, each drawing comfort from the thought that he wasn't alone, that he had come with friends.

The three started to undress, reluctantly stripping off long coats, vests, shirts, and underclothing. One of them, naked except for his hat (he was wearing it due to his piety and the holiday, but mostly to postpone going down into the dark, cold mikvah), said, "Maybe we should go bathe in the river after all, eh? What do you think?"

A dog appeared in the open doorway. He stuck his muzzle inside and snuffled around as if he'd never before smelled such an empty, desolate place without even a morsel of food. He seemed confused by this strange house and its strange humans, with their heads like other people's but looking like some other kind of creature from the neck down. Baffled, he stared at the scene, then suddenly tossed back his head, raised his snout, let out an ululating howl, and scrambled off. The man who was wearing nothing but his hat shouted after him: "The hell with you!"

This man—his name was Avrom Hersh—wasn't wearing his hat just because he was religious, but to be last in the mikvah. He wasn't quite sure what made him so anxious, but he fervently hoped his companions would go first. When they eventually got moving, Avrom Hersh trailed behind. The men walked step by step, one step at a time, across floorboards that were cool under their bare feet, each board transversed lengthwise by a gutter—this wasn't a typical floor; the beams were too thick. And there, at the far end of the room, was an opening that let in the wan outdoors light.

A heavy odor wafted from the standing water in the mikvah: a blend of the dense, sour reek of human sweat and the fermented funk of human bodies. The water below was invisible, so lost in darkness the eye couldn't capture where the shadows ended and the water began. The windowless wooden walls surrounding the mikvah disappeared into the shadows below, plunging deep underground like the walls of a well. They were spattered from top to bottom with mushroom-like growths: slick gray buboes, some of them so old and desiccated that they'd started to crumble away like clay shards.

"Maybe we should go bathe in the river," Avrom Hersh said again. It wasn't so much that he wanted to bathe in the river but that he didn't want to go into the mikvah: he was overcome by an unfathomable terror of descending into that black water. Left to himself, he would have dressed in his clean clothes and gone straight home.

But suddenly—"No harm can come to those who fulfill the commandments," he blurted out, and trusting in his faith and the precept he'd just quoted, he gathered his courage, plunged down the steps as if dragged by the arm, and disappeared into the water below. The two men waiting above heard a splash. One of them, wondering if they should follow, asked, "Is everything all right?"

"No . . . I don't feel so good," came the reply from below.

It was a few hours before sunset. The sun in the western sky shone brightly but gave little warmth: a late-afternoon sun at the end of summer, the final day of the year. Women were lighting candles in honor of Rosh Hashanah. In some houses—you could see if you looked out your window—the candles were lit by a man, a widower whose wife had just died. Motherless children who'd cried themselves out long ago burst into fresh wails while their fathers stood there in their holiday long coats, frozen into statues, unable to go on.

After the holiday candles had been lit and blessed, memorial candles were removed from the windowsills on which they'd burned day and night, not because their light was needed, but as symbols of remembrance. Their flames, gazing blindly into the sunshine, burned faint and dispirited, longing for rest. Now, before the holiday's arrival, the little lamps with their little flames were taken from their windows, snuffed out, and put away.

Later that day, as the men in their long white holiday robes and prayer shawls gathered in the synagogue, the first thing they heard was the chilling sound of weeping and wailing in the women's section. It was obvious how many women were missing—you could count the many empty seats there, and in the men's section, too. Those unfortunates sitting next to the empty seats felt even more uncomfortably crowded than they had when the seats had been occupied by their owners. To the men in their white robes and prayer shawls, it seemed not only that the synagogue was fuller than usual, but that every new arrival made it smaller and more cramped. One man, who'd slipped in for Mincha, the late-afternoon prayer, walked over to the pulpit and in a reverent, mournful voice quoted the words of the Psalm: "Blessed are those who dwell in Your house; they shall praise You forever."

Avrom Hersh's family—he was the man who'd felt sick in the mikvah—was among those absent that evening, a sign he'd become very ill. In the hours between Erev Rosh Hashanah and that morning, various fantasies had spun though everyone's minds. Some spread the rumor that Avrom Hersh himself had said he'd seen Moyshe—his lodger, who'd died a few days before—down in the mikvah. Others told a different story: as Avrom Hersh was descending into the water, he'd felt a breeze, but since the mikvah was completely enclosed, there wasn't anywhere for a breeze to come from, so it couldn't have been a breeze at all—it must have been death itself, the Destroyer, flying by, ready to take him.

That evening in synagogue, with the holiday about to begin, the crying and wailing almost drowned out the prayers. One man after another, each in his prayer shawl and long white robe, popped into the women's section and shouted angrily or asked sympathetically for silence. The women's loud keening distracted everyone from the holiday's usual mood of reverential awe and flooded them instead with the terror of dying. The only thing congregants felt, doubled and multiplied, was the horror of impending doom. They knew their Day of Judgment was at hand, and hardly anyone could concentrate on the prayers. Many couldn't sit still for even an hour. A steady stream of people—men in prayer shawls and white robes and women in white headscarves—slipped outside and ran home to check on their children and the older girls left in charge of them. Although Erev Rosh Hashanah was supposed to be a fast day, quite a few congregants, afraid weakness from fasting might lead to the plague, went home for a quick bite before or during the prayers—even when the Torah scrolls were being taken out of the Ark. They ate furtively, like strangers in their own houses, as if they didn't belong there and were trying to hide from themselves, their children, even the very walls and windows. Some returned to synagogue late for the final, most sacred blasts of the shofar; others missed its summons entirely. They ran up and down the street, legs heavy, panting for breath, feeling as lost and displaced as if they'd suddenly tumbled into a non-Jewish environment. Their own familiar town seemed foreign, and the familiar Jewish houses seemed foreign too, emptied of adults and occupied only by young girls and children. Their windows, gazing sorrowfully at the hurrying people in the street who shouldn't have been there, expressed the gentle longing of an important and awe-inspiring holiday when Jews should be spending more time in the synagogue than out of it.

Here and there some girl, busy with the ordinary task of cooking the festive meal, paused to look out her window. Here and there the light shining from an open door or onto a front porch fell on a girl with a child in her arms. On the other side of the street, Jews hurrying back to synagogue walked past their Gentile neighbors just as they did every day and were reminded of the everyday Christian world that surrounded them, a world in which they had no place.

Yitskhok Aron too was spending more time outside the synagogue than inside it. He wandered around outdoors, all by himself, his prayer shawl draped over his shoulders, and missed all the most important prayers. When he finally went inside, the service was almost over. Everyone knew just by looking at him that he'd had something to eat before he came in, and they also knew it wasn't because he was flouting the rules, but to stay strong for the sake of his health. They could have excused him if they'd been sure his behavior would save him. But eating on a fast day wasn't his only crime—though no one would make him admit it, everyone knew he hadn't prepared for the holiday in the usual way. His wife had baked challah, and he'd ordered little jugs of milk, sour milk, and sour cream to go with the bread so that, contrary to tradition, his family would celebrate Rosh Hashanah with a meatless meal.

What a man Yitskhok Aron was! Everyone had something to say about him. Tonight, for example, he was wearing his sunglasses. Was he trying to hide his eyes? If so, a mask would have served him better—it was frightening how much his face had changed. If people hadn't known he was Yitskhok Aron, they wouldn't have recognized him: he looked like a stranger. Every day his face grew more and more drawn and more and more pale, his black beard blacker and bushier and his blue glasses bluer and darker in contrast with his thin, wan face.

A little while earlier, Yitskhok Aron had been standing all by himself next to a fence just outside the synagogue, looking at a garden. Although only a few plants had been harvested, the orderly rows and tidy blooms of early and midsummer were no more. Yitskhok Aron, his spirits heavy, contemplated the vegetables. Thin support stakes stood overgrown by vines, some bare and some leafy, all stripped of their beans. Here and there round, heavy-bodied watermelons lolled on the earth, sheltered by leaves like parasols, their long, green prickly stems sprawled all around. There were a few overgrown cucumbers, yellow and rotten. Stalks of maize, their bulging husks topped by black withered beards, bore long leaves like palm fronds. Some husks revealed kernels like rows of grinning yellow teeth browned by the sun, while others gaped emptily, their kernels pecked by birds. The unpicked, decaying vegetables were stark reminders of this unprecedented time: because of the laws against eating fresh produce, the town's gardens had been left to decay. Yitskhok Aron looked over the fence, and what he saw terrified him. The ruined garden with its abandoned, rotting harvest looked bleak and derelict, even more so than if it had been stripped entirely bare.

Yitskhok Aron was so absorbed in his thoughts that he didn't hear the loud voices raised in prayer in the synagogue. But he did hear a rapping at the window and a voice summoning those outside for Unetaneh Tokef, the Rosh Hashanah prayer that asks whose name will be inscribed in the Book of Life and whose in the Book of Death.

This night at the beginning of the new year was warm, a little humid, and pitch-dark. The new moon rose late, the new moon of this blighted month of Tishri, which, with God's blessing, must return every year in the cycle of time. In the deep darkness between two months, one just ended and one barely begun, the town lay enveloped in a celebratory glow of candles and candelabras that brightened tables set for festive meals. In Jewish houses all over town, a major holiday was being celebrated, a sorrowful holiday, a holiday of mourning and grief.

The synagogue stood dark and abandoned, emptied of candles, light, and celebrants. But now, in the middle of the marketplace, a lantern suddenly flashed, its heavy framework casting onto the earth alternating bars of darkness and light that spun and rotated with the lantern's motion. There had been a new death in town. Encircling the lantern, flashing in and out of its bright beams and deep shadows, legs milled around: a group of men marching to the cemetery.

Four men had changed from their holiday long coats to their ordinary clothes, left behind their families and the festival celebrations, and now, on this night of a major holiday, were on their way to do a sad workaday task. With a lantern lighting their path and pickaxes slung over their shoulders, they were going to dig a fresh grave in the cemetery for a man who'd just died: Avrom Hersh, who'd gone into the mikvah trusting in God, who'd expressed his faith with these words: "No harm can come to those who fulfill the commandments."

The townspeople had closed their shutters early, before blessing the wine, before eating dinner, and long before bedtime. The windows of poorer houses were hung with old moth-eaten shawls or everyday long coats. It seemed as though each house wanted to detach itself, close itself off from the outside world, distract itself with domestic cheer from the misery of others. Everyone knew Avrom Hersh had died that day, but nobody wanted to think or talk about it.

Yitskhok Aron was eating his holiday meal. He found the meatless fare depressing—it sustained neither his physical nor his spiritual being and left him doubly unsatisfied. Though he was sitting in his usual chair at the head of the table, he felt a little estranged, not only from his wife and children but even from himself. He had a strange new feeling somewhere inside, and it frightened him. He ate as he normally did, and no less than usual, but at fleeting moments he felt that it wasn't he who was eating, but someone else, some stranger. Every once in a while he rubbed his hands together and carefully examined his nails.

Eight candles in eight candlesticks lit up a table around which eight people were sitting. A lamp burned overhead, and in its light the milk-based food looked pallid and lifeless, even paler than milk. Yitskhok Aron was suddenly struck by the vague feeling that his name wasn't Yitskhok Aron, that he didn't have a name at all, that he was some nameless creature.

In the early morning of the second day of Rosh Hashanah, people discovered that during the night two little sisters in one house had fallen ill with the plague. Everyone in synagogue that morning was talking about it. Each person claimed to have heard the story first, before they even got to the synagogue, and everyone told the news to everyone else. No one could sit still—all were on tenterhooks, buzzing with nervous agitation, glancing out the windows repeatedly, afraid that any minute now they'd be hearing screams and wailing in the street outside.

The dayan, distracted by everyone else's distraction, was more upset and inattentive than any of them. The congregation clearly didn't have its mind on the service, and that scared him; if people didn't concentrate on their prayers, the plague would get even worse. He was also discouraged because not one of his remedies had worked. He'd done everything he could think of, and the plague hadn't weakened a bit—in fact, it had grown stronger. He was horrified at the death of his dearest friend, Avrom Hersh, who'd suddenly been snatched out of this world: in the blink of an eye he'd gotten ill in the mikvah, and the very next day it was all over—he was dead and buried.

When it was time to ceremoniously open the Ark for the removal and public reading of the Torah, the dayan remembered that every year on this day, the second day of Rosh Hashanah, Avrom Hersh had been called up for the honor of reciting the blessings. The dayan, standing by the open Ark of the Covenant, couldn't stop thinking about it. He wanted to focus on the ceremony's sublime prayers, but he couldn't concentrate. Then, suddenly, he thought he saw a dazzling light, and he knew it was Avrom Hersh's soul, wandering through this sinful world for seven days and nights before finding its rest in Paradise.

The dayan passed his prayer book to the cantor, who was that day's *baal kore*, or Torah reader, and then pulled the heavy, embroidered upper edge of his prayer shawl over his head as he followed along with the prayer. When the cantor laid the prayer book on the bimah and began the recitation of "God will help, protect, and save all that trust in Him," the dayan whispered something into his ear. The cantor broke off, his face suddenly as pale as a freshly plastered wall. The dayan stepped back so that between himself and the cantor there was enough room for a third person. The cantor carried on with his recitation, but now his voice was faint and wavering. Then he broke off. In a voice barely louder than a whisper, he called out the traditional invitation: "Let Avrom Hersh, son of Naftali, arise."

A chill fell on the congregation. In silent awe, hair prickling with fear, everyone glanced around, looking for the man who was there, but invisible—who, after death, could see but could not be seen, who'd maintained his bond with the living world and had been invited to say the blessing over the Torah. They stared in breathless horror at the vacant space between the dayan and the cantor, imagining it was occupied by an unseen, silent presence, and in their minds that presence recited the blessing, and every person repeated the unspoken words to himself: Praise the One to whom our praise is due, now and forever.

After the inaudible blessing, the cantor said "Amen" and began reading the weekly Torah portion. When he'd finished, another silence emanated from the empty place between the cantor and the dayan, a silence the length of the closing blessing. Again the audience listened intently. When the silence was over, the cantor, instead of making the usual blessing over a person who's just blessed the Torah, recited El Maleh Rakhamim, "God of Mercy," a prayer for the dead.

Then the dayan read from the Torah, and after him the cantor took his turn. With the resumption of the usual service, the congregation cheered up a little. But the dayan clearly had something more up his sleeve. Sure enough, the minute the Torah scroll was replaced in the Ark, the dayan slapped the top of the bimah to get everyone's attention and, his voice a little unsteady, announced, "Now we'll say Yizkor."

This was unexpected. Everyone knew that Yizkor, the prayer for the dead, was never recited on Rosh Hashanah. The congregation glanced around uneasily. Because of this break with tradition, those few people whose parents were still living didn't know whether to leave during the prayer or whether they should stay where they were. Unsure what to do or if they needed to ask, they tentatively headed for the door, leaving behind the great majority of congregants—all of them, far more than before the plague, mourning one or both parents. Among the bereaved were many small children.

A heavy, oppressive sadness suffused the synagogue. From the women's section came crying and wailing. Men drew their prayer shawls over their heads, and a murmur of tearful prayers arose. Here and there a man standing next to his little son recited the Yizkor prayer with the child, word by word: "May God remember the soul of my mother . . ." For some time the mourners stood absorbed in prayer, tears falling onto their prayer books and blurring the words on the paper. When Yizkor was over, the motherless little boys, still sheltering under the comforting warmth of their fathers' prayer shawls, leaned against their fathers and, happy to be helping their mothers' souls find their way to Paradise, earnestly repeated the words of El Maleh Rakhamim, "And she shall rest peacefully in her resting place. Amen."

The people who'd left the synagogue for the remembrance ceremony filed back inside. The prayers had brought a melancholy comfort to the bereaved, and, sensing the mood, a few of the newcomers gave one or another little orphan a kindly pat. Then the congregation prepared for the Mussaf service. The cantor, enveloped in his white robe and prayer shawl like a corpse in its shroud, took his place by the lectern and submerged himself in the serene words and melody of the introductory prayer, Hineni, "Here I am, impoverished in deeds and merit." The congregation, deep in meditation, was carried away by his singing, eagerly anticipating each soaring, thrilling note. And then . . . suddenly, from somewhere in the forgotten world outside, they heard someone yelling and screaming. The reverential mood was broken, and everyone in the synagogue, the entire Jewish population of the town, shot out the doors, poured into the street, and dashed over to where the terrifying noise was coming from.

Two houses sat across the street from each other. A woman had fallen ill in one house, and in the other, where two people had lain suffering since the previous day, a third person, a woman who'd been lodging there, was also afflicted. The people crowding outside were startled by a sudden noise from within—someone was banging for help on the inside of the window. They could see a hand, as pale as a drowned person's, with clawed fingers and yellowed nails. It beat against the windowpane like a frantic, fluttering wing, as though death and life had come together in that hand to beckon the dying woman to death and the living to save her. Then a face appeared, hovering among the flowerpots on the windowsill, the face of the woman condemned to die. The face disappeared and then appeared again. Its dull, watery eyes held a shocked, confused look, and in those eyes you could see the onslaught of death. The eyes gazed into the street with an inward expression, indifferent to the land of the living, as if the world were an alien place they were viewing for the first and last time, a world in which a woman—her name was Feyga—had lived and died. The corpse within the woman was looking out of her eyes, and what was knocking at the window, pleading for help, was the blind, fading life of the already-dead Feyga. In the street outside, prayer shawls, long white robes, and women's white silk headscarves clustered in confused disarray as the displaced congregation huddled together under the open sky, shouting and crying in a horrifying holiday display of terror.

The cantor, who'd remained in the synagogue, stood at the lectern, gazing around at the sudden void. Abandoned prayer books lay open, their letters and lines black with sorrow, with only empty air to read them. Here and there a fallen prayer shawl lay in a tangle, its fringes dangling. The synagogue seemed as wide and cavernous as if giant hands had forced apart its walls. In the silence of the empty synagogue, the cantor could hear the cacophony outside, a rush and tumult like running water that seeped into the empty building and smothered it in the sound of muffled screams.

The cantor stood paralyzed with fear, afraid to step away from the fragile security of the lectern, waiting for the congregation to return. He saw Yitskhok Aron appear in the doorway and step silently, heavily inside. He wore a long blue coat, loosely belted, and a yarmulke—clothing too informal for the holiday but too formal for home, as if he'd rushed away during or right after his prayers at home—or as if he hadn't been praying at all.

"Yitskhok Aron, it's you!" the cantor exclaimed, and waved a finger, motioning Yitskhok Aron to go back outside and retrieve the escaped congregation.

Yitskhok Aron looked at the cantor, or at least his beard pointed in the cantor's direction—his eyes were invisible behind his blue lenses. He didn't say a word but just stood there nervously as if he was forcing himself to remain still. He was trembling but made no effort to sit down, as though he'd forgotten how. Every movement expressed a deep, dramatic sense of loss. He looked woebegone, on the edge of tears, like a man who wanted to plead and scream but was afraid to. In an effort to gather his strength, he took a little vial of smelling salts from his breast pocket. He opened it with difficulty and put it to his nose, faltering as though his hands were independent of his will, as if they and his nose belonged to two different people. Then he was gone.

The cantor tore himself free of the lectern, ran over to the doorway, and stood there with his legs braced apart. He looked around and, as if his words were a prayer that had to be recited all in one breath, shouted into the street, "Yitskhok Aron! Yitskhok Aron! Yitskhok Aron!"

All that night, candles and lanterns burned in people's houses. Bright bars and little blobs of light forced their way through closed shutters and covered windows as if the anxious families inside were sending lonely signals to the dark moonless night, messages that spoke of a town that rested without resting and slept without sleeping in the firelight that illuminated and protected the sleeping and the wakeful alike. The bright stripes and little blobs of light told a tale of helpless, defenseless people who feared the night and its darkness, people who'd burrowed away to avoid seeing or hearing or fearing any disasters that might befall their neighbors. It was quiet outside: a living, breathing quiet, enfolded in night, darkness, and the horror of death.

During this time of night and darkness, sleep and wakefulness, anxiety and dread, four people—two adults and two children—departed this life and this world. All four, who'd fallen ill that day under the light of the sun, ended their struggles by firelight. Four people in two houses across the street from each other—three in one house and one in the other—died in mortal terror. Now, from the outside, both houses looked peaceful. The dead were at rest after their agonies, and the survivors were done with the anxious labors that they'd kept up, without a break, almost around the clock. In both houses the living hovered around the dead, unable to sit still, speechless, suffering, and exhausted, knowing perfectly well they'd done everything possible, and full of sorrow and despair because nothing they'd done had helped.

Some distance from these two houses was a third house, one with doors and windows on all four sides. In one half of the house, which had its own front door and windows and smelled of medicine and fried pork, lived a Gentile feldsher, and in the other half, under the same roof as the feldsher, lay Yitskhok Aron, wrestling with death. His body burned with the heat of constantly replenished hot-water bottles, while the many loyal hands of his large, devoted family had practically massaged the skin off his arms and legs. Yitskhok Aron's brother-in-law, Abraham Barabanchik, had stood by his side the whole time he'd been ill. Everyone had great hopes that Abraham Barabanchik would save him. Barabanchik was a man of unusual strength and determination, and his unyielding efforts made it seem possible that through sheer stubbornness he could tear his brother-in-law out of the hands of death.

While all this was going on, a certain rich household, having made plans to leave town, smuggled themselves out of their home under cover of darkness. A horse-drawn wagon waited in front of the family's red-painted house, whose shutters were closed and doors locked to make it look as if the inhabitants were sleeping peacefully inside. Only the back door leading to the courtyard and stable stood open, revealing a faint light, just enough to see by. The light dimly illuminated a sturdy porch on which a ladder stood leaning against the house, extending as high as the chimney and looking out of place, an alien object attached to the familiar side of the house. Like deserting soldiers preparing to abandon a battlefield, people tiptoed in and out of the open door with packages in their arms, loading them onto the wagon. The horses, long familiar with standing and waiting, patiently chewed their bits while the pile of packages grew on the wagon behind them and people climbed aboard one by one. Finally, the wealthy couple and their children got in, found their seats, and drove off, leaving the locked and bolted house, with instructions to keep it that way, in the care of relatives, a poor couple who found themselves the owners of everything and nothing—since the house was locked up against them as well as everyone else. Overnight they'd become a new kind of pauper, heavily burdened with responsibilities, and now they felt poorer than before, when they had only their own home to worry about.

Before dawn, when everyone got up for the Selihoth penitential prayers, the congregation heard the news: four people had just died, Yitskhok Aron was fighting against death, and a rich family had slipped out of town and bribed the watchman on one of the outbound roads. As people gossiped, the prayer house filled with fathers and their little boys, who'd been roused from their deepest sleep and brought to synagogue to say kaddish for their dead mothers. The little kids sat side by side, yawning and shivering from waking too early in the autumn's damp chill. This was a new world for them: the world of the dawn-time synagogue, full of men, candles, and lanterns. The yawning children breathed in the dim light of the early-morning synagogue and the sorrow of the early-morning prayers while the grown-ups gossiped incessantly about the four new deaths, Yitskhok Aron's illness, and the rich family's escape. Later, people turned from that discussion to another topic: the Fast of Gedalia on the third day of Rosh Hashanah. In a time of plague like the present one, when weakness from hunger could prove fatal, were people permitted to abstain from the fast? Some were for the idea and some against, and a quarrel broke out over the matter, each participant eager to show off his expertise and learning, either for or against.

"So what'll you do on Yom Kippur, eh? Are you planning to fast or not?"

"Yom Kippur and the Fast of Gedalia have nothing to do with each other. The Yom Kippur fast is commanded by Torah, but the Fast of Gedalia is from Talmud, from the rabbis."

"Listen to what he's saying. He thinks Talmudic law isn't important," one pious old man retorted. "The rabbis didn't make things up out of their own heads, you know. Everything the sages said, they either deduced from Torah or were inspired by God."

"To save a life, it's permissible even to violate the Sabbath," interrupted another man, who also knew a thing or two, but the angry old man refused to let go of the argument: "What makes you so sure? You think violating the Sabbath can save someone's life? Maybe it can't. Fasting and prayer—you think they won't help? If eating on a fast day could keep the plague away, then Yitskhok Aron wouldn't be dying right now as we speak. Who took care of his health better than Yitskhok Aron? He didn't even serve a proper Rosh Hashanah meal—not a scrap of fish or meat—may God, blessed be His name, send him a complete cure. But what Yitskhok Aron did was useless! You can see that, can't you? It didn't help him one bit."

Then another man jumped in and said the dayan should issue a rabbinical authorization. This year, people should be allowed to eat on the Fast of Gedalia—in fact, they should be forbidden from fasting.

It was dawn. Roosters crowed sleepily, knowing their days were numbered, reminding those who heard them of the approaching Yom Kippur holiday and the Day of Judgment to come. Crowing came from all directions—young and old roosters, united in concert, each mourning its own short and uncertain life.

The men in the synagogue moved closer to each other. The roosters' crowing brought the same image to each mind: the marketplace's broad expanse and the narrow alleys where houses cuddled right next to each other, some with long ladders extending from ground to chimney, joining the ground to the rooftops, vacant and abandoned, their owners gone, their rungs empty and the spaces between them blank. Narrow alleys and the open marketplace: a town with rabbis and neighbors—and also the deadly cholera. In the center of the marketplace stood a slate tablet on which was written a tally of the town's population—how many men and how many women—and every day the town had fewer people, but the numbers on the slate tablet remained the same.

There came a sudden sound: hands clawing at the far side of the door, fumbling and groping in search of the doorknob. Eventually, the hands found what they were looking for, and the door opened. A woman, panting in her haste, stumbled into the synagogue, practically falling through the door as though someone had shoved her inside. Struggling to catch her breath, she gasped: "Yitskhok Aron just died!"

They'd all learned one thing, plain and simple. If Yitskhok Aron, of blessed memory, could come down with the plague and die of it, that was a sign that none of the practical things he'd done to protect himself and take care of his health would work. So one group of people concluded that they obviously needed to become even more pious and redouble their prayers and pleas to God for help. Their opposition—though more practical, they were still good Jews, not heretics, heaven forbid—argued that the community had already tried being more pious, but it hadn't helped. If a man like Abraham Moyshe, they pointed out, a good Jew without a stain on his character, a man who was so religious he prayed with two sets of tefillin, a man who was more devout on ordinary days than other people were on Rosh Hashanah and Yom Kippur—if a man like that could be felled by the plague, then being religious was no remedy either.

The first side, those who favored the more pious response, countered with a passage from the Torah: *As long as Moses held up his hands, Israel prevailed.* They went on, "As long as we look to God for His blessings, as Moses did by raising his staff when Israel fought against Amalek, we'll prevail against our enemies. The Holy Torah teaches us not to turn away from God by letting our hands fall to our sides—we have to make an effort to carry out His will."

The opposition came back by quoting the rest of the passage: *And when Moses lowered his hands, Amalek prevailed.* When Moses grew tired and lowered his arms, the enemy gained strength. But then he got help from Aaron and Hur, who supported his arms in the air until, with God's blessing, Israel eventually triumphed. "So the Torah supports our argument," they continued, "or rather, to put it the other way around, we're saying exactly what the Holy Torah says. People have to be ready to receive God's blessings but they have to help themselves as well, and if they don't, then the plague wins."

"But that's exactly what Yitskhok Aron did!"

"And he's the *only* one who did. If we'd all taken care of ourselves like Yitskhok Aron, he wouldn't have died."

"And if we'd all been as observant as Abraham Moyshe, of blessed memory, Abraham Moyshe wouldn't have died either. He died because of the sins of others. A saint is always punished for his generation's sins."

The opposition flew into a rage. "What are you ranting about? Are you saying we're not observant enough?" And they started listing examples of how upstanding and pious they were, as if more virtuous people than themselves couldn't possibly exist.

The first side conceded that whatever had been done up to now hadn't helped and went on to say the town couldn't afford to wait until tempers cooled—they had to do something immediately. And there was only one remedy remaining that hadn't been tried yet, and that was to hold a wedding in the cemetery.

There was already a likely couple at hand—actually, they'd been around for ages. If the community had provided the means to help them get married fifteen years ago, that would have been a great good deed, but there hadn't been a plague at the time so no one had bothered. Even back then the young man seemed middle-aged, with a thick beard so matted you could practically hammer nails into it, and the woman looked like she'd already borne a half-dozen children.

The community had supported the two all their lives. Everyone fed them, and they never went hungry, eating a meal in one house, a snack in another, and always wanting more. Senderl worked for the town government as an outdoor laborer; Yenta worked indoors as a maid. They were rivals and despised each other. When Senderl walked into someone's kitchen and found Yenta there, he bristled like a tomcat who'd wandered indoors and run into the female who'd scratched out his eyes in the garden. Sometimes the pair found themselves working at the same house at the same time without knowing the other was there. Senderl would be chopping wood or sweeping out the stable, and Yenta would be inside washing floors. As long as they didn't know the other was on the premises, their work went well, but the moment they learned the other was nearby, they'd make a mess of things. He'd begin chopping the wood too thick or too thin, and she'd start splashing dirty water all over, slopping her washrag in the bucket whether she needed to or not, and smacking the floor with the filthy rag until her legs were soaked up to the thighs.

Everyone knew how the couple felt about each other, so if someone wanted to annoy Senderl, they'd just have to say, "Yenta sends her greetings." If they wanted to tease Yenta, they'd say, "Senderl says hello." But despite knowing how much the two hated each other, people were convinced they were about to perform a mitzvah, a righteous act, by marrying them off—and by the heavenly merit they'd gain by this mitzvah, the plague would surely be ended.

What a pair these two were! Yenta never stopped smiling. She could stand in the same place for hours on end, arms crossed over her chest, grinning at the whole world. She'd stare in wonder at every pig or dog that trotted by, following it with her eyes and smiling as if she'd never in her life seen such a creature. What she especially loved was watching a rooster chasing a hen. She made sense when she spoke, but she talked like a six- or seven-year-old, about buttons and scraps of broken pottery—things like that. The gift of an empty matchbox was enough to make her happy.

Yenta's husband-to-be, Senderl, was a serious man. If you told him to dance, he'd dance, and if you told him to sing, he'd sing, but he'd never crack a smile. He had a weakness for matchmaking.

"Senderl, tell me who I'll marry."

Senderl would close his eyes, wrinkle up his forehead, raise his hands in a gesture of exaggerated piety, wag his forefinger from side to side, and mumble to himself. Then, his eyes still closed, forehead still wrinkled, and finger still wagging, he'd announce the name of the future husband or wife. He always did a good job; often the couples he'd matched would get engaged, and whenever he saw a newlywed couple who, in his opinion, weren't suited to each other, he'd say, "Phooey! Get rid of them. I'll find you someone better to marry."

Yenta always wore a headscarf with her hair showing around its edges, like a married woman who wasn't too bothered about looking modest. She walked around barefoot eight months a year, and each of her toenails was as long, pointed, and black as the head of a pickaxe.

Now and again Yenta changed her mind about Senderl, especially when he distinguished himself in some unusual way. He was an expert chicken catcher, better than anyone else in town. Whenever a chicken went missing, its owner would get Senderl to find it, and he'd go straight out and retrieve the lost bird from whatever godforsaken place it was hiding in. At such times Yenta recognized Senderl's worth and rare talent, and would have died for a glance from him. She especially admired Senderl when he showed up like a magician in the marketplace with a dozen or more eggs to sell. Everyone knew they weren't his, but they could never work out where he'd gotten them. Not from some house or chicken coop: Senderl was no thief. He found his eggs out in the open. There's always some wayward hen who lays her eggs in some half-wild corner surrounded by bushes and weeds—to the annoyance of her owner, who can hardly ever find them in their secret hiding place. But Senderl was an expert. It didn't help to threaten him with seven years of poverty for stealing eggs—he carried right on. Sometimes he even went down to the river for goose or duck eggs left behind when the mother went for a swim.

During the summer Senderl managed to earn quite a bit of money, and Yenta was jealous. She'd sometimes go looking for hidden "treasures" herself, but her efforts were fruitless. Her only revenge was the thought that each one of Senderl's thefts would earn him a punishment of seven years' poverty. In Yenta's muddled brain, poverty on account of the eggs Senderl was taking was somehow completely different from the poverty he actually had.

So the town decided to marry Yenta and Senderl off to each other, and the week between Rosh Hashanah and Yom Kippur was taken up with meetings about the wedding. Heads of wealthier families haggled to decide who should contribute more and who less, and the town was enlivened by the thrilling affair. Even before everyone knew how things would all turn out, young and old were congratulating the soon-to-be-married couple: "Mazel tov, Yenta! Mazel tov, Senderl!" And the two went on sniping at each other: she sneered at him when she was congratulated, and he did the same. Senderl was huffier than usual, and even Yenta stopped smiling at everyone she met.

At first, when the community leaders told Senderl they'd decided to marry him off to Yenta, he recoiled as if the news were a poisonous snake whose tail he'd just stepped on. For a while he wouldn't hear of it, but later he said he'd consent to the match if they gave him a hundred rubles. They argued him down to seventy-five, and he had the good sense to demand the dayan be given the money to hold until after the ceremony.

The wedding day was delayed for a week, until the third day of Sukkoth, the harvest festival, while the bride and groom were prepared for the wedding. The townspeople organized a collection of goods the new couple would need in their married life. Synagogue assistants went from house to house, and everyone gave what they could: a shirt, a pair of underpants, a handkerchief, a quilt cover, a sheet, even a handful of feathers taken out of some woman's own quilt. Those who were better off donated more valuable things: shoes, trousers, a couple of long coats, overcoats for summer and winter, a few caps, some vests, nearly a dozen arba kanfoth—undergarments with ritual fringes—and a half-dozen pairs of socks, both long and short. Among the five or six dresses collected for the bride was one of white silk, donated by a wealthy young woman who wanted the pleasure of seeing Yenta wearing it. There were so many goods that some women were envious of the new couple, who overnight had become positively affluent. No one else in town had so much linen or so much clothing, and that wasn't even counting the wedding gifts to come.

Everyone was anticipating the big day as if it were a special holiday. They were all impatient to see Senderl and Yenta under the chuppah, the traditional wedding canopy. Everyone got ready, because it was everyone's wedding.

A few wealthy young bachelors, who'd amused themselves by learning fiddle or clarinet, volunteered to play the wedding music. They even found an amateur poet to serve as a badchan—a wedding entertainer—who promised to joke and sing as well as any professional. A day or two before the wedding, the musicians and a few of their friends dressed the bridegroom in his new clothes just to see how he'd look in his high stiff collar and bow tie, and then, with a lot of banging and clattering, they paraded him into the synagogue like Hasidim with their rebbe. Smiling faces appeared in the little windows of the women's section, craning to catch a glimpse of the bridegroom.

In synagogue on the second day of Sukkoth, that day's baal kore, or Torah reader, honored the bridegroom with a call to recite the blessings over the Torah before the congregation. Everyone in the women's gallery poured into the men's part of the synagogue, and as the baal kore was blessing the bridegroom, the women showered them with cooked beans and kernels of grain. Wealthier women threw handfuls of nuts. Kids flung themselves onto their hands and knees, scrambling for goodies on the dirty floor and stuffing their mouths and pockets.

Long before dawn the next morning, thick smoke was already pouring from the chimney of one of the Jewish houses. Its kitchen window was brightened by candles and lamplight until well into the day. A half-dozen women were hard at work in that kitchen, each for the sake of the mitzvah. A little later that morning, two women, wives of the synagogue assistants, went to the cemetery to invite the souls of the bride's and groom's parents to the marriage ceremony.

It was a beautiful day for a wedding. Dawn arrived with a brilliant fanfare of light and birdsong that heralded a bright, warm morning, and the cloudless sky and windless air promised the rest of the day would be just as pleasant. Silky strands of silvery spiderwebs wafted above the grass as if they were alive, floating in the balmy air like placid babies newly born along with the morning.

Each sukkah snuggled up to its house like a cherished child snuggles up to its parents. Some of the sukkahs were built against the house's front door, hiding it from view, and others against a window. The little huts looked delicate and fragile, their walls made of boards with wide gaps between them so that the interiors were barely separated from the outside world, as if little shelters had been carved out of the outdoors, small rooms tucked away from the open air in honor of the festival of Sukkoth. Protective flaps covered with roofing material, which could be lowered over the sukkahs' roofs in bad weather, now stood wide open, suspended on ropes or propped on crooked poles like wagon shafts. The sukkahs' widely spaced roof slats were covered with branches and leaves, and when you looked up from below, you could see thin stalks of maize with their long leaves lining the roof and green thatches of reeds hanging down inside.

Gabriel, the synagogue's caretaker, left his house right after dawn. Carrying the etrog and lulav, plants symbolizing the holiday, Gabriel trotted down the festive streets, rushing in and out of people's houses as fast as he could, less like a man bringing the holiday spirit into each home and more like the festival of Sukkoth itself embodied in a man—a religious Jew with a beard—and in the long, green, pointed fronds of the lulav.

A little later the young folk appeared, sleepy-eyed and in a buoyant mood, to visit the bride and bridegroom and have some fun with them. When they got to their homes, they did whatever they felt like doing. A gaggle of girls clustered around Yenta, holding up her donated clothing, one piece after another, to see how they'd look on her. They sprinkled the bride's face with powder, and, using the red paper envelopes that cigarette papers came in, they colored her cheeks, spitting on the brightly colored paper and rubbing it over her skin. As for Senderl, he was surrounded by a flock of young unmarried men who, as the women were doing at Yenta's house, held up the bridegroom's donated vests, hats, and coats, measuring each garment against him and laughing so hard that they practically choked.

There was still some time to go before the wedding, but the musicians, instruments in hand, had already lined up behind the badchan in the street and mimed a silent, comical march. The fiddle players scraped the backs of their bows against the strings, while the clarinetists held their instruments' mouthpieces to their lips and danced their fingers over the silver keys, pressing and releasing them in silence. The band set off down the street playing their inaudible music. It was a brilliant idea, and everyone who saw the procession was overcome with hilarity: even people in mourning, unable to sit shiva on account of the holiday, smiled as they watched the strutting, soundless pantomime. Then, when the band reached the house where the bridegroom was staying, the performers burst into a loud marching tune that lifted everyone's spirits even higher.

The musicians, still playing, filed into the house. But the music trailed off as soon as they went through the door: it was so crowded and noisy, there was no room to play. The house was packed with little kids, the bridegroom standing in their midst with a flustered expression. He looked completely lost—clearly he had no idea what to do with himself or with the gang of children besieging him. He stood there helplessly, all dressed up for his wedding, looking more like a fool than ever, as if he'd suddenly lost his sense of self, his sense of being Senderl, and become something else, and he didn't know what that something else was—whether it was better than the old Senderl or worse. He stood there like a newborn baby with no identity, clothes disheveled, hands hanging limp at his sides. The musicians chased out the kids, who banged and clattered through the door, scrambled out the windows, and stood around the house yelling and screaming.

A bit later, when the adults started to arrive, things quieted down. Even the children started to feel the gravity of the moment: this wedding was no joke, but a very serious matter indeed. As each man entered the room with the self-important air of a father-in-law, the band greeted him with a hearty rendition of "Mazel Tov," to which the badchan replied theatrically—like all badchans at all weddings—"Now *that* was an excellent 'Mazel Tov,' performed in honor of Reb . . . ," adding the name of each new arrival in turn.

The groom sat at the head of the table, surrounded by the wealthiest and most pious men, everyone drinking whiskey, making toasts, and eating honey cake. The same thing was happening at the bride's house—Yenta was surrounded by women, all of them making a fuss over her. Men pushed to get closer to Senderl, and women pushed to get closer to Yenta. Everyone was eager to partake in the mitzvah of honoring the couple and even more eager to earn the heavenly merit to escape the plague—may God help them all!

A few hours before nightfall, the musicians struck up the wedding march. The bridegroom and his visitors, with braided havdalah candles flickering and smoking in their hands, left the house. Senderl, in a long, black frock coat worn over a white robe that peeked out at the throat and hem, looked like a widower about to marry his second wife. Some ways behind him, a group of women led the bride, her face veiled with a white folded scarf. The couple and their escorts were accompanied by the entire Jewish population of the town, from children to old folks. The poles of the wedding canopy swayed above the heads of the procession. Their feet trod up dust that swirled around their heads like thick fog in which long, curling strands of smoke from the havdalah candles twined and interlaced. The band played lustily. Joy and sorrow intermingled: a couple was on their way to the cemetery, the place where the dead were buried, to be married under the chuppah. Everyone's eyes were drawn to the tall poles that stuck up over the heads of the crowd. For some reason they looked a bit different than usual.

Within minutes, the cemetery was full of people. Most of the crowd, too impatient to squeeze through the narrow gate, clambered over the fence, from boys to adult men. Everyone wanted to get near the chuppah for a close view of the bride and groom, and to see their expressions as they were married. Some kids climbed trees and perched in the branches. Here and there among the crowd you could hear the words of the funeral prayer, *El Maleh Rakhamim*, sung with all the embellishments—people were praying for the couple's parents.

The four poles of the wedding canopy were separated. Each corner of the square canopy was fastened to a pole, and the chuppah was held aloft. The bride and groom were escorted beneath, where they recited the psalms "Teach us to number our days" and "The vanity of worldly riches" seven times each. After the wedding was over, the musicians struck up a march. The bride and groom walked arm in arm back to town, and just as before, when everyone wanted to be first in the cemetery, now no one wanted to be last, and they all scrambled out over the fence.

It was still broad daylight, but everyone knew evening would soon fall. The sun stood in the West, just as clear and pure as when it had risen that morning. Surely, a warm night would follow this lovely, heaven-sent day. The townspeople walked back with complete faith that an end had come to the plague. And though they normally wouldn't have dreamed of cavorting or carousing, each person laid a hand on another's shoulder, right there in the middle of the street, and they all danced straight into the synagogue, where tables and benches were being set up, to spend the entire night celebrating their delivery.

Section 3

Women

Rosenfeld has an uncanny knack for getting into the minds of his female characters, whose inner lives are richly imagined and realistically depicted, with no attempt to flatter the egos of male characters or readers. While some of the concerns of female characters—for example, their pressing desire to marry—may seem a little old-fashioned to some contemporary audiences, we must keep in mind that women's financial and social independence is a recent phenomenon, far from universal, and something we should not take for granted. In these stories, Rosenfeld handles women's rites of passage—love, sexuality, motherhood, and aging—with insight and sensitivity, understanding that women's roles in patriarchal societies are often traps from which they cannot escape.

Zelda, in "Call It Destiny," is engaged to a young man about to be sent off to war. Her feelings are conflicted: Should she marry him or break off the engagement? What exactly does she want from this fragile relationship with a man she does not even love? Zelda is drawn simultaneously to the security of marriage, the longing for romance, and the drive to independence. Neither she nor the people around her are fully aware of her contradictory, unspoken motivations.

Readers of "A Mother" understand that Mrs. Koyfman is trapped in a loveless marriage to a bullying husband. According to the laws and customs of her society, she cannot escape from her marriage. She longs for a child to love, but her attempts to become a mother only deepen her loneliness and humiliation.

Miss Leder, the protagonist of "Nero," a successful businesswoman, is unhappily single. She is afraid of losing her independence and therefore frightened of her own sexuality, the expression of which, by the standards of her time, must lead to marriage. Unable to face her internal conflicts, she displaces her erotic feelings onto her beloved cat, Nero.

"Miss Bertha" tells the story of a woman who, effacing her own needs and desires, lives only for others. Eventually, she meets a smug, entitled "celebrity," who takes advantage of her passivity and attempts to rape her. She bravely defends herself, but is defeated by her own unexpressed—and misplaced—longing to be seen and loved.

Finally, "A Respectable Woman," a simple story with complex themes—women's sexuality, aging, sexual predation, and consent—raises a number of uncomfortable questions. Is it acceptable for a woman to pursue a much younger man—her son's friend, who is barely more than a boy? What if neither of the two is able to articulate their confused and conflicted feelings? And who should we hold responsible for the outcome of the story: Mrs. Belemer or the young man?

Call It Destiny

It seemed to be destiny: Zelda, who was well past her prime, had just gotten herself engaged when God sent a war to the world, and her fiancé had to go serve in the army. He and Zelda had met just a few times altogether, and while she wasn't thrilled with him, she *was* thrilled with being engaged, so deep inside she felt grateful.[1]

When the rumor started going around that they'd be drafting people his age with temporary exemptions, Zelda's fiancé went to see her and talk things over: Should he get out of service by injuring himself? That's what he'd done a few years previously, which is why he had an exemption, though now he was all better. But Zelda wouldn't hear of it. She preferred that her fiancé be a soldier, because if he got out of the draft, people would think the man she'd chosen to marry had something seriously wrong with him. It was in God's hands, she thought; if she *were* destined to marry a cripple, let it happen without her participation. If he were wounded in battle, she wouldn't break off with him, but in that case, no one would have anything to gossip about because she'd obviously chosen a healthy man in the first place. And if he managed to stay healthy, that would be even better from her point of view.

"If you want my opinion, I'd say don't do it," she told him, her tone cool, as if she were a distant acquaintance of his, not the woman

---

1. An earlier version of this story appeared in the 2019 *Pakn Treger Translation Issue* (https://www.yiddishbookcenter.org/2019-pakn-treger-translation-issue/call -it-destiny).

he was going to marry. "It's nothing you can understand—it's in God's hands. If it's your destiny . . ."

That was all she had to say. She could hear the insincerity in her own voice and was afraid he'd hear it too. But was it her fault that she didn't feel anything for this man, that he was a stranger to her, that she'd accepted his proposal only because he'd wanted to marry her when nobody else had? No, she'd made up her mind: God would decide. If her fiancé came back alive from the army, he'd be her destined husband. Even if he came back wounded, she wouldn't leave him, because if that were to happen, she'd obviously been destined to marry an invalid. But who could tell?—a little flame suddenly sparked in a corner of her mind—what if he came back safe and sound? What if he came back as a hero with medals on his chest, gold and silver in his pockets? Suddenly, the man sitting across from her vanished as her feelings welled up for the man who'd come back to her decorated with medals, wallet full of gold and silver. Maybe this whole situation was the opposite of what she'd thought at first. Maybe this war was a stroke of luck for her.

A light sprang up in her brown eyes, dull as spoiled cherries, eyes whose light had been snuffed out long ago, and its glow suffused her spinsterish face. At that moment, she looked like an abandoned house in which a person with a burning lamp appears, suddenly, at night.

Zelda's fiancé just sat there glumly. You had to feel sorry for him: here he'd come to talk things over with this woman he'd met only two months ago, a woman whose advice he depended on more than the advice of people he'd known for decades, and things had turned out so strangely.

"Does this mean you're saying I shouldn't?" Those were the last words he spoke to her.

"No, you shouldn't," she answered fervently, as if she were focused on nothing but his own good. But she was only delighted he was asking her what to do, and that his fate, the fate of a young man, lay in her hands.

Every morning Zelda went to the post office to ask if she had a letter. She walked proudly, her expression serenely confident, as if her fiancé had found a good job out of town. Standing on the post office's porch were other young women and wives, together with older men and women, waiting for letters from fiancés, husbands, and sons in the army. Many of them had the washed-out expressions born of long, anxious waiting; their eyes looked lost and their arms hung limp, as if their lives had lost all meaning. Zelda stood placidly in their midst, pleased to be like the others now: she had a fiancé; she was getting his letters. As far as she was concerned, that was the whole point of her being there. So every morning she pretended to ignore the other people, to be entirely occupied with her own thoughts, to be interested only in the man who was writing to her.

His letters were always exactly the same: one day he was here; the next he was somewhere else. His health was good. He forgot to inquire after Zelda's health, which she found quite annoying. He seemed to think nothing was going on in her life, and even if there had been, it wasn't important; only he was important, his life, his health. Zelda was always disappointed in his letters; she kept looking for something about herself, hoping to see the words a man should write to his fiancée. She looked for a tender word, some expression of warmth, and she never found any, and whenever she finished reading one of his letters she felt vaguely resentful.

The letters eventually stopped coming. Oddly, it didn't occur to Zelda that her fiancé might be somewhere dangerous, his life in continual peril; she only thought he'd simply quit writing her. She was so convinced of this idea that she tried to impress on everyone that she thought he'd been killed, and deep down inside herself, she hoped this story, not her hidden suspicion, was the truth.

Nevertheless, she kept up her daily trips to the post office. She went because there were other people who hadn't received any letters for a long time either, and they were still going.

One day there was a letter for Zelda. But to her great amazement, when she glanced at the address, she saw that the handwriting wasn't her fiancé's. She opened the letter right there on the spot, and again a stranger's writing met her eyes. Her heart started to pound; her eyes blurred so that she couldn't read. Like anyone else in her situation, she wanted to devour the letter in a single breath but was so impatient she couldn't understand a thing. When she did manage to make out a word, it stood out all by itself, rolling around in her brain like a button in a sewing box, which is theoretically useful but never actually needed because there's nothing for it to be sewn to.

Slowly, Zelda fumbled her way off the porch, still holding the letter open in her hands. She was far too anxious to bring it home and read it there. But after a few steps she stopped. Who was this "unknown, esteemed young woman"? She glanced at the signature: a stranger's name, a name she didn't recognize. She took in a few words from the letter's middle . . . they were incomprehensible, they had nothing to do with the man whose letter she'd been expecting, and nothing to do with her.

"Having gotten to know your fiancé," she reads, "with which we've lived very well"—no, she's skipped a few lines. "I'm completely alone." What is this? Why is this man saying such things to her? And what about her fiancé? No, she can't read any more. She's trembling, and the words she's just read are spinning in her brain . . . strange words that a stranger had written to his friend's fiancée . . .

The people who'd been waiting had dispersed, leaving the post office porch and the street in front of the building empty. Some had left with letters and others without, some with good news, others bad, and now no one remained on the street except Zelda. Yes, she'd gotten a letter, but it wasn't from her fiancé, but from her fiancé's friend, and she didn't know what he'd written, and she was afraid to find out. Over her head hung the gray autumn sky, dripping scattered, chilly drops, and everything around her, all of nature, was empty, naked, and dark.

Still holding her letter, Zelda wrapped her shawl around her arms and hurried off home. The minute she opened the kitchen door, her mother, who'd been standing by the stove, demanded, "Well, did you get a letter?"

Without answering, Zelda walked straight into the next room. Her mother followed her, ladle in hand, repeating, "So, did you get a letter?"

Zelda pulled off her shawl, and her mother, seeing the letter she was clutching, knew the answer to her question. But Zelda's distraught expression worried her mother more than if there hadn't been a letter at all. She went straight over to her daughter and, looking deep into her eyes, stammered, "What's he written?"

Zelda wanted to answer that the writer was someone else, not "he," and she would have said so if only she'd had a clue what the "someone else" had written.

"I got a letter," she murmured quietly, as if speaking to herself, "but I haven't read it yet. I'd rather read it myself first." Then she turned to her letter, reading silently. She did her best, using all her determination, to read slowly and carefully, not skipping lines, not leaving anything out. The letter went like this. He, the writer of the letter, had served in the same military company as Zelda's fiancé. They had bunked together and gotten along well. Zelda's fiancé had read him all the letters he'd received from Zelda, and also the letters he'd written to her.

"Let me hear already—what's he written?" Zelda's mother raised her voice impatiently, seeing by her daughter's expression that the news wasn't good. Zelda was getting impatient herself, but she held tight to her resolve to read everything in the right order. "He was a fine and decent young man," she read further. "Was!" That word leaped in her mind. She burst into tears and flung herself down in her bed.

"Oh, no . . . was he wounded?" her mother quavered.

Just at that moment Zelda's younger brother Leyzerke came in. He was a skinny young man who'd had to register for the army; he was so gaunt he looked like a beanpole in the autumn after you've stripped off the vines. He walked in without saying a word, as if he already knew what had happened and wasn't surprised by his sister's tears because he was so weighed down with his own problems. He sidled over to his sister, plucked the letter out of her hand, and began to read it to himself.

"I want to hear too!" their mother demanded.

But Leyzerke, who was completely absorbed with his own troubles, paid no attention to his mother and calmly went on reading. His mother, seeing his unruffled expression, forced herself to wait until he'd finished and was ready to tell her what the letter said. Finally Leyzerke tossed the letter onto the table.

"Well?" she said.

"What an idiot!" he proclaimed, giving his sister a long, pitying look.

"What do you mean, 'idiot'?" their mother asked, looking relieved, and after thinking it over a few minutes, she added, "Thank God . . . but what does he say, then?"

"What does who say?" snapped Leyzerke impatiently.

"How should I know? You're reading the letter, and you're asking me who wrote it?" his mother retorted.

Leyzerke, still deep in his own worries and too impatient to think about anyone else's, raised his voice. "It's not written by 'him.' It's written by somebody else!"

"Somebody else? What for?"

"You mean you don't know?" Leyzerke was losing his temper.

"Stop torturing me!" the old woman yelled, slapping her head with her hands. "Just read it! Read it. I want to hear!"

So the young man, subsiding under the weight of his problems, calmly read the letter while his mother and sister cried. Its author described how he'd buried Zelda's fiancé according to Jewish ritual, but he went on to say a lot more about himself than about the dead man. He wrote that the dead man had been his one and only friend, and now he was completely alone—he'd lost all his friends, everyone he knew, when the enemy captured their city. Now he didn't even have anyone to write to, and without that, his life in the army, which was difficult enough, had become simply unbearable, so he was imploring the young lady to write him as soon as she recovered from the blow she'd suffered; he was begging her from the bottom of his heart. He'd answer her letter as soon as he got it.

"Well, what are you crying for?" Zelda's brother asked. "Maybe the person you're actually destined to marry is *him*."

A few days later, Zelda answered the stranger's letter. Oddly enough, after she'd written the first line or two, she realized she didn't feel like writing the words she knew she ought to write to a stranger; instead, she wanted to tell him things she'd never wanted to tell her fiancé. Her heart ached with pity for this man who'd been torn away from his relatives and friends, this solitary man for whom her solitary heart longed. . . . Could it be that this was her real destiny? In the back of her mind, a thought stirred to life . . . could it be?

Her pen raced. She didn't have to think about the words—the letter wrote itself. Each syllable was imbued with warmth, kindness, yearning. She didn't think about what might come of her letter; she expressed her feelings completely, and the result was a beautiful, emotional letter in which one lonely heart called out to another.

A week later, Zelda went back to the post office. She went every day, and the other people there, knowing her fiancé had been killed, were surprised: Who was she expecting a letter from now? But these days, nobody else mattered to Zelda. Her thoughts were all for the man, and her eyes were bright with longing.

A Mother

Before Mrs. Koyfman got married, she loved to imagine her future baby—a girl with big blue eyes and blonde hair in ringlets, just like the doll she'd had as a child. But now her wedding was ten years in the past, and Mrs. Koyfman was still, to her great despair, childless. She was inconsolable.

One night as Mrs. Koyfman lay in bed wishing there was a baby sleeping beside her, a thought popped into her head: she could buy a doll, one that looked like her fantasy child. She knew the idea was a bit odd—but it was also oddly attractive.

That morning she woke up more cheerful than usual, her mind fixed on the thought of buying a doll. She surrendered herself completely to the fantasy, even though there still seemed to be something not quite right about it. It was that not-quite-right feeling that made her hesitate. It would be embarrassing—people would guess why she'd done it, and her husband would certainly ask. What could she say? And the maid would laugh behind her back. But then Mrs. Koyfman realized there was nothing to worry about—neither her husband nor the maid would find out. She'd think up a plan.

When she'd finished her cocoa and eaten her breakfast, she washed up, put on her black dress with its silk-lined bodice, threw her oversize handbag over her arm, and, feeling as carefree as a girl, left the house and ran down the short flight of stairs to the street. She stood there a few minutes waiting for a droshky, but wasn't much bothered when she didn't see one. She walked along happily, the silk lining of her dress swishing. A hard frost made the trees and rooftops as white as if they'd been sprinkled with a light powder of snow.

As soon as Mrs. Koyfman entered the toy store she saw five girl dolls sitting on a shelf, displayed among the boy dolls. Some had blue eyes and some dark; some had blonde hair and some black; all had little arms that reached out to her. Her heart started to race. Among the dolls she spotted one bigger one, the height of a four- or five-year-old child. She asked the clerk to pass it over. The clerk—a large, sturdy-looking young man—reached out, grabbed the doll by one foot, and pulled it off the shelf. Before showing it to Mrs. Koyfman he brushed the dust off its plump pink cheeks, wiped off its shiny legs, shook its knee-length dress, and finally pulled the dress up to dust underneath. Mrs. Koyfman looked on with exasperation, annoyed by the clerk's rude behavior in front of a lady and irritated that he was handling the doll as if she were just any ordinary piece of merchandise.

At length Mrs. Koyfman took the doll and examined her. The first thing she did was gaze into the big, wide-open blue eyes that closed when she leaned back and opened when she stood up; then she spent a few minutes stroking the blonde curls that covered her forehead and lay over her shoulders. She examined her legs up to the knees, but no higher than that.

"How much does this cost?" she asked.

"Fifteen rubles," said the clerk.

The manager, who'd been standing behind the counter, pushed his way through a herd of rocking horses with long manes, walked over to Mrs. Koyfman, plucked the doll out of her hands, and began to praise it: "If I may point out, Ma'am, this doll is imported. Look at the coloring of her face; it's extraordinary. She's completely life-like." Mrs. Koyfman handed over her money and happily took the doll home.

That first night at bedtime, Mrs. Koyfman undressed the doll to her undershirt as if she were a real child. But lying under the covers, holding the hard, cold, smooth little body in her arms, she was sorry she'd undressed her, and the next night she put the doll to bed in her clothes. Before she lay down herself, she spent a long time combing the doll's hair, trying out different hairstyles. Every once in a while she'd hug her tight and say aloud, "I love you so much. I'd give up my life for you." Then she put out the night light so she wouldn't have to see the small painted face. After cuddling for a few minutes, Mrs. Koyfman felt the little dress warm up, and she could almost convince herself that she was holding a real baby in her arms. She gave herself over to her motherly role, going so far as to offer the doll a breast so she could nurse.

Mr. Koyfman slept in his own room, so it was easy for Mrs. Koyfman to keep her bedroom door locked. She carried the key in her pocket, and now and then during the day she'd pop into her room and lock the door behind her. Then she'd pick up the doll, sit down on the bed, stand the doll on her lap, stretch out the little arms, look deeply into the wide blue eyes, and gaze at the little red lips frozen in a sweet, childish smile. From time to time she let go of the doll's hands so that she could stand up by herself—then she'd catch the doll with a start before she could topple over. Mrs. Koyfman was pretending, in a nebulous kind of way: she wasn't so much afraid that the doll would be broken as that her baby would be hurt. Afterward, she'd hug the doll tightly, covering the blonde hair with kisses.

But as time passed, Mrs. Koyfman began to grow frustrated. She found the doll's stubborn silence troubling, and she worried more and more: Why wouldn't the doll say "Mama"? The more she thought about it, the more anxious she got. The continual silence weighed on her nerves to the point that sometimes she felt like punishing the cold, dead thing. One day she ended up flinging the doll onto the bed. It lay there with its arms stretched out and its eyes closed while Mrs. Koyfman paced the floor in agitation, her tall, matronly figure giving off an air of utter misery. Her dark eyes burned with fury, and from time to time she glared at the doll. Finally, she snatched it up and shoved it under the bed. Then she stormed out of the room, locking the door behind her. But a few minutes later she went back in, gently took the doll out from under the bed, and began playing with her again.

One night at bedtime, Mrs. Koyfman got so carried away playing with her doll that she spoke out loud. "I love you so much. I'd give up my life for you." There was a knock at the door.

"Who's that?" she said.

"It's me," growled her husband.

Mrs. Koyfman was startled. "What do you want?"

"I want you to open the door."

"I don't have to listen to you," she retorted.

Mr. Koyfman started kicking the door. Mrs. Koyfman hid the doll under the bed and turned the key in the lock. In roared her husband like a thunderclap. He rushed over to the bed, ripped off the coverlet, reached under the bed, and yanked the doll out by her hair.

Then he smiled. "So you've been talking to a doll." He looked it over and said with a smirk, "What a cute kid, very pretty. I had no idea. Mazel tov." He flung the doll to the floor and stalked out.

Alone in her room, Mrs. Koyfman wept.

Nero

Miss Leder sat in an armchair by the fireplace, her legs stretched out to the fire and her feet resting on a soft plush cushion. She wore a Persian shawl around her shoulders, not so much for its warmth, but for its style and the aesthetic pleasure it gave her. She watched the fire as it brightly burned, its heat on her legs lulling her into a doze. From time to time she closed her eyes, the flickering light still visible under her lowered eyelids. She was finely attuned to the silence in the dining room around her, as well as the utter stillness that filled all three floors of the flat she lived in. It seemed to her that the stillness was particular to that place: a physical, conscious stillness that lingered all day long, despite the tumult and clamor of the dozen or so little girls who worked upstairs in her workshop and clattered up and down the stairs with the energy of youth. After work, when they'd gone home, the silence came right back, flooding the lower floor and rising to the very ceiling of the topmost corridor. There wasn't a sound in the house—only the quiet, genteel outside noises that filtered indoors, and from time to time the heavy, massive sounds of buses rushing past on their hard rubber tires.

Miss Leder could sense the maid on the other side of the thin wall dividing the dining room from the kitchen. The maid was sitting quietly in the kitchen waiting to go home, and Miss Leder could hear her silence—the restless silence of a woman who, her day's work done, was waiting for the appointed minute that would give her the freedom to leave. Miss Leder glanced at the clock: yes, it was almost nine o'clock . . . any second now . . . there it was. On the other side of the wall the silence came to life. A scrape, the movement of a

chair, and then footsteps: one, then another, a third, and then a few
more . . . and then the silence was right there, knocking at the door.

"Come in!"

It was the same every evening: the maid announced her departure
and said good night. Miss Leder knew the routine from experience,
but still every evening she greeted her employee before she left with an
inquisitive look and a vague hope that tonight might bring something
different. She detained the maid for a few minutes while the woman
waited with stolid indifference. She was a typical Englishwoman, tall
and thin—although, ironically, she had a typically Jewish name. Ethel,
she was called. She had a long, pale face with coarse, almost masculine features. She'd been working for Miss Leder for two years, during which time she hadn't changed a bit: always the same phlegmatic
apathy, like a creature without emotions—a fish in a human body.
When she'd first hired Ethel, Miss Leder thought she was an innocent
young thing, but she soon discovered her cold fish of a servant was
more licentious than the worst "Gretchen" in Germany. At the beginning she'd been a live-in maid and slept in Miss Leder's flat, but she'd
entertained male visitors at night, and Miss Leder refused to put up
with that. As an older unmarried woman, Miss Leder, like many others of her kind, was cautious, even prudish to the point of going out
of her mind when, one morning, she'd found a tomcat in the house
with her female cat. She'd sworn she'd never have a female cat again.

Ethel, the Englishwoman, had quite a few boyfriends, and Miss
Leder knew about them all. Ethel got depressed at the end of every
affair and perked up again when she started a new one.

"How are you doing, Miss Ethel?"

Ethel thanked her for asking, and Miss Leder, realizing her maid
had no desire to linger, gave her a few shillings so she could do some
shopping next morning on her way to work. Ethel said good night,
and Miss Leder replied, "All right, Ethel. But before you go, tell
me—what's the old gentleman upstairs doing? Is he at home, or has
he gone out?"

Every evening before Ethel went home and left her employer
alone in the house, the same question popped out of Miss Leder's

mouth, though she never got an answer. Why was she so interested in the old gentleman? Well, it wasn't so much that she was interested in him—she didn't care about him at all—but she wanted to know if she was alone in the house, all by herself, or if the lodger was home, the old stranger who lived upstairs on the third floor in the room he rented right next to her bedroom. . . . And where was Nero? The cat had vanished again. He usually sat with her before the fire, which gave her a comfortable, cozy feeling. But for the last few evenings, he'd abandoned her to loiter outdoors, courting his ladies, so she had no choice but to sit up by herself and tolerate his whims. Otherwise, he'd have to spend the night outside. The devil alone knew what dirty deeds he was getting up to out there—and when he'd come in, he'd sleep in her bed. She'd tried several times to shoo him out, but it never worked. It was her own fault; no one had forced her to let him into bed with her . . . but he wasn't much more than a kitten . . . how old was he, anyway? She'd had him long enough to feel he belonged to her, yet at the same time he was old enough to be drawn to other cats . . . but . . . it was odd . . . she felt . . . though it was only a vague feeling, she felt a dim sense of . . . was it resentment? Could she be a bit—just a tiny bit—jealous of her Nero? But . . . only the devil knew what he was up to. Where could he have gotten to, and how long would she have to sit here waiting?

Miss Leder walked over to the sash window, raised the bottom half, and called in a loud, sharp voice, "Nero! Nero!" Craning her neck to look upstairs, she tried to see if a light was on in the third-floor window. She didn't see one, but that didn't necessarily mean the old gentleman wasn't in his room.

The street below had sunk deep into the darkness of a winter's evening. Lit-up windows cast their light into the shadows of the empty street, making it seem like two worlds were wrapped around each other: one world of bright houses that struggled to illuminate the empty outdoors gloom, and another, outer, world with an inde-finable, murky gray sky above and moist darkness below, punctu-ated here and there by the glow of windows and streetlamps. From time to time an automobile rumbled by, its wheels leaving wide, dull, dry-looking tracks on the damp road. Passersby walked up and down the sidewalks, the thick soles of their overshoes clattering. And from everywhere came the sound of cats yowling like the voices of children wailing over some disaster or lamenting the endless, tantalizing, tormenting absurdity of life.

"Nero!"

Miss Leder quickly lowered the window and, shivering with cold, sat down again by the fire. Really, she wasn't at all worried about not being married. The only thing that bothered her was that other people thought she minded. Those authors who write about old maids and their dark, somber lives . . . what liars they were! It wasn't so terrible at all. Take her friend Mr. Zanfil, for example. Every time he came to visit he'd take off his glasses and look at her that way— without his glasses—but when he was with other people, he'd look at them through his glasses. It intrigued her: Why on earth would he take off his glasses just to look at her? He was a gentlemanly, soft-hearted man. . . . Maybe he'd take pity on her and decide to marry her. They were already good friends. He'd drop by out of the blue, uninvited and unannounced, to sit for an hour or two before her fire, where quite often he'd nod off in his chair, and she'd leave him sleeping. She'd tiptoe out of the room, go upstairs to her bedroom, light a fire, make herself comfortable, and enjoy its warmth. The fire would glow, and she'd glow too, with warmth and pleasure. She'd imagine, as vividly as if she were actually seeing it, his waking up and realizing he was alone in the room. An hour or so later, she'd come back downstairs and he'd still be there. She always felt sorry for him—he'd look so upset as he groped around for words to excuse himself.

"It's quite all right, Mr. Zanfil!"

But his embarrassment bothered her. She knew very well *he* thought it was rude to fall asleep right there in front of her, but she didn't mind at all—she wasn't the least offended.

But maybe he was coming to see her with a particular goal in mind: he was a warm, compassionate man, of course, and maybe he felt so sorry for her he'd ask her to marry him, and it would never occur to him (if he really was thinking along those lines) that she'd refuse him. That thought would never even cross his mind. And why should it? She was ten years older than him, after all.

Miss Leder got up from her chair, opened the door to the corridor, and glanced up the stairs. She thought she'd heard footsteps—maybe the old gentleman was coming downstairs, despite its being so late. . . . But no . . . she'd only imagined footsteps on the stairs, which happened quite often when no one was there, because the old man walked so softly he didn't seem like anyone at all—so, when there really *was* no one there, Miss Leder sometimes thought it was the old man. . . . And why was he living in her house in the first place? Before she'd decided to rent him the room, she'd thought like this: everyone said the only kind of lodger she could have was an old man because she was an unmarried woman. Now a woman lodger . . . but she hated the idea of a woman lodger, for one reason or another—she didn't even know why. These steps were alive all day long under the feet of the dozen little girls and the three Misses and one Mrs. who worked in her little corset factory upstairs. Her flat was lively all day long, with the doorbell ringing and the rapping of the brass knocker. Real English people don't like to use the bell; they prefer to knock. . . . Was the old man home, or wasn't he?

Here came another question—an out-of-the-way one this time, something novel. Why was she living alone here in a three-story flat with a busy factory employing more than a dozen workers—why did she need the headache? . . . Well, the answer was simple—things were that way because she was an expert in the business, and because women need corsets, and because what she'd be doing otherwise wasn't so very different from what she actually *was* doing. And maybe some of them, some of her gentlemen visitors—maybe some of them were thinking of marrying her for that very reason, because of the business. . . . Maybe even Mr. Zanfil. . . . He didn't have a very important job, after all, working in the Zionist office.

Yes, there really did seem to be someone walking down the stairs. How odd that she'd think so when no one had gone up or down for a couple of hours, and she didn't even know if the old man on the third floor was home. And even if it *was* him, you couldn't hear him anyway. Perhaps it was Nero: maybe he was carrying on a romance, running up and down the stairs with his chosen female—or one that had chosen him—maybe the one that sat for hours outside on the windowsill, looking in at him.

"Neeerooo!"

A door quietly opened upstairs, and a face appeared, dimly illuminated in the wan light that filtered up from the downstairs hall. Its eyes, looking like two dark blotches in the dimness, peered down over the banister. "Yes, miss?"

Miss Leder apologized profusely. "I'm sorry," she said—she'd been calling her cat.

Miss Leder came from Courland, in Latvia. Her parents had died when she was young, but by then she'd learned her trade. She left Latvia, and by the time she was twenty she'd traveled all through Scandinavia, from country to country and city to city. She made good money wherever she went, and because she was earning so much she couldn't risk settling down and losing business. Eventually, after years of rootless wandering, she realized she was too old to get married. The years had slipped by unnoticed, leaving her with nothing but constant watchfulness—the instinctive reaction of a female who, finding herself surrounded by males of her species, each wanting her as a mate, defends herself and won't surrender to any of them. Because she was living among foreigners in foreign countries, Miss Leder was forced to protect herself constantly, with the result that she stayed more innocent, with less experience of men, than the most prim and proper girl in her hometown.

Miss Leder wasn't concerned with the values of middle-class respectability. By the same token, she made no secret of her innocence . . . but for years on end now, she'd felt discouraged and resentful because no matter where she went or whom she met, people had exactly the opposite impression of her. None of her friends believed she was chaste because they all knew how much traveling she'd done—so how could she still be untouched? No one took her seriously, and no one asked her to marry him. So for years on end, loneliness burned in her virginal heart, mixed with a hellish fury at men, until it got to the point that she kept her embarrassing innocence to herself because it had caused the predicament in which she found herself without even noticing how she'd arrived there. Now she regretted her past: the many happy moments she'd let slip by when she could have made something of her youth and her girlish vivacity. She especially regretted one man she'd ardently loved. That had been seventeen or eighteen years ago, in Christiania, Norway—a cold country nine months of the year, but the skies were so beautiful, and for much of the summer the sun shone almost twenty-four hours a day, setting and rising again at almost the same moment, an unending day of eternal light and perpetual youth. Those day-like nights drove Miss Leder out of her mind, stirring up in her all kinds of longing mingled with pleasurable melancholy. She'd stay awake all night, eyes wide open, never weary of gazing into the nighttime daylight, which, at times seemed a beautiful, bright dream, the dream of a never-ending, sunshiny day. The people she passed in the streets looked like they too were caught up in a dream of tranquil sweetness, as though they'd crossed into another state of existence, hypnotized by the unending days that lived out their twenty-four hours under the light of the sun.

It was there, in Christiania, that Miss Leder fell in love, with a man she trusted more than the rest because he was Jewish. Even though Miss Leder didn't know much about being Jewish, she was alone in a foreign place and felt closer to one of her own people. He never told her he was Jewish and she pretended she didn't know, and she didn't tell him about her own background either. But as time went on, she became aware that he was trying to take advantage of her love and trust. She thought it over, but not for long. She left the city, went to Germany, and settled in Berlin, where she lived a number of years. After that she moved on to stay briefly in several other German cities, and at last she crossed the sea to London, where she'd lived now for a dozen years and would probably stay a while longer. She loved London: it seemed the kind of place where a single person would feel less lonely because loneliness seemed to be everywhere, part of everybody and everything—the whole city, buildings and people alike, was gloomy and gray, as if sunk into grizzled senescence. Almost everyone looked too old to get married: there were elderly spinsters and thin, ancient bachelors, every one of them grave and taciturn. An entire race of buttoned-up, dull, quiet people. Yet she liked them: their very faults appealed to her. She saw great beauty and integrity in the English, and at times she thought even their faults were great virtues.

Miss Leder knew she would have been unhappy if she'd stayed in Courland. Here, though, on this British island, things were different—she didn't know why, but they were. Here she knew how to handle herself. She always behaved correctly, and she had to keep behaving that way, because . . . well, because . . .

"It's already late, Mr. Zanfil. You should be getting back." Miss Leder was a little miffed with him. What a strange man he was! She'd told him she was forty years old, and his response was no, she couldn't even be thirty yet. He was the only person she knew whose company she disliked—he was always rubbing her the wrong way. Though he was one of her visitors, he was her least favorite guest because he wouldn't leave her at peace with her unmarried state. Sometimes he'd do or say something that would pry loose a brick from the wall around her pent-up heart, letting in a dazzling ray of light that scorched her; he disturbed old, well-preserved sorrows that she'd long forgotten, reviving sad, painful longings. And why should he care whether she was thirty or forty years old? All right—she wasn't quite forty; she was thirty-nine—but for some reason she'd told him she was forty.

Sometimes they'd be talking and, as occasionally happens, a delicate subject would come up, and Mr. Zanfil would avoid using certain expressions out of respect for Miss Leder's unmarried state. That would annoy her no end. It wasn't because of her age—women of a certain age don't need to be protected from such words. She'd protested more than once: "Why such modesty, Mr. Zanfil? Say whatever you want. I'm not a naive young thing." True, she always blushed when she said this, and she had to struggle not to turn away. Every time she proclaimed herself no innocent, she'd regret it, yet she'd say the same thing again and again.

Miss Leder was sitting in her armchair by the hearth, her legs stretched out toward the fire, just as she had yesterday and the day before yesterday and every evening of the eight or nine months of the year when the fireplace was lit. Nero sat nearby on the rectangular plush rug that lay under the table and chairs, completely submerged in a sweet torpor of warmth, watching the fire through narrow slitted eyes.

"Nero, you're not going outside anymore. Do you hear? I won't let you. It doesn't become you, Nero. You're an aristocrat, after all—how can you run around with those filthy street creatures?" Miss Leder always talked to Nero that way. He turned his head and looked at her in silence, his huge eyes glowing with love and light, and as he sat in serene and majestic repose, holding her in his gaze, his eyes gradually narrowed into slits and his lashing tail gradually slowed its movement until only its very tip was twitching from side to side. That nervously twitching tail expressed the essence of feline egoism, proclaiming that deep inside the motionless, satiny black body lived the soul of a cat, a solitary creature of no account to those who walked on two feet, but of great interest to others of its kind. The sound of yowling came from outside the window. To Miss Leder, it seemed like children crying—but Nero knew better, and his ears pricked up. He listened intently, ears quivering. Despite his sedate demeanor as he sat by the fire, nothing outside escaped him. He heard every yowl, and his ears quivered with each one. He knew very well what they signified, even though he himself never yowled—in fact, he hardly ever made a sound. Yes, he was an aristocrat, but that hardly mattered—they were his own kind, after all, and deep in his feline marrow, imprinted in his innermost being, was an overpowering lust, a magnetic attraction to others of his species, which, it seemed, hadn't concerned him until recently.

Nero was eight or nine months old. Miss Leder had bought him seven months ago from a curio shop that sold rare birds and animals. She'd been out walking, and as she passed the display window she'd been brought up short by a pair of huge bright eyes that were staring out at the street with bewildered, kittenish charm, their gaze so innocently sweet that Miss Leder was galvanized with love for the tiny creature. When she went inside to buy him, the shopkeeper told her his complete pedigree: the kitten had come from a cold region of Canada where the skies high above were always clear and blue, which was why he had such huge, amazingly beautiful eyes. The man also told her the breed was distinguished by an especially good memory and that before too long he'd understand every word she said to him.

Miss Leder dignified her kitten with the name "Nero" because he never left the fire, and she always kept a fire burning in the dining room just for him. He loved to sit there in placid tranquility, his shining eyes, narrowed to slits, staring at the flames. Only from time to time, when the fire did something out of the ordinary—if it crackled or whooshed or if a little ember rolled away—would he open his eyes wide to look suspiciously at the hot, bright flutter of flames, and at those times it was obvious that even when Nero was napping, his instincts were alert, warning him that he was resting beside something that, though pleasant to be near, wasn't entirely trustworthy.

Again it was nine o'clock in the evening. Again the maid had just left, and again Miss Leder didn't know, but wished she knew, if her elderly lodger was in his room, and again she couldn't explain why she was always so eager to know. Miss Leder had taken off one of her slippers and was stroking Nero's head and back with her bare foot. Through the thin silk stocking she could feel the fine, soft smoothness of his satiny pelt, and while she stroked him she spoke to him tenderly, her words as sweet and soft as the fur under the foot that was gently gliding over his head and back: "That's enough, Nero—I won't let you sleep with me again!"

There was a knock at the window. Miss Leder got up, walked through the kitchen, and opened the back door. She already knew who it was: Mr. Zanfil was the only one of her guests who felt comfortable enough with her to knock at the window so he could be let in through the back. "Hello, Miss Leder!"

Miss Leder led Mr. Zanfil into the dining room, where he promptly took off his glasses, put them on the table, pulled over a chair, sat down by the hearth, crossed his legs, and gave the cat a pat on the head, greeting him by name. Nero, sitting between the two chairs, didn't even bother looking around to see who'd just patted him.

Miss Leder offered her guest a glass of tea. He thanked her politely, but refused—this time he'd brought the treats himself. He stood up, removed a big box of candy from the pocket of his overcoat, opened it, and offered it to Miss Leder. He'd never done that before, and the gesture made her a little nervous. His happy smile vaguely disturbed her. She took a piece of candy and, looking Mr. Zanfil straight in the eyes, asked what the occasion was. He answered, still smiling, that he might be treating her to candy again someday.

He was standing right next to her, as close as a brother stands to a well-loved sister, and his nearness added to her uneasiness. The whole time she'd known him, he'd never stood so close to her. Miss Leder felt that the barrier of reserve he'd placed between them had suddenly dissolved and that he'd suddenly become as relaxed with her as her other friends were. Up until now, that bit of reserve in his character had let her feel closer to him than to anyone else she knew. Now, however, he'd allied himself with all her other male friends, married or unmarried, as friendly as all the others, and with his casual friendliness he'd become a stranger just like them.

Mr. Zanfil went on to explain one of the most prominent Zionist leaders in town had taken him under his wing, which meant he was in line for a better job, one that would bring him six or seven pounds sterling a week. Deep down, Miss Leder felt a bit displeased by this news, but at the same time she breathed more easily, because— again, deep down—she'd been dreading something worse. Mr. Zanfil cheerfully put the box of candy on the table next to Miss Leder and, settling his glasses back on his nose, asked if a person could live comfortably on a salary like that.

"Yes, of course," Miss Leder said brightly, knowing perfectly well what he was getting at. She spoke in a firm, assured tone so that he wouldn't think she was trying to talk him out of what he was planning to do. "You'd be doing very well on seven pounds a week."

Miss Leder impulsively laid her foot on Nero's back and pressed down hard. The cat, lithe as an acrobat, flattened himself and slithered out from under her foot. He stood up tall and arched his back; then he stretched himself out, belly to the floor, all four legs extended as far as they could go, and opened his mouth in a gaping yawn, exposing sharp white fangs and a flat red tongue that trembled and fluttered like a pennant of soft, flexible fabric. Behind his tongue one could see the back of his throat with two holes leading to his insides. Then Nero straightened up again, took a few steps toward Miss Leder, and pressed the entire length of his beautiful body against her legs in their striped stockings of thin silk. As he gazed into the flames, it was hard to tell from his eyes what he was thinking or which of the two he loved more: the fire or the legs he was rubbing. His tail waved in the air. A couple of times it gave an unexpected jerk so that it looked like a living being separate from its owner, a thing with its own mind and its own sinister impulses.

Miss Leder lifted Nero into her lap and picked up his upper body so that his front paws hung in the air; then she hugged him close with his head tucked under her chin. Mr. Zanfil took off his glasses, smiled at the charming tableau, and stroked the length of Nero's body. Ten peaceful minutes ticked by. Outside the window cats yowled like wailing babies. Miss Leder, sunk into a deep melancholy, listened, barely aware of what she was thinking: she had the foggy notion that she'd been torn away from her everyday life and plunged into a mystical world where—it seemed—the caterwauling was the cries of children yet unborn, wandering souls searching for a place deep within her female being where they could fulfill their destinies by being born into this world.

At length Mr. Zanfil started speaking again. He picked up the thread of what he'd been saying and went on to explain he'd just gotten engaged to a certain Miss Herlekh.

"Well! Congratulations, Mr. Zanfil!"

Nero chose that moment to try to jump down from Miss Leder's lap. With a flash of anger, she grabbed him and squeezed him tight. "No—I won't let you out tonight!"

Nero glared at her, his eyes glowing phosphorus. She felt his wiry body uncoil under her hands and knew he was getting ready to squirm out of her grip. "No, sir, you're not going anywhere!" The cat started to writhe and struggle in earnest, whipping his agile body from side to side. It took all Miss Leder's strength to hold onto him, and as his struggles grew wilder and more relentless, she clutched him tighter and tighter.

Woman and beast wrestled with each other, each motivated by pure instinct, while Mr. Zanfil stood there watching with a smile on his face. He had no idea what was going on, where the cat was trying to go, or why Miss Leder wouldn't let him down. At first he thought it was just a game, but when he saw Nero's increasing violence, he started warning her to let go of him. Miss Leder glared at her guest each time, her face full of hatred and contempt, and with increasing obstinacy she squeezed and clutched at the cat, until finally Nero opened his mouth wide and sank his sharp fangs into her hand.

For an hour and a half, Miss Leder cried hard without stopping. For the first time in her life she knew, without the shadow of a doubt, that she'd wasted her life. It was gone forever . . .

Miss Bertha

The boarders considered Miss Bertha one of their own, a guest like all the other guests, even though her brothers were the owners of the Sunshine Boardinghouse resort. In fact, it went further: the boarders liked Miss Bertha even more than they liked each other because, despite being the owners' sister, she behaved like a boarder, eating her meals and spending her time with them. But what the boarders liked best about Miss Bertha was that they could badmouth the owners right to her face, just as they did among themselves. She was a real treasure, particularly in the opinion of those guests who, in return for their twenty-two dollars a week, would eat up the whole place if they could—people who think that no matter what or how much they eat, the food is lousy and there's not enough of it, considering the money they've spent. So the boarders complained to Miss Bertha about the owners, but their slander didn't count as slander because they were speaking to a relative of the people they were complaining about.

Miss Bertha was a loyal, devoted friend to all the guests. She was patient even with mothers who came with, and for the sake of, their children. Every one of these mothers wanted her children to eat and drink as much as she wanted, which was considerably more food and drink than the children wanted—because, after all, they were in the countryside.

"Miss Bertha, what can I do with my kids? They won't eat or drink a thing."

Sometimes a mother would be sitting on the grass with her child, struggling to pour a glass of milk down the kid's throat when Miss

Bertha would come walking by, and the mother would turn to her and ask, "Miss Bertha, could you give it to him? Maybe he'd drink it then."

The women who stopped Miss Bertha weren't completely to blame for interrupting her walk—in fact, Miss Bertha always walked in such a way that you could see she wasn't walking for pleasure, but circulating on purpose from person to person. Whenever somebody stopped her, she'd stay for a while, spending so much time with that person you'd think she'd planned her visit from the start. When it was a mother with a child who stopped her, Miss Bertha would get so involved with the kid you'd think she'd come by with the express purpose of taking over the mother's responsibilities.

You can devote yourself to strangers the way Miss Bertha did only when the boardinghouse belongs not to you but to relatives who give you the same comforts that the boarders pay for. It wasn't that Miss Bertha's brothers had burdened her with the job of taking care of the guests and making sure they were satisfied. Not at all: the brothers did the minimum required to meet their obligations to their paying guests—no more and no less than they had to, about the same as other boardinghouse owners did for their boarders who were paying the same fees the brothers charged. Beyond that, they didn't give a damn about anyone. Miss Bertha, however, was kind to all the guests. She honestly cared about every single one and wanted them all to be happy.

Miss Bertha welcomed every new boarder, male or female, with open arms, as if that person were her personal guest, someone who'd come to her family home as a visitor, not as a paying boarder. She'd greet them as enthusiastically as if she'd been looking forward to their visit for months. For the first few hours she'd keep a watchful eye on each one and acquaint them with everyone who strolled by, stopping passersby to introduce them to the newcomer: "I'd like you to meet Mr. So-and-So" or "I'd like to introduce you to Miss Such-and-Such."

But there were always some loners among the guests, who, either from pride or for some other reason, kept to themselves. Miss Bertha was saddened by these people, not on her own account, but because their attitude might offend others. She found the arrogant standoffishness of one particular man, a well-known personality, especially worrying. Her brothers had gone to a lot of trouble to attract this celebrity to their resort to advertise themselves and the business, but the man did more harm than good. He rubbed everyone the wrong way, and no one could stand him. Miss Bertha didn't beat around the bush; she begged him to make friends. Wherever he went she'd turn up at his elbow, complaining, "Still alone, always alone, forever alone! Aren't you bored?" Then, if a young woman happened to pass by, Miss Bertha would call her over to join her and her standoffish companion. Eventually, quite a crowd would accumulate, and so, whether he wanted to or not, the man was forced to spend time with the people Miss Bertha had gathered so skillfully—but only as long as Miss Bertha was there. As soon as she left, the crowd fell apart and he was alone again.

More than one young woman came from the big, tumultuous city, having worked hard all year to earn her two-week vacation, wanting a holiday to relax and eat her meals surrounded by mountains, trees, and fields—but mainly looking for a holiday from herself. She'd come to vacation among strangers, to play the role of a fun-loving girl, and to haul in a fun-loving young man who was looking for the kind of girl she liked to imagine she was. But when two or three days—a significant time in a short vacation—go by without anything happening, the girl gives up, gets depressed, and starts talking about leaving before the end of her two weeks. Then along comes Miss Bertha to keep her company. She does everything she can to cheer up the girl, bringing her over to join this or that group of young men or women, and the girl stays all the way to the end of her holiday.

Every season, there were a few young men and women who stuck close to Miss Bertha and acted as her aides and messengers, carrying out her every whim—not her own personal whims, of course, but those of the boarders, since it was Miss Bertha's whim to take care of and entertain them all. These young men and women didn't turn up just by accident; they came to the boardinghouse every year and were good friends of Miss Bertha and her brothers. When the longtime guests got together, it was impossible for anyone to feel bored. With whoops and yells, they'd drag some young woman into their circle dance or deafen her with songs and music, and it often happened that such a girl, who'd arrived in stylish clothes with her nose in the air, pretending she couldn't speak a word of Yiddish, was transformed into a down-to-earth Jewish girl once she was drawn into their company, singing Yiddish songs along with the rest and leaving happily when her holiday was over.

All kinds of people came to the Sunshine Boardinghouse, not all of them looking for a break from their lives. Some of them were perfectly content with their lot. There were blissful couples who were so ecstatic, it was obvious that they weren't married to each other, which is why they were so happy. Miss Bertha didn't have anything against these people, even though she herself was a decent, respectable woman. It was none of her business, she thought, if people did things she disapproved of, because no doubt they had their own reasons. She sometimes went so far as to defend behavior that other people, even those who were nowhere near as respectable as she was, would consider immoral. For example, there were two men who'd come to the boardinghouse with a young woman. For the first few days no one knew how the two men were related to the girl or to each other, but when people found out they weren't related at all but that the three of them lived together, it all became clear and tongues began to wag. Miss Bertha alone came to the young people's defense, even though she was more embarrassed by their three-way relationship than anyone else. Because she couldn't even imagine that people were capable of indecent things, she figured that whatever kinds of indecent things people *were* capable of, this wasn't one of them.

The girl who lived with the two boys confessed all to Miss Bertha: she said she was in love with both young men and they were in love with her, so their only option was to live together as a threesome. Miss Bertha was on her side—really, she thought, what else could they do, seeing as the girl loved the two boys and they loved her? What other alternative did they have except for the one they'd found?

The only thing that surprised her was that the two boys weren't jealous of each other. That topic intrigued her so much that she asked the well-known personality who was boarding there if such a thing were possible: Could two men love the same woman and live with her without being jealous of each other? The celebrity said it was out of the question. If both men loved her, he said, or if even one of them did, that man wouldn't be able to tolerate the relationship between the other two.

Miss Bertha figured the celebrity was right, since she herself was now thinking along the same lines. Earlier, before she'd learned his opinion, she hadn't been so sure. Perhaps the girl who lived with the two boys was right that both of them were actually in love with her, because otherwise why would the girl do what she was doing? But after talking things over with the celebrity, Miss Bertha decided that if the girl really thought that's the way it was, someone should open her eyes to the fact that she was mistaken—that it wasn't possible for two men to love and live with the same woman without at least one of the two romantic heroes being jealous. And that's what Miss Bertha told the girl. The first thing next morning, the three of them got up and left the resort a week earlier than they'd planned, and a few days after that, one of the guests said hello from them, saying he'd seen the threesome in another boardinghouse in the neighborhood. Miss Bertha felt bad about the whole situation—it was her own fault the three young people had left for another resort.

"Who are you looking for?"

Whenever Miss Bertha saw boarders wandering aimlessly by themselves, she understood they were looking for someone, and it was her job to sort things out. She took a personal interest in the first person's meeting up with the second person, and off she'd go to find them. She'd sniff around like a bloodhound, obsessed with her mission, single-mindedly trying to track down whoever the person she'd just met had been looking for. Her long face with its wide, innocent eyes and pointed chin wore an expression of guileless naïveté, and if you were to see her bumbling among the trees and across the lawns, you'd think she was the embodiment of the proverbial simpleton, blundering knee-deep in other people's silly human sins and passions, asking right and left of everyone she met, "Have you seen Mr. So-and-So? Have you seen Miss Such-and-Such?" and calling out their names.

Sometimes while she was running around asking questions, the well-known personality would pop up beside her or come up from behind, and with an expression and tone of voice that said he'd been looking everywhere for her, he'd inquire, "Bertha, sweetheart—who are you trying to find?" She never knew what to answer, because she'd suddenly realize she didn't know the answer, and she'd be embarrassed and turn back, and he'd call and shout after her, "Bertha, sweetheart!"

So she'd walk away and join some cheerful group of people where she'd always be welcome because she was never any trouble—they could say or do whatever they wanted, just as if she weren't there or as if she were just one of the crowd. Sometimes one young man or another would flirt with her, just for the fun of it. She wouldn't resist, but she wouldn't flirt back, either. She'd be in the young man's game but a nonparticipant at the same time, as if she weren't the person he thought she was, but the person she'd been before he'd started flirting, a person who deserved respect, so she'd feel calm and detached. She was less calm about the woman who was standing somewhere far away, a woman who could hear, somewhere in the distance, someone calling her name: "Bertha . . . !"

In the evenings, all the young people and older folks who weren't too old to have fun got together in the casino to dance. Miss Bertha would be one of the crowd, having fun and dancing along with the rest, but with one difference: the others were having fun and dancing on their own account, for their own pleasure, but Miss Bertha was doing so for the sake of others. She'd stand around, ready to make up a twosome with anyone who needed a partner. She was especially useful when it came to the broom dance, where she was as important as the broom itself. In the same way that the broom never chose a partner to dance with but was just there to be grabbed by some man or woman who had no other choice (that is, no human partner), people would grab Miss Bertha when their only other option was to dance with the broom. That's why Miss Bertha was in the dance—she never chose a partner, but was grabbed and pulled into the dance with everybody else, and the moment the piano and fiddle broke off in the middle of a song and the broomstick crashed to the floor, she'd stop and stand there passively, waiting for someone to grab her in preference to the broom.

The well-known personality, the celebrity boarder, danced along with the rest. A man in his fifties, he was (it goes without saying) perpetually eager to grab the youngest and prettiest partners. Miss Bertha had often seen one or another of these women choose another woman to dance with rather than falling into his hands, so she was always ready to step in. She figured it was better for him to dance with her rather than some woman who'd just be miserable. And when Miss Bertha was whirling around the floor with him, she'd think that despite the fact that he chased other women, his behavior with her showed he was pleased to be with her. She reasoned that the other women avoided him because he'd stick his legs between theirs while they were dancing, and she liked to think she was helping them avoid such unpleasantness.

One night while dancing with the celebrity, Miss Bertha asked (because the other women were eager to know) if he was married. Instead of answering, he pulled her tight against the entire length of his body and made an indecent suggestion. Miss Bertha was so surprised that in the heat of the moment she couldn't figure out who she was—was he making his obscene proposal to her or to some other girl? She was so confused it didn't occur to her to be offended, so she kept dancing, pressed tight to his body, locked in his arms. But when the dance ended, she walked straight out of the casino and started to run, not knowing where, through the deep grass. She could hear someone running after her. She couldn't see who it was, but she knew it was him.

She tried to hide in one of the canvas tents that stood nearby: white, slanted, sharply angular tents like torn-off roofs, with gaping black openings into attic-like darkness. She dashed inside, but a moment later he came in after her, bursting through the opening like a boogeyman, and made straight for her.

"What do you want?" she gasped. Her heart was pounding, and her voice was the voice of a woman who does in fact know what a man wants in a situation like theirs, but pretends not to know because she herself isn't so far from wanting exactly the same thing. In fact, Miss Bertha wasn't that woman at all. She knew what he had in mind—he'd just told her, after all. But for some reason she couldn't bring herself to believe him. She had a hazy notion—a darkly impenetrable, incomprehensible notion—that he hadn't been talking to her, or maybe he'd meant something other than what she knew he'd meant. The celebrity didn't say a word but grabbed her roughly, as if he knew the time and place were right and he didn't need to bother convincing her. Miss Bertha felt completely lost . . . but then, in her helplessness, she came back to herself. It happened by accident: as he was forcing his heavy, masculine weight onto her, she felt something sharp poking into her breast, and she suddenly remembered she was wearing a stickpin brooch. She yanked it out of her blouse and stabbed it into him. He snarled like a wild animal and was gone.

It was late when Miss Bertha went to bed, still in her clothes. She lay awake for a long time. In the silent darkness around her she could hear the whooping voices and wild dancing of the merrymakers, glutted with food and hilarity. Every now and then, as she started to doze off, she'd imagine a certain stranger—one who was intensely familiar to her in his unfamiliarity—flinging his arms and legs out more wildly than the other dancers, and she thought the raucous whoops were coming from him, and she'd snap out of her doze and wake up with a shock. Now she was afraid of him, even though she knew the threat was past. In fact, now that it was over, she was afraid of him for the first time, much more so than when she'd really been in danger. She was frightened—but not angry, as she should have been. She was even sorry, at fleeting moments, that she'd stabbed him with her stickpin. She knew she could have prevented the whole unpleasant situation some other way.

The next evening, a car drove up to the Sunshine Boardinghouse, the car that brought guests back and forth to and from the resort. It pulled up, emitted a puff of smoke, stopped, and sat there waiting.

It was after supper, and people had just left their tables after the third large meal of the day. The diners, stuffed to the gills—most of them were full even before they'd sat down to eat—were scattered in couples and groups along the dusty, gray gravel road that stretched off to either side of the resort, leading in both directions to mountains and valleys, farms and boardinghouses. The tallest mountain, the most imposing of those in the area, cast its enormous shadow as it did every evening, and although it was still early—a few hours until sunset—a twilight pall had fallen over the Sunshine Boardinghouse, while up on the mountain's high face and on its peak, crowned with dense trees, patches of sunlight slanted over the wooded darkness. You could easily imagine that those bright patches had drifted down from some alien, fantastic world to visit the mountaintop in all its majesty. Now, even more than usual, the mountain seemed a high aerial world unto itself, having detached itself from mother earth to shoot skyward with its own distinct forests and trees, knowing nothing, and never to know anything, about boardinghouses or boarders.

Miss Bertha came outside with a small bag in her right hand, followed by one of her brothers and a sister-in-law of the other brother, who'd stayed behind in the house. She seemed lackluster and grumpy, avoiding everyone's eyes, though many of the boarders were crowding around, telling her and each other how upset they were over her sudden and unexpected departure. When she'd settled into the car, they showered her with gifts: flowers, variously colored leaves, twigs, and plants—nature's rich summer bounty. But Miss Bertha sat in the car as if she weren't even there, as if it were all happening to someone else. She was too embarrassed to look up, and only when the car started moving did she glance around and smile crookedly at the boarders who'd come to see her off. She couldn't get her bearings—who were all those people who'd come out to see her with their friendly good-byes? They were strangers, after all, even though hardly any time had passed since those unknown people had been so close to her. She'd taken such an active part in the personal, intimate lives of so many; she knew their deepest secrets, which, she reflected, she'd found so interesting only a few hours ago. Now she was taking that baggage away with her, like an unwanted, hateful burden . . . but what did anyone know about her? Nothing, that's what—and nobody could be bothered to find out, treating her as if she didn't have her own personal life, as if she were nothing but an empty vessel waiting to be filled with the problems of strangers. Here she was, leaving the resort, and not a soul knew she was looking around, hoping to see someone—the man who'd brutally attacked her. He wasn't there, for obvious reasons. But she wanted him to be there with a deep, inward longing she couldn't show on the outside because . . . well, the real reason was because now, after all that had happened, she was in love with the man.

They showered her with gifts: flowers, twigs, all kinds of wild, blooming plants, and they called after her, "Good-bye, Miss Bertha! Miss Bertha, good-bye!"

And away she drove.

A Respectable Woman

When it comes to their husbands, most women run neither hot nor cold. Rather, the temperature of their love rises or falls according to what's going on around them. A woman's commitment or lack of commitment to her husband has nothing to do with her innate personality. One woman can act like she's devoted to her husband but betrays him the first chance she gets, and another can dislike her husband intensely but still refuses to be tempted by another man. A woman's attitude to her husband, whether it's positive or negative, is almost always a result of external circumstances. For example, a faithful wife might come home with a loving expression and a smile because some man walking past in the street just looked at her with desire in his eyes, while if the same thing happened to an unfaithful wife, she might lash out at her husband. There's a kind of kinship between a respectable woman and one who's not so respectable. In fact, respectability and disrespectability are very close in-laws, as I'll show you, to the best of my ability, with this story.

Mrs. Belemer was always in a cheerful mood with her husband. Why? Because she knew other men were constantly eyeing her up and down. The more men who were around and the more eyes that were on her, the more faithful and devoted she was to her husband—and that's why she looked forward to the two months each summer she spent in the mountains. There, surrounded by men, new life was breathed into her loyalty and devotion to her husband. She was delighted she had a husband to be faithful to, but deep down she was even more delighted at the many opportunities to show off her commitment in front of other men. It's generally accepted that what's typically known as "respectability" should be acknowledged by strangers—outsiders, that is—who are consumed by jealousy. Many men wanted Mrs. Belemer, and that gave her a special feeling of pleasure—she could flaunt her unavailability in front of them all, which, of course, means she was faithful only because she could tease other men with her respectability, and that in itself means she was faithful not for the benefit of her husband, but on account of strangers.

Every Saturday evening Mr. Belemer arrived at the holiday resort in his car. As soon as he drove up, he stuck a fat cigar into his mouth. His pretty wife was waiting for him at the top of the flight of stairs in front of the boardinghouse, which was perched on the crest of a little hill. He slammed the car door and ran up the steps, full of the self-importance due to a man of his status, and clasped her tight in his arms, holding his smoking cigar behind her back as they kissed.

Mr. Belemer behaved like a big shot, a true-blue Yankee, as if it were nothing to have his own car and his own wife, neither of which anyone else could touch. He knew his wife well and trusted her completely, and that feeling of security in his wife's commitment to him, even when they were apart, radiated from him. He looked insolently right into the eyes of other men as he escorted his wife along the short paved path that led up to the boardinghouse, his thick, smoldering cigar jammed firmly into his mouth as they walked.

The couple would spend Saturday evening and all day Sunday in each other's company, eating together, going for walks together, and sitting together, the two of them entirely wrapped up in each other and standoffish with everyone else, as if they were saying, "Don't bother me and I won't bother you." This was true especially of Mr. Belemer, whose every look and gesture expressed perfect self-sufficiency. He was his own master, and everything he owned, including his wife, belonged to him and nobody but him.

Mr. Belemer left early Monday morning, full of smug self-satisfaction. Ignoring the other vacationers, he kissed his wife repeatedly right in front of everybody, climbed into his car, and slammed its door. He started the engine, and the car came to life with a warm smell of gasoline. He called good-bye to his wife one last time, and the car slowly pulled away, accelerated, and was gone.

Even after the car was out of sight, Mrs. Belemer stood at the top of the hill, gazing after it with proud, watchful eyes. Her bearing was graceful, with the assured confidence of a woman who's completely convinced of her powers of attraction. She knew the man who'd just left would come back every weekend, so in the meantime, she needn't miss him.

She waved for a long time, holding her hand high in the air over her head where it fluttered as if it had a life of its own, a delicate little animal with thin, bloodless fingers that looked even paler and daintier than usual. Her husband could no longer see her waving, and she knew it, but she was no longer waving for his benefit, but for that of her onlookers.

Eventually, like a young mare who's just been released from her harness, she turned her graceful, lively body—a well-built body full of life and the ripeness of a woman who knows what life is—and walked away, favoring every man she happened to see with a bright smile, every now and then turning to wave and call out, "Good-bye!"

Years passed. Mrs. Belemer's forties were now behind her, and she couldn't help but notice the ranks of her male admirers had grown somewhat thin. At her age, she no longer needed to prove how respectable she was, so there was no point in flirting anymore, neither with her husband nor with anyone else—and gradually, almost without noticing, she began to lose interest in advertising her unavailability, because, after all, all women her age are assumed to be unavailable anyway.

The last time Mrs. Belemer went off to the boardinghouse, whatever devotion she'd had for her husband was dead within her. Her heart was hollow, an empty perfume bottle that once emptied remains forever empty, retaining only an afterimage of scented liquid like a nostalgic memory of what had once been. Mrs. Belemer too was empty, just like that bottle, with only a longing in her heart for the years gone by that had slipped away unnoticed like the perfume from a bottle, one drop at a time.

From her lonely room in the boardinghouse she wrote a letter home, inviting her boy to visit. He was an only son—after his birth she hadn't wanted another child. When he was little, she'd taken him to the country with her. Later, though, as he began to get older, she hadn't wanted anyone to know she had a son of his age, so she'd started leaving him behind.

Mrs. Belemer's son, who was beginning a two-week vacation, brought along a friend, another young man who was also on holiday. The minute the two arrived, they flung themselves into local life like good swimmers plunging into the water with the unthinking bravado of youth. Wishing to make the most of every moment, they rushed headlong into their brief vacation, and within an hour or two they'd gotten to know all the young women in the boardinghouse, laughing and joking with each one.

Mrs. Belemer followed her son with a mother's sharp, experienced eye, like a cat watching her kittens play at hunting mice: she knows the game well, and she plays like an expert. So Mrs. Belemer watched the young people's lively sport, their game that electrified the air with youthful energy. Their every gesture was lustful, full of desire, yet everything was said and done with great decorum, as if they were thinking about anything and everything except for the one thing they actually *were* thinking about.

High mountain peaks loomed all around like the petrified bodies of gods, soaking up the last of the daylight as the sun sank behind them and a long, early twilight settled into the valley. There were trees on the mountains and more mountains behind the trees with the blue sky arching overhead. It was impossible to tell which was the older eternity and which was the younger. Even in the old eternity you could feel eternal youth, the everlasting richness of nature and the infinite appeal of life.

Various men came up to Mrs. Belemer to ask about her son—was he in fact her son? They knew the answer but asked with feigned amazement, pretending they thought she was far too young to have a grown-up child. Mrs. Belemer knew they were flattering her, and she knew why, but she wasn't interested. Those men were too old—they were her age, and they didn't appeal to her. She'd fallen into a vague fantasy of her past youth—a time before she was married, before respectability and playing at respectability had a place in her life. But those days were long gone, and she didn't know what would come next. She found herself in a dilemma. She had no idea what she wanted, but somewhere in the fog of her feelings a yearning sensation nagged at her.

What happened next happened that night.

Midnight had come and gone. Middle-aged men and women who'd stayed up late began to disperse. Wives went without passion to their husbands who were already asleep in their roomy double beds, and husbands went to their wives who were likewise in bed, and everyone tripped over the long grass under the weak glow of the electric lights that lit up only the small space around them, outside of which lay the dark night in whose embrace hills, trees, and all the natural world flowed together. Among the other vacationers, but slightly apart from them, walked the respectable Mrs. Belemer with two young men by her side—her son and her son's friend. She could sense the fresh young life in them, and she felt for them.

She took the young men into the boardinghouse's kitchen for a glass of milk, arm in arm with both as if they were her sons. She didn't forget for a second, however, that one of the two was *not* her son, and she was curious: Could a boy like that feel anything for a woman like her?

The enormous kitchen was as roomy as a walled garden. Mrs. Belemer poured two glasses of ice-cold milk, and the two young men gulped them down, all the while looking at each other over the rims of their glasses, their mischievous, laughing eyes full of youth and high spirits.

As they left the kitchen and went back outdoors, Mrs. Belemer took the two friends by the arms and in a motherly tone asked if they were tired. Then she gently scolded her son because he hadn't given her even a half hour of his time.

"Is that the way you act with *your* mama?" she asked her son's friend.

"I like my mama a lot," the young man replied awkwardly.

At that moment, a girl ran past them, a little distance away but not too far, as if she were trying to show herself and keep out of sight at the same time: a short, slender young woman who slipped past as if she were running down a narrow corridor and didn't want anyone to recognize her. Her white blouse and white shoes betrayed her in the darkness, but the rest of her body, everything between the blouse and shoes, was invisible, as if she were hiding in the shadows. Both young men, as if they'd planned it in advance, started after her. Mrs. Belemer instinctively dropped her son's arm but kept her grip on the other young man. A moment later, when the girl and her son had vanished, she asked her companion if he wanted to follow them. "You'd better believe it," he said, stammering a little, hardly knowing what he was saying or what he'd meant to say.

Mrs. Belemer knew the young man was feverish with excitement, and his suffering pleased her. She enjoyed her little revenge; she knew he couldn't escape even though he was attracted to the younger woman, and it was her own sudden whim that was keeping him beside her. She walked on, holding the young man's arm as they strolled far away from the electric lights, and as the night around them grew dark their eyes adjusted so they could see the thick profusion of trees and shrubs by the sides of the path. It seemed that at night, in the dark, all these growing things were living a different kind of life, one that was much more mysterious than the lives they lived by day, a hidden life turned forever inward on itself.

Mrs. Belemer kept walking, leading her companion by the arm. She didn't know where she was going or why, but one thing was clear—his youth, which set him so far apart from her, was stirring up feelings of envy, sorrow, and loneliness. So just like Samson the hero, who prayed to God, "Strengthen me and give me courage, just this once," Mrs. Belemer determined to test her powers for the last time. But now things were different, and she couldn't tease this youth— scarcely more than a boy—with her unavailability. Now, at her age, she could attract a young man and stir up his passions only by letting him think he had a chance with her.

She could sense his excitement. It wouldn't take much to divert it to herself, but her maternal feelings held her back. She could easily imagine that afterward the young man would meet up with his friend, the son of the woman who'd . . .

So now what? Were they at that point already? No . . . she hadn't the slightest intention of letting things go so far. It was out of the question. Yet she didn't want the boy to walk off on his own, either. She cast around for a topic of conversation and was surprised to find that this young man, who'd been so clever at coming up with all manner of silly jokes when he was with people his own age—especially when there were a few girls he could flirt with—this same young man seemed to have entirely lost his wits in her company. Obviously, she thought, despite her first impressions, he must be a fool. If he was smart, he'd surely . . . but maybe . . . maybe that girl her son had run after, maybe a girl like her would . . . but if that were true, she really *did* feel sorry for her young companion.

"It's a shame to keep you any longer," she said. "Why don't you go back?" But she didn't really mean to let him out of her hands. She was playing with him, like a cat with a mouse.

In the meantime, Mrs. Belemer and her companion were walking farther and farther away from the boardinghouse and its inhabitants and deeper and deeper into untamed nature, which is so beloved by—and so foreign to—city people. They could hear the ceaseless rippling of a little nearby stream, hidden behind a screen of trees, saplings, and undergrowth, and the stream, the trees and shrubs, and the surrounding mountains made them feel that the eternal silence and the eternal secrets of the living world were silently murmuring, and the silence and the murmuring were so similar to each other that it was hard to perceive which was the most silent. . . . Was it the actual silence, or was it the rippling of the stream? The air all around was glittering with fiery little points that sparkled here, there, and everywhere, flickering in and out among the trees and branches and hovering in the thick, deep darkness just above the ground. The fiery dots sprayed out of the dark night, and it seemed that each fiery spray was a new secret emerging from its dark hiding place—a secret that revealed nothing, but just made the darkness blacker and more mysterious.

Mrs. Belemer was overwhelmed by the life around her and all its mysteries. And within her, two strong emotions hammered and seethed: she was drawn simultaneously to behaving as a married woman her age *should* behave and doing something she knew was wrong. She wanted to fall on the young man's neck and bewail her lost youth, and she also wanted to do something reckless, something only the most reckless woman was capable of . . . or, to put it another way, something as reckless as the most respectable woman was capable of, as reckless as only a respectable woman can be when the time is right.

"You'd better go," she said sharply, as if issuing an order.

The young man, who was essentially no fool, but simply a young man who'd blundered into a ridiculous situation—one in which even the brightest person wouldn't know what to do—knew perfectly well that he couldn't just go off and leave her there. Simple courtesy dictated that having walked so far with this woman, he'd have to walk her back.

"Go on back! I'm not worried about myself. I'm thinking of you. *I'm* not afraid." Mrs. Belemer was making sure she was the object of his attention, and now she pressed her advantage. "What are you doing? Why didn't you go off with that girl when you had the chance? Why are you here?" She had one desire: to toy with his feelings, to lead him on, to speak and act in such a way as to suggest the possibility of satisfying his lust. Mrs. Belemer had changed completely—years before she'd drawn men to her with her unavailability, and now she was using quite another tactic to reel in her son's friend. But she didn't feel any less respectable deep inside than she'd felt when she was younger. She didn't love the young man—she felt nothing for him. There was only the deep, unconscious desire to put an end to the game of flirting she'd been playing for so many years, extricate herself from the chaos of her previous life, and enter into a respectable old age in which she could lead a restful, tranquil life.

As if by magic, a narrow little trail suddenly appeared off one side of their path. Faintly visible in the dark, it wound through the thick growth of trees, saplings, and bushes, disappearing among them. Mrs. Belemer stopped at the fork where the little trail branched off and peered ahead, trying to see where it led. Something drew her into that convoluted tangle of undergrowth that melted into the darkness. Deep inside she felt a kinship with it all—the darkness and the complexity it embraced, the sum total of living things all enfolded together in the night. She had the vague sensation that she herself, her entire being, was a detached part of the arbitrarily entangled lives around her and that only by accident was she something that was called a person—a woman. Her life was as mysterious to her as the lives of the plants—beings that also live and grow—were to them. What was the mystery behind this arbitrary growth, this capricious existence?

Mrs. Belemer walked down the trail, and the young man followed. He felt thoroughly ridiculous, the very personification of a bumbling fool. He knew something was in the air, but anticipation of what lay in store made him stupid; he didn't know how to set things in motion, how to take the first step: the unexpected and mysterious step of approaching a woman her age. . . . What an idiot he was. He caught up with the woman and took her arm, aware of the silly expression his face was making. The trail was narrow, too narrow for two people to walk side by side, so the woman walked along it and the young man walked through the undergrowth beside her, fending off branches, tripping over grasses and vines, and dodging among bushes that bent under his feet and sprang up in his wake with the sound of beating wings, rustling for a while until they regained their former shape, rearranged their twigs, and settled down behind him. Eventually, he noticed a large rock. It was barely visible in the darkness where it sat among the trees as if it were lost, looking, with its flat top, like a kugel just out of the oven. "Would you like to sit down for a while?" the young man asked his companion.

Mrs. Belemer knew he was electrified with desire—she'd been aware of every movement, and she'd been listening to his breathing. And now she began to play the role of a naive, innocent girl. "No, why? It's late—we should be getting back." She started to turn around, but he was directly behind her, blocking the trail. She heard him standing there and sensed him watching her. Now she was nervous. She walked on ahead, hesitant to keep going but knowing she shouldn't stop, either. Just then, off in the distance, she saw a gap in the darkness as the trail opened up, like a beckoning door, to the broad path leading back to the boardinghouse.

Behind Mrs. Belemer came the sound of hasty footfalls, and a minute later she was imprisoned in the young man's arms, pressed tightly to his hot, strong body. She could feel his pounding heart and his rapid breathing. And the question occurred to her: Should she give in? Or should she put up a fight? It was a rational question, asked in cold blood, and she couldn't decide—she was both in favor of and against giving in. She had no particular reasons one way or another—she wouldn't become more respectable if she put up a fight, or less respectable if she didn't. But then she remembered her son, and she started to struggle.

It was too late. She'd kindled the young man's lust, and her struggles inflamed him further. She felt the unyielding strength of his young, untamed passion. She knew she'd fought long enough to make him feel guilty, and there was no point in resisting any longer. So she gave up, and let him take what he wanted . . .

Section 4

The Call of Life

In fiction as in life, men as well as women are limited by their social roles. Rosenfeld's male protagonists are typically unable to navigate their sexuality, caught in social expectations against which they inwardly rebel, and confused about women and their feelings about them. They are trapped in a morass of helpless, inarticulate desires and fears from which they cannot escape.

The narrator of "The Little Brothers' Place," a passive, introspective young man, is intrigued by a robust, confident woman, a political agitator who enjoys dressing in men's clothing. Sadly, he lacks the confidence or the ability to act on his desires. Mr. Zafran, the protagonist of "A Singular Man," is an even more awkward lover: unable to express his love for Manya, the tailor girl, he blurts out nonsense and, despite running a successful business, lacks even the most basic social skills.

"The Artistic Temperament" and "On Vacation" explore the damage that the desire to conform to external pressures can do to a relationship. In "The Artistic Temperament," Rosenfeld examines the relationship between Philip Trop, an artist, and his wife, a woman he's embarrassed to admit he's still in love with, six months after their marriage. How can Trop face his bohemian friends? Mikhl, in "On Vacation," works in the city during the week, and on weekends visits his wife and adult daughters, who are vacationing in the countryside. Mikhl's love of nature and the outdoors clashes with his wife's desire to conform to the behavior of her neighbors.

In life, there are many men like Rosenfeld's male protagonists: outwardly successful to one degree or another, yet woefully inept when it comes to social relationships.

The Little Brothers' Place

We'd met for the first time just yesterday, but during our walk this evening she allowed me to take her arm. I knew she was the kind of girl who'd let me do that the first time we went out, without—God forbid—getting annoyed with me.

I met her at the little brothers' place. That's what everyone called the two men because they looked like twins, even though they weren't even from the same family. Not only that, but the "brothers" seemed to enjoy looking alike so much that they took it even further, as though they'd agreed between themselves to work in the same place, go on walks together, and even dress alike, right down to their shoes and hats.

So that's where I met her, at the little brothers' place. But what was she doing there? I haven't got the faintest idea. All I know about the little brothers' place is that it's a kind of refuge. Let's say a young man wanders into town from somewhere or other, a guy who's either on the run or come of his own free will, hoping for a lucky break. Where does he go? The little brothers' place. If some other guy arrives in town with his beard and whiskers shaved off, saying he's a Jewish artist—who takes him in? The little brothers, of course. And if a person like that—or anyone else—needs a few rubles for expenses, everyone knows that raising the money is up to the little brothers, and no one else. Like the others, the girl had arrived at the little brothers' in some mysterious way, and the pair of them let me know right away she was somebody special, even though I'd long ago stopped believing anything they said because they loved making a huge fuss over everyone who ended up with them. But this girl was different somehow.

As soon as I finished preparing my lessons, I tidied myself up at the mirror, grabbed my walking stick, and headed straight over. The night before, she and the little brothers had told me she'd been deported as part of a group of seven young men and herself, the only woman. When I arrived, I found her sitting on a white packing crate. Her legs were splayed out as if she were a man, and she was wrapped in a cape—a mannish black cape—topped by a big black hat with the red glass beads of two hatpins poking out like the eyes of an animal. She was talking to the little brothers, who were standing at their work—they were bookbinders who ran their own business—the three of them chatting and laughing together. She laughed the most, showing white teeth like pearls and rocking back and forth together with the crate she was sitting on. When I saw her in her cape and hat, I assumed she'd put them on to go out, but later I found out she always dressed like that, even indoors.

My first thought, though, was "Whose cape is that?" I have no idea why I was suddenly so interested, but I *do* know that was the reason I liked her—because she was wearing a man's cape. I doubt anyone would believe me if I told them that when I held her arm, I took a kind of piquant pleasure in the man's cape that hung between us. I don't know why, but it's true. I'll even admit that my hand, the one that was holding her arm, was playing with one of the cape's buttons at the same time.

We wandered around until late at night. Well, I shouldn't really say "wandered"—we were practically running. She was such a fast walker, she wore me right out. My heart was racing, but I couldn't tell her that. I would have told someone else, but not her—this girl in a man's cape—because from time to time it seemed to me that I was the girl and she was the young man, which wasn't surprising because I was a bit of a weakling and she was the picture of health. "Let's slow down a bit," I pleaded. "What's the point of running? It isn't polite to run around like this." (That's what I said. Do you think I'd admit I was out of breath?) She didn't even listen, but began spouting propaganda—people have to be self-sufficient, they need to think for themselves, they should be this way or that way—those pie-in-the-sky fairy tales that make me sick whenever I hear them. But what choice did I have? I had to hear her out, and who knows how long she would have gone on in that vein if we hadn't met up with the little brothers. They stopped us in the street and said that a certain Shloyme had been looking all over the place for her, and while they were telling her this they were eyeing me—if I'm not mistaken—with unfriendly expressions because I'd run off with their "treasure." It's worth mentioning here that the little brothers had bad luck: as soon as their guests got to know other people, they'd stop having anything to do with the two of them. The brothers must have had their feelings bruised many times. They were jealous that way.

When the little brothers had told the girl Shloyme was looking for her, it occurred to me that the cape she was wearing must have belonged to him, so for some reason I suddenly got interested in the guy. I guess I was jealous. I could hardly wait for the minute I could get her alone to ask her, "Who the heck is Shloyme?"

"He's one of the people who was deported along with me."

"Really? He must need his cape."

"What do you mean?"

"I mean you're wearing his cape, and it's cold out—isn't that why he's looking for you?"

"What on earth makes you think this is his cape?" she asked in surprise. But just as I was about to answer, a chubby little face materialized in the darkness before us, as abruptly as if it had popped out of a hole in the earth. The face's owner probably tried to shake my hand (it was hard to see in the dark), extended the same hand to the girl, and said impatiently, "It's been two hours already. I've had the heavens of a time finding you."

"Listen to him talk!" I said to myself. Such a classy young jerk— he's too polite to say "hell of a time," so he says "heavens" instead. And suddenly I understood: My God! This must be Shloyme! But why had I imagined Shloyme would be tall and refined-looking, and why had I been so certain the cape was his? Now I saw that the little guy could have wrapped it three times around himself. But what really annoyed me was the way he was cozying up to the girl. I wasn't the least bit jealous, but for some reason his chummy behavior was a blow to my self-esteem.

We stood there a few minutes like three dots on a page. I was looking forward to him leaving, and he was probably thinking the same thing about me. Eventually, as if we'd reached some unspoken agreement, we started walking. I don't know who was the first to move, and maybe there wasn't a "first" at all, but the three of us set off at a trot. I could feel my ears burning with humiliation. I wouldn't have been embarrassed if I'd been walking with him on his own— what embarrassed me was that the girl was there, walking between us. *That Shloyme!* A couple of times the thought popped into my head—it's Shloyme all right, but the cape isn't his. He must have a cape of his own, a teeny tiny one. . . . Suddenly, I broke out laughing.

"What's so funny?" asked the girl, and the little guy made a questioning face and leveled a long look at me. But I wanted him to figure it out for himself. "I was just remembering something," I told the girl, at the same time giving her arm a squeeze.

It was late. The weak, sleepy clang of a bell off in the distance told us it was eleven o'clock. The street was dead quiet. Here and there, like a dark clotted shadow, a shopkeeper sat quietly next to a shop's locked door, thin strips of light showing from its cracks, waiting for a customer to come in and buy a few pennies' worth of goods. Wooden lanterns cast a dim, somber light that did nothing to brighten up the street—in fact, the thick black shadows cast by their posts made the dark night darker yet. A light, cool breeze blew, stirring the leaves of the trees.

"It's time I went home," I said, stopping and letting go of the girl's arm. I was about to say good-bye to her, but she asked in surprise, "What, you're leaving already? Why—are you worried you won't get enough sleep? It's so nice out."

The little guy was about to throw in his own two cents, so just to spite him I took the girl's arm again and we started off. But about ten minutes later the loud banging of his walking stick on the cobblestones began to grate on my nerves. I started rapping the stones hard with my walking stick too, but unfortunately, his walking stick was thicker than mine so his rapping was louder. That annoyed me even more, so I handed my stick to the girl. "Here," I said, "this will go with your cape." She took my stick, carried it along for a minute or two, tapped it on the stones a few times, and handed it back. She didn't like it: it was a thin little stick, she said, made for a woman. She preferred a thicker one. The little guy leaped to attention and gave her his stick. Taking it, the girl rapped it so hard on the cobblestones that the dull crack echoed the length of the street. "Now this is a walking stick!" she said. "This I can understand—this feels good in my hand!"

I couldn't walk any more with this masculine woman who'd insulted me so painfully—just being with her made me feel awful. So I said good night to her and shook hands with them both, and in a downhearted mood I set off home. When I got there, I threw myself into bed and fell asleep. All night in my dreams I kept seeing the little soul in her long cape and big hat with two red glass eyes, holding a walking stick in her hand. And then suddenly, without warning, she was gone.

A Singular Man

Mr. Zafran fell in love the minute he glanced through the display window and saw the tailor girl approaching the store with her bundle of merchandise. Even earlier that day he'd had the feeling she wouldn't be the girl who usually made the weekly delivery, and the first sight of her made his soul light up. When she came through the door and walked over to Mr. Zafran to give her report, he knew his eyes hadn't deceived him. The vague thought crossed his mind that all these years he'd been on the lookout for a girl like her, and the only reason he'd been single so long was because the girl he'd been waiting for hadn't arrived . . . and now, in his thirty-eighth year, here she was at last—though a little late, to be sure.

The young woman finished her update, and the older of Mr. Zafran's two employees, a tall young man who fancied himself a wit, came over and began joking with her as he'd always done with her predecessor when she came every Friday. His intrusion made Mr. Zafran feel like a religious Jew who, sitting down to the Passover meal, spots a slice of forbidden bread on the table, desecrating the feast. A dull shock of disappointment went through him, blotting out his joy. There was only one hope of saving the situation, he thought, and that depended on the girl having the self-confidence to put the other man in his place. But she failed to rebuke him. Mr. Zafran could tolerate the horseplay as long as his employee confined himself to verbal teasing, but when he flung a cape around the girl's shoulders and spun her around to face him, saying she'd make a good model, Mr. Zafran couldn't hold back any longer. "Why not? What a brilliant idea!"

The young woman blushed, looking confused: Should she take his comment as a compliment or an insult? Mr. Zafran waited for the moment she'd lose her temper and let him have it, but she didn't say a thing. Her submissiveness made him think less of her. He gave her a long, thoughtful look and said sharply, "Well? Why don't you speak up?"

The girl looked puzzled. "What do you want me to say?"

To Mr. Zafran's ears those words were freighted with the inept stupidity of the working classes. Although he was a liberal person by nature, for the first time in his life that kind of ignorance repelled him, and the minute the young woman left the store he burst out with some sneering remarks about her, all the while repressing his attraction of a few minutes earlier. Figuring that since his boss was making lewd comments about the girl, he could too, Mr. Zafran's employee, mockingly quoting the Song of Solomon, said, "What a pair on her—just like two big handfuls of grapes." Mr. Zafran was pained by the words, but he plastered a smile on his face, which, the minute he felt it, made him think he must look ridiculous. So he changed his mind and arranged his features to convey the impression that he'd forgotten all about the girl and what he'd just said about her, hoping the young man would follow his example, forget about her too, and put an end to his ribald comments.

Mr. Zafran called over the boy, his younger employee. He thought for a minute, then said, "Go get me a glass of soda water."

From then on, Mr. Zafran's Fridays were pure torment. All day long he'd watch the clock, waiting for the girl (her name, it turned out, was Manya) to arrive, and the whole time he was waiting he couldn't have told himself which he hoped for more: that she'd show up or that some sort of miracle would occur and she'd stay away. Both desires were tangled up together, as if they could somehow come true simultaneously.

One Friday, despite the fact that Manya was still in the store, standing right next to him, Mr. Zafran asked his employee, "What do you think—could you fall in love with her?"

The young man put his hand over his heart and gave Manya a good long look. With a sincere smile, he asked her, "Is there really such a thing as love in this world?"

Mr. Zafran stood there expectantly, as if Manya's answer to the whimsical question held the key to something important—though what that something was, he had no idea. He looked her straight in the eye and waited. The young man, however, gave her no opportunity to speak. He launched straight into a long, spicy story about something that had happened to him: there was a time he'd wanted to fall in love, he said, but couldn't—that is, he'd tried to fall in love with a girl, who was, according to his own assumptions, someone you couldn't help but fall in love with. He went around with her for a few weeks, but it didn't go anywhere. So he tried fasting—he went hungry for a whole day, hoping that would make him fall in love, and when it didn't, he tried staying awake all night—because, he explained, he'd heard that people who were in love couldn't eat or sleep.

Mr. Zafran thoroughly enjoyed the young man's comic tale and jumped in with his own anecdote about a love affair that hadn't gotten off the ground. He told a story about the time he'd been head over heels in love with a girl, but the girl hadn't believed that he loved her.

"Why not?" Manya inquired.

"Because she was a hunchback, and she didn't believe that a man like me could fall for someone like her."

The tailor girl laughed and asked, "Didn't you tell her you were in love with her?"

"Many times. And that's not all. In the beginning, even before I got to know her, I used to blow her air kisses from my balcony, but as soon as she saw me she'd hide in her house."

"Are you sure you weren't just making fun of her?"

Mr. Zafran delved deeper into his role. He explained that there's no great art to falling for a pretty girl, but it's quite a trick to fall in love with someone like the girl he'd fallen in love with. He clearly remembered that all his neighbors, everyone who lived on his courtyard, would look at him as if they'd never seen anyone like him before.

Manya heard him out with interest and gave him an admiring look, encouraging Mr. Zafran to keep spinning out his crazy story: "Some years ago I met this stunningly beautiful girl. Everyone who set eyes on her fell head over heels, but I couldn't stand her. It really annoyed me that she never even noticed—it never entered her mind that some creature like me, a man who despised her, could live on the face of the planet. Do you know what I mean? The first woman, the hunchback, couldn't believe someone like me existed—a real man who loved her. But the second woman was just the opposite—she couldn't imagine anyone disliking her."

"Well, that's the way things are," remarked Manya with a luscious little smile. She got up from her chair, ready to leave. Suddenly, the tall joker pushed between them and announced, "Everything Mr. Zafran said is true. He didn't make up a word—it's all worth its weight in gold."

Mr. Zafran stepped back from the two of them, stood there a minute looking them over, and finally said, "What a good-looking couple you make."

Manya's father was blind. He'd go out most days and, tapping his stick with every step, make his way from store to store, begging for alms. The blind man had his regular rounds: some people gave him a weekly handout, and others gave by the month. One of the weekly contributors was Mr. Zafran, who'd inherited the blind man from his father, just as he'd inherited his store, his house, and his furniture. Since the blind beggar had been entrusted to him, Mr. Zafran stayed true to his father's tradition and gave the old man a generous donation every Thursday. When he found out the old man was Manya's father, he began greeting him more effusively. He also increased the beggar's weekly "salary," even though he knew Manya would never find out—for the simple reason that she had no idea her father was going around begging for handouts. Still, Mr. Zafran treated the old man to whatever he could give him. The father was as ignorant of his daughter's doings as she was of his: he had no idea she came into the store every Friday, and he constantly bragged about how pretty and well brought up she was. Mr. Zafran pretended he'd never met her, and sometimes, when the blind man had finished singing his songs of praise, Mr. Zafran would ask why some rich guy hadn't fallen in love with her, given that she was so pretty.

One Thursday when the blind man dropped by for his weekly handout, Mr. Zafran put him off. "I'm very sorry, but there's no money today. Can you come back tomorrow?" and he named a time. Mr. Zafran was hoping the father and daughter would run into each other in his store. Why? It was hard to say. In essence, Mr. Zafran didn't have anything against the girl. In fact, he had no idea why or for whose benefit he'd decided to make both father and daughter miserable.

The blind man arrived at the arranged time. Mr. Zafran sat him down next to his own chair behind the counter and kept him waiting until Manya arrived. As soon as she opened the door, Mr. Zafran took a gold five-ruble coin out of the till and, pressing it into the blind man's hand, said loudly, as if the man weren't only blind, but deaf as well, "Listen. I want you to know this isn't a copper coin—it's a gold fiver. Here—put it into a pocket all by itself so you don't mix it up with your small change and give it away by accident."

The blind man was stunned. In all the years since he'd lost his sight, he'd never received a handout like that from anyone—he'd never even heard of a beggar getting such a generous donation. He rubbed the coin between his fingers . . . yes, it was real. Mr. Zafran wasn't trying to fool him. He could feel by the coin's weight, too, that it was gold.

Just then the beggar heard someone at the doorway. As the footsteps crossed the threshold, they stopped abruptly, as if whoever had just entered was trying to hide the fact that they were there. The blind man, confused, got up to leave, turning his head from side to side as he tried to hear what was going on and tapping the floor in front of his feet with his stick. Mr. Zafran led the beggar to the door, and as soon as he'd let him out he turned to Manya.

"That man just told me he has a very pretty daughter—he talks about her every time he comes in. I think he's telling the truth. I believe him more than I'd believe a normal father who brags about his daughter, because all fathers are blind when it comes to their own children. But that man really *is* blind. So other people must have told him what his daughter looks like, and if they can see that she's pretty—well, then, it really must be true."

Just then the tall young employee came in from the street. He sneaked up behind Manya's back and put his hands over her face, covering her eyes with his fingers. The girl, agile as a snake, squirmed out of his arms and stood there fuming, her eyes filled with angry tears. Then she turned on Mr. Zafran. "You shouldn't have let him do that," she said, her voice unsteady. "And now you're just standing there smiling. It doesn't suit you, Mr. Zafran. It's rude! The only reason he grabbed me is because he knows you'd put up with it."

She said her piece and left without a good-bye. Mr. Zafran watched for a short time as she stalked off down the street. Her footsteps were loud and angry as they quickly receded, the footsteps of a woman who utterly rejects the place she has just left, and the furious way she walked made it clear that she wouldn't return. And it suddenly dawned on Mr. Zafran that he'd never see her again.

In the following days, Mr. Zafran found time in the breaks between customers to sit and obsess over what had just happened. He'd had a straightforward path to the girl, an easy and obvious one: "I'm almost twice your age, but not so old it should be a problem. I'm a rich man, and you're a poor girl. I love you, and I'm asking you to marry me." Why hadn't he done that? Why? What kind of devil had led him off down the zigzag road he'd taken?

He'd never felt so lonely before. It was especially bad when he got home, a "home" consisting of six rooms that he lived in all by himself (or, rather, that no one actually lived in), and where he was always aware of his unspoken obligation to the memory of his parents. His mother and father had left him behind, just as they'd left their property, as if they expected him to carry on just as they'd done themselves, to preserve forever their bond with the living world. They'd looked forward to his wedding but hadn't lived long enough to see it. They'd left him a wealth of possessions, including a house furnished with beds and everything else a married man with children could possibly need.

Whenever Mr. Zafran walked through his door, it seemed that every piece of extra furniture—furniture a single man doesn't need, that only a family man needs—every one of those useless sticks of furniture was begging him, "Get married—it's depressing living here with just you." He felt as though his parents were speaking to him through the furniture: "You're a grown man now. Get married!"

What a disheartening effect it had on him, this orderly arrangement of belongings that remained after his parents had left this world . . . it was dreary, always the same, yet he couldn't make up his mind to change things around. He had all the money he needed, and there was no need to sell anything, so the house and its contents ceaselessly nagged at him, wordlessly demanding, "Get married!"

He'd never felt so sad before he'd gotten to know Manya. He'd imagined that by now he'd be a happily married man, the head of a family, and that his home would be a cheerful, lively one. Now his sense of loneliness was so piercing that he was afraid to sleep alone, all by himself in such a big house.

Mr. Zafran brought the apprentice boy home to sleep over a couple of times, but after one or two nights he lost patience—there was no point spending time with the boy or trying to have a conversation with him. He tried a few times: "It's kind of boring here, eh?" The boy was tactful enough to reassure his boss that no, it wasn't boring, and Mr. Zafran knew he was lying but didn't know why. "You think I don't know you're trying to butter me up, but I do know! I can see it in your eyes. And what if I were to ask you what kind of person you think I am, a good one or a bad one—would you even stop to think about it for a minute? Or would you just blurt out . . . well? Why are you so quiet?"

"You're a good person!" the boy said impulsively.

"Really? A good person? A really good person?"

"You gave that blind man five whole rubles!"

If the boy hadn't been so young, Mr. Zafran would have welcomed the opportunity to open up, tell him the whole story, and explain why he'd given the money. But he couldn't tell him the whole story. "Yes, that's right! A big, beautiful handout—five whole rubles! But I've lost more than that five rubles. I've lost much, much more . . . I've lost a treasure, a fortune, a gold mine . . . because of that five rubles, I've thrown it all away." Then he clasped his hands behind his back and began to pace, and after crossing the room a couple of times, he sat down in an armchair by the big oak desk and stared at the little flame of the fat wax candle burning in the candlestick.

The gray hairs sprinkled through Mr. Zafran's Spanish beard made him look old, so he went to the barber and told him to shave it off. As soon as the barber began, Mr. Zafran closed his eyes and kept them closed until the job was finished. He wanted to see the change in his appearance all at once.

Mr. Zafran, looking transformed without his beard—and also a few years younger—left the barbershop and paused in the street outside. He felt like a new man. Thanks to his alteration on the outside, he felt different on the inside, too. He was overcome by a sudden longing for a completely different life, a life far removed from the staid, middle-aged life he was living. After all, he thought, he wasn't old yet. He was old for a bachelor, true, but if he were to get married he'd stop thinking about how old he was. He'd shaved off his beard, which made him look a few years younger, so no one would take him for an old man (or even an old bachelor), and if nobody thought him old, then he *wasn't* old and he could still look forward to getting married, given his material circumstances.

He looked at the passersby walking back and forth down the street, strangers who didn't know him and couldn't see how he'd changed after shaving off his Spanish beard. He was only annoyed that he hadn't done so a few weeks ago . . . although, of course, there

was no possibility that anything with the girl could happen now, so
he may as well have kept the beard . . . so why, and for whose benefit,
had he just shaved it off?

He had no desire to go home, but neither did he feel like wandering the streets in a state of unmarried loneliness. Certainly, he mused,
he had the means to live a life of lavish extravagance, yet . . . though
he owned and ran his own store, his situation was different from
that of other businessmen, most of whom were able to lead lives as
gentlemen and respected citizens because they were constantly chasing after profits to maintain their businesses and their reputations in
an effort to impress even bigger merchants and bigger profiteers. But
Mr. Zafran, who wasn't the type to chase after money, still needed
to maintain the business he'd inherited from his father and run it as
his father had. He was no cheapskate. For example, he sometimes
dealt with a poor wagon driver who once in a while delivered a few
thousand rubles' worth of fabric from the factory to make coats.
Mr. Zafran in turn passed that fabric on to the tailor. He didn't
know and couldn't figure out why he worked with that driver; he
wasn't desperate to save a few pennies, because the pennies he saved
weren't worth anything to him. But then he didn't work with the
wagon driver because he wanted to. His father had done business
with the man, so Mr. Zafran felt he should do the same.

Mr. Zafran had one confidant: Lyova, a man he'd once worked
with when they were employed in the same store. Lyova was always
happy to see him, but Mr. Zafran hardly ever visited. He had nowhere
else to go for reasons apart from official business, and he was always
a welcome guest, but he rarely went over to Lyova's because Mr. Zafran suspected that Lyova's wife thought he was attracted to her, so
he felt obliged to play along and pretend he actually *was* interested
in her. He flirted to please her—he couldn't help but see she enjoyed
it. He didn't have a personal stake in flirting with her, and he wasn't
looking for one because he was devoted to his friend. Also, he knew
Lyova's wife was a respectable woman, despite the fact that she played
the coquette. It was odd, he mused, that such things were happening
in his life: he had to hide his indifference from the woman he was

indifferent to, while at the same time he had to hide his love from another woman, the one he was in love with. . . . But what if he went to Lyova's house and poured out his heart to his wife? No matter how she took it, she was Mr. Zafran's friend too, after all . . . or maybe he should confess to her husband? No, it wouldn't do to talk to a man: men are more cynical. But now wasn't a good time to talk to the wife, either—Lyova would be home, and if he wanted to confide in her, her husband couldn't be around. So he'd have to wait for another time.

Mr. Zafran caught sight of a young woman who'd just slipped past and was walking on ahead of him. She was wearing an unfamiliar dress, but he recognized her gait and the shape of her body. It was her, Manya, the tailor girl, though in the first split second he couldn't believe his own eyes, simply because he'd just been thinking about her. When you happen to meet someone by chance, it's an accident, but when you run into somebody at the very moment you're thinking of them, it's something else altogether.

Mr. Zafran began following the young woman, striding rapidly down the street, even though he didn't know what he'd say or how he'd act if it really was her. His only goal was to catch up with her, and he fervently hoped it was really her and not some stranger. When he was just behind her, she suddenly stopped, turned around, and said hello. He was surprised at her greeting—he thought she was still angry with him.

"Who am I?" he blurted. Manya studied him, perplexed. Of course, she couldn't help but see how different he looked without his beard. His chin was plainly visible, looking paler than the rest of his face because his beard had covered it up for years, keeping off the sun. Still, he was far from being unrecognizable . . . so, assuming she'd noticed his missing beard the moment she saw him, he hoped she'd mention it. Manya, however, didn't know Mr. Zafran well enough to jump in and start discussing something personal like his beard, so she completely ignored the whole thing. "I don't understand," she said. "What are you talking about?"

Suddenly, Mr. Zafran remembered his cousin who lived in a faraway city. He'd come for a visit eighteen years ago, and the two young men had looked so much alike that their own parents couldn't tell them apart unless they were right next to each other. With this cousin in mind, he plowed straight ahead, making things up as he went along: "I'm not talking about anything. I think you've made some mistake."

The young woman looked confused and embarrassed, and Mr. Zafran found himself playing a new role, one he didn't quite understand himself. He vaguely sensed he was putting on a performance, but even he wasn't sure what kind of performance it was.

"If I've made a mistake," Manya said, mystified, "who are you then?"

"I'm not from around here—you wouldn't know me. I've only been in town five or six months. But I know why you think you know me. I have a cousin who lives here, Isaac Zafran, who looks just like me. We're so much alike, our own parents couldn't tell us apart."

"But how do you know me?" Manya countered.

"One time I saw you leaving my cousin's store. Since then, I haven't been able to get you out of my mind."

Now the young woman's suspicions were aroused. "So tell me," she snapped, "if it's not too much to ask—what do you want from me?" She asked so forcefully and so decisively that Mr. Zafran was taken aback. Should he carry on in the role he'd just assumed, or should he be honest—admit everything and tell her he loved her? He felt like a man wearing a mask: the man behind the mask is fully aware that everyone knows who he is, but he still feels free to joke around in a way he never could without the mask.

"I love you so much I can't stand it," he blurted.

Manya, instead of doing what she might have done in other circumstances—analyzing her own feelings and deciding what to say in return—was too busy trying to figure out if the stranger had meant what he'd said. When a woman can't figure out if a man's serious when he says he loves her, she'll string him along—she won't turn him down, even if she doesn't love him back, until she knows whether he means it or whether he's mocking her. All woman are like that, no matter how bright or unintelligent they are. Even if a woman's answer is "no," she needs to know that the man who's confessing his love is sincere, and she'll refuse him only after she's decided. Until then, a woman has about the same scruples as a prison official who sends a sick prisoner to the hospital so he'll be in good health when he's hanged. Manya, the simple and unassuming tailor girl, was clever enough to behave the same way: she said nothing, but simply smiled.

Mr. Zafran decided to go visit his friend Lyova's wife and confide in her: spill his soul and confess he was in love with this girl, and so on and so forth. He figured that apart from helping him express his deepest feelings, his confession would have the added benefit of getting Lyova's wife, once and for all, to understand that he wasn't in love with her. Why should she go on thinking he loved her, even though he'd given her no cause—and why, and for whose benefit, should he go on feeling guilty in front of his friend? All told, it was a brilliant idea. It would be worth seeing her, just to get the fantasies out of her head.

As it turned out, Lyova was away when he dropped by; unknown to Mr. Zafran, he'd left town that day on an urgent business assignment. But when Mr. Zafran greeted Lyova's wife and asked where her husband was, she gave a clever, roguish smile, implying that Zafran himself was a clever rogue to pretend he didn't know that her husband wasn't home. "My husband? He'll be home any minute. Have a seat."

The wife was wearing a tightly fitting blouse, which gave Mr. Zafran the impression that she'd dressed up as if to say "yes, all this could be yours," but he wasn't sure. Her flaunting her breasts and body, her smiling, and her flirtatious eyes made it clear she was perfectly aware of her assets. Mr. Zafran, observing the harmonious interplay of the wife's looks and behavior, didn't have the faintest idea what was going on with her. He'd always thought she had a good life with her husband—she loved him and he loved her—but nevertheless, here she was, all dressed up, possibly expecting that any minute now her husband would walk in . . . but that would mean she'd gotten dressed up for her husband, while at the same time she was ready to flirt with another man.

"Did you think I'd forgotten you?" she said, putting her hands on Mr. Zafran's shoulders and sitting him down. "Do you think it hasn't once occurred to me: 'If only he had the sense to come visit, we could go for a walk somewhere, or for a drive in the park'?" He looked at her, and she saw the way he was looking at her and added, "Why are you looking at me like that?"

"I thought Lyova would be home." Zafran was telling a half-lie, though he couldn't have said why. The truth was, he'd come an hour earlier than the time they'd arranged because he wanted to confide in her, and that would have been uncomfortable in front of her husband, because men are cynical . . .

The servant carried in a brightly polished, round-bellied brass samovar and stood it on its little table next to the dining table, which was already set with small plates and little bowls full of many kinds of snacks, quite enough for a whole meal. Lyova's wife poured tea into a couple of glasses and invited her guest to the table.

"Lyova and I were just speaking about you. We were wondering why on earth you're still single. We thought we might kidnap you and marry you off."

Mr. Zafran smiled to himself. He truly envied his friend—what a pleasure it would be to come home every evening to such a nicely turned-out little woman, a wife who dressed up for her husband and their visitors, who welcomed him with a laden table as if he were an honored guest. He'd thought it many times, and now he thought it again: his friend was so lucky.

"Do you always eat by yourself, before Lyova gets home?" Mr. Zafran asked, watching her help herself to a full meal—far more than just a snack. He was eager to eat too, but he held back, waiting for the man of the house.

Up until now, Lyova's wife had assumed Mr. Zafran knew her husband was out of town. When she saw he wasn't eating, though, she remarked, "Do you think I should go hungry until my husband comes home next week?" Then Mr. Zafran realized his friend was off traveling, so he felt free to tuck in. Starting with a sip of this and a nibble of that, he ended up eating a full meal, which he washed down with a drink. His young friend, though she had no ulterior motives—she wouldn't have dreamed of cheating on her husband—was also enjoying having a dining companion. Of course it was more fun to have a guest for the evening meal than to dine alone . . . but even in that there was a certain amount of cheating going on, a genteel kind of cheating, a tiny little amount, the kind of cheating that happens even when a husband's right there. After all, how many times had she asked her husband to bring Mr. Zafran home for dinner?

Truth be told, Lyova's wife would have been quite indifferent to Mr. Zafran if he hadn't been so indifferent to her; his indifference and his unusual behavior that evening excited her.

After dinner, Mr. Zafran poured out his heart to Lyova's wife, and she listened with shining eyes and a series of wry little smiles that Mr. Zafran didn't even notice. He was happy he'd confessed everything, and he was delighted that his friend's wife finally knew he was in love with another woman, not her.

Mr. Zafran received a nasty shock. A printed notice had suddenly appeared in the window of the store across the street, which had been empty for a few months, announcing that the major firm Landesman was about to open a store selling women's coats in that location. Landesman was the company where Mr. Zafran's good friend Lyova worked as head manager of their retail outlet, so Lyova must have had a hand in this development, and if that was so (though it was less a question of "if" and more a matter of "definitely"), did that mean his friend wanted to bring him down? But why? What had he done to hurt Lyova so badly that he'd stab him in the back?

Mr. Zafran wanted to go see Lyova and talk it over, but then he changed his mind and decided it would be more straightforward to write, and then, after he heard what his friend had to say, he'd have a better idea what to do.

A half hour ago he'd told his older employee to lower the shutters over the door and windows, and as the shutters came rattling down he'd taken the keys from the man and asked his younger employee, the boy, to accompany him—though the request was really an order. Mr. Zafran was very upset. Even before he left for home, he knew he'd find it hard to be alone in the house, but at the same time he knew he couldn't stand having anyone around, so the boy suited his mood. Mr. Zafran didn't think of the boy as an actual person, but he was alive and that was enough.

When he got home he sat right down at his desk, lit a lamp, and tried to write a letter to Lyova. But his efforts went nowhere. That is, something got written, but what he'd produced seemed silly—the words that flowed out of his pen weren't at all what he'd thought to write beforehand. So what was the use of trying? If he couldn't write what he wanted to write, he wouldn't get what he wanted to have, so he may as well not bother at all.

A few minutes later Mr. Zafran changed his mind again. He decided this whole idea of writing had been a silly notion right from the start. Even if he did manage to write what he'd wanted to write, it would still be no use. What did he think would happen—would Lyova be fired on the spot? If the Landesman firm had already decided to open a new branch somewhere or other, what reasons would be enough to make them back out? Also, Lyova was his friend—he must have seen in advance that he'd be thumbing his nose right in Mr. Zafran's face, and that still didn't stop him. So maybe the best thing was to honestly ask straight out, "My dear friend, what have you got against me? What have I done to you that makes you want to ruin me?"

Suddenly, Mr. Zafran jumped up and snapped at the boy: "Why aren't you a few years older? The hell with you!" He poised his inky pen over the paper for a moment, then started scribbling all over the clean white sheet, scrawling at random, without sense or logic, and after he'd covered the page top to bottom with scrawls, he showed it to the boy and asked, "Would you like to have a lot of money?"

The kid's reply was both clever and practical. "What's that got to do with me?"

"Look: no matter how old or young they are, everyone wants to get rich." Zafran was babbling, not knowing or caring whether he was speaking to the boy or to himself. "Just tell me, you little devil—haven't you ever thought of sticking your hand under one of my cushions to see if there's any money there? Don't be afraid, don't worry, you're not the only one who's thought that. We're all thieves. The only difference between a thief and a respectable person is that the thief can't control his desires, or maybe he's less of a coward than a respectable person. I know you're a good boy, but still, when you go past a big store with gold and silver watches hanging in the window, don't you think, 'Oh, if I could only cut a little hole in the windowpane and stick my hand in and take out one gold wristwatch, just one—and no one, not one person, will see me'? And later, when you grow up, you'll think the same thing when you walk by a bank: 'If I could only sneak inside so that no one sees me, if I could only perceive but be imperceptible' (that means you'd be able to see other people in the bank, but they couldn't see you)—and then you'd stuff all your pockets and even your shirtfront with money and then you'd leave. . . . And after you die, people will pay you compliments: 'Oh, what a fine gentleman he was . . . ' But really, why am I talking this way to you? Do you have any idea?"

Mr. Zafran got out of his chair and began pacing the length of the room. Every time he turned his back to the lamp, his shadow stretched out ahead of him so it looked like he was chasing the shadow, and when he turned around and faced the lamp again, the shadow was behind him so it looked like the shadow was chasing him. After he'd walked back and forth across the room a few times, from one wall to the other, he halted in front of the boy and demanded, "Should I write a letter or not?"

"To whom?" the boy asked with innocent curiosity.

"Do you think, even though it's not quite time yet . . . do you think you'll be able to find a new job?" Mr. Zafran said abruptly.

"The Zafran company's about to go under. We've got six months, maybe a year. . . . After thirty-six years in the same premises! Of course, we'll put up a good fight—but meanwhile, while there's still time, we have to plan ahead. Don't worry, I'll do everything I can, but eventually I'll have to leave . . . and maybe it'll be easier to leave sooner rather than later."

He was speaking to the boy, irritated with himself for addressing the kid as though he were grown up. At the same time, he also knew he could be frank with the boy precisely because he was a boy, and that if a sensible adult were there instead, Mr. Zafran wouldn't have said a thing. He could never confide in an adult as he'd confided in the boy. It was all so painful and embarrassing, yet at the same time . . . Who would care that the Zafran store, which had been in the same premises for almost forty years, would go bankrupt in a year or so?

"Get to bed!" he suddenly yelled and glared at the boy until he left the room, walking through the open doorway and disappearing into the darkness beyond, from which, a few minutes later, Mr. Zafran heard the big old-fashioned clock striking the hour. He counted each clang, even though he was wearing a watch and already knew what time it was. When the last clang died away, he plunked himself down in the armchair from which he'd gotten up a short time ago and began to write a letter to his friend Lyova.

A few days later, Mr. Zafran got an answer to his letter—an answer so shocking that at first he couldn't believe his own eyes. He'd never seen anything like that letter before. When he first started to read, he couldn't even make out what the words were saying—he thought that either he or the writer must be out of his mind.

The letter began with a tirade of insults and abuse. In the very first line, the writer addressed him as "swine"—that is, instead of the usual salutation, "Dear So-and-So," his friend called him "swine," and that word was enough to throw Mr. Zafran into a tizzy. He read on without understanding a thing. "Swine" hovered over every word and every line, and quite some time passed before he could force his brain to concentrate and figure out what the rest of the letter was saying. In a torrent of abusive, venomous words, Lyova was accusing him of coming to his house—having bided his time until he, Lyova, was away on business—and entering his home with the aim of seducing his wife.

Mr. Zafran, who'd been sitting in his shop behind the cash box, jumped out of his chair as if a snake had crawled up behind his back and bitten him. He yelled for his employee, shoved the letter under his nose, and waited while the tall young man read it to the end. The employee, who fancied himself a wit, had no idea what it was all about, but he understood—as anyone who'd read the letter would have—that his boss had gotten himself into a scrape with a woman, and he smiled to himself.

Mr. Zafran knew his employee didn't know the whole story, and he also knew, since the man was obviously no clairvoyant, that he couldn't possibly understand the true situation. Nevertheless, he fell into a rage, snatched the letter right out of his employee's hands, and hollered, "You idiot! You have no idea what's going on!"

"But I was just reading it!" the employee said defensively.

"It's complete nonsense, it's a lie, that's not what happened! I don't love her one bit! It never even occurred to me to . . ."

The employee smiled, and you could see in his smile that he didn't believe a thing his boss had said: surely, the accusation must have some basis. Mr. Zafran saw the smile and went out of his mind with fury. "Get out of here! Drop dead—get away from me!" But as the man started to walk away, his boss grabbed him by the collar, pulled him back, and started to speak, his plaintive voice quavering. Like a prisoner who's been sentenced to death pleads with the chaplain in his final moments before execution, protesting his innocence of the crime he's about to be punished for, Mr. Zafran, with emotion that brought tears to his eyes, told his employee the whole story.

Poor Mr. Zafran—he was in a terrible state. He knew that even if he yelled as loud as he could for twenty-four hours without stopping, "Whether you believe me or not, I'm telling the truth!" no one would listen. And his misery was intensified by the fact that he didn't even know himself which was worse: the pain of not being able to convince anyone that he didn't love his friend's wife or the pain of not being able to convince anyone that he loved another woman instead. He didn't know which of the two women he should concentrate on—should he try to convince the clownish young man how much he hated Lyova's wife (before, he'd been indifferent to her—now he hated her), or should he try to convince him he was really in love with Manya?

Mr. Zafran sat back down, propped his elbows on his office desk, put his head in his hands, and thought deeply about the whole confusing situation that he'd gotten himself into and that he couldn't see any way of getting himself out of.

"Yes," he admitted, "I'm in love, it's true, but not with her. I'm in love with Manya."

The clownish employee stuck out his tongue, shrugged his shoulders, covered his mouth with his hands, and crowed like a rooster, "Kukuriku, ru, ru, ru!"

"What?"

"Some love affair. You were always making fun of her. Now she'll never come back, and it's your own fault."

Mr. Zafran saw there was no use trying to convince the young man he was in love with a girl he'd mocked mercilessly. This guy would never believe he was in love with the girl he really was in love with or that he wasn't in love with the woman he really wasn't in love with.

"Are you saying you think I'm in love with my friend's wife?"

"I don't mean to say anything at all."

"I don't believe you. That *is* what you think." Mr. Zafran paused for a moment and then burst out hotly, "But I'm asking you, how could Lyova's wife possibly think I'm in love with her when I told her I'm head over heels in love with Manya, and I even asked her advice about what I should do . . . how *could* she believe it?"

"Well, maybe she thought . . ."

"What did she think? What *could* she think?"

"She could have thought you meant you were in love with *her*, not the other girl."

"How could she possibly think that when I told her who the girl is?"

"I don't know."

"How could she think I meant I was in love with her, when she's never heard me say even one nice thing about her?"

"So maybe she's offended by that."

"Well, so what? Does she have to lie about it—tell her husband I told her I'm in love with her?"

"I don't know anything about it," the tall young man said dismissively with a mock-serious expression, slowly backing away from his boss. "What do I know? When it's time for me to get married, I'll get married. When you put off getting married for too long, who knows what might happen?" Then the young man's mock-serious expression became truly serious. Flinging out a hand in an impulsive, one-armed shrug, he pulled a droll, sour face (which looked funny in and of itself) and said that, all things considered, he didn't understand the point of falling in love. He knew people had to get married, but love . . . he didn't get it. He had no idea what love even was.

"I know that when I get married I don't want to hate my wife, even if I don't love her. And I don't want to be a worse husband to my wife than some guy who gets married because he's head over heels."

Mr. Zafran experienced a strange feeling, a feeling of envy he'd never had before. He envied the young man because he was and always would be indifferent to Manya. He decided to forgive his employee for being so nonchalant while he, Zafran, had been suffering the pangs of love. "Listen!" he said impulsively. "Do you know why Manya left? She left because I threw her out."

"You did? What for?"

Mr. Zafran thought for moment. "Anyone would have to love a girl like her, but I didn't. That's why I threw her out. I knew any man should be able to love her, but I couldn't stand the sight of her."

In the half-open doorway, partly blocked by the shutter that had been lowered against the sun to cool down the store, Izak the tailor appeared. He'd been one of Mr. Zafran's workers, but now, like most other tailors, he was hanging around with nothing to do, waiting for the winter season's work that was due to start in a few weeks. As soon as Izak entered the store, you could see he'd been walking the streets unemployed and empty-handed. He took off his cap, pulled out a handkerchief that he'd obviously put into his pocket just before he'd left home, and used it to wipe his forehead, turning the clean white handkerchief damp and dirty with sweat and dust.

"Is it ever hot!" Izak slipped behind the cash table and stood at Mr. Zafran's side.

"It's all right for you," Mr. Zafran said. "You can walk around outside when you don't have work, but when we're not bringing in any money, we're still stuck in the store."

"That's not true, Mr. Zafran—you had a really good season. What more do you want? Your customers have cleared out your shelves."

Mr. Zafran asked Izak if he knew that the Landesman firm was just about to open a new branch right across the street.

"Why—are you worried about it?"

"Tell him!" Mr. Zafran said to his tall young employee. "You tell him what the problem is."

But Izak interrupted. "What's the story with you and Manya? She was going on and on about you—you tried to talk her into believing that you weren't yourself but you were someone else, and so on and so forth, the devil knows what, I can't even begin to remember it all."

Mr. Zafran stared at Izak, trying to figure out what to do. Then he came to a decision: he told Izak to send Manya over to his house either today or tomorrow at closing time because he had something important to discuss with her. If she didn't want to come to his house, she could meet him somewhere else, a little park or city square.

"What am I—a pimp?" Izak retorted with a trace of irritation. "If you want to tell her something, you can go to her place yourself— or send someone else."

"That's not it! Izak! Izak, I'm just talking about business. I just thought up a plan—she can help me save my store."

"Save it from what?"

"From going under, from the competition right there across the street that's giving me a huge headache."

Izak, with a quizzical look, said he didn't understand what Manya could do to help.

Mr. Zafran curtly interrupted: "What's it to you—you think I'm crazy? I'm perfectly sane, and I know what I'm talking about."

"So what will I tell her if she doesn't want to meet you?"

"You don't have to explain anything. Just send her to me. . . . Let's see, tell her you're having some sort of problem with me. Yes, that would be easiest—just make something up and send her over to my house. It's no big deal—don't worry, I'm not going to eat her."

Izak fanned his face with his hat and looked over at the sturdy shelves full of thick winter fabric, lying there ready and waiting for his shears. Two mannequins stood stiffly in the middle of the floor, giving off the air of blank emptiness common to all inanimate objects that look like living people. Although Izak the tailor had no claim on anything in Mr. Zafran's store, he felt completely at home in it because he had the same things in his own workshop: the mannequins, the fabric, and the coats—everything in the store had gone through his hands too, and because he was so much at home he felt free to tell his boss, "Ah, you're useless, you know!"

The tall, clownish young man broke into a long, clownish laugh.

The chandelier with its heavy glass clusters hung in the middle of the living room ceiling. It hadn't been lit in years, ever since the real heads of the household had gone to their eternal rest, but it was glowing now, illuminating the large room with crystalline light. It was hung so thickly with glass that the electric lights scattered within were completely hidden, as if the dozens of faceted icy droplets were shedding light all by themselves, light that burned deep in their translucent bodies.

The chandelier had been lit in honor of the guest Mr. Zafran was expecting. For weeks now, he'd been keeping the furniture's plush cushions dusted; he'd spared neither money nor effort to make the room look comfortable, as if it had a lot of visitors.

Finally, he could hear the light patter of a woman's footsteps, and his heart started to beat hard. What comfort and intimacy, what a joyful spirit there was in the footsteps of a young woman! He could almost believe she was his already. He couldn't figure out exactly what she meant to him, but here she was, a woman he loved, and even before she entered the room, it seemed to him that something in it had changed, that the room itself had sensed the woman's approach. Mr. Zafran was so captivated by the sound of her footsteps that he forgot to open the door for her. He'd had every intention of doing so just a few minutes ago, but then he forgot until he heard the soft ring of the electric bell.

He asked Manya to sit down, and she thanked him for having invited her. She took a seat and said that Izak had sent her to see him for some reason, and just to be on the safe side, she'd asked another girl to wait for her outside.

"But since you're already here, I'd like you to stay a little while. There's something very important I have to discuss with you. If you like, I'll go downstairs and tell your friend you'll be here for some time so she'll wait a bit longer—or she can just leave."

The tailor girl thanked him and said not to go to any trouble because she wouldn't be staying long. She'd just take whatever he wanted to give her for Izak, and then she'd be off.

"But don't you know my whole future depends on you?" Mr. Za-fran noticed her impatient movement and realized what she was thinking, so he quickly reassured her that he hadn't meant what she thought but something completely different: he'd had a stroke of ter-rible luck, he was about to be ruined, and she was the only person who could save him from going under.

Manya opened her eyes wide, thinking this was another one of his made-up stories, some brand-new, crazy fantasy that had popped into his mind, and she asked with an ironic half smile, "Really? Are you talking about yourself, Mr. Zafran? Or someone else—your cousin maybe? Which one of you is about to go under?" And she broke into a wide grin.

Mr. Zafran suddenly understood the complete mess he'd managed to get himself into. He tried to defend himself: God only knows he hadn't meant any harm. Back then, on the street near the barbershop, he hadn't intended to do anything wrong; he'd had no ulterior motives, and all he could tell her now was that at the time he couldn't believe, or couldn't let himself believe, his luck—the chance to go ahead, like any other man on this planet, and frankly admit he was in love with her. Otherwise, he would never have tried to deceive her. After all, it was only by way of his little deception that he'd been finally able to open up to her.

Manya was willing to believe Mr. Zafran was in love with her, but his behavior, ever since she'd started making deliveries to his store . . . and most recently, his fantastic story about the other Zafran . . . She told herself that she'd sensed he was sincere when he said he loved her, but what could she possibly make of that sincerity when this man, who'd spoken so sincerely, had played that ridiculous practical joke on her—a joke that completely contradicted his words? Still, Manya was like every other woman: whether she was interested in the man who was talking her ear off about love or felt nothing for him, she still wanted him to mean what he was saying, so despite her suspicions that he was setting up yet another practical joke, she put on a serious face and said, "How can I help you, Mr. Zafran?"

"Just one little thing: I'd like you to go with me to someone's house and say . . . or no, you don't need to actually say anything, I just want you to be there. I'd like to introduce you as my fiancée."

"That's it? No more, no less?"

Mr. Zafran explained the whole sorry situation. The girl, who had already heard it from Izak, still couldn't imagine what any of it had to do with her. Was this another one of Zafran's wild fantasies? It made no sense at all—something didn't fit. He said he'd confessed everything to Lyova's wife (if that was even true), so why would the wife go and tell her husband that Mr. Zafran had said he was in love with her?

"Maybe they'll just believe you without me there," Manya said lightly.

"If you don't want to come, I'll invite them here."

Manya looked blank, so Mr. Zafran went on. "To our engagement party."

The girl got up from her chair and calmly, with biting irony, said, "I'll think about it."

Mr. Zafran hurried to stop her. "Manya! My life is in your hands!" Then he added, "I know—it's my own fault you can't take me seriously. You must think I'm still joking. But I'll swear on anything you like that even back then, when I really was joking, I was serious, too . . . a thousand times more serious than other men are when they talk to the girl they love."

"Do you need to give me something for Izak?" the girl asked coldly as she put on her coat to leave.

Mr. Zafran stood there for a few minutes in bewildered frustration. Finally, he asked, his voice pleading, "So your answer is no?"

"Listen, Mr. Zafran! That's enough of your silly jokes—I would never have thought it of you. And why on earth is it my job to fix your problems? Go find someone else." Then she headed for the door. Mr. Zafran stared at her like a prisoner who's been sentenced to death stares at his judge—the only man who can save him from the gallows and, at the same time, the man who's sentenced him in the first place. The prisoner pleads with his eyes, though he knows it won't help in the least and that the sentence will be carried out in full force.

Manya opened the door. Mr. Zafran ran after her, planted himself in her path, and yelled into her face, "All right, it's a lie—everything I've just said to you . . . it's all lies! You were right all along—I made fun of you on purpose! Look, I'm laughing at you!" And he broke into loud guffaws.

From the room next door, whose dark, open doorway looked into the room where Mr. Zafran and Manya confronted each other,

came the clanging of the large wall clock. The clock started striking at the exact moment the girl closed the door behind her, as if its
chimes that sang out the hours were accompanying the girl into the
past, from which—just like the vanished hours the clock had rung
away—she would never return. At the same time, Manya's staccato
footsteps echoed in the corridor as she ran from him. When they
ceased, Mr. Zafran was left with the sensation that the girl's footsteps had been absorbed into the lifeless air of his lonely bachelor
home . . . they would never fade; they would remain there forever,
suspended in still, sorrowful silence.

The Artistic Temperament

The painter Philip Trop woke up at dusk in a pessimistic mood. He sat up and spat across the floor as far as he could, just like a peasant. Then, catching himself, he tried to rationalize his spontaneous action: for years on end, his studio had been filthy with litter and dirt, he told himself, and he'd gotten used to it being that way. But now things were different. He'd been married for six months, and he still couldn't adjust to his studio's new state of cleanliness because it constantly reminded him there was someone else in his life. In order to feel inspired, he needed to know he was alone—that the only spirit to fill the air of his artistic environment was his, and only his.

With one long glance, Philip measured the length of the attic and its glass roof made up of many windowpanes and a short wall in the front, most of which was also glassed in. He felt a sense of estrangement and remoteness from the city and its people, although the room in which he sat was in the city center. In the attic studio the daylight lingered longer than in more ordinary dwellings; the room glowed with natural light well after lamps had been lit in the surrounding apartments, and the days slowly extinguished themselves in drawn-out death throes until night fell completely. The artist luxuriated in his time alone in the long twilights, and since he'd gotten married he loved his isolation even more, knowing he'd never be lonely; he could have company whenever he wanted.

He could hear footsteps under the attic's thin floor, the brisk tapping of high heels as his young wife, confident of her privilege and status, bustled around the apartment. The artist reflected that only wives who know their husbands adore them walk around so boldly, as if every step of theirs is of vital importance.

Half a year into his marriage, Philip was still surprised to discover the sound of those footsteps hadn't yet lost their magic, their magnetic hold on him. If someone had told him beforehand he could live with a woman for six months and still be in love with her at the end of them, he wouldn't have believed it. He'd gotten married because his wife-to-be refused to live with him unless they were married legally, and now, all these months later, he still loved her. A whole six months of loving the same woman—it was embarrassing. It was even more embarrassing when he was with his friends. Whenever he got together with them, he'd brag that he'd stopped loving his wife ages ago, and soon, any month now, he'd throw her out. And whose fault was it that he'd been with her for such a long time and was still in love with her? Wasn't that what old people did? He couldn't work out if getting married was something young people did or if it was a sign of old age.

The artist was twenty-five years old, but his great popularity made him feel much older. Then there was his bohemian lifestyle, in which days blended into nights and nights blended into days, and his intimate relationships with many women. He'd already had his fill of life, and if it weren't for the calendar, he'd have thought he was at least fifteen or twenty years older than he actually was.

Philip threw off his plush blanket, and a second later he was on his feet and stuffing his pipe with tobacco. Puffing on the pipe, he walked across the floor and stood at the window, his gaze skating across rooftops covered with a thin layer of fresh snow that lay spread out like a bedsheet, giving off an air of white, wintery melancholy. Flat-topped, short brick chimneys poked out through the snow, mindlessly spewing smoke into the cold, bleak air.

The windows under the snowy roofs were illuminated with lanterns and electric lights. They shone blankly with the indifference and isolation of people who live their own little lives in the midst of a big city. The artist watched the squares of light and the people who appeared in them. They were walking around, occupied with their own concerns, though the painter couldn't see any of them actually doing anything, which gave him the impression their only purpose in life was standing around or wandering from one room into the next.

He left the studio and took the stairs to the level below where he'd rented two rooms. As he entered the dining room, he glanced at the door leading to the bedroom. It was closed, and below it, between the door and the floor, lay a thin strip of light like a bright knife that divided the dark room in front of it from the bright room behind. He wanted to go into the bedroom but hesitated, reminding himself he was in the habit of knocking first. But that was silly, he thought. Had she ever said he couldn't come in? So why the ceremony? Was it to show her that even after all this time he still respected her feelings? Well, if that was the reason, he could drop the formality. Let her think that . . . that by now, after all . . . well, really, wasn't it time to put an end to all this politeness? A silly habit like knocking didn't suit an artist, a free spirit like himself. Was he a bookkeeper with finicky manners or some sort of high-class gentleman? And aside from all that, right now he wasn't in the mood for sentimentality.

So Philip hesitated behind the door, thinking about it—should he or shouldn't he?—and coming to no conclusion, he jerked open the door, and there stood his wife, half-naked.

Mrs. Trop, who was startled by the sudden opening of the door but not at all embarrassed, glossed over her surprise, though she felt it necessary to point out her husband's error: "Are you forgetting your manners, my dear Philip?" The artist carelessly looked away, wanting her to think he was completely indifferent to her half-clad state. After a short pause he turned back to her and with dramatic, impassioned seriousness stated, "I'm bored to death with the whole thing."

"Bored with what?" the artist's wife asked with puzzled disquiet, at the same time impulsively crossing her bare arms over her bare breasts that peeked out from above her corset. She didn't quite understand what he'd meant, but she didn't want him to look at her unclothed body just then, either. "What are you bored with? Tell me what you mean," she urged.

Philip looked with growing excitement at his wife's well-built torso with its womanly allure, then at her graceful stockinged legs and her feet, clad in patent leather sandals with high heels, which made her feet seem even smaller and daintier than they actually were. His glance sprang upward, and he stared, unable to tear his eyes away from the slender, pale throat threaded with fine blue veins that made her look so young, naive, and innocent. Then he took in the thick cloud of hair on her delicate, oval-shaped head, and at last her little face with its wide eyes. All these things retained the same magic that they had six months ago, before they were married, and even nine months ago when he'd first set eyes on her. But now he was embarrassed to show her how he felt, because his interest in her had lasted such a long time—so, still gazing at her with the pent-up fascination of an artist and a man, he put on a frown and repeated what he'd just said: "Bored! Bored! I'm bored to death with it all!"

She'd figured out by then what he meant, but she still didn't understand the reason for his sudden, unexpected outburst. In his behavior up to now he'd never given her cause to suspect . . . and just a few hours ago they'd decided to go to the theater . . . so what had come over him all of a sudden?

"Philip, is something wrong? Philip?"

"I'm fine. What makes you think anything's wrong?"

"What's going on then?" She hesitated a moment and added, "Should we stay home?"

"Why don't you just go ahead? Why not?"

"What about you?"

Philip drew on his pipe and sulked, "I don't want to go. I don't feel like it."

"Then I won't either." But suddenly Mrs. Trop caught his meaning. "What—you mean you want me to go without you?"

The artist's attack was sudden and unexpected. "What kind of stupidity is that?" he snapped. "Just because I don't want to go, does that mean you shouldn't? Why? If you feel like going, why shouldn't you go even if I don't want to?" He stopped to draw on his pipe, then went on, "Is there some sort of law that says a man and his wife always have to do exactly the same thing—if one goes to the theater, the other one has to go too, and if one stays home, so does the other? You can go and you *should* go, because you feel like going and I don't. I feel like staying home."

"Philip!" she wailed. "Don't you love me anymore?"

The artist brushed off her question and got deeper into his role. "It's best that you know this now and not later. I'm no better than any other man—that goes along with an artist's intuition. It's not his fault if he can't act like a bookkeeper or a watchmaker and tie himself down to his wife. And you have the right to do whatever you want, too. A man and his wife . . . even when they love each other, they still don't have to act like some guy who owns a well and won't let anyone else use the water. Because if he does that, no fresh water gets in, and then the well goes stale and the water tastes bad."

His wife, like all beautiful young women, was herself an artist by nature. Her pride was wounded by her husband's behavior, and her love for him retreated deep inside. Her face took on an expression of cold indifference. "You're right," she replied.

"You see?" said the painter. He wasn't too happy his wife had agreed, but he suppressed his annoyance. "See, you understand my point."

"Yes, I do. I have nothing against you—as long as you give me the same freedom you're about to take for yourself."

Mrs. Trop quickly finished getting dressed and, leaving her husband behind, went to visit one of her girlfriends. The artist went to a café, and the two didn't meet again until each got home around midnight. And though both still burned with love and passion for each other, they lied: she told him she'd had a wonderful time with some man, and he told her he'd been partying with some woman, and resentment and jealousy ate at both their hearts. But neither admitted a thing to the other. They both pretended to be happy in their new, promising lifestyle that—so it seemed—they'd just begun to live.

On Vacation

It was Friday evening when Mikhl—a small man sporting a short forked beard—arrived at the cabin. As soon as he entered the little house with its dirt floor and its roof that, plastered inside, doubled as the ceiling, he pulled off his Shabbos jacket, sat down, fanned himself with his hand, and wiped the sweat from his face. Then he turned to his three daughters. "So what's new?" he asked. Bontsie, his wife, was standing at the stove. She dipped the last fish in flour and put it into the pan to fry. The hot oil spat with a loud hiss, adding more fumes to the haze of bluish smoke that filled the room and drifted toward the two little windows where it was suddenly tugged outdoors, as if it were the souls of the fish making their escape.

Mikhl fanned his face with his hat and glanced at his daughters, then turned back to his wife and watched as she cooked. He longed for some fried fish with salad, but it wouldn't do to ask before dinnertime.

His daughters were hard at work too. Their hair was mussed, their blouses unbuttoned at the neck, their foreheads damp. Little drops of sweat, like beads on a rosary, stood on their upper lips. Their hands moved faster than seemed possible, and as the sewing machine clattered away, they kept exchanging glances with each other.

At sunset they all went to bathe in the ocean. Mikhl undressed behind a rock not far from the women. As he waded in, he accidentally caught a glimpse of his wife and daughters wobbling into the water like a gaggle of ducks. Mikhl turned away, flung himself down, and swam off. He surfaced after a few minutes, then swam a bit farther and looked back to see if the women were watching. He showed off a little: "Brr, brrr, brrrr!"

Mikhl's silly behavior embarrassed his daughters. They smirked at each other and promptly sat down, submerging up to their necks. But Bontsie called to him: "Where are you going?" Mikhl's heart leaped like a child's who's been given a hug right after a spanking. He started swimming again, even harder than before, glancing back at the women as he went. Then he dunked his head, dove straight down, and stayed underwater, holding his breath as long as he could, until his chest was about to explode.

After his swim and a good Shabbos dinner, Mikhl, in a contented mood, decided to get some fresh air. He dragged two chairs outside, sat down on one, and invited his wife to join him. She said no and gave him such an odd look he was almost sorry he'd asked. Making the best of things, he put his feet on the empty chair, leaned back, and raised his face to the sky. His cheap detachable shirtfront had come undone from his vest and twisted to one side, and his chest, covered with black hair, showed through a gap in his shirt. A little breeze blew; it played over his shoulders and made its way under his shirt, stirring his chest hair like wind in the grass, tickling him.

His daughters had gone out for a walk. They hadn't said a word to him at dinner, answering in monosyllables when he spoke to them. He hated that. The least they could do, he thought, was ask what he'd done during the week.

Mikhl was starting to get depressed: Why did his daughters treat him so badly when all he wanted was to talk with them? Sorrow bubbled up inside him. He felt like crying, hugging the girls, kissing them again and again. "What do they have against me?" he wondered. "Don't I give them whatever I can? Sure, they want . . . all girls need to get married . . . but why blame me? Back when I was making good money, what did I do—waste it all drinking?"

Bontsie knew what was going on. His wife was more to blame than their daughters. She was the one who . . . if it weren't for her, the girls would be different. They sneered at him, treated him like a dog. All she had to do was say, "Girls, that's not nice . . . He's your father." What a shrew she was—she even encouraged them. Kids . . . what do they know?

A full moon, glowing fiery red, was rising on the distant horizon. The night brightened a little, revealing the faraway silhouettes of people wandering here and there, walking back and forth from one cabin to another. The moon got smaller and whiter as it rose, and the night paled at the same time, as if it were afraid of the unexpected intruder.

Mikhl, who'd been nodding on his chair, suddenly opened his eyes. For some reason he was thinking about the moon rising overhead. He looked around wonderingly, crossed his arms over his chest, and let his eyes and mind wander across the clear sky with a deep sense of pleasure. He forgot that one day soon the sky would be hidden behind clouds, the trees would be thin and bare, the earth covered with snow. The day was coming when he'd argue with his family and they'd throw him out of the house. None of that mattered now. All he felt was the breeze caressing his face, playing in his beard, creeping under his shirt. A relaxed, enjoyable shiver went through his body. Like a trusting child in its mother's lap, he surrendered to the pleasant sensations, to the little catnap that strayed into his brain, padding along quietly, softly, as though on small quilted paws. His eyes kept closing and opening again, like a chick's when you stroke its head, and the sweet trilling notes of a distant mandolin spun out and intertwined like silk threads, weaving together in his drowsing mind and intermingling with his thoughts, and it seemed to him that everything, the entire world, was music, everything, everywhere was music . . . and he was there too, floating, drifting with the melody . . .

"Mikhl!" Bontsie's voice startled him awake. She was sitting inside by the door, looking out at him. He didn't answer.

A minute later: "Mikhl!"

Again he said nothing, so she got up with a scowl, walked over, and gave him a poke.

"Mikhl, Mikhl, come on. I've already asked you."

"In a moment," he answered, eyes still closed.

"Mikhl!"

He heard her but found it hard to speak, annoyed that she'd woken him.

For a minute or two there was silence. Bontsie took a few steps back and forth, like the vacationers he'd seen earlier walking to and fro. She was thoroughly annoyed with Mikhl for ignoring her when she'd tried to wake him, so this time she didn't even say his name. She just walked over, yanked his sleeve, and snapped, "Get up!"

Mikhl looked at her and said, "Do you know what I'd like? More than anything? To sleep outside."

"Do you know what I'd like? More than anything?" Bontsie mocked. "I'd like you to come in and go to bed."

"But it's so nice out here."

Eventually, Mikhl rose to his feet, both he and his chair emitting a groan. He went inside, wobbling like a drunk, and fell onto the mattress lying ready for him on the floor.

Bontsie sat by the door, waiting for the girls. "It's already so late," she thought, listening for them and peering into the darkness. Everyone was asleep in the other cabins. "I'll bet they're at Moroskin's. Yes, that must be it," she thought. "Girls, kids. Where are they? They should be getting some rest. What a handful. Kids today, you can't tell them anything. Well, today's Shabbos; they can sleep in tomorrow, but what about the rest of the week? When do they sleep? They stay up all night . . ."

"Bontsie!" Her thoughts were interrupted.

"What?" she said, startled.

"The girls—are they back yet?"

She didn't answer.

Mikhl lay on his back, scratching his chest, tossing fitfully on his mattress. He didn't feel well. He kept falling asleep and waking up again, itching all over in the unbearable heat. He was lying in a puddle of sweat.

Bontsie was trying to remember something. She remembered that she'd just thought about something important, but she couldn't remember what it was.

Mikhl's idea popped back into his head: Wouldn't it be nice to sleep outside? He mulled it over a minute or two, then called Bontsie over and suggested it to her.

"Nobody cares what you want," she snapped. "Why are you nagging me?"

"Why are you getting so upset?" he said, stung.

"Have a fit and die."

"Witch," he muttered under his breath.

Suddenly, he jumped up as if someone had poured boiling water over him. He stuck his pillow under one arm, jammed the mattress and sheet under the other, and headed for the door.

"I hope you have nightmares and never wake up! You're out of your mind!" Bontsie cursed. She grabbed the mattress and tried to yank it away. Mikhl hung on tight, trying to pull it out the door. Both were breathing hard. Mikhl kept muttering, "All I want is to sleep outside, and she says I can't."

"We'll see about that. We'll see," Bontsie spat. They struggled over the mattress, squaring off like a couple of chickens fighting over a worm. Both were white in the face, their arms and legs trembling with effort. But they were equally stubborn: neither would give in.

"Let go!" She grabbed at the pillow.

"Not on your life," he sneered.

"So we'll just stand here?"

"I guess we will."

"Even if it takes all night?"

"Even if it takes all night."

Bontsie threatened her husband with the thought of their daughters. "They'll be home soon," she said.

"Yeah, so?"

The couple renewed their battle with fresh energy, pummeling each other's hands and arms, each trying to wrest the mattress and pillow from the other's grip, but neither would let go. Finally, Mikhl caught his second wind. He gave a mighty heave and ended up in possession of the prize. He flung the mattress to the ground outside the cabin, propped the pillow against the wall, and lay down. But he couldn't sleep. He heard his daughters arrive home. He heard his wife complaining about him, cursing him. His heart sank and a few tears came. He told himself he'd rather die than spend another night in the cabin—if he came back at all.

In the morning they found his mattress—empty.

Section 5

Rivals

"Behind the Veil" follows a family—a lathe operator, Leyb, and his two daughters—and their hired worker through the weeks leading up to and following Passover, one of the most important of the Jewish holidays, which commemorates the Exodus, the escape of the Israelite slaves from Egypt. In its three major sections, the story explores the tensions and rivalries between family members, employers and employees, men and women, Jews and Christians. Like the ancient Israelites, Leyb and his family must navigate difficult terrain: poverty, isolation, and the necessity of maintaining their Jewish identities against the relentless pressure to assimilate. These broad themes underlie a domestic drama: the two sisters are rivals for the affection of their father's employee, while at the same time they attempt to fend off the unwelcome attentions of their wealthy, entitled neighbor.

For those with an interest in pre-Holocaust Jewish history, "Behind the Veil" also provides an intimate, almost ethnographic portrayal of workers' lives in an unnamed east European city.

Behind the Veil

It happened on one of those days as winter gives way to spring. The weather, typical of that time of year, featured a battle between two seasons, two forces of nature. It began with a playful skirmish when the sunny morning was interrupted by a brief hailstorm that whitened the muddy earth. The sun managed to break out again but was quickly veiled by a cloud as hail once more battered the ground and the walls and windows of people's houses. The pattern repeated several times until the game intensified into a real war. Snow and rain battled it out, each hurling itself against the other, intermingling like opposing armies struggling to capture the other's position. Here and there, icy white winter prevailed for a few minutes, only to be washed away by the rain—and then, a few minutes later, in the same place or somewhere nearby, another temporary drift of snow appeared. Everything and everyone caught up in the conflict got thoroughly, miserably drenched. The whole world dripped, flooded, and drowned in water.[1]

The storm blew around a dozen men, one after another, into Leyb's workshop—pitiful refugees with their umbrellas flipped inside out, so soaked that bodies and umbrellas alike poured streams of water. The broken umbrellas looked like wings of the storm with their jagged edges like those of huge, squashed bats.

---

1. An earlier version of the central portion of this translation appeared as "A Holiday," in *Have I Got a Story for You: More than a Century of Fiction from the Forward*, ed. Ezra Glinter, 278–89 (New York: W. W. Norton, 2017). It appears here with the *Forward*'s permission.

As each new arrival entered Leyb's workshop, he was invited to stand near the iron heating stove that warmed the wide corridor where the workbenches were set up. The apprentice boy filled the square, gaping mouth of the oven with kindling, and on top of the kindling larger pieces of wood with big knots in them, and the refugees, survivors of the storm, warmed and dried themselves by the red-hot sides of the iron stove while their broken umbrellas were mended.

New people kept arriving, blown in by the storm one after another, and later, as the storm died down, they began to trickle out. The departure of these men, who'd stopped by to warm and dry themselves in this familiar place before setting off for their various destinations, left a strange atmosphere in Leyb's workshop, an empty, unfamiliar feeling.

Among the refugees from the storm was a certain young man whose umbrella had flipped inside out. Both he and his umbrella looked as though they'd escaped a catastrophe—an earthquake, perhaps. The young man stood by the door with a bewildered look on his face, smiling a little to himself at his predicament: drenched through and through with a ruined umbrella dangling from his hand. But then he saw the window that opened into the corridor workshop from the living quarters behind it, and the faces of two young women gazing through it. His face took on a friendly expression; a soft, good-natured glow showed in his large black eyes, and it seemed he'd completely forgotten his discomfort. A few minutes later, he handed Leyb his wrecked umbrella, asked how long it would take to repair it, and strolled over to the heating stove to dry off, all the while keeping his eyes on the corridor window that framed the heads and shoulders of Leyb's two daughters.

It took Leyb about ten minutes to do the repair. When the umbrella was mended, Leyb expertly opened and closed it and then announced "Finished!" to the stranger drying off by the stove. Just at that moment the storm died down, which meant the young man could leave even without his umbrella—and now that it was fixed he had even less reason to linger—but it was plain to see he wasn't eager to go on his way. Was that because he hadn't finished drying off yet or because he couldn't tear his eyes away from the girlish faces on the other side of the window? The girls' father, Leyb, thought the latter might be the reason and turned to his daughters in irritation: "Why are you standing there staring like two little nanny goats? Don't you have anything better to do?"

The girls vanished from the window, and a few minutes later the unknown young man reluctantly turned away, paid Leyb for fixing his umbrella, and started to walk out. But then he turned, looked Leyb in the face, and in a quiet and surprisingly casual voice asked, "Would you happen to have any job openings?"

Leyb was startled—the young man didn't look anything like an artisan, and, a bit confused, he answered with a question, "Are you a skilled worker?"

"Yes, of course," came the confident reply.

"A lathe operator?"

"Obviously, given that I'm asking you for a job."

"Then you could have fixed your umbrella yourself."

The young man stood there a few minutes with a perplexed frown on his face, and then replied hesitantly, "I know the work."

"I don't understand," growled the boss.

"I left my last job," the young man answered.

Leyb stared at him for a long time, as if looking would give him the answer to the question he wanted to ask, but of course he couldn't inquire about a thing like that. At length he spoke: "One time I hired a man like you, who wanted to learn the trade and paid me to teach him. He was well-off and didn't need to work—for him, it was just a hobby. But afterward the trade came in handy. The business he owned went downhill, so he opened his own workshop. Now he's got twenty-five lathe operators working for him and he's laughing at us all."

The young man said nothing but simply smiled to himself under his thin black mustache. Seeing he wasn't going to get an answer, the boss said, "Well, what do I know—I don't know a thing. Drop by in a couple of days. Right now I don't have any work for you."

As soon as the young man closed the door behind him, Leyb turned to the window overlooking the corridor workshop and spoke to his daughters on the other side: "What a strange person. He doesn't look anything like a working man."

A few days later the young man showed up with a polite little smile on his face like someone dropping into a house whose inhabitants don't know him, though he knows them. Leyb, who had in fact forgotten all about the worker, greeted him genially: "Well! And what might a young sprout like you have to say for himself?"

As soon as the "young sprout" reminded Leyb he was looking for work, the boss remembered. "Oh, so it's you!" he said cheerfully. He paused, then added, "I don't know. Things are slow right now. I'm not sure . . . Maybe later, a little closer to Passover, some work might come in. I have an empty workbench. If you're willing to get paid by the piece, maybe . . . it's all the same to me; it makes no difference. But if you want to get paid by the week, you'll need to come back next week, maybe in ten days."

The young man said he was willing to get paid by the piece.

The boss looked him over, sighed, and grumbled to himself, "So how's this going to turn out, eh?" Actually, Leyb didn't much care—he knew he wouldn't get rich no matter whether he paid the worker by the piece or by the week. Either way, Leyb would stay poor. And with that unhappy thought, he blurted, "I don't get a bit of good luck! And nothing can help without luck. It's like being a doctor," he went on. "There are doctors who can treat anything. No matter what your problem is, they'll fix you up. If you need to have a tooth pulled, they'll do it. If you've got an earache, they'll treat it. If you come in with a bellyache, they know what to do about that, too. Sounds like a good way to make a living, eh? Nope—turns out it's no good at all. Doctors like that are a dime a dozen. To get ahead, you need to specialize in one thing."

In truth, Leyb was talking not about doctors, but about himself. He could do anything and everything involving his trade—he knew it all, yet he was going straight under. At the same time, other lathe operators, men who specialized in one product, were constantly in work and making good money.

"Do you know what I mean?" Leyb said victoriously to the young man, pleased with himself for having managed to bring out such a deep thought.

Leyb's daughters were looking out the window into the corridor workshop, listening to their father's lecture and smiling, proud of their clever father, and—as Leyb thought—waiting expectantly for the young man's reply. The visitor, however, preferred to keep his opinions to himself. He strolled over to the empty workbench—the one no one was using—and pressed his foot on the treadle until the wheel with its four holes around the rim started spinning. Then he used his hand to set the uppermost wheel turning, and after that he turned to the tools, picking them up one at a time to inspect them. There was no telling from his expression whether the machine and the tools satisfied him or not, but one thing was clear—he was none too happy that, for the time being, he didn't have any work to do. He couldn't stay in the workshop if there was nothing to do—but it seemed he had no desire to leave, either, on account of the girls who'd been watching the whole time from their window. But he said good-bye eventually and walked out.

The young man was back the next afternoon, and even though there was still no work for him, he got the lathe ready and sharpened his tools. When he was done, he sat at the workbench and lit a cigarette. "Have you been apprenticing here long?" he asked the boy, who was busy at his own lathe.

"A year and a half."

"You know the trade yet?" he asked, keeping his voice low.

But the boss overheard and cut in. "More than a corpse does."

The young man smiled good-naturedly, looking patient, embarrassed, and a little helpless as he sat there with his cigarette. Realizing he was at loose ends, the apprentice stepped in with a suggestion:

Could the worker sharpen a chisel for him? The young man jumped at the chance: he got to his feet, started his lathe, and began whetting the tool. As he worked, a thin, fiery thread of sparks peeled away from the hot metal. From time to time he dunked the scorching chisel into cold water, making it squeal like a puppy with food stuck in its throat.

While the new man was working, his back turned to the window overlooking the corridor, Sheyndele appeared behind the glass. She looked over at the apprentice with a little smile, which, however, had less to do with the boy and more to do with the man who was standing with his back to her, not seeing her—or pretending not to see. A few minutes later, Sheyndele's sister, Tsilye, appeared beside her with an angry comment: "Why are you standing there staring? Get back to work!" The two girls vanished. The apprentice, as a way of thanking the worker for sharpening his chisel, said into his ear, "The girl who was just in the window is Sheyndele. She's the younger sister, and the older one is Tsilye."

Spring burst free of winter's shackles ahead of schedule. By Purim, the days were already beautiful—sunny and warm—and as Purim passed and Passover drew near, the days got even sunnier and warmer. The southern sky rose high over the big city, arched above the tall churches with their cross-topped spires, and towered above the lofty poplars, scattered in great numbers among many lesser trees. The air grew more humid every day, and that in itself—the earth exhaling winter's last breath—bore witness to the fact that winter was over.

Here and there in the city parks and along the boulevards, fragile lilac trees began to put forth their tender buds. Chestnut trees flamed with red swellings, looking, with their bare spreading branches, like burning candelabra. The new season made its presence known not only outdoors, in the free air, but even in the darkest cellars, where the potatoes left over from winter—humble vegetables fated to be cooked and eaten—suddenly revealed themselves as alive, putting out pale snouts and roots that gleamed white in their dark prisons, as if threads of daylight, like phosphorescent worms, were growing out of the shadowy gloom. Onions played the same trick. These pungent vegetables, hanging in a braid or lying in a bucket in some dark corner, also returned to life, extending bristly, whitish green (or greenish white) whiskers.

Tradesmen, too, began to feel the preholiday mood as more work came in day by day. Leyb's new hire, however, didn't react as expected. As long as there'd been no work, the young man had been enthusiastic about the job, coming to the workshop each day in search of something to do. But as soon as orders started to flow in, it became clear that the idea of earning money wasn't much to his taste. He stood sedately at the lathe and worked lethargically. Leyb hadn't minded during the slack season, but later that spring, closer to Passover, when one job after another needed to be done, the worker's indolence didn't appeal.

The man was one of a kind. His hands were slow, but every piece of work that left them was a treasure—a skill that became a fault, however, when the work wasn't done by the time he'd agreed to. From time to time Leyb tried to hurry him up—politely, of course. He had no rights in the matter since the worker was getting paid by the piece, but he was sometimes forced to prod him along. "You're too fussy; you're tickling the work. If it's not exact to the hair, that's all right."

The young man may have been overly scrupulous, but his continual lateness was even worse. Leyb couldn't tolerate that, and he'd complain every morning before the worker arrived: "This isn't an office. He can't just show up at ten o'clock like some bookkeeper. What can I do with him?"

"Tell him you don't like him being late."

"What good will that do? And besides, he's getting paid by the piece, not by the hour."

"So tell him the holiday's coming up."

"You think he doesn't know that already?"

"Tell him you'll fire him and hire someone else," the older daughter, Tsilye, said in exasperation.

But that was the problem. The boss was reluctant to fire his newest employee because very few people were willing to do piecework. And there was no point hiring a worker by the week, because aside from the days leading up to a holiday, there was rarely enough work to go around, so it just wasn't worth it. Apart from that, Leyb paid his new employee very little. You might think the boss was an idiot who didn't know he was being led around by the nose, but that would be a mistake. The young man revealed as much when Tsilye, the older daughter, drew his attention to the fact that he was producing very little work: "That's got nothing to do with you. Your father's keeping his mouth shut—maybe he likes things just the way they are."

The days leading up to Passover were Leyb's favorite preholiday days—not because Passover was his favorite holiday, but because that's when his favorite work came in: taps for wine barrels, which he made from red wood in the wine cellars. People came from all over the city, wanting him to make new taps, while others brought him old taps that needed new handles. Despite the fact that he'd have to work fifteen- or eighteen-hour days in the weeks before Passover, Leyb was happy. Fussing over the work gave him an almost spiritual pleasure. After he finished each tap, he'd test it on his tongue to see that no air was getting through. This was the culmination of his finest personal accomplishment: if the tap didn't let any air through, it wouldn't let any wine leak out either. When Leyb lifted the tap from his tongue, it would give a resounding pop, just like the sound of uncorking a bottle of soda water.

Making and mending wine taps was the work Leyb loved best, and he wouldn't entrust it to anyone else—though he did bring it up with the worker—who, the family now knew, was called Elye: "Would you like to try your hand at this? What do you think?"

Elye, it seemed, knew how to make and repair wine taps, but he didn't show any particular interest in doing so, and the boss, as if it weren't enough that Elye's apathy was costing him time and money, was insulted that the young man turned up his nose at the work that Leyb found so pleasant. He lost no opportunity to express his opinion. Every time Elye turned away from the workbench for a minute or two, Leyb would ask despairingly—addressing no one in particular—"What am I supposed to do with this guy?"

When God was in a good mood and the sun was shining, Elye would stop working, put down the piece of wood he'd been turning on the lathe, go out into the courtyard, find a box or something to sit on for a while, and light a cigarette. There he'd sit comfortably, wreathed in smoke. This drove Leyb right out of his mind, and he'd go to the window overlooking the workshop, whether one of his daughters was there or not. "Just look at him sitting there. You'd think he was relaxing in his father's vineyard!"

Of course Leyb's reaction was perfectly natural. Here he was going practically blind looking for any job he could lay his hands on, so it wasn't surprising he'd want his employee to do a decent day's work. Still, one question lingered: Why didn't Leyb fire Elye? There were two ways of looking at it, and neither gave a satisfactory answer. If there was no work, Leyb obviously didn't need an employee, but if—with God's help—he survived until the holiday and the work came in, was Elye lightening his load, even a little? Not really—so why keep him around? To that question there was only one answer: the boss kept Elye around because Elye clearly didn't need the work, and given that he didn't need the work, he must have another income. And if he had another income, it would be interesting to know how much and where it was coming from. Was the money enough to make Leyb consider marrying off one of his daughters? Was the worker a rich man in disguise? So, Leyb cautioned himself, he must be patient and suffer in silence.

Sheyndele started preparing the house for the holiday a few days earlier than usual. She threw herself passionately into her work with so much energy you'd think that showing off her youthful agility was her only goal. You could see in her eyes and her expression that she wasn't working so enthusiastically on account of Passover, the holiday everyone celebrated, but on account of her own private holiday—her own private celebration of womanhood, which the onset of spring had awakened in her. Her inner springtime had been buried deep within until the coming holiday suddenly brought it to life, making her eyes shine with a young woman's full, yet untapped, energy.

Without telling anyone, Sheyndele started bustling around the house one morning, and the days preceding Passover descended into their usual chaos and clutter. She got up early and, all in a rush, ran into the wide corridor, which was flooded with dazzling daylight. She stood inside the glass door that led into the courtyard to put on her headscarf and broke into a huge, glorious smile. Her face became one with the joy of the holiday. Youthful innocence radiated from her tender skin as if her whole body had been purified or as if she'd been transported to a higher, more spiritual plane of existence. At the same time, she felt a glow of the pride you often see in the daughter of a respectable family who's busying herself about her home.

Sheyndele was the first one in her family's courtyard to begin the chores that had to be done in the days leading up to Passover. One at a time she hauled boxes and bundles from the house into the courtyard in preparation for a thorough cleaning. Several days later her neighbors joined her with their own household goods, and everyone started beating, dusting, and scrubbing. Every day the courtyard got more and more crammed with beds and bedding, kitchen chairs, tables, and cupboards. All day long you could hear the thumping of carpet beaters. Plumes of dust filled the air, mingling with the vapor rising from the buckets of hot water used for steam-cleaning beds and kitchen furniture. Housewives scoured and flayed the surfaces off whatever tables and chairs had the misfortune to be unvarnished. Young wives, older women, and girls of all ages—even little kids— worked themselves to the bone, filthy with dust, dirt, and mud. They were all wearing their oldest blouses, which had been packed away since the year before—blouses that were again honored to cover the bodies of their owners.

Like everyone else, Sheyndele had decked herself out in her oldest blouse, which, worn and faded as it was, actually suited her. In it she seemed younger, more like a child, a mischievous, charming girl. The blouse made her look shorter in the waist, so it seemed that her lower body had lengthened and grown from her dust-covered ankles up to her waist, and she looked like a little girl wearing an older girl's skirt so people would think she was all grown up.

Sheyndele did the same work that everyone else was doing, but with a charming playfulness that made it seem she was working just for the fun of it. She wielded her beater on pillows and blankets with carefree abandon, waving it teasingly at whoever came near. Every once in a while she glanced at the corridor window as if she were thinking about someone in the workshop on the other side of the glass.

In the midst of all this chaos, Yoshke Futran stepped onto the balcony of his apartment across the courtyard from where Sheyndele was working. Yoshke was the son of a wealthy family. He walked out suddenly, with the breezy self-confidence of a young man who's well provided for, a young man who doesn't work and needn't worry about making a living. The minute he showed his face outdoors, he dropped a few choice remarks down to Sheyndele. That's the kind of guy he was.

Elye, inside in the workshop, heard what Yoshke was saying. He pricked up his ears, and a wash of color played over his cheeks.

Tsilye came to her sister's defense. "You'd be better off if you came down and helped." she yelled up at the balcony. "Aren't you embarrassed, always hanging around with nothing better do?"

A minute later, Yoshke was down in the courtyard. He walked straight up to Sheyndele as if they were close friends, grabbed the beater right out of her hands, and began to smack the pillow that Sheyndele had been beating, watching her gleefully the whole time. Doing housework was beneath him, but he was working for the fun of it, not because there were chores that needed doing. He was beating the pillow purely out of youthful spirits and was proud of his clumsy attempts. As he battered away, he ogled Sheyndele and made faces, wagging his big handlebar mustache up and down and back and forth.

Elye's eyes started to glow. His ears turned red, and his hands, which were holding a chisel to the piece of wood he was turning on the lathe, stiffened and froze. He stood there like a lifelike statue, a worker hacked out of marble, until suddenly he stepped away from the workbench, went out into the courtyard, sat down on a box under the corridor window, and lit a cigarette, watching Yoshke's antics with angry slit eyes like those of a bird of prey just before it attacks.

"So that's where you are!" Tsilye's voice rang out. "Look at him, just sitting there while his work goes to hell. You call that a worker?"

About fifteen minutes later, Leyb left the workshop and stood in the doorway, gazing at Elye and shaking his head ruefully. Finally, he said, "If you don't care that there's work to do before Passover, try putting yourself in my shoes. *My* calendar says the holiday's coming up. It's the middle of the day—how can you turn your back on it all and sit down for a break? It doesn't make any sense! Cut it out! That's enough!" Leyb finished with a poisonous little smirk, and, pointing at Yoshke Futran—who was still pounding away at the pillow—he went on, "Look! Even Yoshke's getting ready for Passover!"

They went back into the corridor, Elye in the lead and his boss trailing. Yoshke Futran, who'd tossed his beater aside, trotted after them into the workshop and contentedly lit a cigarette as if he'd just finished doing an important job. He sat down, made himself at home, and fanned his face with his hand. "Whew! I'm tired right out!"

"What if you had to earn a living like me—twelve, fifteen hours a day—what would you be complaining about then?" Leyb grumbled. Then, as if he wanted to show the lazy do-nothing how hard he worked, the boss went straight to his lathe. He turned the back wheel with the smaller wheel above it back and forth, not full turns, but half forward and half back again. He was fitting a new handle into an old wine tap. As he squeezed the handle into the hole of the tap, it emitted a grating screech, a groaning wail that seemed to describe the cheerless, toilsome life of the family who lived in that house, who'd been living that difficult, joyless life for so many years. Leyb worked almost automatically, the whole time watching his daughters through the window overlooking the courtyard. They were slaving away, veiled by clouds of dust, yelling and carrying on like the other women.

"That's how it goes," Leyb sighed, and a minute later, seeing Sheyndele use her beater to whack the Futrans' maidservant over the shoulders, he banged on the window with a piece of wood and shouted angrily, "Why are you clowning around out there? The hell with you, and the hell with your ancestors too!"

The day before Passover, Elye said good-bye to his boss and his daughters, wishing them a happy holiday. Leyb walked him to the door, saying, "Drop by over the holidays—anytime!"

The sisters didn't invite him back for a visit, thinking that if he wanted to see them, he'd do so on his own, without an invitation. They looked him straight in the eye and smiled, wanting him to see how pleased they'd be to welcome him back as a guest, even though they weren't openly inviting him.

A half hour after the worker left, the apprentice left too. The girls invited him back: "Come by for a visit!" they said in unison.

The first two days of Passover were spent in the holiday atmosphere of cleanliness and peace. The family rested and ate. The first morning, Leyb got up after noon. He'd had a good night's sleep and was bored already. You could tell by the way he yawned, every yawn accompanied with a "khe-khe-khe" or a "kha-kha-kha," as though with each one he were exhaling the two-thousand-year diaspora. He'd worked hard before Passover and was tired of having nothing to do. His limbs, used to constant movement, ached from inactivity, and as for his spiritual being, he took no pleasure in the holiday. He was no small-town Jew whose soul is more than satisfied with Shabbos and the holidays, who takes both physical and spiritual pleasure from the days of rest. Everyone knows religious Jews are never bored on holy days—they have plenty to do to fill the empty hours. But for Leyb, like any person of any nation who's worn out from work, those days were days to rest and nothing more. The spiritual pleasure that pious Jews feel every Shabbos and holiday was nothing to him; his rest was only physical.

Leyb upheld the "thou shalt nots." Like pious Jews, he didn't work on Shabbos or holidays. But he didn't do what pious Jews do when they brush off the obligations of the workweek, and that's why Leyb felt so empty and bored—he had nothing to fill up his empty hours.

The second day of the holiday Leyb took a nap after lunch, and by two o'clock in the afternoon, with the sun still high overhead, he was standing as he normally did in the evenings at the corridor's glass door, looking into the courtyard and yawning hugely. Every time he yawned, his mouth opened so wide that his nose turned up and his eyes filled with tears, brimming like a Havdole wineglass, and his teeth—the missing ones and the rotten ones that remained— bore witness to the fifty-something years of his life and the miseries of his old age.

Leyb stood there, wearing only his trousers, bare feet jammed into a pair of decrepit galoshes that looked their age and bore witness to the wet, muddy seasons they'd seen.

No visitors came. Father and daughters, left alone in each other's company, began to feel like strangers—strangers who knew each other so well it was depressing. The daughters longed for men they hadn't yet met, and Leyb felt estranged from them. They were his daughters, his family, but just now he didn't understand something he understood perfectly well on any other night of the year: why (was it for their sake or his own?) he'd made the sacrifice of not remarrying.

The workbenches, covered with old bedsheets and tablecloths, gave off an air of unhappy boredom. Their being hidden away for the holiday didn't put anyone in a festive mood; rather, it seemed that the bedsheets and tablecloths had stifled the workweek and the usual workaday tumult. And because father and daughters weren't getting anything out of the holiday except resting and eating, and because resting and eating bored them already, they were starting to long for the clatter and noise of the ordinary workdays . . . and also for the stranger, the worker who'd insinuated himself into their everyday lives.

The girls looked forward to seeing Elye. They hadn't invited him to visit over the holiday, but they expected him anyway. They were pretty sure he'd come, though they didn't know when, so they refused to leave the house in case he arrived while they were out.

Having yawned until he couldn't yawn anymore, Leyb went into the kitchen and washed himself. Then he got dressed in his traditional holiday clothes and went out for a walk, thinking he'd drop into a synagogue somewhere for afternoon prayers.

He paced slowly down the street, step by step. He wasn't headed anywhere in particular—he'd just gone out for something to do— and his feet felt uncertain, as if the ground was shifting below them. The bright sunshine made him feel like a stranger newly arrived in the city: he wasn't used to walking the streets in the middle of the afternoon.

When self-employed tradesmen like Leyb venture into the street in broad daylight, they always feel a bit out of place. They live out their lives in the city, but at the same time they feel estranged from it and the people in the streets. The city noises and turbulence are foreign to them. You can pick out such men in a crowd, no matter how well they're dressed: they carry themselves differently, their footsteps are halting, even clumsy. So Leyb, walking down the street in his good holiday clothes, looked a bit pathetic.

He didn't always seem that way. In his own home, wearing his work clothes on regular weekdays, he was full of confidence. There was a sense of intimacy between himself and the six workdays of the week, a kind of belonging, a decades-long peace between himself and his work. He'd gotten used to it, as one gets used to a wife. The work had become a part of him, a piece of his identity, and he'd become part of the work. He felt at home at his workbench, joyful even, if he happened to be working on a high-quality product.

Leyb wandered down the street for quite a while, but since it was still a long time until afternoon prayers, he turned back toward home. As he approached his house, he spotted his daughters sitting on the steps outside the door and yelled at them, "What are you two doing, sitting around like that? Why don't you go out for a walk?"

On the fourth day of the holiday, two guests came to visit: the apprentice and his father. Out of respect for the father, the boy was invited to sit at the table with the boss and his daughters. The girls, amused at the idea of treating the apprentice like a grown-up, smiled at each other. In fact, the apprentice did look a bit grown up with his hair trimmed and the peach fuzz shaved from his cheeks. Now he looked older and more masculine. Before he'd shaved, you could see that all he'd had was a bit of peach fuzz—but now, afterward, you could believe he'd once had a beard.

"If I'd seen him in the street, I wouldn't have recognized him," one daughter remarked.

"Me neither!" said her sister.

The daughters prepared the samovar. This was the first time the apprentice had been in the house when they'd done the job that was normally his. He was given the honor of carrying the samovar to the table, though, and he was pleased to have his old job back—it made him feel more at home. He carried the samovar carefully, at arm's length from himself and his new suit, giving the impression that he wasn't carrying the samovar but rather that it was floating in the air ahead of him, tugging the young man in its wake: a newly hatched young man in a new outfit. The samovar pulled him to the table, placed itself in a brass tray, and released him. There it sat, flaunting itself, the glowing coals at its base making the water in the tank bubble and hiss.

The girls poured tea and put some nuts on the table. The apprentice was thrilled, as though he'd just entered into a new kind of existence—it was quite something to sit at the table with his boss and the two daughters, and with a bowl of nuts on top of it all.

The girls sensed his state of mind and kept urging him, "Have some nuts—don't be shy!"

"Is there still a little wine?" Leyb asked Tsilye.

Yes, there was—there were plenty of treats in the buffet, but Tsilye hadn't put them on the table. She wasn't being stingy, but she didn't know what sort of guests the visitors were, so she treated them as she always treated the casual visitors who dropped in during the holidays and had to be given something. She assumed a glass of tea and a few nuts would do for people like them.

Apart from that, Tsilye was a bit nonplussed that it was the apprentice who'd turned up instead of the man she'd been expecting.

She felt as though the boy, little more than a child, had been sent from the world of men in order to mock her, which made her resent him a little. But at the same time, he was an emissary from the masculine world, and she liked that idea. She was disappointed he'd come instead of the worker, but all in all, Tsilye welcomed the apprentice as someone better than nothing. She was like a hungry infant who wants the breast but instead gets a finger to suck. The finger doesn't soothe the baby's hunger—rather, it stimulates its digestion—but sucking on it makes the baby happy so it hangs on tight and won't let go. Tsilye felt a bit like that—as if the boyish apprentice were some kind of substitute for a man.

The two men, Leyb and the apprentice's father, sat there with nothing to say. Actually, the boy's father did have something he wanted to discuss; he was there not just to exchange holiday greetings but to get Leyb to do something on behalf of his son. There was never enough time during the week, so he'd put the discussion off until the holiday—but now he sat there in silence. He couldn't just come straight out with why he was there, especially on a holiday when he'd been welcomed as a guest.

Leyb, of course, knew the boy's father had come to ask a favor and was waiting for him to come out with it so they could both relax and Leyb would be able to pass time with the other man as if with a family friend. But as long as the boy's father had something to say, a barrier stood between them. They sat together at Leyb's table like strangers, even worse than strangers, and didn't say a word.

"The holiday's half over," Leyb remarked.

"Time flies," the other man agreed, combing his hairy fingers through his thick, rounded beard, neatly trimmed in honor of the occasion.

"Have some nuts," Leyb said. "They're good with tea. And you"—he turned to the apprentice—"what are you sitting there for? Are you waiting for a handout?"

Sheyndele scooped a double handful of nuts from the triangular glass bowl, went over to the boy, told him to hold open his jacket pockets, and poured them in.

"He's growing up," Leyb said. Like any employer, he knew his apprentice's wages depended on his age, and obviously, over the next year or two, the boy would grow up even more.

"Yes . . . but then what?"

The apprentice's father stopped cracking nuts. Crumbling their empty shells between his fingers, he got down to business. To the girls, this was even more boring than before, and each in turn slipped out of the room. The boy got up from the table to stand by the window, where he remained the whole time his father and his boss debated and argued over him, cracking nuts one at a time in his bare hands and eating them. Ten minutes later Tsilye came back in, and, getting her attention with a quick smile and a wink, the boy put a nut on the windowsill and cracked it with his forehead. The nut smashed into pieces, revealing its innermost heart, which looked like a shattered brain.

Passover ended with the beginning of Paska, the Christian Orthodox Easter. Processions of Christians carrying lanterns and candles poured freely into the streets, backed by the power of Christian beliefs and Christian authority. The Christians paid no attention to the many young Jewish people who, while celebrating their own holiday, were drawn into the new festivities and swept along into a foreign Christian world. These temporarily assimilated "children of freedom," as it says in the Passover ritual, let themselves be absorbed into the celebrations, walking among the Christian majority as if they'd lost their independence and their sense of Jewish identity. They mingled with the Christians and their religion, with foreign people in a foreign world.

Among the hundreds of Jews who'd fallen in with the thousands of Christians were Tsilye and Sheyndele. They'd left home that evening to go out into the street, where they blended in with a stream of Christians whose faces and throats, and those of the people on either side, were illumined by the candles in their hands. The sisters, like the other Jews who were pulled along in the wake of the

Christian crowds, weren't carrying candles, and this, they felt, gave away their origins, though their Jewish identities lay hidden deep inside. Outwardly they were part of the closely packed crowd, but inwardly they felt quite separate, as if the crowd were composed of a different kind of human being than themselves. The differences between themselves and the others made them uncomfortable, but they were still glad to be out of the house; their discomfort helped them forget how bored they'd been at home over the holiday, especially over the last day or two.

The church bells were hushed now, and their silence seemed deliberate. At midnight, the darkest hour, the bells would ring out wildly, urgently, to impress upon the assembled devotees that the most important moment of the holy festival had arrived. Now, in the provisional silence, people were quietly filling the length and breadth of the cobbled sidewalks, gravitating to the streets and squares where the churches stood far and near among the houses, their high stone walls crowned with pediments and crosses. Their spires towered above, lost in the vast, dark air, while beneath them tall, narrow windows were illuminated so brightly they didn't even look like lit-up windows, but seemed like sheets of bright, living, translucent color marked into squares by black iron grates. They looked like transparent doors with iron grates forged into a tall, many-storied prison.

Tsilye and Sheyndele were drawn along into one of the churches, where they felt like they'd fallen into an alien, multicolored world—so much brightness, so many candles, and so many people—everything as a whole and each individual detail calling attention to itself with its frightening strangeness. The girls wanted to leave, but there was no escape—they were completely walled in by a densely packed, breathing, motionless crowd. Everything around them was foreign: even the air was different, Christian, too strange and too heavy to breathe.

The girls could hear the priest in some distant place of honor, his mumbling voice sometimes accompanied and sometimes interrupted by a shrill, shrieking choir. The people around them kept trying to stretch out their arms to cross themselves, but they were packed together so tightly they couldn't even reach their own chests. Instead, they piously made the sign of the cross on their foreheads. The sisters, standing right beside them, felt as if their foreheads were being crossed, too.

Tsilye and Sheyndele stood pressed tightly against each other, breast to breast. They looked at each other and smiled, finding comfort and familiarity in each other that they'd never felt in their own home. It was an honest, Jewish comfort.

They got home very late. Their father opened the door for them and lit their way inside with a candle.

The Passover holiday still lingered in the house. Pieces of matzo and a few Passover dishes lay on the table, evoking a melancholy feeling, as though an old grandmother had just died. During her life she hadn't been useful to anyone and nobody needed her, but you miss her a little now that she's dead. The family hadn't gotten a thing out of Passover, aside from lazing around and getting bored, but they were still a bit sad it was over.

Each sister took a small piece of matzo and bit into it. They weren't particularly hungry, but they ate automatically, for comfort and the love of their own holiday.

The church bells rang out, reminding the Jewish tradesman that all around him lies a widespread Christian world full of Christian life and its bells whose ringing inspires joy and passionate devotion in Christian hearts. During Christian holidays, the Jewish tradesman feels even lonelier and more isolated from the outside world. He's more distant from Gentiles than he is on regular working days, and at the same time he's more separate from other Jews, especially the ones who don't work with their hands but run stores and other businesses and so, whether they like it or not, have to close on Christian holidays.

Under the clamor of the church bells, Leyb got up much earlier than he did on holidays and workdays alike. He was dead tired and feeling lazy after eight days' rest: too lazy to stay in bed and far too lazy to work. He got up early so he could have an hour's free time before starting his workday.

He went into the workshop and stood by the glass door that opened to the courtyard. Jaws wide open, he yawned into the rising sun. The morning light stirred the workshop to life; it shone into Leyb's gaping yawn, illuminating a mouthful of neglected teeth, rotted before their time. His eyes, watery from yawning, glittered like glass lenses. The church bells rang continuously, stirring longing, loneliness, and sadness in his Jewish heart. He looked at the covered workbenches and fleetingly recalled the thirty-five years he'd known them. He'd wanted to wash his hands of them at least five times in the past but hadn't been able to manage it.

Leyb uncovered the three workbenches one by one, as though he were unveiling the workweek: three dirty, blackened workbenches. As he lifted their covers, he felt that after a long separation he'd been reunited with something of his own, a piece of his own life. Turning one machine wheel, then another, he felt as though he were touching a part of himself, a part not much loved, but intimate nevertheless. It seemed to him that the holiday, which had come for eight days and then gone, was also one of his own, but it was . . . yes, it was like an aristocrat who condescends to drop in on his poor relatives once in a while, and when he goes back home he leaves behind a lingering discontent: his relatives resent his visit and its ending, too. That's how Leyb felt after the holiday—it had brought both good and bad things into his life, and now that it was over, he missed them both, the good and the bad.

Leyb went into the house and got ready to pray. He wasn't a freethinker, but he was no zealot either. He prayed because his father had prayed and because he himself had prayed all his life, and because in his opinion only aristocrats and boors didn't pray, and because things weren't going so well for him that he shouldn't pray, and also because now, in his old age, it was too late to stop.

Touching the tefillin, which he hadn't held in his hands for eight days, he felt he was touching the workweek, the week that seemed holier than the holiday just then: holier and closer to his heart. Laying the cold tefillin on his bare arm, he felt a biting chill go through his body and, tightening the leather strap, in the early-morning stillness, in the early-morning workday after the holiday, standing among the Passover dishes and the other remnants of the holiday that hadn't been cleared away yet, he began the weekday blessing for laying tefillin: "Blessed are You, Lord our God, King of the universe, who has sanctified us with His commandments and has commanded us regarding the commandment of tefillin."

In the room where the Passover things were still lying around, Leyb stood in his tallis and tefillin, praying the weekday prayer in the weekday style, muttering the words mechanically, without paying attention. Only when the sounds of the church bells carried to his ears did he remember he was in the middle of his prayers, and as if to protest this symbol of Christian piety and Christian foreignness, which stirred a particularly Jewish melancholy in his heart, he began to pray more earnestly.

Later on the apprentice arrived. His boss could scarcely recognize him because he'd changed so much during the eight-day holiday: his lips were plumper, his cheeks pinker. Dressed in his torn old work clothes, he looked like the sun hidden behind a bank of clouds—he glowed like a spring morning, radiating freshness and life. Feeling somewhat awkward on account of his eight-day absence, he looked at the floor and shyly said, "Good morning."

Leyb said nothing to the apprentice about his being late. He understood in an indistinct kind of way that after eight days of rest, the boy would have to be late on the ninth. Actually, his coming to work was a novelty in and of itself: normally he didn't arrive at all, since every other day of the year, aside from Passover, he lived with Leyb's family. Now here he was, coming to work like a regular employee, and that notion made his boss smile.

Pulling off his jacket and cap, the boy laid the belt over the wheel, dampened and oiled it, gave the wheel a turn with the foot pedal, and asked his boss what to do next. Leyb told him that for now, he should get the samovar ready.

The girls got up around noon. Despite having slept more hours than they usually did when they went to bed early, they looked like they hadn't gotten enough sleep—or rather like they'd slept far too long, much longer than they were used to. On this first day of the Christian holiday, they got up feeling depressed, bone lazy, and not in the mood to do anything, even though they had a lot of housework to do. They had to wash all the Passover dishes, dry them, and store them for the next year, and then do everything again in reverse: bring the everyday dishes out of storage and wash, dry, and put away every one of those, too. It was a regular workday, but because it was the first day after the Jewish holiday and the first day of the Gentile holiday, it seemed more difficult than a usual workday, and the girls felt heavy and dull.

The girls walked into the sun-drenched corridor where they looked at each other's tousled hair and the morose expressions on each other's faces. They felt as though they'd brought the night and nighttime sluggishness from their beds in their shadowy rooms into the blinding light. Neither had washed yet, and both were still in their underclothing, their legs practically bare. One of the sisters had jammed her bare feet into a pair of old galoshes spattered with whitewash, and the other wore slippers cut down from a pair of worn-out everyday shoes. They stood at the glass door and gazed through it into the courtyard, their open mouths revealing pale, dry tongues and young white teeth.

"Didn't you get enough sleep?" their father asked sarcastically.

"Have we missed anything important?" Tsilye retorted, and Leyb looked up at the ceiling, remarking, "Someone got out of the wrong side of bed."

"Wrong again," said Tsilye. "It was the right side, actually."

"And what were you doing out so late?" Leyb asked indifferently. As a father, he had to ask, though he knew he wouldn't get an answer.

"Do you really need to know?" Tsilye answered with equal indifference.

"You were in some church somewhere, eh?"

"So what if we were?"

"You know they'll catch you one day. They'll chop you up, grind up the pieces, and burn them. That'll teach you to go sneaking into churches."

Tsilye, paying no attention to her father, stood gazing into the courtyard, watching the people coming and going. Gentile children ran around clutching big pieces of paska, yellow Easter bread, and stuffing their mouths. It was just like the previous day, only then it had been the Jewish children running around with their pieces of matzo.

The girls turned back into the house and surveyed the mess, but neither lifted a hand to do anything. They weren't so much sleepy as despondent. Yawning, each sister poured herself some tea from the Passover samovar into a Passover glass at the Passover table, and it seemed to them that the Jewish Passover had fallen asleep and was sleeping into the workweek and into the Gentile holiday. Or perhaps Passover was dead, lying there like a corpse, and until a person's body is carried out of the house they're both there and not there at the same time.

In the workroom, the week was already under way. It was as busy as usual, though the worker, Elye, hadn't arrived yet. His workbench stood between Leyb's and the apprentice's in stunned, silent immobility, and shavings from the other two workbenches showered onto it like hail on a dead horse.

"For everyone else, Passover's eight days long, but when it comes to me, it's nine," Leyb grumbled. He was thinking of Elye, wondering why the man hadn't arrived yet. The work itself wasn't bothering Leyb, because there wasn't much for Elye to do. What he was really annoyed about was that the worker hadn't bothered to visit during the eight days of the holiday.

After eight days of doing nothing, Leyb felt too sluggish to work. An hour and a half later, he got up from the workbench, shook the shavings from his beard and clothes, went into the house, sat down as he usually did after a full day's work, and watched his daughters, who were finally busy clearing away the holiday things. He watched the workweek taking shape in the house and felt only boredom. From every direction, far and near, he could hear the unceasing clanging and clamor of the church bells. They were no longer tolling with deep religiosity as they had last night at midnight. Now the sounds were different: the bells clanged happily, impetuously, without the order, sequence, or rhythm that rouses faith in the hearts of believers. Now the bells inspired gladness and pride: they summoned the Christian world to the spirit and joy of their holiday.

And here, in Leyb's house (as in the homes of hundreds of other Jewish tradesmen), people ushered out the Jewish holiday and ushered in the workweek, surrounded by the clanging of church bells. They barely felt the subtle pressures of assimilation; they only felt, in a dim sort of way, that the coming workweek was neither here nor there—not a typical workweek, but not a holiday either. The foreign holiday, like a current of water flooding into a poor Jewish house, sapped the will and hands of their strength to work, and people sat there enervated, in a state of suspension, not doing anything but taking no pleasure in idleness. Instead, they felt only an apathetic discontent with their own holiday, which had just ended; with the Gentile one, which was just beginning; and with the coming week, which had just arrived to be met with the joyous sounds of a foreign holiday and a foreign, Christian life.

Nobody bothered to cook lunch. The family ate Passover leftovers with fresh-baked bread and matzo, a couple of cold, stale little kugels, a little borscht (also left over from the holiday and warmed in an everyday pot), and a few chicken cracklings covered with hardened fat, which they smeared on matzo. After lunch, Leyb lay down for a nap, and the two girls disappeared for a couple of hours. Neither Leyb nor the apprentice heard or saw them. They didn't know if the girls were sleeping or sitting quietly, feeling dispirited after Passover and listening to the church bells ceaselessly ringing out their message of jubilation from a foreign Gentile world and life.

The apprentice was working alone in the corridor when Yoshke Futran, the deadbeat, walked in, the son of the Futran family who lived in the upstairs apartment with the balcony. Yoshke, that do-nothing, was dressed up for the holiday: every day was a holi-day for him, whether other people were working or not. The stupid expression on his face and his flushed cheeks gave away the fact that he was drunk, and when he walked up to the apprentice, the boy could smell it on his breath. Yoshke had come on an important mis-sion, one that only a hedonist with too much time on his hands could have thought up. He wanted the apprentice to make something on the lathe for him—something that no decent female should see—so he could sneak it into the handbag of a certain young woman. The apprentice was too embarrassed to take on the job, so Yoshke sat down at Elye's workbench to make the love offering himself. He mounted a piece of wood on the lathe and scraped away with his chisel, but all that happened was that the piece of wood got thinner and thinner until finally it snapped in half, flew into the air, and smashed into the windowpane that overlooked the courtyard.

Just then Elye appeared on the other side of the broken window. He peered into the workshop, discovered Yoshke, and glared at him. Leyb, followed by his two daughters, ran into the workshop, and see-ing Yoshke inside and Elye outside, with the broken window between them, the three of them stood there staring and asking each other what in the world was going on.

Several days passed, and Elye still hadn't returned to work. Leyb nagged at his daughters: "Why don't you talk to him?" It wasn't that Leyb needed a worker—it was already well past the holiday rush—but he was rankled by the man's disappearance and complained over and over, "He knows the trade—he can do the work! He's a good worker!"

Tsilye, the older girl, advised her father to fire Elye. "If there's no work, why do you need him? And if a job comes in, you can always hire someone else."

"So he's obviously smarter than both of us combined. He didn't waste a minute waiting for me to fire him—he just left on his own," Leyb retorted.

On the third day after the holiday, a job did come in: more than a dozen ivory billiard balls, worn and dented, that needed to be restored on the lathe—an exacting job that could be done only by an expert. When the order arrived, Leyb hesitated for a long time—should he take on the job or not?—and then, after the man who'd brought in the order had left, Leyb asked his daughters anxiously, "So what should I do now, eh?"

"What—don't you know how to do the work?" Tsilye asked.

Leyb took offense. "What do you mean? Of course I know how. But what about my eyes? I need to make the balls perfectly spherical—round to a hair's breadth."

"If you already knew you couldn't do the work, you shouldn't have said yes," Tsilye scolded. "You know very well that even if Elye were here, you can't depend on him—not that he *is* here, anyway."

Leyb flared up. "You know very well that I can't see properly, so stop telling me I don't know how."

Sheyndele, who'd been silent up to now, put in her two cents. "So get a pair of glasses."

Like many plain, uneducated men, Leyb couldn't stand the idea of wearing glasses. He glared at his daughters and spoke: "My whole life—fifty-two years—I haven't worn glasses, and now you want me to saddle my nose with a couple of lenses stuck together with wires? Not in my lifetime! Why? Just in case a job like this turns up once in a blue moon? You think I'm a professor, walking around in a pair of glasses?" He lapsed into silence, then added, "I'll wait out the rest of the day, and if Elye doesn't show up, tomorrow I'll send the apprentice back with the balls, and that's that. The hell with the whole business."

"And I'm telling you, he's not going to show up, and there's no point waiting until tomorrow. You may as well send them back right now," Tsilye retorted.

That evening Sheyndele wrapped herself in a shawl, went out to the courtyard gate, and with anxious impatience looked up and down the street, hoping to see Elye. She had the perfect excuse: she wasn't looking for Elye on her own account, but for her father's sake, because he'd taken on a job he couldn't do because of his weak eyes.

If she ran into Elye, she'd tell him that was the reason she'd been hoping to find him.

Sheyndele's face peered out from her shawl, a sweet, still gravity in her eyes. She looked like a young nun pondering a world from which she'd detached herself, turning away from all the pleasures of life.

Fifteen minutes later the apprentice came outside, noticed Sheyndele standing there, and said, "You're looking for Elye, eh?"

Sheyndele eagerly caught her breath. "I am, yes. How did you know?"

"What do you mean, how do I know? I know," the apprentice replied with a sly little smile.

Sheyndele replied apprehensively, "If you happen to run into him, tell him my father needs him—he should come back to work." Then she turned on her heel and went into the courtyard.

Elye showed up the next day. It was early evening, after the workday was finished, so evidently he'd dropped in just to show his face. Leyb was in the workshop, and Sheyndele happened to be there too. When she glanced through the window and saw Elye in the courtyard, she darted into the house. The minute she left the corridor, Tsilye walked in, looking so nonchalant that you'd think she was there just so she could pretend not to notice the worker's arrival.

Tsilye took her time before greeting Elye. "Well, look who's here!"

Elye stood by the door with a childlike smile and an expression of shamefaced innocence. He glanced in turn at the boss and his daughter, clearly suspecting that they'd agreed beforehand to be together when he walked in. The young man cleared his throat once or twice and finally asked Leyb, "Has any work come in?"

Leyb didn't look at Elye, but spoke into the air: "Hmm, so now he wants to know . . . is there work or isn't there? He doesn't have work so he must need some. Of course if he *wanted* to work, he wouldn't have vanished for three days. But if he *doesn't* want work . . ."

One corner of Elye's mouth tweaked in a smile. He made no attempt to defend himself, and Leyb carried on with his little sermon as if he were talking to a third party. "Of course if God helps a person get by so he doesn't need to work, that's all very well and good for him. But what do *I* get out of it? How can I make money off an empty workbench that's just standing there not doing a thing? If a man doesn't want to work, he should tell me straight to my face: 'Hire someone else—I quit.'" Then Leyb turned to Elye and spoke his last words in a high-pitched voice trembling with emotion: "Where's the justice, eh? There's absolutely no justice in this world—not a bit, eh? People just made up the idea that there's justice. Because if there really *were* justice in this world, why can't you give me a little? Even a crumb?"

Elye tried to defend himself—it wasn't his fault; something had happened, and he couldn't come in. Leyb's resentment was already starting to die down, but he kept right on yelling and complaining. "So what happened—where? When? Who stopped you? Your wife or children wouldn't let you come? One of your kids got sick? Your wife got sick? Come on! You're not even married! You don't have a family. Have you ever heard anything like it—he couldn't come? Why on earth not? Do you expect me to believe you?"

Sometime later, Leyb showed Elye the billiard balls, which were lying on a workbench wrapped in a rag. "Look at these—they arrived yesterday. If I'd known you weren't coming, I'd never have taken the job. I thought—well, who knows, sometimes a man gets sick and can't come in. If you'd done that ten years ago, it would have bothered me as much as a cat yowling outside—I'd have put them on the lathe, and that would be that. But now I can't see so well, and I don't wear glasses. It's a good job—what do you think?"

It ended with a handshake and an agreement that Elye would come back first thing in the morning to lathe the billiard balls, but before he left, Tsilye stuck him with one last barb: "You'd better leave us a guarantee."

The next day Elye returned early, even earlier than most workers start their days. He looked fresh, well rested, smiling. Leyb had already gotten up but hadn't gone into the workshop yet. When Elye came in, Leyb flung open a window and said a friendly, cheerful good morning, a smile appearing between his beard and whiskers.

It was a rare bright, sunshiny morning. The air streaming in through the open window carried the freshness of the recently born day and the sweet, delicate warmth of spring in its full, nurturing ripeness.

Elye took off his cap, peeled off his jacket, sat down at the workbench, and got ready for work. His preparations alone required great skill. First he had to drill a round hole into a piece of wood that would hold a billiard ball. The hole had to be exactly round, perfectly smooth, and uniform to a hair—it couldn't be even a shade larger or smaller anywhere, or the billiard ball wouldn't fit, and if it jumped out while it was being worked on, it would be ruined, and that would be twenty-five rubles down the drain because the balls were ivory and very expensive.

Leyb stood in the house in his tallis and tefillin, forgetting his prayers and instead looking through the window into the workshop with a little smile on his face, completely absorbed in Elye's preparations for work. When Elye's preparations were finished and he began his work on the billiard balls, Leyb, still in his tallis and tefillin, went into the workshop and stood off to one side, gazing at Elye with the eyes of a devotee looking at a saint who was performing a miracle.

"Don't hurry. Take your time—there's no rush," Leyb urged, then turned to glare at the apprentice, yelling, "Keep your eyes on your own work!"

Later that morning, when his daughters got up and tried to look through the window into the workshop, Leyb pulled it shut. "The less you stare, the better it'll go."

It took a day and a half to smooth over the fifteen billiard balls, and the whole time the work was going on the house was in absolute silence. Everyone tiptoed around and spoke in whispers. They all felt a kind of lofty seriousness, a reverential awe, as if the high priest in the Temple in Jerusalem were among them, immersed in some sacred ceremony.

When Elye was finished with the billiard balls, Leyb told the apprentice to set up the samovar, and when it was ready Tsilye invited Elye for tea, adding, "You've never been inside our house."

Evidently, father and daughters had agreed beforehand to invite the young man in, because the house had been tidied up for a special occasion, with a white tablecloth spread on the table—but of the two girls, only Tsilye was in a festive mood. Tsilye, who'd consistently agitated against the worker, was all dressed up, while Sheyndele wore her everyday clothes as if she wished to remain in the shadows.

Though it was still broad daylight outside, they lit the lamp in the guest's honor. Leyb took Elye's arm and invited him to sit while Tsilye poured tea and arranged the glasses on the table: four glasses in four places. There was an awkwardness when the family sat down—they didn't seem to know if they should sit in their usual chairs or in different ones. Sheyndele looked particularly uncomfortable, perched on her chair as though she were the guest, as though she, not Elye, was visiting for the first time. Tsilye helped her sister out a little: she took on the role of hostess, and in general seemed much more relaxed in the young man's presence than her sister was.

"So this is the first time you've been in my house," Leyb remarked. "You were waiting for an invitation, eh? Well, that's all very fine and good—and even if you hadn't waited for an invitation, you'd still be a fine young man. It's not like it was in the old days. Other bosses have workers who invite themselves in far too often. But my daughters aren't like those other girls. Tsilye—there she is, my older daughter—if she has something to say, she just comes out with it; she's not embarrassed. And the other one: you can see she's a little more bashful—that's what I figure, anyway. She's so quiet you'd think that she can't even count to two. She takes after her mother, may she rest in peace."

"And what about me? You always say I take after Mama," Tsilye retorted with a coquettish toss of her head.

"Do you want to take after your mother?" Leyb replied. "Go ahead." He turned back to Elye. "They both want to be like their mother. One says she takes after her mother, may she rest in peace, and the other says the same thing. It's only their mother they want to take after. You work yourself to the bone—you sacrifice your life for your children, and they'll begrudge you even this one little thing. Well, never mind . . . it makes no difference to me. You say you take after your mother"—he said to Tsilye—"and so be it." Then Leyb turned to Sheyndele. "And what about you? You don't want to take after your father either, do you?"

"Of course I do," Sheyndele scoffed in a tone that said she wasn't agreeing with her father to please him, but rather to spite him.

Elye stared at Leyb, threw a quick glance at Sheyndele, and with a knowing little smile murmured, "No . . . she's not like you at all."

Tsilye got huffy, as if Elye had given her sister a compliment. She pressed her lips together, then yelled at her father, "So, tell me exactly how I take after you—huh?"

Leyb broke into a laugh and answered, "Who told you that? All I said was that your sister takes after your mother."

"Yes, I know. And you also said I take after you."

Now Leyb was feeling a bit uncomfortable. He turned the conversation back to himself, though everyone knew he was still really talking about his daughters. Heaving a sigh, he said to Tsilye, "Ah, look what old age does to a person. If you'd known me before you were born, you wouldn't be so mad at me. All the girls used to chase me. I was a good-looking man when I was your age." He was trying to compliment Tsilye by implying that since she took after her father, who'd been a handsome young man, she was obviously a beauty too.

After a short pause, Leyb ran his hands through his beard and asked Elye resignedly, "And now what? Just because I'm old and gray, everyone forgets I'm here." He ended with a huge yawn.

While all this was taking place, Yoshke Futran strolled into the workshop, making himself right at home with the easy confidence of someone who doesn't have to work for a living so thinks he can go anywhere and do anything he wants. He set up a little piece of wood on one of the lathes and began to scrape away at it. The apprentice told him to stop—he'd just swept out the workshop and would have to clean up behind Yoshke all over again.

Sheyndele got up from the table and went into the corridor. Yoshke gave her a courtly bow that managed to convey the mocking contempt men like himself feel for lower-class girls. Sheyndele, who'd always received his exaggerated, overenthusiastic salutations with indifference, this time returned his greeting with a joking curtsy of her own and walked over to stand next to him with the casual friendliness a girl shows to a close friend or family member. Sheyndele knew, of course, that Elye was watching from the house through the open window. Her father and sister had also seen her approach Yoshke as if she knew him well, and must have thought her behavior odd. Even the apprentice noticed and thought she was acting that way because she was being watched—or, to be more precise, that she'd cozied up to Yoshke on purpose, just so they'd see.

As for Yoshke, he reacted to Sheyndele's unexpected friendliness by putting a hand on her shoulder and bursting into the love song from Tchaikovsky's opera: "Onegin, I won't hide it from you—I'm in love with Tatyana!"

The apprentice, who felt a particular sympathy for Elye and who hoped the worker would get together with Sheyndele because the boy liked her too—she was always nice to him—didn't care for the way Yoshke was fooling around with his boss's daughter. The only way he could think of to stop him, though, was to bustle between Yoshke and Sheyndele with his cleaning rag to sweep up the splinters Yoshke had made at the lathe. Yoshke, offended by the apprentice's rudeness, pushed the boy back so hard that he almost fell over. The apprentice glared at him. "What makes you think you're so important?" and then added, "I'll tell Elye. He'll rip out your guts." Then he leaned down to clean under the workbench. The minute he bent over, Yoshke kicked him right in the face.

The apprentice yelled and practically passed out. He straightened up with warm blood gushing from his nose, and an instant later Leyb, Tsilye, and Elye had dashed out of the house and into the workshop. Yoshke tried to defend himself: he hadn't meant any harm; he'd just wanted to tease the apprentice by poking him with his foot. But he didn't have time to finish his story. Elye grabbed Yoshke's lapels with one hand, gave him a few hearty smacks with the other, and shoved him out the door. Then Elye left too, without a good-bye, walking away with long, hasty strides.

Sheyndele fussed over the apprentice for a long time. She gave him cold water to snort up his nose, and later, when the bleeding had stopped, she kept hugging and patting him, her eyes damp with sympathy. "You hate him—Yoshke—don't you? Do you hate him?"

"Yes," the apprentice answered.

"And who do you love? Is it Elye—is that right?"

"Yes," the apprentice answered. "And I thought you loved him too."

Sheyndele was silent a few minutes, and then, her voice trembling, she ventured, "But Yoshke's better looking, isn't he?"

"Sure—but Yoshke doesn't love you."

"No? How do you know? And what about Elye?"

"Elye loves you."

"How do you know—is that what he said?"

"No, he never said. But I can tell."

"That's not true. You're wrong—he's in love with Tsilye." Sheyndele uttered the words in the tone of a judge handing down a sentence that was distasteful even to himself. She flounced off, went into the courtyard, and sat down on one of the two steps that led down from the door.

She sat there until late into the night, hunched over as if she were trying to curl into herself, to hide her womanly feelings from the night and the darkness and the moon, which swam out into the middle of the yard around eleven o'clock, pouring its wan light onto walls and windows and into the empty places that divided one wing of the courtyard from the other. Sometime later, the Futrans' servant girl came out and sat down beside her. In a piercing whisper, as if she wanted to be heard and not heard at the same time, the maid began to bad-mouth Yoshke—he was constantly bothering her; he never left her alone for a minute; she couldn't hang enough locks on her door to keep him out at night. And she was, she said, speaking for Sheyndele's own good when she declared, "Believe me, I'd rather have no job and nothing to eat on Shabbos but a piece of bread than put up with it all. When they think you're only a maid, they turn into animals. They can do whatever they like to you."

Far off in the distance, but clear as crystal, the city clock struck midnight. Each clang rang out into the silence and hung trembling in the air until the next strike of the bell drowned it out. The twelfth and final clang faded slowly into a melancholic, whimpering reverberation as if it were whooshing into infinite space in search of its eleven wandering brothers who were lost in that vast, silent ocean of air. And when the last tremulous clang finally faded, the silent night was more silent yet. It was as if midnight had ushered in the true time of silence, and only now was the nighttime silence beginning.

A door opened on the far side of the courtyard—the door that led upstairs to the Futrans' apartment—and an indistinct human form appeared, detached itself from the shadows around the entranceway, and after a short hesitation came striding across the courtyard toward Sheyndele and the servant girl. Sheyndele stood up and went into her house, leaving the servant girl sitting on the steps. When Yoshke came up to her, he said politely, "I've just come to tell you it's time to go up to bed. It's very late."

"None of your business," snapped the girl. She got up and walked away as Sheyndele had just done, leaving Yoshke behind in the courtyard with just the moon for company.

Elye had vanished again. This time, as though he'd never existed, no one so much as mentioned his name. However, the girls looked so woebegone it was plain to see they hadn't forgotten their father's employee—in fact, they obviously missed him. They were so bored and miserable, they didn't know what to do with themselves.

Once, when their father was out in the courtyard on some errand or other, the sisters fell into conversation. There was no point in staying with their father, they agreed, living under his roof, eating at his table, and just waiting around for a husband to turn up. "Papa thinks he's doing us a big favor by supporting us," argued Tsilye. "If only he'd sent us out to work in a factory, we'd have been a thousand times better off. Factory workers meet other young people; they get together. But here—who comes here? Who sees us—who knows us? Even if you were the most beautiful woman on earth, what does it matter if no one ever sees you? I think even the Futrans' servant girl has it better than we do. The Futrans have visitors, and maybe one of them will fall in love with her."

"Look, you know Elye's in love with you," Sheyndele said unhappily. "What more do you want?"

Tsilye was silent for a while, and then, hesitating a little, replied, "You've said so before, but I don't see it. And even if it's true, what good would it do me?" She fell silent, then added as if to herself, "I could say the same thing about you."

"What?"

"I could say it's *you* he's in love with."

"What makes you so sure?" Sheyndele retorted.

"What makes you think he's in love with *me*? I think it would be easier for someone to fall in love with you than with me." Tsilye fell silent, and a few minutes later she asked, with real curiosity in her tone, "Do you like him?"

"No," Sheyndele said sharply. "I like Yoshke."

"Really? Does Yoshke like you back?" Tsilye asked.

"I don't know," Sheyndele answered, her voice tight.

Tsilye heaved a deep sigh and said, "If I were you, I'd have had Yoshke eating out of my hand ages ago." Then her eyes filled with tears. She turned away from Sheyndele and stared into the emptiness of the wide, bright corridor.

Almost two weeks after Elye had vanished, a customer came in with a substantial order—a consignment of stair balusters—for three hundred rubles. This was an unexpected windfall: so much work and so much profit, not to mention fifty rubles' down payment on the spot.

Leyb and his daughters had a huge celebration. Only one thing disturbed the holiday mood: the job had to be done by a deadline that Leyb and the apprentice wouldn't be able to meet on their own, so whether they liked it or not, they'd have to consider taking on an additional worker.

"What should we do?" Leyb asked Tsilye in a worried tone. He was thinking about his vanished employee.

"How would I know? Do whatever you think you should."

"So now, all of a sudden, you don't know," Leyb fired back. "Other times you stick your nose in whether you need to or not, but this time you have no opinion?"

Now Sheyndele stepped in. "Why are you chasing after Elye? If you're having problems with him, you can always hire someone else. Get the wood ready and do whatever else needs doing, and if he doesn't show up on time . . .'"

Leyb, who wasn't interested in Sheyndele's opinion, interrupted his younger daughter: "But what do *you* think, Tsilye?"

"As far as I'm concerned, you should fire him right now and hire someone else," Tsilye said, only to be cut off by her sister. "That's not true, Papa! Papa, that's not true! That's not what she wants! She wants Elye to work here—that's what she really wants!"

Leyb patted Sheyndele's cheek. "Do you really need to tell me? You think I don't know? Of course I know! Why do you think I put up with him? If I hadn't known, I'd have thrown him out ages ago."

Sheyndele was dumbfounded. "You knew all along? What did you know?"

"You two think your father's nothing but a fat, ignorant slob, don't you? Well, you should trust me more." Leyb fell silent, and then, looking pensive, said, "But how will it all turn out? Do you even know where he is—who he is? That young man's a complete mystery." He paused, then added, "But I don't want to interfere. I won't make any promises. I know you feel that . . . how can you understand? If it's what you want, I can put up with him a while longer, and if it's not, I'll hire another worker tomorrow."

Tsilye made no reply. Leyb glanced with a smile at Sheyndele, and murmured as if to himself, "Well, never mind. Time will tell. I'm going out to buy supplies. If he doesn't show up tomorrow, we'll have no choice—we'll have to hire somebody else." He put on his good coat, picked up his walking stick, clapped Tsilye playfully on the shoulder, and said, "Don't worry, God will help us! A few more big jobs like this one, and we won't have to worry about a thing!" And off he went.

A few hours later, two enormous cart horses with a man leading them by the bridle nosed through the gate into the courtyard. Eight heavy hoofs clopped resoundingly on the cobblestones as if counting themselves off one at a time, and behind the lumbering hooves rolled four massive wheels under a huge wagon loaded down with long pine planks, and behind the wagon walked Leyb, wearing his Shabbos best with his walking stick in his hand. Only his cap, which was pushed back over his forehead, gave him something of an informal look.

The wagon driver began to throw down planks one by one. Each length of wood hit the ground with a bell-like, resounding clatter that reverberated through the courtyard, each clatter a statement of the boss's new status: the wood he owned, the important job he was about to do, and the profits that would soon come his way. You got the sense that with this fresh opportunity—this enormous order—the life of Leyb the lathe operator was about to veer off in a new direction. Tsilye and Sheyndele stood next to their father, not speaking but smiling happily, and with every clang a plank produced as it clattered onto the growing pile of hard, dry wood on the ground, their smiles grew more radiant. Tsilye held her father's cap and used a handkerchief to blot the sweat from its damp sweatband, and when that was done she wiped her father's forehead while Sheyndele amused herself with one of the horses, stroking its muzzle with her fingertips, enjoying the silky softness under her hands.

"Look at this—see how smooth it is," she said to her sister with childlike artlessness.

It was then that Elye chose to make his appearance. Leyb and his daughters, as if by previous agreement, pretended they hadn't noticed him enter the courtyard. As the three of them stood there, frozen in place, they looked like pieces on a chessboard after a player has finished his turn and left them that way. Sheyndele had a slight advantage over the other two. She was still standing in front of the horses and patting their noses, and from her position, partly hidden by their bodies, she may not have seen Elye arrive and walk toward them. That, however, was impossible for the other two. Not only could they see anyone entering or leaving the courtyard, but they certainly couldn't fail to recognize someone as familiar as Elye. As for Elye, the frozen tableau of the three people and the horses made him smile, and so he could enjoy the sight of them standing there, ignoring his presence, he retreated a few paces to watch. Who knows how long this game of blind man's bluff would have gone on if the apprentice, who was also in the courtyard, hadn't shouted, "Look who's here—it's Elye!"

Leyb gave Elye a sidelong glare and said sarcastically, "We have a visitor! Greetings! What have you got to say for yourself?"

"I see some work's come in," Elye replied, a bit confused by Leyb's reception.

"Yes, so?" Leyb snapped, then suddenly he flared up. "Do you have any idea, Elye, what I'd like to say to you? Don't hold it against me—but go work somewhere else. I've had enough. You're too hard to get along with, and I'm done with you. I'll be honest, Elye: I can see by the way you work that you don't need to work and you don't like working. The way I see it, you can get along without working. So what do you want? I have no idea. This whole situation isn't going anywhere, so it's time to say so long and take care of yourself. It's like the way people avert the evil eye: 'I don't know where you came from, and I know even less where you're going.' We're through. I won't hold anything against you, and I don't think you should hold anything against me, either."

Elye stood there gaping at Leyb like a defendant in court who listens, stunned, as the judge hands down a heavy sentence. In the meantime, a tremendous banging and clattering arose as the two cart horses started maneuvering their massive bodies, turning the huge, empty wagon toward the gate so they could leave the courtyard. As they ponderously set off, Elye tore himself away and strode behind the slowly moving wagon as if he belonged with it. But when it had vanished through the gate and the worker had almost disappeared from sight, Sheyndele, with burning cheeks and fiery eyes, dashed after him, grabbed his arm, and pulled him back.

Elye stood there like he was chained to the spot, and, looking down at Sheyndele, he drew a deep breath and in an unsteady voice said, "Sheyndele, let go. It's better this way. Let me go. Let go!" At the same time, despite his own words, Elye took Sheyndele's hands in his own and held them in a tightening grip, drawing her strongly to himself. She tried to pull back and step away from him, but he moved toward her, trying to tug her closer, his face growing paler with every passing second. His wide eyes bore an expression of resolve and submissiveness, spirit and humility at the same time, while he kept murmuring, hardly knowing what he was saying. "Let go. Let go!"

Now it was Tsilye's turn to get involved. She'd stood there the whole time like a third wheel, as if she didn't care a bit whether Elye stayed, but now she said to Sheyndele, her voice sullen, "Why are you begging like that? Just look at you, schlepping him by the arm. If he wants to go, let him go—some other boss will get a bargain. You'd think he was the only worker in the world."

Then Leyb came up, and, like a neutral arbitrator, someone who doesn't take anyone's side, he said to Elye, "You've come to work, right? Not just to say, 'Good Shabbos.' So why stand on ceremony? Take off your jacket and get to work." With this announcement, Leyb grabbed Elye's jacket sleeve with both hands and began to yank it down his arm. Elye helped his boss pull off the jacket, and throwing it over his left arm he went into the workshop.

Elye worked for two weeks straight without a break. On the last day, the day the job was due to be finished, Leyb's family celebrated with a late lunch to which Elye was invited. It was a big party for a big job, with a net profit to Leyb of around two hundred rubles.

A few hours earlier, well before quitting time, Leyb had clapped Elye on the shoulder and announced, "Elye, today you're going to have lunch with us!" The girls must have known even earlier, because even a stranger could have told by their vigorous bustling in the kitchen and the celebratory, rapid-fire clattering of plates an hour and a half before lunchtime that they were cooking a meal for somebody special.

Tsilye had dropped into the workshop a few times that day, cheeks pink and eyes shining, the picture of one of those respectable daughters who stays home to cook lunch while her mother's off in the synagogue. But Sheyndele hadn't put in an appearance, and the men in the workshop hadn't even heard her voice in the house. Only once did she quietly step over to the window overlooking the corridor and glance at Elye, but all she could see as he stood at his lathe was his back—his unseeing back that was turned to the window. Sheyndele's expression was wistful, as if she were sorry Elye hadn't even noticed she was there, that his back had no eyes to see what was happening behind him.

While the family and their guest were eating lunch, Tsilye went into the workshop, handed the apprentice a ten-kopek coin, and told him to run out for a siphon of soda water. "Tsilye," the boy remarked, "look at you—you're shining like the morning star!" It was true. But oddly, despite the fact that Tsilye and her sister looked as different from each other as day and night, their thoughts just then had a great deal in common.

The apprentice returned with the siphon. Leyb drew himself and his guests half a glass of soda water each, and raising his own he said, "Lehayim! To life! To health, wealth, and happiness!" Of course, only people who've already had a drop or two can jokingly propose a toast over a glass of soda water. Leyb had already had quite a few "drops or two," which was plain to see in his flaming cheeks—half covered by the hair of his beard—and his squinting eyes that, in spite of his poor vision, were lit up with joy.

Leyb downed his soda water and turned to Elye with a friendly smile. "And as for *you*, only the devil knows who you are. You've been working here four months already. That's how long I've known you, and I don't know you at all. But never mind—I trust you anyway. And why's that? Who knows? Even I don't know—I don't have the faintest idea! You know, if a man happens to be a crook—a thief, let's say—he'll try to hide it. But it's the exact opposite with you—you're afraid to admit you're a respectable man. Am I right, Elye? What do you say?"

Elye picked at the label on a box of matches, all the while smiling cheerfully. Tsilye looked from her father to Elye and back again, her face shining with secret, happy anticipation. Sheyndele sat at the table as if she weren't part of the family but a stranger who'd wandered in by accident. She wore an expression of intense boredom.

"Say something, Elye. Don't be afraid," Leyb pressed on. "You're a fine young man—I know that. So why so quiet? Out with it!"

"All right," smiled Elye.

"So, I've finally wormed something out of him—God be praised! Now answer me this: Why are you sitting there like butter wouldn't melt in your mouth? You're no fool, and there's no need to act like we're strangers. Do you feel like a stranger here? Do you think it's nothing but the whiskey talking through me? No, you're wrong, Elye. For a long time now, I've wanted to talk to you the way I'm talking now. *So what do you want to say*, you're asking me? Why haven't I said it yet—and why now? Well, it's an old story, and maybe this *is* the whiskey talking. But I've been waiting a long time to tell you this. And besides, since God has seen fit to send me—no evil eye—more than a little bit of work, a good two hundred rubles are about to fall into my lap, and you know a man with money feels better, he's in a better position, he can afford to say what's on his mind . . . so what do you have to say about that, eh?"

"I think so too," Elye agreed.

There was a long pause. Then Leyb gave a half-serious chuckle. "What a scoundrel you are! You know why I say that? Because . . . you want to know why? If a man's a scoundrel and hides it, he really is a scoundrel. But a good man who hides his goodness is an even bigger scoundrel than the real one."

"Papa, you're not making any sense," said Tsilye, getting up from her chair. Her father looked at her for some time, nodding and stroking his beard.

"Not making sense, eh? Do you think I really think he's a scoundrel? Would he be sitting here at my table if that's what I thought? I'm just speaking the truth—I'm telling him what's on my mind."

Tsilye and Sheyndele started clearing the table. Every time they went back to the kitchen with a load of dishes, they stayed away longer. While they were out of the room, Leyb relaxed more and more, and he looked less and less happy whenever they came back, until at last he snapped at them: "How long are you going to hang around?" Then he jerked his head at the apprentice and said, "And you, what are you doing here? Are you looking for something?"

The boy returned to his workbench, but from the window he could hear the entire discussion: everything the boss said to Elye and Elye's occasional, terse answers.

"What's going to happen, Elye?"

"What do you want to happen?" Elye replied.

"How long will this go on? It's got to end sometime."

"What has to end?"

"What do you mean, what has to end? As if you don't know. Do you think I don't know? I'm telling you, I know. I've been around a while."

"What do you know? I don't know what you know." Elye sounded a little uneasy.

"Listen, Elye! If I tell you I know, I know! If I didn't know, I wouldn't talk about it. I know that these days, when it comes to these things, a father shouldn't get involved. Today's children aren't like previous generations."

"I have no idea what you're talking about, Reb Leyb." Now Elye sounded thoroughly confused.

"Do I need to draw you a picture? And how do I know you won't tear it up?" There was a lengthy silence. "Listen, Elye—they know I know everything. Yes, I know everything, and it all depends on you. She's ready and waiting. Are you listening to me? She told me herself."

"Reb Leyb!" Elye exclaimed, a strange, joyous tone in his voice, and Leyb cut him off: "Shhh, quiet, not so much noise! Sit down, relax, I'll call her in now, and what I've started, you'll settle between yourselves. Just be quiet, take it easy, and we'll count our lucky stars. . . . Tsilye!"

Three days later a new employee was installed at Elye's workbench. He was an insignificant, almost boyish looking man, but because he was a fully qualified worker, not an apprentice, he gave off an air of smug self-satisfaction. His manner at the lathe was casual: he joked around and constantly sang silly ditties, and his joking and singing trivialized and cheapened the family and their home. Just the sound of his voice was common and vulgar. You almost felt sorry for the old man, standing at his lathe next to the youngster, who was forced to listen to his warbling. The newly hatched little worker brought an unfamiliar atmosphere into the house, and the fact that the father and his daughters felt estranged from each other seemed to be his fault.

For days now, the family had barely spoken. The more the slight young man filled up the length and breadth of the corridor with his yodeling, the quieter and more repressed the family became. Almost every time he broke into his full-throated song, the windows slammed shut one at a time.

There, behind the dark, closed windows, the daughters of the house tiptoed around in silence, having shut themselves in with the unspeakable, shameful tragedy that had played out just a few days ago. From time to time you could hear the footsteps of one or the other—the quiet, sad sounds made by two people silent together in the same room who want no one to know how silent they are.

It was hard to decide which of the girls was more miserable. But though neither spoke, it still seemed that Sheyndele's silence was deeper somehow, more heartfelt. Her darting eyes were those of a trapped animal, alone and desperate. As for Tsilye, she gave off an air of lethargic despondency, a kind of listless exhaustion. She seemed to have grown several years older during the past few days.

Things improved after a while in that the sisters finally left the house where they'd shut themselves up, but they went no farther than the corridor or the short staircase before the door, where they'd sit for hours on end sewing or doing some other household task.

Leyb kept an eye on his daughters and spoke to them now and then, but it was clear that something was bothering him and he'd call over to them, "Why don't you go out for a little walk? Have you ever seen girls doing nothing but sitting at home?" And the boyish new worker kept right on whooping it up:

I once had a friend, a lawyer friend,
Who impounded my little machine,
The machine I used to rent.
What kind of machine? My sewing machine!
The one that helps me sew,
Whose wheels turn 'round as they go.

"Can't you sing a little quieter?" said Leyb with a fierce scowl.

The family's peace was unexpectedly interrupted by a shocking scandal, as if a thunderbolt had fallen from the sky into their midst. In fact, the thunderbolt did actually fall from above—from a strange, unfamiliar house, a house where people lived a strange, unfamiliar life quite foreign to Leyb the lathe operator and his daughters. That's where the scandal occurred, and the news was brought by the servant girl who worked there, in the Futrans' house upstairs, where Yoshke lived with his parents.

Early one evening the servant girl burst into Leyb's house and flung herself on Sheyndele like a mad dog burst free of its chain. It was a long time before the sisters could get her to say what had happened. Every time Tsilye dragged the servant girl away from Sheyndele and told her to explain the whys and wherefores, the servant girl, snarling with venomous hatred, wriggled away and pounced on Sheyndele again, while Sheyndele just stood there piteously, pale as a freshly plastered wall and trembling, literally trembling, unable to utter a word except for the occasional, almost inaudible, "What? Why are you . . . ?"

Eventually, the servant girl burst into tears and wails about the terrible thing that Yoshke Futran had done to her, and Sheyndele collected herself enough to ask why she, Sheyndele, was to blame. The servant girl answered rudely, "You—it's all your fault! He would have married me! I would have shown him . . . and I *will* show him . . . but he says he's in love with you and you're in love with him, too."

"Well, and so what, even if you're right?" Tsilye interrupted. "How does that make Sheyndele guilty? You came here once to ask her advice about Yoshke, and she listened to you, and now here you are with your problems. Who told you to be such an idiot?"

Suddenly, Sheyndele grabbed Tsilye's hand and pulled her away from the maid. Her face white, her legs trembling under her, she asked the girl, "Did Yoshke tell you, or did you figure it out yourself?"

"Figure out what?"

"That Yoshke and I are in love."

"Of course he told me. If he hadn't told me, how could I have known? And why else would I be here—what else have I got against you?"

"Tell Yoshke I said he's a liar."

Tsilye broke in again. "Why? Why are you so scared of her? You don't owe her anything. Is it your fault she's stupid?"

"Tell him," said Sheyndele stiffly, measuring out her words like an automaton, one at a time. "Tell him I said he lied to you."

"But I know it's true!" Tsilye broke in. "I know it is!"

"Tsilye, you don't know a thing."

"What are you talking about? You told me yourself!"

Sheyndele's face twisted with effort. She took a deep breath and said, "Listen, Tsilye. I'll tell you one more time why I said that about me and Yoshke and why I wanted you to believe me. But"—she pointed at the servant girl—"it has nothing to do with her, and she doesn't need to know the details. All she needs to know is that I've never been in love with Yoshke and I don't think he's ever loved me either—and even if he *did* ever tell me he loved me, that's what all young men say to girls, and I never paid any attention. He probably said the same thing to you"—here she turned to the servant girl—"but I never encouraged him by showing any interest in him, and I don't think he thought I *was* interested. I think he lied to you about him and me just so he could get away from you. So tell him I told you he's lying, and if he doesn't believe you, I'll tell him to his face."

The girl left just as furious as when she'd arrived. Just a few minutes later, a frightful racket could be heard from the Futrans' upstairs apartment. One after another their windows slammed shut, but that wasn't enough to muffle the uproar—even through the closed windows, you could still hear yelling and screaming. At one point the servant girl ran onto the balcony, shouting, "I don't care if it kills him—or me! It's *me* he'll get married to!" Then Mrs. Futran, Yoshke's mother, ran out and dragged her back inside.

Tsilye and Sheyndele stood there in the half-dark corridor workshop watching the drama, and finally Tsilye said, "Respectable people know what's what. He'll never get away from her. Believe me, she's done a better job of it than either of us did, and that goes for other girls like us, too."

"Do you envy her?" Sheyndele asked.

"What do you think? If you think I'm any less humiliated than she is, you're making a big mistake."

Sheyndele sat down at one of the workbenches, propped her elbows on the machine, and buried her face in her hands. She didn't cry—it was even worse than that. She shook all over as though she were having a fit, and only after a while did she break into soft sobs so heartrending you'd think she'd been born an orphan. She looked like an orphan, too: the sole survivor of a large family or the last person on earth. Tsilye gazed at her sister in shocked surprise, and as she looked, something slowly dawned on her, a realization that grew more and more horrifying. Eventually, she bit down hard on her lower lip, as if trying to hold in the terrible secret she'd just discovered. Slowly, silently, she walked over to Sheyndele and laid a hand on her shoulder, and just as slowly she silently gazed into Sheyndele's face, still half-buried in her hands: one tragic mask gazing at another. "Sheyndele?" There was no answer.

A few minutes later, Sheyndele got up from the workbench, went into the house, and came out again wearing her shawl. She walked through the corridor like a woman tired beyond exhaustion, went out into the courtyard, and sat down on one of the two little steps in front of the door. Tsilye put on her own shawl and followed her sister, leaving the workshop with the lost expression of a refugee who's discovered for the first time that, though she can't stay where she is any longer, there's nowhere else she can go. Step by careful step, her posture stiff, she set off for the gate to the street, but after a few steps she turned and walked back, now with the defeated look of a person returning home because she has no other choice. Slowly and carefully, she sat down next to Sheyndele, and in a trembling voice she murmured, "Why did you do it? Why?" She paused, then added, "At least *you* could have been happy." She looked as though she were about to cry.

Section 6

Myself

Like many authors past and present, Rosenfeld occasionally reflects on his own role as an artist: a perceptive witness of his fellow human beings and reteller of their stories.

Isaac Hershenhorn, the narrator of "The Layabout," is a flaneur, an observer who wanderers through society but remains detached from it. He is also a writer, like Rosenfeld himself, who lives in his own world but is deeply engrossed in his art and sensitive to the relationship between himself and his readers.

In "The Literati," the final story in this collection, Rosenfeld imagines his own funeral and, with a good measure of self-deprecating satire, considers his legacy to Yiddish literature. In the opinion of his fictionalized colleagues, his stories were good, but not *that* good—and definitely (as some of Rosenfeld's real-life critics complained) too long-winded. One fictional colleague, recollecting a previous conversation with the now-deceased Rosenfeld, remarks that the author admitted a particular story (probably the one appearing in this collection as "Behind the Veil")[1] was too long and offered a surprising reason for its wordiness: it was "for the critics"—those snarky Yiddish reviewers who, in

1. The Yiddish title of "Behind the Veil" is "Hinter a Shlayer," rendered parodically in the Yiddish original of "The Literati" as "Hinter di Shayern" ("Behind the Barns"). For "The Literati," I translated "Hinter di Shayern" as "Behind the Bale."

Rosenfeld's opinion, seize on a story's one fault and ignore its strengths. The story ends with a plaintive lament that seems to sum up Rosenfeld's feelings about his own difficult life: "Wouldn't it be better if we all had a little more respect for each other while we're still alive?"

The Layabout

A long time ago, someone told me that writing comes from laziness—in other words, walking around with nothing better to do. He put it simply: "If my head were as empty as yours, I'd be a writer too."

I don't know how true that is, but I do know it's true I'm a layabout—and also a writer. I'm not choosy. I write articles for the newspapers, and once in a while I'll send in something witty, but at the moment I'm interested in writing a story. Whether it'll work out or not—I'll decide that later, once I've finished. I have nothing to lose; I've got the time, and writing will save me the trouble of walking the streets. I'm so tired of these streets! It seems like everyone's watching and pointing their fingers: "There goes the layabout!" The storekeepers in particular must know me—they're always standing in their doorways, damn them to hell!—but do you think they ever stop me to ask if I want to buy anything? Picture this: a woman's sitting in the street outside her shop door until late spring, warming herself by a brazier, a woman with a pregnant belly and red, watery eyes, a woman who won't let a single, solitary soul walk by without trying to drag him into her store—and even *she* doesn't take the trouble to lure me inside. I have to admit, that bothers me more than anything. . . . On the other hand, though, when I think of it, maybe it's not so surprising—she knows me, so she knows I don't need anything she has to sell . . . but that in itself annoys me. Why does she have to know me? So as soon as I get a few steps from home, I pick up my pace. Let everyone think I'm going somewhere on business.

As you, my dear reader, will soon see, my story's going to be about me—that is, I'll be its hero. I'll describe myself. I don't think it

makes any difference to readers whether the author describes somebody else or his own self. The story needs only to be interesting. I
can't be certain, but it seems to me I'm a very interesting subject. I'm
thinking of calling my story "Notes of a Layabout"—and no matter
what you might think about that, right now, sitting here at my desk, I
feel pretty good about my profession. I can honestly say there's something original in me, something particular to myself, and no clerk or
tradesman—or anyone who spends all their time working for a living—can be what I am, or what many others like me are.

Perhaps that man was actually right—the one who said you need
an empty head to be a writer. You tell me: Is anyone as impression-
able as a layabout? Who else notices every little thing, whether or not
it's of interest? Not a single sound escapes my ear; everything I see
and hear sinks deep inside me, finds its distorted mirror image in my
mind, and settles down for a long stay.

Imagine this trifling event. I was walking past this house—I'd
been walking past the same house for about four years already—and
this one time I saw a young woman in the window. She was weeping. She wasn't making a sound—her tears poured down in silence.
She must have been hiding from her family. It was autumn. Clouds
hung low over the houses; the ground was black, deep in mud. It
wasn't raining, but from time to time a cold drop fell on my face,
and I couldn't tell if it was falling from the sky, the telegraph wires,
or the leafless trees above . . . or maybe the air itself was weeping icy
tears. Now you tell me: What's going on? A young woman's standing there crying. Who cares? She's a stranger—I didn't know her or
anything about her. If I'd known the woman was crying because she
didn't have anything to eat, or because her husband had insulted
her, or because—who knows what makes a woman cry?—I wouldn't
have been so affected. But her tears weren't for those reasons. Who
knows how many such tears are shed in silence, with not a single
soul ever knowing about them? The tears a woman cries in front of
other people are water; the tears she cries on her pillow at night are
blood. . . . But that's enough about the woman.

They call me Isaac. My family name is Hershenhorn. I'll tell you
right now that both names are made up, but that shouldn't bother
anyone. I'm of middling height, neither tall nor short. I'm twenty-
three years old. I was on the verge of being drafted three times but
got out with a medical exemption. I have a long, narrow face, but I
look young, almost boyish. My cheeks are always flushed, my face
bright red from my cheekbones to my ears—small ears, set lower
than other people's, almost at my neck. I have thick black hair shorn
down to my scalp. I shave my beard and mustache, and I trim my
sideburns short in the English style. Sometimes when I'm in the
mood I let them grow. Then, after I shave, no one recognizes me,
and I find that amusing. I dress in the latest fashions: a coat with two
buttons done up, a collar with a long handmade bow tie, shoes in the
American fashion, and flared trousers.

My father runs a tavern; he's friends with the security constable
at the post office. When the weather's bad, the constable comes over
to our place, pulls himself up to the counter, and strikes up a conversation. My father never has much to say, so when the two of them get
together I have no idea where all the words come from. I should also
point out that when his friend is over at our place, my father won't
say a single word in Yiddish, even to his family—anything he has to
say, he says in Russian, and we have to answer in Russian, too. But
after our "noble guest" has had a drop or two, everything livens up.
The constable curses his own people; he enumerates their various
failings and says that the best, most upright, and finest people are
Jews. And my father says just the opposite. Christians, he says, are
good people, but Jews make him angry enough to spit. He describes
how Jews fight with each other: one man takes food out of someone else's mouth; a second betrays someone; a third wants to drown
someone else in a spoonful of water. The constable doesn't understand this last, purely Yiddish, expression, and he innocently asks,
"Can you drown in a spoonful of water?"

My father started to hate Jews when one of them opened a beer
hall across the street from us and lured away many of our clients, in

particular the railroad employees who were the source of a lot of my father's income. The reason they crossed the street was that my father refused to buy their goods, things they'd stolen from the trains.

I don't have a mother. She died when I was just a little kid. Oddly enough, though, there's a picture of her somewhere deep inside my brain, like a negative that developed I don't know how long ago. I think she was taller than average, fine-boned with a long face and black eyes. It's possible that this picture appeared in my brain when I was a baby at her breast. When I tell my father I remember my mother, he laughs at me. He says I wasn't even a year old when she died. Why does he think it's so funny? I can even remember how she died—to this day, I have an eerie feeling of dread somewhere inside.

But more than anything else, my father hates it when I tell him I remember the great fire. Then he loses his temper—how can I remember that, he says, when I hadn't even been born yet? My mother was only in her seventh month with me. But I remember it all the same. I shouldn't say "remember": rather, I feel it physically, like something unique, something horrifying; there's a dull, wordless fear sitting somewhere inside me, stamped deep into my soul. Sometimes, when I immerse myself in this vague feeling, I can even see the flames, not just red ones, but black ones too. In a vast area of the sky, over the roofs of unfamiliar houses, I see the fluttering of black rags.

It goes without saying that since I don't have a mother, I have an "auntie" instead. My father never had any children with her, but there's a daughter from another man. This daughter is the same age as me, but she's so small and thin that she looks a lot younger. I didn't think much of her when we were kids, but the older we got, the more I hated her. What irked me the most was that she never even noticed. I have a habit: when I don't care for someone, I want that person to feel it—and especially her. I might not have wanted this so much if I could have known that once in a while she thought I was in love with her. But who knows what she thought? Maybe all along she'd been working out a plan to marry me. And maybe her mother knew too, and maybe that's why they were so nice to me. I worry about that. I don't know for sure, but I think if the two of them were to suggest we get married, I wouldn't be able to refuse. Why not? That's something else I don't know.

The girl's name is Grisl, her mother's Nekhoma. But I think both of them should have the same name, because in all my life I've never seen a mother and daughter look so alike—if they were the same age, you'd never be able to tell them apart. If you ask me, a likeness like that is possible only if a woman had a child all by herself, with no man involved. For some reason—I don't know why—that thought depresses me. No, it's not depression, but some sort of eerie feeling takes hold of me when I see the pair of them jump up to do the same thing or come out with the same words at exactly the same time. Their two bodies seem to have a common soul, their thoughts held in lockstep by an electric current. Often, when I'm sitting in my room, one of them will open the door and stick her head in, and then a few minutes later, the other will, too. What's remarkable is that both of them open and close the door exactly the same way—that is, neither of them knocks softer or louder than the other, and when I ask what they're looking for, the mother says she's looking for her daughter, and the daughter says she's looking for her mother. I wonder: Why do they always look for the other in my room when neither of them has ever once dropped in for a visit? They hardly ever come in, only when they want something important.

One time, when Grisl stuck her head into my room, I got up from behind my desk and nodded for her to come all the way in. She stared in astonishment, and I thought her mother would have looked exactly the same way if I'd suddenly invited her in, too.

"What is it?" Grisl said.

"Nothing. Are you afraid to come in?"

"Afraid?" she repeated, quickly closing the door and at the same time pulling a face that made something turn over inside of me. I looked her over for a few minutes and eventually said, "Why aren't you married yet? How come?"

"Why aren't I married?" she repeated coldly, as if she'd been expecting the question.

"No, really, I mean it."

Grisl didn't say a thing. In reply, she pulled a pin out of her lapel, stuck it into her blouse, and sauntered out of the room.

The Literati

One of the better-known writers had just died, and his funeral was over. On their way back from the cemetery, a number of his colleagues walked into a café and asked the waiters to push some of the small tables together. The men sat down around the resulting big table, and each proceeded to order whatever took his fancy—which, on this occasion, was something much more extravagant than usual, for the simple reason that they'd just buried one of their fellows. Most of us do the same thing after we've seen a friend or acquaintance off to the next world. We tend to completely forget we're alive until someone near us dies; then it's as if a black line has been drawn under our own life, making it more vivid, something to appreciate.

So each funeral-goer gave himself permission to eat and drink as much as he wanted, feeling deep down (notwithstanding the heartfelt, overwrought speeches beside the dead man's open grave) that he was cleverer than his dead colleague, for the simple reason that he was still alive. That was each man's justification for indulging himself: to affirm the life that animated him. The company glowed with happiness, not because—heaven forbid—their friend was dead, but because they themselves still lived.

The group was composed of two unequal segments: the "immortals," that is, the literary writers (some familiar names, a few better-known names, and a couple of famous names), together with a larger number of "mortals" (journalists, publicists, and columnists). Those lesser creatures are much more eager to go to the funerals of their more illustrious fellows than they are to attend their banquets or jubilees. Whenever an immortal dies, the mortals turn up at their gravesides in much greater numbers than they do for their own mortal brothers.

The café's daytime atmosphere was sleepy and lackluster—typical of a first-rate establishment that's packed to the rafters at night. One seat was occupied here, another was occupied there, and a few couples sat half-hidden in their corners as though yesterday's festivities had cast them up like flotsam to drift aimlessly into the next afternoon. They had nowhere else to go because it was only here, in this café, that a trace of yesterday still lingered. Even the couples sat huddled together like refugees from the past, as if the past were all they had in common.

As soon as the dead man's colleagues sat down, they began rummaging through his bequest to Yiddish literature, dissecting his stories one at a time. You could see immediately that what they really thought about their fellow writer was a far cry from what they'd just heard in the eulogies at his open grave.

"I'd like to know something," someone announced. "What I'd like to know is why we suddenly turn sentimental the moment one of our colleagues dies. We completely lose our sense of perspective. Now a man can't hear when he's dead, so he doesn't care what we say, but still, we have to say something. Only why do we have to rhapsodize over him? I wouldn't mind if we praised people while they're still around, but when it comes to complimenting someone who's alive, even our biggest spender is thrifty—he always holds something back. When that same man gives a eulogy for someone who's died, though, he'll say whatever pops into his head, and it's 'genius' and 'brilliant,' and 'our very own,' and 'our very best,' over and over again."

"People do the same thing at banquets," someone interjected, taking a sip of his black coffee.

"No, there's no comparison. They're two completely different things. At banquets, people exaggerate—they'll turn a flea into a sparrow and a sparrow into an eagle. But at a funeral, people turn a flea into an elephant!"

"That's just imagination. We've got no shortage of that."

"What d'you mean, imagination? It's a simple, barefaced lie."

"No, I don't accept that." One of the better-known writers, a man who looked like Ibsen, spoke up in his quiet way. "You heard the eulogy I gave at the funeral, and I dished out more compliments than anyone else. I admit I exaggerated quite a bit, my friends, but at the time, while I was speaking with such great emotion, I didn't think I was overdoing it. I reject the word 'lie.' 'Imagination' is a much better word. We all use imaginative exaggerations in our writing—so, my question to you is, why shouldn't we use them when we speak, especially at a colleague's funeral? That's precisely where we *should* let ourselves go, with no holds barred. Our imaginations take off and soar, and nothing we say has anything to do with the merits of the departed person. Why? Because—listen to what I'm saying—because now the dead man has earned a new merit, which is death itself. In the Talmud, Raba says, 'I am dust in my lifetime, all the more so in my death,' but we don't really believe him. We feel a deep respect in the face of death—we can't help it. You can't have respect like that for any living person in this world, even if he's the most brilliant, the greatest person alive. And this respect, I maintain, which we can only feel for someone who's no longer with us, makes a deep impression on our very souls, on every one of our senses. Even a dead animal makes us feel that way. Even if a person was a complete nonentity in his lifetime, he's important after he's dead. Whenever you think of a dead person, your thoughts are serious—you can't think about that person as casually as you did when he was alive. So, why is it so remarkable, friends, that when we stand beside the open grave of a friend of ours, a friend we respected when he was alive, given that he's now associated with death itself . . . is it any wonder we exaggerate?"

"It's a shame corpses don't write," remarked one man who had written quite a lot, though no one had written about him.

Another writer, a humorist, looked mockingly at the man who'd just spoken and remarked, "Well, I consider *you* a corpse, but I've never had anything good to say about you."

His target paled with anger, but because it was the humorist who'd mocked him, he decided to treat the insult as a joke and replied lightly, "Oh, you won't be such a bad guy when I'm dead. I'm sure you'll say a couple of kind words over my grave."

"By all means. You'll have earned them honestly by then. Dying will be your finest achievement for Yiddish literature." The humorist looked around triumphantly, eyes and spectacles flashing, smiling happily because he was the only one in the room who could tease as much as he wanted without anyone getting angry at him. Then he settled his gaze on his victim, ready to slap him down if he opened his mouth again. His victim didn't reply, so the humorist patted his shoulder and said, "Don't be jealous of our colleague just because we heaped praises on him at his funeral. One person even called him a 'lion of our literature.'" The humorist patted his victim's shoulder again and added, "And we all know, as it says in Ecclesiastes, that a living dog is better than a dead lion."

The whole gang broke up laughing, but though they all took the humorist's last remark as a joke, each of the men was still happy the humorist was joking about the other man, not him.

Everyone had finished their food and drinks, and the smokers were done with their pipes and cigarettes. Smoke drifted overhead as the daytime ennui settled back into the café. The only difference was that a few people had left and a few others had wandered in, but even the new arrivals looked as if they'd brought the previous day into the café with them to continue it there. The daydreamy, melancholy strangers seemed to have a lot in common with the man who'd recently been laid under a mound of earth: they belonged to yesterday, just as he did. Only the colleagues who'd accompanied their friend to his eternal rest looked like today's people, because they radiated the joy of being alive.

"Well, guys, are we going?" one asked.

"What's the matter, are you in a hurry?" another answered. "We've paid enough to sit here a while longer."

The humorist stood up and propped a foot on the seat of his chair. He put his elbow on his knee and poked the damp bit of his pipe into his mouth, saying, "Just imagine, gentlemen: if our colleague were to climb out of his brand-new grave and see us sitting here, enjoying ourselves in such comfort, he'd . . ."

"Die all over again!" someone interrupted.

"Oh, come on, he was no idiot," a third man spoke up. "He wouldn't be that shocked."

"So he was a pretty smart guy, eh?" the humorist asked, biting on the end of his pipe with a roguish little smile.

"Oh, yeah," a couple of others chipped in. "Smart and talented too—what else is new?"

No one said anything. The humorist, still nibbling his pipe between his front teeth, broke the silence. "So we're all in agreement. Clever? Yes. Good-looking, polite? Yes. But when the word 'talent' comes up, no one has a thing to say."

"Because he didn't have any talent!" one of the better-known writers called out.

"That's not true!" The tall writer who wrote long stories and had been a writer for many years fumed with indignation. "He was a very talented person."

"That won't help *you* any!" Ibsen smirked.

"What's that supposed to mean?"

"Tell him what I mean." Ibsen turned to the humorist.

The humorist explained. "He means you're taking our departed colleague's grievances personally—because when you die, people will say exactly the same things about you."

The tall writer exploded. "Your jokes all stink, and you're a boor who's asking for a smack in the face. Listen here, if you open your mouth again, I'll give you something to remember me by!"

A couple of listeners leaped to Ibsen's defense, but the tall writer said it was all right, that it wasn't Ibsen he was mad at—he just couldn't stand the smell of the humorist's jokes.

The conversation circled back to the dead man and the question of his talent. The crowd split into two factions: one said that he'd had talent, while the other maintained that he hadn't. A few people admitted that he'd had *some* talent, but a couple of stubborn individuals wouldn't allow even that "some."

"Nothing but a windbag!"

"A real hack!"

"I've never been able to read his stuff all the way through."

"I'll concede one point, gentlemen," said the tall writer of long stories. "He was always long-winded."

"That didn't help him live any longer," someone put in.

"Please don't interrupt," the dead man's defender retorted. "I want to tell you all something he once told me. We were discussing his story "Behind the Bale," the one that made him famous. You probably remember all his stories. When I told him "Behind the Bale" would have been a masterpiece if it hadn't been so long-winded, he said to me, and I quote: 'I know.' So I asked him when he'd figured that out—right after it was published? And he said no—he knew even before he sent it in."

"Really?"

"He said he'd done it on purpose."

"What for?"

"For the critics."

"What are you talking about?"

"Listen, it's inspired. He did it because of the critics. If the critics want to pick on a story, he said, they should at least pick on its weak points. He knew that critics are always on the lookout for some kind of fault in a story, no matter how good it is. So to stop them from criticizing the good parts, he stuffed it full of padding, and if a critic wants to attack that, let him."

"Brilliant!" someone murmured, and after a short pause added, "Seems like that critic taught him something."

The tall writer continued, "Here's another analogy. Only a great writer could think up something like this. A sixth finger—that's what he said—is completely redundant, but once in a while it can come in handy. Imagine, he said to me, you've been attacked by a ferocious dog and can't get away. Stick out your extra finger and shove it right down its throat. Go ahead, take that! Choke on it!"

"Bravo, bravo!" There was a round of applause.

"Keep cheering," Ibsen spoke up. "Since we already know about the great love our colleague had for his critics, I'm inclined to believe that what we've just heard really was his own idea, and we must give full credit to the source. And now that the source is departed, his words carry more weight than ever."

"Look, I'm warning you . . . if you barge in again with your . . ."

Ibsen's face flamed, and he jumped to reply. "What have I said this time? That's not what I meant. . . . I mean that it's . . . if you think that's what I meant, well, please excuse me." He spoke politely, but his face flamed with malice.

It's hard to say which one of the two men would have boiled over first, but just then one of the listeners got to his feet, walked over to the two angry men, and in the portentous voice of the messenger in An-sky's play *The Dybbuk* he announced, "In the name of our recently deceased colleague, I, Judge Whatevermynameis, pronounce my judgment. You will stop fighting immediately, and not only will you stop fighting, but you're also sentenced to shake hands and forgive each other. This is the judgment that I, Judge Whatevermynameis, pronounce upon you in the name of our colleague, whom we have just accompanied to his eternal rest. Go on, shake hands."

It was a suspenseful moment; nobody knew if Judge Whatevermynameis had been serious or if the two angry men would obey his command. Either way, the adversaries—you had to feel a bit sorry for them—found themselves in a farcical situation. On the one hand, they'd lose face if they obeyed Judge Whatevermynameis, but then again, they couldn't *not* obey him either, because he'd ordered them to forgive each other in the name of the deceased man, whom the tall writer had defended, and if he didn't do what Judge Whatevermynameis had said, it would look like his defense hadn't been sincere. Ibsen, for his part, had a great deal of respect for the deceased man, so he couldn't just shake off the words of his colleague who'd ordered them to make peace on behalf of the departed—but he couldn't give in, either, or he'd look ridiculous.

The two opponents glared at each other for a minute or two, each waiting for the other to hold out his hand first. Finally, the man with the greater respect for the dead man extended his hand, and the other walked over and clasped it.

"In honor of our departed colleague!" someone called out. Perhaps he was teasing Ibsen because of his great regard for the man who'd just died. But a few minutes later he added, "Wouldn't it be better if we all had a little more respect for each other while we're still alive?"

A somber mood fell on the company for the first time. Only then did it really sink in that they'd just come from a funeral.

Bibliography of Stories in This Collection

"The Artistic Temperament": "Kinstlerlishe Kaprizn." In *Geklibene Verk*, vol. 4 (*Umfarmaydlekhe*), 219–25. Vilnius: B. Kletskin, 1929.

"Behind the Veil": "Hinter a Shlayer." In *Geklibene Verk*, vol. 2 (*Eygns*), 171–235. Vilnius: B. Kletskin, 1929.

"Call It Destiny": "A Basherte Zakh." In *Gezamlte Shriftn*, vol. 3 (*Froyen*), 277–86. New York: Yonah Rozenfeld Komite, 1924.

"In a Dream": "Tsu Kholem." In *Geklibene Verk*, edited by Chaim Grade, 55–61. New York: CYCO-Bikher Farlag, 1955.

"In Transit": "Komunistkes Untervegs." In *Geklibene Verk*, vol. 7 (*Vos in Lebn Kon Pasirn*), 258–64. Vilnius: B. Kletskin, 1929.

"The Layabout": "Der Leydik-geyer." In *Gezamlte Shriftn*, vol. 2 (*In Shotns fun Toyt*), 141–48. New York: Yonah Rozenfeld Komite, 1924.

"The Literati": "Tsvishn Shrayber." In *Geklibene Verk*, vol. 7 (*Vos in Lebn Kon Pasirn*), 18–27. Vilnius: B. Kletskin, 1929.

"The Little Brothers' Place": "Bay di Briderlekh." In *Gezamlte Shriftn*, vol. 1 (*Tsvishn Tog un Nakht*), 265–71. New York: Yonah Rozenfeld Komite, 1924.

"Miss Bertha": "Mis Berte." In *Gezamlte Shriftn*, vol. 6 (*Oyf di Grenetsn*), 65–79. New York: Yonah Rozenfeld Komite, 1924.

"A Mother": "Muter." In *In di Shmole Geselekh*, 75–79. Warsaw: Velt Biblyotek, 1912.

"Nero": "Nero." In *Gezamlte Shriftn*, vol. 6 (*Oyf di Grenetsn*), 133–51. New York: Yonah Rozenfeld Komite, 1924.

"The Old and the Young": "Elter un Yugnt." In *Geklibene Verk*, vol. 6 (*Basherte Zakhn*), 220–26. Vilnius: B. Kletskin, 1929.

"On the Riverbank": "Baym Breg Taykh." In *Gezamlte Shriftn*, vol. 3 (*Froyen*), 9–36. New York: Yonah Rozenfeld Komite, 1924.

"On Vacation": "Datshnikes." In *Gezamlte Shriftn*, vol. 1 (*Tsvishn Tog un Nakht*), 85–92. New York: Yonah Rozenfeld Komite, 1924.

"A Pair of Glasses": "Oygn-Glezer." *Geklibene Verk*, vol. 7 (*Vos in Lebn Kon Pasirn*), 191–97. Vilnius: B. Kletskin, 1929.

"A Plague of Cholera": "Di Kholyere." In *Geklibene Verk*, edited by Chaim Grade, 170–233. New York: CYCO-Bikher Farlag, 1955.

"A Respectable Woman": "An Orentlekhe Froy." In *Geklibene Verk*, vol. 4 (*Umfarmaydlekhe*), 226–37. Vilnius: B. Kletskin, 1929.

"A Singular Man": "Eyner a Mentch." In *Geklibene Verk*, vol. 4 (*Umfarmaydlekhe*), 52–84. Vilnius: B. Kletskin, 1929.

Jonah Rosenfeld (1880?–1944) was born in Chartorysk, Volhynia, Russian Empire (present-day Staryi Chortoryisk, Ukraine). Before his thirteenth birthday, his parents died of cholera, after which he apprenticed as a turner in Odesa and worked in that trade for the next ten years. He began writing in 1902, and his first published story appeared in 1904.

In 1921 Rosenfeld emigrated to New York, where he was a major contributor to the leading American Yiddish-language newspaper, *Forverts*, until 1935. He was a prolific writer and highly regarded by his contemporaries. He died in New York in 1944.

Rachel Mines received her PhD in English from King's College London (UK) and retired from the English Department of Langara College, Vancouver, Canada, in 2020. She began studying Yiddish language and literature in 2007 and was a Yiddish Book Center Translation Fellow in 2016. Dr. Mines has published translations from Yiddish in various print and online journals, including *Pakn Treger*, *In geveb*, and the anthology *Have I Got a Story for You: More than a Century of Fiction from the "Forward"* (2017). Her first book-length translation, *"The Rivals" and Other Stories by Jonah Rosenfeld*, was published by Syracuse University Press in 2020.

Printed in the USA
CPSIA information can be obtained
at www.ICGtesting.com
CBHW030830170324
5400CB00004B/4